EXECUTABLES

Lisa Cindrich & Jay Sparks

UNMOORED PRESS

First Unmoored Press print edition published 2016

www.unmooredpress.com

ISBN 978-0-9982431-1-5 (paperback)

« CHAPTER 1 »

DURING NINE YEARS AND 362 DAYS of incarceration, Tori Jennings had worked almost every job in Glynn River Penitentiary's poultry processing unit: chiller hanger, lung gunner, vent cutter, skin puller, drawhand, backup cropper. Live hang, she thought, was the worst. And she was in her eleventh straight hour of it.

Chickens shrieked in stacked crates against the wall. Dust and feathers blurred the murky air. The artificial lights dimmed in a futile effort to calm the birds. On the other side of a pair of swinging doors, Tori glimpsed the loading dock. Inmates hustled more crates crammed with scraggly chickens from the backs of trailers. She paused and rubbed her lower back through her sweat-drenched jumpsuit. Bringing her hands forward again, she winced at a fresh cut in the meat of her left palm.

"Better look lively there, Jennings." A guard tapped her shoulder with his baton. His lips stripped back from his gums in a threatening smile. "How many days you got left in here?"

Tori jerked away. "Three." She held herself stiffly and stared at the shit-streaked conveyor belt that rattled in front of her. Overhead, the hang line jerked and clanked.

"Well, you start slacking now, Jennings," the guard said, "and I might have them cut it down to two. Get your ass back to work." The guard strode away.

Tori sagged and let out her breath. Her hands shook. Three days. She tried to push the thought away, but it kept forcing itself into her mind. They'd release her in three days. She'd walk out of the prison into the hills of central Pennsylvania. Free, but never really free. An execution company would be waiting for her outside the prison. No one had told her that for certain, but she knew it. She lowered her head, trembling. What chance did she have? What chance did any Executable have?

Nearby, other inmates dumped birds onto the conveyor belt. It moved at a ruthless pace, demanding machine-like efficiency from the inmates who strained to hang a bird every two to three seconds. Grabbing a chicken from the belt, Tori wrenched it upside down as its claws seethed and grasped. The cut on her hand burned. She stretched to snap the bird's legs into a pair of swaying metal shackles. Blood slid from her palm to her wrist, and turned the edge of her gray sleeve a splotchy brown.

Trying to numb the terror that the guard's taunt had stirred inside her, she fell into the rhythm of the line. She focused intently on each empty set of shackles, ignoring the already-dangling birds that flopped and struggled against their restraints at the edge of her vision.

By the time the shift change whistle blasted from the kill room, the muscles in Tori's back felt brittle as old elastic. Sweat coated her plastic-encased feet; they ached as if the bones were grinding through her skin.

"Move!" Guards herded her and the other inmates through the exit at the back of the kill floor and into the next room where icy air crept out from the chillers. Enormous paddles drummed inside the thirty-foot steel tubs. Those paddles could crush a skull or ribcage, snap arms and legs. She'd seen it happen and sometimes, in nightmares, she heard their incessant, swiping rhythm.

The inmates shuffled through a dank corridor that led to the showers. In the sudden quiet, away from the blare of machinery, a high-pitched ringing sang through Tori's ears. In her early years at Glynn River, the ringing had been intermittent, but now it never completely went away.

She undressed with the others. Nude and barefoot, she slopped through puddles stagnating in hollows of the uneven floor and stood waiting beneath the showerheads that arced from the concrete walls. Bored guards, male and female, stared from a catwalk overhead. A ripe green stink uncurled through the humid air.

Water erupted, frigid, drilling spikes through Tori's skull. She squeezed her eyes shut as she rubbed a bar of caustic brown soap across her roughly-cropped hair. A grudging lather seeped down her body, frilling the puckered scars that curved across her left ribs. The cut on her palm blossomed pink as the icy water poured over her.

The water cut off without warning before she could rinse herself clean.

"Get it in gear, ladies." A guard repeatedly looped his hand toward the exit as if directing planes on a tarmac. "Today would be nice."

The women dressed in a rush, elbows stabbing. There were no towels and as soon as Tori pulled on a jumpsuit, the fabric turned damp and stuck to her skin.

The exit door at the rear of the shower room shuddered open. Tori, in the middle of a clot of prisoners, scuffed into the corridor.

Dull thuds echoed from an intersecting hallway. Screams. Tori's gaze flicked that direction; her head turned a bare inch. Fifty feet away, a guard bent over a prisoner curled into a tight ball on the floor. The guard's baton rose and fell with an even, unemotional rhythm. Another guard barely restrained a Riker's Doberman—a Hellhound—that snarled six inches from the woman's neck. The dog's enormous jaws snapped at the air. Poisonous saliva drooled onto the floor. The guard gripping the leash laughed.

Most of the prison's dogs were regular Dobermans and German Shepherds, but somebody had thrown a few Hellhounds into the mix. Tori had heard about the dogs years ago, before she was in prison, but she'd never seen one until she came to Glynn River. Border cartels originally engineered the dogs, giving them jaws that gripped like a pit bull's and toxic saliva guaranteed to bring down the healthiest man within days, if not hours. Some confiscated Hellhounds went to penitentiaries. The guards loved them, of course. Loved the power the dogs gave them, the panic the dogs inspired, more intense and degrading than a gun or club could inflict.

The woman begged, her words wet and thick, pressed through a mouthful of blood. "*Ayudame. Ayudame.*"

Tori silently translated the Spanish—*Help me*—and closed her eyes. No one could help.

Then someone grabbed Tori from behind, snatched her arms to the small of her back.

"Hey!" Cuffs clamped around her wrists. Tori twisted her neck to one side. A pair of guards had her, one at each elbow. "*No!*" They pressed her down a side corridor, away from the other women, and down a flight of stairs slippery with fungus. Mold speckled the walls like tufts of stained white fur. The air smelled of wet leaves and sour vegetable peelings. Tori's chest squeezed tight.

What if they'd decided to release her early? What if they were going to push her outside right now? They couldn't do that, she tried to tell herself, but she knew the truth: they could do whatever they wanted.

What if hitters were already in position around the Glynn River perimeter with their rifles trained on the entrances, just waiting for her to stumble outside?

That image snapped through her with the white-heat of panic. She wrenched one arm free. A baton cracked against her lower back just beneath the ribs, dropping her to her knees. She pressed her hands against the floor and struggled to breathe. A stunner touched the back of her skull. Heat sizzled deep into bone. Her teeth clicked hard together and tears jolted from her eyes.

"I have three days left." Her voice floated somewhere outside her body.

"Move," one of the guards said. "*Now*."

"I'm not leaving yet. I'm *not*."

"You hear this one?"

The stunner jabbed her shoulder. A convulsion rolled through her body, left her limp.

The guards dragged Tori onto her feet and thrust her into an even murkier corridor. She staggered and fell onto one knee. The shock of bone on concrete shot through her leg, temporarily paralyzing her.

"Don't worry. You're not leaving early." One of the guards hawked up saliva from deep in his throat and spat. The warm glob oozed down the back of Tori's neck. "And, no, it's nothing special for you, Jennings. Standard operating procedure."

The other guard sighed, sounding bored. "Suicide watch, Jennings. It's just suicide watch."

Another wad of spit struck the back of Tori's neck and clung there. Her skull buzzed like the grimy fluorescent light overhead.

The guards pushed her into a cell. The door slid shut.

The cell was small and freezing. It smelled like a basement: dank, metallic. The lack of windows made sense if it was underground although the other cells she'd been assigned, sometimes four or five levels above the main factory floor, never had windows either.

Trembling, Tori dropped onto a thin pallet on the floor. No sheet, no blanket, no pillow. The more she tried to stop trembling, the harder she shook, sudden spasms of cold and dread that half-convulsed her.

4

She'd spent the last decade crammed with a half-dozen women into a cell intended for two. For ten years, she'd listened to screaming nightmares, shouts, fights, beatings, the slam and echo of doors. Privacy sounded like heaven.

But as the minutes—hours—crept past, the quiet of this new cell left her breathless and gut-sick.

She eyed the door with its two narrow horizontal slots, one at the floor and the other at eye-level. Overhead, a camera chirred behind heavy wire screening. The screen was dented as if a previous inmate had tried to punch through it.

Was someone watching her? What did any guard care about an inmate's suicide except for the physical mess and the paperwork? Easier to release an E-felon off prison grounds and let hitters finish the job.

Tori ground her fists against her eyes, killed the tears that threatened to overwhelm her. Three days and nothing could stop the countdown. Three days to do what? Cry? Beg? Pray?

Say goodbye to her father.

In ten years, they'd never allowed a visit, a cell, a package, a message, a single word.

E-class felons are not allowed communication with persons external to the penitentiary. That's what they'd told her during intake and they'd meant it. She didn't know if her father was dead or alive, healthy or sick, or if he still lived in their tiny Philadelphia rowhouse two blocks from the North Philly no-go zone fenced off after a terrorist's biobomb exploded. Ten years and not one damned scrap of news.

God, she missed her dad. After Mom died when Tori was six, Dad taught himself to braid Tori's hair, the twisted strands slightly less lumpy and lopsided every day. He'd stumbled through his own embarrassment to buy Tori tampons and bras when she hit puberty. He'd searched for her when she dared to break curfew, didn't let her hang out till two a.m. like the other girls, the ones who ended up pregnant or synthheads or both. He'd managed to find a ride into Philadelphia every day during the trial and sat through every minute of it, given Tori encouraging nods when everyone else in the shabby courtroom showed her nothing but disgust.

They'd never let her speak to him after her arrest. She'd never been able to tell him that she hadn't killed the child. He couldn't have believed that she was guilty. Could he? No matter how the evidence looked? Ten years was a long time, a third of her life. Maybe her father had brooded about the accusation—the conviction—so long now that he wasn't sure what to believe about Tori's guilt or innocence.

And now they thought she'd walk out of here and die without knowing if he was okay? Without ever getting to tell him that she was not the murderer everyone said she was?

Anger foamed up.

She pushed herself away from the bed and pressed herself against the freezing door. "Hey!" she shouted, peering into the blackness of the upper slot. When no one came, she slammed her fists against the steel.

The slot finally slid open. A pair of pale eyes stared at her. Tori pushed her face hard to the slot. "I want to talk to my father."

"Not allowed."

"I need to send him a message."

"Against regulation."

"Come on!" Tori smacked the flat of one hand against the door.

The eyes didn't shift. "You're an Executable. You're not going to be meeting up with your father again."

"I don't have to see him." Tori's voice cracked. "Just know he's alive. Tell him—" She didn't finish that sentence—*I love him*—didn't want to expose those words to the guard's mockery.

"Look," the guard said. "Last year we released 44 inmates, class E. Three made it out of the immediate area."

Tori's throat felt like someone had stitched it shut. She could barely squeeze air through it.

The guard raised his fingers into view. His nails were clipped severely back so that the tips of his fingers bulged, red and bald, above them. "Gunshot. Strangulation. Bayonet. Crossbow." His fingers counted off each demise with the exactness of an accountant balancing a ledger. "I wonder what it'll be for you?"

Someone laughed in the corridor behind him, and Tori's heart twisted, a sickening, sideways lurch.

"Hey," said this other person, still out of view. It was a woman, another guard Tori assumed, her voice dark and velvety as petals. "You wanted a safe, quick death here in Glynn River, you should've blown up an airport."

The first guard snorted. "Or killed yourself a few cops. Not that we advocate that sort of behavior."

The female guard's laughter was as dusky and rich as her speech.

The slot snapped shut.

« CHAPTER 2 »

TORI DREAMED OF NOOSES and razor blades. When she woke—with no idea if it was morning or midnight—the caged bulb glared with an arctic light. She hunched over, her hands working at each other, a headache squeezing her skull and sending queasy ripples all the way to her stomach.

The guard was right, about plenty of things.

If Tori were a terrorist or if she'd been convicted of killing a cop, the court would have handed her the death penalty, straight up and administered right here in Glynn River's cell block H. No chance for survival, but no chance of suffering a long torture session of a death either. It didn't seem like a bad trade off, at least not at the moment.

If she were twenty years older, if she'd been convicted in 2022 instead of 2042, she'd be a lifer. Back then, a couple of death row exonerations had led to a complete suspension of the death penalty. The suspension didn't last long, not with the cartels pressing farther and farther north, leaving headless, amputated corpses in their wake. Then, after the biobombs started, with the mutations and contained plagues and the areas lost to no-go-zones, public mood had spun a fast 180.

But, from the way a fellow inmate had once explained it to Tori, by the time the public was clamoring for death row again, the government was out of cash. Stone broke, or just about. A death sentence was expensive and drawn-out, and the government wasn't willing to foot the bill except in the case of terrorists and cop-killers. The prisons were already half-sweatshop, half-cage and the companies involved in running them saw a "fresh profit center." That's what her old bunkie, Hazel, had called the Executable business. Hazel of the political manifestos and a frequent resident of 'the hole' over in cell block G.

"All it took," Hazel had preached, over and over, "was a bunch of lobbyists and business big shots with handfuls of cash—yeah, and of course the usual shit-for-spines in Washington, and there you are. And there was an extra bonus—the Army snipers laid off when they cut down all those battalions to save money? Shiny new jobs for them. Pretty steady work too. There's always another E coming down the pike and out the prison gate. Turn it into a lottery. Turn it into a vid. Tell everybody: hey, we've got the DNA now so you can rest 100% easy that the guilty are guilty. Nothing for anybody to feel bad about."

Tori's conviction date was July 18, 2042, with sentencing the same day. No death row, no life without parole. Instead, Executable status, full and complete.

Stumbling to her feet, she paced the cell's eight-foot width. The guard was right about the hitters too, how they could kill her in a hundred different ways. Images followed her as she paced: beatings, throat-slashings, disembowelings. Tori blinked away a barrage of images: sunlight crashing through branches; men with smeared green faces crouching in blinds; hunting knives leveled at her chest. Squeezing her eyes shut, she still saw the shadowy hitters, saw her abdomen blasted open, her intestines spilling like drenched ribbons over her hands.

Her eyes jerked open. The muscles in her arms and legs quivered and ticked as if electrodes sparked against them. Her face froze beneath an icy sweat.

Every conflicting rumor she'd ever heard about Executables surged into her mind. The hitters had to stay at least 150 yards off prison property. Or 300 yards. Or 500. Hitters weren't allowed to shoot in the direction of the prison. Hitters shot wherever they damn well pleased. Executables were released barefoot and forced to run full-speed across whatever lay outside the prison: gravel, burning desert. Sometimes guards helped them sprint faster by sending a few rounds after them. The same person who'd insisted Executables were sent out barefoot also whispered that Glynn River's staff liked to spread broken glass directly in the Executable's path. Ninety-nine percent of Executables died from bullet wounds; no, only about half were shot to death and the rest died far more gruesome deaths. Hitters mined the release area with steel traps, preferring to catch Executables alive in order to inflict hours of torture before killing them.

And if, by some miracle, you got past the hitters, then there were grabbers ready to lame you, tie you up and ransom you over to the execution company.

Death could take five seconds. Five minutes. Five hours. It was all up to the execution company and their clients, usually the families of the victims.

The smart Executables found a way to kill themselves before release.

She'd thought of it before, of course. There wasn't an inmate in Glynn River—Executable or not—who hadn't. During numbing hours when she'd worked the hang line or the kill line or the evisceration line, visions of death rose that were so real and enticing that they nearly stopped her breath with a desire for oblivion. Death seemed like an eternal forgetting, and forgetting sounded like paradise itself.

She backed against a wall and stood there, scanning the cell. Barren as it looked, she knew that if she really wanted to kill herself, she could find a way. One inmate she'd bunked with years ago had strangled herself using nothing but her jumpsuit and the bed frame. Another bunkie had broken off the handle of a plastic spoon and flayed her wrists with it. And Tori had heard stories of others—true or not—who'd ripped the arteries out of their arms with their bare teeth or smashed their skulls against concrete. If nothing else, there was always the option of attacking a guard. *That* never ended well for the inmate.

She turned her palms up and stared at the work-scarred flesh of her forearms. Could she really do it? What would they tell her dad? *Would* they tell him? Her stomach churned. Vomit rose in her throat.

She flung her gaze from the walls to the lightbulb, from the empty pallet to her bare feet. Not much to work with. She had her jumpsuit, the mattress—if you could call it that, a quarter-inch thick. Maybe it was stuffed with some sort of toxic pellets.

Crouching, she felt along the stitching for a good spot to tear the thing open.

Both slots in the door slid open. Tori jerked back from the mattress. A smell of burnt toast floated into the cell.

"Hey. Jennings."

It was the same guard she'd talked to before, with the bulging eyes and scalped fingers.

She turned her back to him.

"Hey, about your dad—"

Those words jerked her upright. She stumbled to the door and pushed her face to the upper slot. Crazy, but she half-expected to see her father there, right now, slouching in the corridor the way he did, his hands tucked behind his back, his smiling face creased with far too many wrinkles.

"What?" she cried. "What?"

There was nothing on the other side of the slot but those pale, protruding eyes.

"We're watching you," the guard said. "Remember?"

Tori's insides cracked like glass.

The guard continued. "Don't mess with the mattress. There's nothing inside it that's going to help you off yourself." His sigh was world-weary. "Other E's have tried it. Just pisses off admin."

"Pisses them off, who cares?"

"Just that they might have a chat with the hitter's company. Suggest that they shoot you up slow, starting with your hands and feet."

Tori's shrug was huge, trembling. They weren't about to let her kill herself. For one thing, the bookies would've been busy, taking bets on how fast she'd die, how far she'd get, what method the killers would use. There were people who'd made more on Executable bets than on Power Ball.

"Oh, hey, and sorry," the guard added. "But word is your father won't be able to make it to your funeral."

Panic struck her. "Why?"

But the guard had already pulled back. "Damn, girl, you're pathetic. They'll slaughter you like a piece of livestock."

Tori hated him with a pure, white flame of anger. She shoved a hand through her hair. "Like hell they will."

"I can tell, just how you look."

"Yeah? Like what?"

"Like dead meat."

A breakfast tray scraped through the slot at her feet. The smell of it sickened her.

Both slots shut. She stalked with the tray to the bunk. What the hell had he meant about her father? Probably all lies anyway.

She sank to the floor, sat trembling, the concrete like a slab of ice. She closed her eyes and saw her father smile at her again, tip his head forward in an encouraging nod, reach out a hand. Her fingers pressed against his palm. She could practically feel his fingers, warm and slender, squeezing her own.

Dead meat?

Screw them.

Picking up the tray, she made herself eat, scooping up crusted oatmeal with her fingers and chewing a blackened sausage patty that cracked between her teeth. She'd need every bit of nourishment, every particle of energy she could gather.

Her nerves felt like someone had shredded them with steel wool. She bit down hard on the last of the sausage and thought about the choice she'd just made.

Life. Or, at least, the last hard-fought scrap of it.

« CHAPTER 3 »

THE LIGHT BURNING ABOVE the sink in the trailer's kitchen illuminated splintered glass and a small golden pool of beer on the floor.

Paige Eisen leaned against the counter, her long legs crossed at the ankles, her short boots gleaming. The man at her feet writhed. The spilled beer near his face simmered, a faint poisonous vapor swirling up from the puddle as it ate through the linoleum.

Paige glanced through the screen door. Pine trees slouched into the darkness of the Oregon forest. A fine rain fumed around the exterior lights of the nearest trailer a hundred yards away.

The bonus on this job was going to be measly, but she was okay with that. The man needed to die. Deserved to be blotted out. Erased. She was glad to be the one to do it.

His cockiness had only made the job quicker and easier. She'd arrived from Philadelphia that morning and had the Executable on her hook at the local bar by nightfall. She shook her head. The man had been damned lucky to get away from the initial hitters even if they were from Omni, one of the shoddier, bargain basement execution outfits. How had he convinced himself that it was now safe to hang out at the town watering hole? Maybe if he'd known the family of his final victim had switched their business from Omni to Regency, he'd have stayed home tonight. But probably not. In her experience, criminals were usually not the brightest people.

A hoarse cry pulled her attention back to the man. White blisters had erupted on his lips within seconds of gulping his first swig of beer from the glass; now, his mouth stretched wide, his equally-blistered tongue stabbing at the air.

Reaching into a pocket of her trousers, Paige pulled out a small bottle. Thick brown glass concealed its contents. "Come on, now," she said, unscrewing the top. Careful not to get any of the fluid on her own skin, she refilled the eyedropper and crouched beside the man. His hand clawed at her left boot. A familiar disgust rose in Paige's gut; a familiar anger clutched her. The hand holding the eyedropper quivered. She closed her eyes and pulled her mouth hard-shut.

She could practically smell that other boozy breath—whiskey, most often—hot on her face. Her foster dad's hand sliding across her hair. His voice deep in his throat: "Just a little goodnight kiss, sweetheart. One little kiss for your daddy."

Paige's eyes snapped open. She forced her hand and her voice steady.

"There's not going to be any mercy bid," she told the Executable on the floor. "How many women *did* you rape before you got sloppy with that last one?" The man groaned and flailed his arms. Sweat glistened like slime on his face. "And just what did you plan to do to *me* tonight? Fuck me? Strangle me? Both?"

Rage detonated inside her.

To hell with the eyedropper. She upended the bottle's contents in a stream that splattered the man from throat to abdomen. The liquid singed through his undershirt and ate into the flesh beneath. His chest hitched up and down, each breath rasping through his throat.

Paige's breathing was nearly as ragged. She inhaled deeply, strode past the dying man, and pushed against the screen door. The tattered wire was cool and wet against her palm. Standing in the darkness on the concrete block step, she let the damp air extinguish her anger and the memory of fear.

Her comm shivered against her hip. She snapped it open, hoping to see Mike. Instead, Merle Edgers squinted out from the screen.

"Paige," Edgers puffed. He looked harried, his eyes scratchy and pink, his hair rumpled. "This a good time to talk?"

"As good as any."

"Remember how I was telling you we potentially had a couple of great jobs coming up? Well, the Victoria Jennings contract just came through. You know, the nanny from hell, the crazy bitch that killed that Senator's grandkid? Remember that? Poisoned the little bastard."

Bitch? A sour taste curdled on Paige's tongue.

Feet dangling an inch above the floor, nine-year-old Paige sat in a chair with faded, ripped upholstery. On the other side of a cluttered desk, the social worker glared at her, muttered "Little bitch!" and stabbed a number into her phone.

Edgers grinned and leaned forward in his leather executive's chair. Although massive, the chair failed to overwhelm him. He was a large man, barrel-chested, with hands like shovels and a head like a roughly-formed boulder. His thick, silvering hair was gathered into a ponytail.

"The Senator's family is rolling in it," he said. "Which means an excellent bonus for one lucky pair of hitters."

Paige glanced back through the screen door.

Maybe Edgers finally noticed the background behind her, because he dropped his voice. "Uh, Portland job underway?"

The body on the kitchen floor was motionless. "Finished. More or less."

Edgers' voice surged from the comm—"Good girl!"—which put Paige's teeth on edge.

"So, the Jennings job," she said. "You're offering it to Mike and me?"

"You have to give me an answer right now. I got Senator Logan to sign the papers yesterday, but then she dilly-dallied today getting the funds transferred. Typical pol...wishy-washy as all hell. Can't make a decision to save her life. We don't have time to fool around. The release is 0600, day after tomorrow."

"Send me the case info, Merle."

"So you can *linger* over it? Or so you can get to Glynn River and set up?"

"You know how we work."

Edgers dragged his hands down his face, leaving a blotchy red-and-white jigsaw pattern on his skin. "I know how *you* work. Mike used to just do his job, one, two, three, done, no trouble, not until you sank your fangs into him. Got him all...what? Scrupulous? That the word? Well, this particular job, there's no time for your crap." Hauling himself to his feet, Edgers lumbered to a small bar set behind wooden panels immediately behind his desk. On the comm's tiny screen, three short shelves of liquor bottles glittered and winked in the background.

Eight years earlier, when Regency still occupied two shabby rooms at the edge of a South Philly slum, Edgers drank moderately. Now look at him. Successful businessman, impressively-appointed offices, and he was—according to the office gossip mill—generally half-soused by midday and deep in his cups by dinnertime.

14

Alcohol wasn't the only change. He used to understand how she worked. Used to respect that, or at least pretended to. Now he'd just as soon lump her in with guys like Geoffrey Whelk and Sergei Chistyakov, sloppy sadists who loved the entire process of killing and never gave a thought to whether the victim had it coming or not.

Gripping a tumbler, Edgers slung himself back into his chair. He pressed a hand against his gut and stifled a belch.

Paige stepped back inside the house and set the comm down on a counter. Kneeling, she touched an insta-vital to the man's neck: no pulse, no brain activity, body temperature falling.

"Paige?" Edgers urged from the comm. Now his voice took on a blustery, flattering tone. "Got the quarterly report yesterday. Terrific work. You guys are really jacking up the international kill stats lately. You know we're at an 86% overseas success rate? And very discreet too, which is much appreciated."

Paige scraped a tissue sample from an unburned area of the dead man's inner arm.

"Got your DNA sample there?" Edgers puffed. "Terrific. Now. About the Jennings assignment, I've gotta have an answer."

"This second?" Keeping her expression neutral and her movements unhurried, Paige took a small sample of blood, sealed it in a plastic vial. "Do you even have anybody else who can do it?"

"What, you think I'm just sitting here praying that the great Paige Eisen and Mike Renz will accept the job? Yeah, I got other staff interested. You kidding? With the kind of payout attached to this one?"

"Who's interested?" Paige stood, picked up the comm, slipped the vial into a pocket. "I hear Geoff and Sergei have been busy boys lately."

Sourness gripped Edgers' features. "Are you trying to imply something?"

"*Another* incident?"

Edgers' shoulders stiffened. "Hey, now. That was a special case. That's why I assigned Geoff to it."

"Really?"

"You know what the Executable in that particular case was convicted of? Well, let me tell you. That particular E burned down a house with the family still inside. When the relatives signed the contract with us, they specified the flamethrower. That's reasonable. And I knew Geoff and his crew could accommodate them."

15

"So they set the place on fire and let it get out of control?" Paige said. Edgers shifted in his chair. "How many buildings burned?" Paige continued. "How many injuries? Come on. There was a riot."

"Very small-scale." Edgers swayed up into a half-crouch. "Bottom line is, Geoff and Sergei bag the kills and give us some very satisfied customers."

"The bottom line, Merle, is how long are you going to let Regency slide?"

Edgers' face filled the screen. The lines around his eyes drew tight. "Regency's got a full plate so I'm going to forget you just insulted me. I've got a lot of work to do, Eisen. Let's get the details on the Jennings hit worked out." He dropped back into his chair again. Picking up a paperclip, he worked it into a straight piece of wire. "Come on, help me out here. You and Mike, the Jennings job, fifty-fifty."

In her mind, Paige saw Mike's sharp blue eyes, his casual grin. She wished she were with him right now, not doing anything in particular, just hanging out together. Those were the only times she ever felt like she could let down her guard, although still not entirely. Never entirely.

"Speaking of Mike," she said, "he told me his bonuses have been pretty light this year."

"Bullshit!"

"I'll have to double-check with him on that."

"He's out on the west coast too right now. Which I'm sure you know since you two are practically joined at the hip. Maybe you can hook up for a little R&R."

"We were already planning on it."

"Of course you were." Edgers gave Paige a subdued leer. "He's on an easy job so he should be well-rested for you."

Paige crushed the leer with her own stare. "Send the specs for me to look over, Merle. Unless you really do have somebody else in mind."

"As a matter of fact, I do."

"Who?"

Edgers glanced away. "Tommy."

Paige laughed. "Your nephew? You're going to send a newbie like that? I've seen Tommy handle a gun. Still can't believe he didn't shoot his own foot off."

"He's done a couple jobs for us. Got his feet wet." Edgers had the paperclip in his fingers again, torturing it until the metal snapped. He flung the pieces over his shoulder. "You think because you did the whole VMI,

16

SEAL training, DIA route, nobody else in the stable can measure up to you? You think Mike is the only one who saw action in Syria and Indonesia and the East Russian sector?" Edgers was blowing like a whale. "I was *trying* to do you a favor. Since you were just in here last week bitching about payouts. I thought, oh, I'll be nice. I'll give her first crack."

"You know my requirements."

"Yeah, well, fuck you too. You've just made Tommy one happy son of a bitch. Have a great vacation, you and Renz. Don't let the thought of all the money you just threw away spoil your fun."

"I won't."

The comm caught Edgers' thunderous scowl. "I'll be sending you some specs for a job in Illinois next week. Cut-rate. Economy package. No bonus. Hell, it's practically pro bono. *Enjoy*."

The screen went black.

Paige flung the comm into her satchel, then lowered the sample containers and the empty brown vial in after it. The satchel swung in her grip as she stalked outside to the rental car and threw herself into the driver's seat. She sat there, her forehead resting against the steering wheel. The sweetish-sickening smell of marijuana seeped from the car's upholstery, courtesy of some previous occupant. It turned her stomach.

Bitch that killed that Senator's grandkid.

She remembered the case because of the 'Nanny-from-Hell' phrase the media streams used to tag the girl, blaring the label whenever they ran a story. She remembered a picture of the girl's face at the end of the trial, too stunned to look pretty, eye sockets hollow and dark in a skeletal face, black oily hair lank to the girl's waist. Somebody should've lasered the lawyer who allowed her to go to trial looking like a skinwaste.

Paige straightened. Poor young women with court-assigned lawyers never got a fair shake. So what? That's life. Not her business what the Nanny-from-Hell had done, or not done. Her hands pushed against the wheel as if she were pushing Jennings herself away.

Little bitch.

Poor kids in lousy foster homes never got a fair shake either. But she'd survived. That was life, too.

The engine turned. She glanced back at the trailer as she pulled onto the road. Every once in a while, people got just what they deserved. It didn't happen as often as it should, but the satisfaction of such moments burned through her with a cold joy.

« CHAPTER 4 »

THEY DRAGGED TORI out of a feverish sleep. Sprawled half-on and half-off the pallet, she stared at the guards above her with blank incomprehension. They were a flurry of motion. Their dark blue caps sliced at the glare of the bald lightbulb.

"What—what are—" she stuttered. But she knew.

Release Day.

They pushed her out of her cell, herded her through a maze of corridors. Her legs threatened to buckle at every step. Her pulse battered at her jaw.

The guards shoved her into a windowless room furnished with nothing but a table and two metal chairs. The weak fluorescent lights gave the man waiting just inside the doorway a jaundiced look. He wore a suit and a comfortable air of authority. A female minister in a dusty black shirt and a white clerical collar hunched behind him. The minister had her arms tightly crossed, like the room was freezing instead of stiflingly hot. She gave Tori a quick, compressed smile.

"Is it . . ." Tori licked her lips. "Already?"

The man in the suit didn't answer her, but nodded at one of the guards.

"Yessir, Warden." The guard picked up a stack of folded clothes from one of the chairs and stepped forward.

The warden nodded at Tori. "You need to get changed."

Heat flared from Tori's chest up through her scalp. The room wavered through a hazy scrim. The same word kept shuttling through her head: Now? *Now?*

How could ten years be gone? How could this actually be the day?

The minister stared at an empty corner. The guards watched, but their eyes were bored. Tori was too numb to care about spectators. She pulled off her jumpsuit, her hands like two chunks of wood. She took the unfamiliar clothes from the guard and tugged a pair of square, masculine underwear up over her hips, then pulled on a stretched-out bra, a pair of too-large jeans that were heavy as lead, and a plain white T-shirt. She had to sit on the floor to pull on sneakers—thin canvas with grimy, fraying laces.

The warden brought out a small plastic device and tapped at the screen. He looked up. "Your felon status is now changed from E-incarcerated to E-released."

"Not for long," sniggered one of the guards.

The warden smiled. "Gentlemen, gentlemen, this is official business here."

"Business?" The minister's voice was low and cool, soothing, like a mother's palm on a hot forehead. "Is that what it's called?"

The warden rocked back on his heels and slid the device back into his jacket pocket. "Ma'am, if this business makes you uncomfortable, you are free to leave at any time."

"Free to leave? Not while God's calling me to be here."

The warden's smile widened. "Excuse me. Guess I didn't hear Him on the line."

The minister's olive-dark gaze shifted to Tori and back. "We get time to talk. That's in your rules, your official business."

Talk? What was Tori supposed to say to this stranger? But the word 'time,' the possibility of even a few precious extra minutes, was reason enough to try.

The warden stepped to the doorway, waved for one of the guards to go with him, motioned for the other guard to stay put. "We can't leave her unguarded, not even with you, Reverend. You've got five minutes."

The door shut. The remaining guard slouched in a corner.

The minister patted the back of a chair. "Let's sit." She paused. "If that's all right with you?"

Tears stung Tori's eyes. Nobody at Glynn River ever asked, "All right with you?" Nobody here gave a damn if something was *all right with you*, or not. In fact, the guards probably preferred not.

The strength went out of her legs again. She half-fell onto the nearest chair and pressed her face into her hands. She couldn't tell if she was going to throw-up or pass out. Her body was numb and alien and soft, like it was made of liquefying jello.

The minister grasped her hand. The woman's grip was tight and damp, trembling slightly. A warm packet of folded paper pressed into Tori's palm. Glancing down, she glimpsed a small square of green, ivory, and orange. Cash. Tori looked up.

"Your father," the minister murmured, and flicked her gaze down at Tori's hands.

The money was from Dad? He was okay? A shock of gladness went through Tori.

The guard rousted himself from his corner—"No physical contact with inmates, ma'am."—and subsided again.

The minister squeezed Tori's hand, released it. Keeping her own hands fisted, Tori lowered them into her lap and pushed the cash into the front pocket of her jeans. Now she was grateful the jeans were baggy.

She leaned forward. The table edge bit into her ribs. "You saw him? He's all right?"

The minister simultaneously nodded and waved the questions away with two upraised palms. "I didn't see him personally. He's been ill, I know. I'm not sure how—" She broke off, started over. "All I can tell you for certain is that he was in Temple's hospital a couple of months ago. One of my old classmates from seminary is a visiting pastor there."

Hospital. Tori's relief drained away. "So he . . . Tori flicked a glance at the guard. He was rubbing one of his knobby wrists, his face puckered up like his wrist hurt him. Tori finished: "He's just sick?"

"I'm afraid I don't know if he's still in the hospital or not."

"But he's not dead?"

The minister's face sagged. "He was still with us in April."

"He believes me, doesn't he?" Tori pressed. She couldn't stop asking questions even though she knew the minister wouldn't have the answers. "He knows I didn't do anything, right?"

The woman's jowls drooped so low they threatened to bury her neck. Her eyes were damp—almost soupy—with apology. "So you *didn't* do anything?"

"No!"

The guard dropped his hand to the polished end of his club. "There a problem?"

Tori sank back onto her chair and shook her head.

"Victoria," the minister said. "This is important. If you have anything to confess. *Anything.* There's not much time."

A sense of suffocation enveloped Tori as if all the air suddenly hissed out of the room. The pulse in her temple drummed. For an instant she was back in the nursery at the Camerons' mansion, deep within an exclusive gated neighborhood outside Haverford. The baby in the crib wasn't breathing, his lips tinged blue like he'd sucked on a popsicle. The nursery— at that first, shocked moment of discovery—had had the same airless, crushing atmosphere as this prison room.

"I didn't hurt Robbie. I would never have hurt him."

The creases around the minister's eyes deepened. "Someone gave that baby antifreeze to drink."

"Well, not me!" Tori shoved herself to her feet. Her chair fell back, slammed against the floor.

The minister rose. "Victoria, I was only—"

"Okay." The guard stepped between them. Tori pressed against the sweating cinderblock wall as if it would pull her in and through, away from all this. She was drenched in sweat, her breath coming in hoarse rasps.

The guard tapped his baton hard against Tori's collarbone. She flinched. Then he jabbed the baton at the door. "Time's up."

"It hasn't been five minutes," the minister protested. "This is important. This concerns *eternity.*"

The guard choked back a laugh.

The minister bit her lip. "Look, every prisoner has a right—"

"She's E-class. No rights."

"But there are still rules—"

"Sorry."

The minister hurried a last few words at Tori. "You won't be alone."

"Yeah," Tori said. "I know. God." She didn't know if she believed in God or not, but if He existed, He sure didn't seem to inclined to help.

The minister looked flustered. "Oh. Of course, God. But I was talking about the Guardian Network. I talked to someone. I'm hoping—"

"Time's up." The guard herded the minister to the door, pushed it open, hurried her through.

The Guardians. Tori had heard rumors about them, how they helped protect E's, helped E's get out of the country. But helping E's was illegal. Interfering with legally contracted execution companies was illegal and probably deadly for everyone involved. Everything she'd ever heard about Guardians indicated that the E had to make it past the initial hitters first, on her own. So even if the minister had talked to actual Guardians, Tori wasn't going to live long enough to see them.

The second guard returned, then the warden with a nod and an "Excuse me, Reverend," as he bellied past her and shut the door. He pulled out his comm. "Quick time check," he told Tori affably as if he didn't know how cruel the comment was. The sweat on Tori's skin froze. How long did she have now? How many minutes?

The warden squinted at the screen, read aloud in a monotone. "Victoria Jennings, you have served a sentence of ten years for the crime of murder in the first degree. By order of the State of Pennsylvania, you are now released from any and all penal institutions managed and administered by the State or its private designees or contractors, and are no longer considered a ward of the State and subject to such obligations. By order of the State of Pennsylvania, in accordance with all federal and state statutes, all rights and privileges once granted you as a citizen of the United States of America are now rescinded."

The warden's recitation fell like blows. Tori's entire body went cold, then flushed. Darkness gnawed at her peripheral vision.

"Have a nice life," one of the guards interjected into the silence. The warden gave him a tolerant glance.

The second guard flung a smirk at Tori. "Too bad they save the old-school executions for terrorists. Bet you'd love a nice toxic cocktail right about now."

The warden pulled a scanner from his pocket. It resembled a magnifying glass, with an opaque screen instead of a lens.

"Jennings?" He gestured at her arm. She didn't move. "Guard."

The closer of the two guards gripped Tori's right hand, twisted it so the palm faced up. When the warden passed the scanner above Tori's wrist, three holo headshots appeared, each taken from a different angle. In them, Tori looked tired, her eyes white and scared. Her coarse black hair stuck up in an ugly buzz. Shadows pooled in her cheeks.

Words rose beneath the holos: name, hair color, height. Tori skimmed the list. Her gaze froze on the last line: *Status: Felon-E.*

Executable. Too bad the clerk hadn't screwed up that particular bit of data entry.

The warden recited: "The E-Class status now encoded on the felon's module supersedes all previous status designations and all prior forms of identification. Law enforcement agencies and employees of licensed execution businesses may, at their discretion, scan—"

Tori cocked her head and squinted, trying to see the time at the bottom of the man's comm. The muscles in her neck felt tight enough to snap. Her wrist burned as if the chip had been injected minutes—and not almost three decades—ago.

"An E-Class ID does not permit access to financial institutions," the warden droned. "An E-Class ID will not allow positive employment verification and permits no—"

Tori's gaze roamed the blank walls. She imagined the forested hills surrounding the prison. Panic drove her heart. "Let me go now," she interrupted.

The warden's face showed no surprise. How many times had he heard this same plea?

"Not permitted," he said.

Tori's voice turned bitter. "Waiting for the hitters to get here?"

The warden glanced at his comm. "I'll tell you when it's time. Till then, you wait."

He began reading aloud again, each word falling like a spade of dirt. Executables were not allowed to vote, not that voting meant a whole lot. They were not allowed to work, at least not legally. Were not allowed access to any social services, including those run by religious or charitable organizations. Were not allowed access to Unihealth. One of the guards pursed his lips and pretended to spit at that last one. Apparently Unihealth hadn't improved in the past ten years.

Executables were not allowed access to educational institutions. Could not hold a passport. Could, at the discretion of law-abiding private citizens, be terminated and harvested by licensed Execution firms, with any proceeds of harvesting to be disbursed equitably, with half divided among the families of the felon's victims and half remitted to the federal Department of Revenue.

Tori's shoulders tightened. She lowered her head. Her stomach churned and a strange, fizzing sensation sizzled on the inside of her skull.

"Steady her," the warden ordered a guard and pulled a small white capsule from a pocket. He crushed it just beneath Tori's nose. A sharp, acrid smell exploded through her nostrils. Her head shot up and she reared back, the inside of her nose practically on fire.

"Better?" the warden asked, almost sounding like he cared. "Head clear?" Before Tori could push an answer through her strangled throat and cotton-parched mouth, the warden continued—"Good"—and took her by the elbow. "Because it's time."

Tori staggered, nearly fell into him. A guard strode up to take her other arm.

"No." Tori shoved him away.

The guard's face darkened. His baton rose, but the warden stopped him with a touch on the shoulder. "She'll get there," the warden said.

Tori managed, somehow, to keep stumbling pace with the warden. He kept his own hand gripped firmly, but not painfully, around her arm as he led her into a short, dark corridor. Her body was awkward and disconnected, absurdly light, about to drift up from the ground.

They passed through two pairs of heavy steel doors. Ten more feet of hallway and then the final door.

With a hushed metallic sound, like scissor blades swiping together, the door slid open. Tori gaped.

Field. Trees. The green was emerald-bright. They'd opened a gate in the tall razorwire-topped fence fifteen feet away to give her an exit off prison grounds. She stared through the open gateway and took in her first unobstructed view of the world in a decade.

The air hung thick with moisture. The strip of grass that stretched between the prison fence and the two-lane rural highway was thick and lush with summer. This was the world: emerald color and the rich scent of damp earth and bark. Tori's eyes filled with tears. Only a few seconds left to breathe everything in.

"Go on," the warden urged. He stood just inside the door. His gaze followed the uneven scallop of treetops edging the ridge of hills in the distance.

On the far side of the empty highway, violets bruised a field of ragged weeds. After the field came the trees. Past the first trees, the forest thickened into a wall. No way to see what those trees might camouflage.

The guards shoved up hard behind her. "*Go*," the warden snapped. "Or we'll have to force you."

A sense of aloneness, keener and more painful than the isolation of her last cell, cut through Tori. She breathed in through her mouth, tasting the air.

One last breath, and she stepped forward.

« CHAPTER 5 »

THE DOOR THUDDED SHUT behind her with a bang as explosive as her heart. The warden, the minister, the guards, the entire world of Glynn River: erased.

Tori's chest heaved, her lungs sucking at the sultry air. Her gaze jumped from highway to field to forest. Her thoughts were jumpy too, and strangely numb. An instantaneous sweat dripped from her forehead into her eyes. She blinked away the sting of salt.

She tried to calm her mind enough to gauge distances. Fifteen feet stretched between where she stood and the fence. Another 40 yards of grass between the fence and the road. The road was two-lane, no shoulders—at least 20, 25 feet across. After that came a wide stretch of uncut weeds and wildflowers—Jesus, probably 50 or 60 yards at least, maybe more—where she would be completely exposed and vulnerable. On the other side of this meadow rose the woods. The first line of trees was sparse and intermittent, but then the forest quickly thickened, the undergrowth turning dense.

She wished to God the warden—or someone— had given her actual legal facts about how far away hitters had to keep themselves—and their bullets—from prison grounds. If she had a 300 yard margin of safety, that would be enough to at least get into the trees. If she had 100 yards, there was no chance. They could take her down before she made it out of the field.

Crazy thoughts flitted through her head. What if she just stayed here? Slept on the prison stoop, ate grass, roved Glynn River's perimeter in search of water and firewood and any scraps left by the guards. How long could she hold out?

Yeah, and the guards'll put up with that, sure. Prod you off the property with stunners and batons, more like. Bring out the Hellhounds. Warden already said you'd better go before they made you.

She considered staying put until darkness fell. *Uh-huh. Only another 15 or 16 hours to go.* The guards weren't likely to allow that much loitering. Waiting for nighttime probably wouldn't help much in any case. She eyed the banks of lights that reared up at regular intervals along the edge of prison grounds. When she'd worked graveyard unloading chicken crates on the dock, the intensity of those lights had been almost blinding. There'd be no sneaking from the penitentiary to the woods under cover of darkness.

She inched forward. Took so long to reach the gate that her heart probably drummed through half a lifetime of heartbeats. A single warning sign hung lopsided from the fence. It depicted silhouetted men thrown sizzling into the air by jagged lines of electrical current. Careful not to touch any wire, Tori paused in the sanctuary of the gateway and surveyed the treeline again.

It was a better view from here, no fencing or razor wire cutting across her vision, but she still couldn't see any hitters. She didn't even know where to look. Would they be crouched in the underbrush or straddling a branch way up high in a sycamore or pine? They'd had plenty of time to build a platform or a blind: ten years, in fact. Hell, they'd had time to put in plumbing, granite countertops, and wall-to-wall carpeting while they were at it.

The door behind her slid open. She looked back. The warden was waving her off with one hand. The other hand raised a stunner. "Better get moving," he called. "Gate's closing in thirty seconds. That happens, we'll be taking you off Glynn River property by force. A lot of force. You won't like that, trust me."

Some mechanism within the gate hummed. The razorwire overhead vibrated lightly.

Tori edged out through the gateway and past the fence. The grass was wet. Dew immediately soaked her canvas shoes. The sunlight striking off the highway was bright enough to make her eyes water.

Just get to the road. It was close enough to be safe territory, almost certainly. Maybe from there, she'd be able to see any hitters among the trees.

Overgrown grass slithered across the tops of her shoes, licked them like poisonous tongues. A single butterfly, pale yellow, blundered past her face. The hot sky pulsed, blue and airless. The sun smothered the field and rippled the air above the highway.

Tori stepped onto the road. The concrete burned through the thin soles of her sneakers. She squinted at the trees, saw nothing...not at first. Then: movement. Green and brown—leaves—no, it was camouflage—shifted in the branches of a pine back behind the initial treeline. Something shiny and silver and long nosed out from the foliage.

A rifle, sunlight smashing against its barrel.

Tori's breath rasped into a ragged whine. Tremors gripped her body and her hands went numb. Thoughts beat against each other like moths. Tears flooded her eyes. She realized, at that moment, that she'd still held onto a shred of hope that there wouldn't be any hitters. That the Senator and her family would have decided that living as an E was enough punishment.

She had no idea what to do.

She squeezed her eyes shut and forced air deep into her lungs. She opened her eyes. The rifle still glinted platinum-bright among the pine branches.

Think.

She took a wobbly breath. Okay. So continuing straight on toward the forest was suicide. Going back was impossible. That left following the highway either north or south. The hitter—assuming there was only one—might at least have to climb down from that tree and attempt a more difficult shot. Unless, of course, she was still in view of the rifle's sight at the moment she passed that 100-yards or 300-yards or whatever-the-magic-number-was-yards mark from Glynn River property. And, for all she knew, the execution company had a dozen hitters swarming the area.

North or south: it wasn't much of a choice.

Or—she snatched at hope—start north or south, then turn, follow the fence around the prison's opposite side and see what waited for her there. Maybe the hitters were all here on the western side, covering the release door?

It wasn't much of a plan—in fact, it probably couldn't really be called a plan at all. But it was all she had.

She turned south. Shifted each leg forward like it was a bit of machinery, not a part of her own living body about to be blasted off. The sun burned against her left cheek. Her peripheral vision caught the movement of the rifle off to her right. Sunlight sparked from the metal in different shades and configurations as the barrel shifted to follow her.

Drops of sweat mixed with tears on her cheeks. She swiped the back of a hand across her dripping nose. Insects in the fields to either side of her kept up a steady saw-blade buzz. Grasshoppers flung themselves from the weeds like oil crackling off a hot pan.

Behind her, tires whined on the asphalt. Tori snapped around, her heart cramming into her throat.

A pickup truck barreled toward her. Two men crouched in the truck bed. One of the men, red baseball cap jammed on his head, raised a gun.

He fired just as the driver slewed the truck into the left lane. The man in the red cap staggered, off balance.

An instant's reprieve. Tori turned west and sprinted for the trees. Her lungs burned and a side stitch gripped her ribs. The high weeds spewed pollen and gnats at her as she smashed through them.

Another crack of gunshots behind her and then the scream of a police siren. Tori dared a backward look. The pickup was off the highway now and bouncing through the field after her. A Glynn River police van lunged across the highway and careened forward in a line to intercept the pickup.

The men in the truck bed crawled out while the truck was still in motion. The burly guy wearing the red cap caught his foot on the tailgate and dropped face first onto the ground. The second man, wearing a neon yellow bandana around his sausage-shaped head, at least managed to stay on his feet. They both lumbered on through the weeds, trailing Tori.

She pistoned her legs and burst through the first line of trees. Something cracked against the massive trunk of an oak a dozen inches from her face. Splinters of bark erupted from the trunk. A couple of them quilled the side of her neck. Tori felt no pain, just kept moving, changing direction and heading parallel to the tree line, hoping the two men— grabbers, they had to be—would assume she'd kept heading deeper into the woods instead.

Her foot connected with something hard. She winced, held in the grunt of pain. Something glinted in the stew of ivy and weed covering the ground. Tori remembered the stories about Executables caught in steel-toothed traps that snapped bone. Her stomach lurched.

She peered through a thick screen of leaves. She could make out Glynn River guards covering the driver of the pickup as he emerged from the cab, hands flat against the top of his head. The rest of the guards were watching the forest, guns in hand, but not making any move to enter it.

Probably didn't care what anybody did once they were far enough off prison grounds. No sign of the two guys from the truck bed.

She found a stick. Gripping it, she poked aside the vegetation.

Not a trap. A gun. Rifle of some kind, the barrel shiny and long like the one she'd seen earlier tracking her from the branches of the pine tree. She stooped to touch it. The barrel was dented badly in the middle. Bent enough that the thing probably wouldn't fire. If it did, there'd be no way to aim the thing. More likely to kill herself by accident than hit a target. Ditto, as far as using the thing as a club.

So, where had it come from? Still crouched, Tori looked up into the branches crowding the air above her. Pines, oaks: nothing but needles and leaves sagging from their branches now, but plenty of those branches looked strong enough to support a man. If this rifle was the same one she'd seen tracking her, then where was the hitter it belonged to?

She squinted through the fractured sunlight. Her gaze skimmed the battalion of tree trunks surrounding her. Something red splattered ivy leaves at the bottom of one of the pines.

Blood: fluid and bright.

Confused thoughts clamored in her head. Was the hitter injured? Maybe the grabbers had shot a deer or some other animal when they were aiming for Tori?

Voices cut the air just to the north. She dropped flat to the ground, the smell of dirt and decaying leaves filling her nostrils. Her pulse jabbered like a lunatic.

"She's gotta be here somewhere," a man said. His voice was thin, scratchy. A whine that instantly scraped at the nerves. "I know we're near the spot. I could see where the shot blew into that oak where we came in."

"Moron!" his companion flung back at him in a tone like a cannonball spinning long and low toward destruction. "I told you to drop her before she got to the trees. Just get one leg out from under her, that's all you had to do."

"You got a gun too. Where the hell was *your* shot?" the first man whined.

They were, Tori thought, probably the noisiest hunters in the state of Pennsylvania, not only their conversation, but their boots crushing through downed branches and weeds.

They were coming closer.

She got to her feet as quietly as she could, flinching at the rustle of leaves as she clambered up from her knees. She walked bent forward, her shoulders hunched, making herself as small as she could as she waded through the tangled underbrush and clambered over fallen trees. Sweat blinded her.

She came across more blood. It stippled the wildflowers and smeared the long leaves of ferns. The quantity frightened her. It looked, more and more, like a trail left by a badly wounded animal. A large animal.

Movement caught her eye. She jerked herself back out of sight, behind a tree trunk. Leaning carefully out, she peered through the gloom beneath a brace of pines.

At first, she couldn't make sense of what she saw: the muddy soles of two black boots, toes pointed skyward and, beyond them, two long, chaotic columns of leaves. After a moment's confused stare, she realized the leaves were fabric, a camouflage print, and the columns were legs belonging to a man sitting propped with his back against the trunk of the farthest pine. Actually, he wasn't so much sitting as he was sagging, losing a battle against gravity as he inched down into the undergrowth like a drowning man sinking beneath the surface of a lake. More blood dribbled the ground in a long line. It might has well have been an arrow painted on the ground, pointing right to his location.

Tori didn't go any closer. Shadows made it hard to see his face, but he was obviously young. His eyes were clenched shut. Hard, like he was in agony. Every few seconds a tremor shook him, sending a shiver through the vegetation that half-covered him. Each spasm made her own stomach tilt, a wave of sickness and helplessness passing through her.

Tori drew back behind the tree again, pressed her forehead against the cool bark. Who the hell was this guy? A hunter? Grabber? She thought of the rifle with the dented barrel. Shit, was this a hitter? He looked like he was about eighteen years old. Had the grabbers shot him by accident? Jesus, if he'd fallen out of the tree, his ribs were probably in pieces, his lungs shredding themselves on the fragments.

The scrapings and stampings of the two grabbers from the pickup circled back in Tori's direction. There was no time to do anything for the injured man, even if she could.

"You missed her," the man with the deep voice complained. Tori started. He sounded much closer than she'd expected. "Missed her with a damn scattergun." More rustling and snapping.

Her heart surged painfully. She glanced around, eyes wild. There was a ravine another 30 or 40 feet through the trees. She headed for it.

The ravine was deep. Its sides were steep, covered with moss and loose rock. Tori climbed down as quietly as she could, cringing whenever she dislodged a few pebbles that rolled to the marshy creek stagnant at the ravine's bottom. The air was cooler down there, and dank with the odors of wet earth and moss.

She crawled through the mud to a large boulder protruding from one side of the ravine and tucked herself into the narrow space beneath the boulder's overhang, burrowing back as far as she could.

At the top of the ravine, boots snapped against sticks, knocking down a shower of pebbles.

Tori pulled herself into a tighter ball. Her ribs clamped around her lungs, refusing to let them expand.

"Maybe she rolled down into that gulch," the whiny man said.

It sounded like one of the men was trying to side-step down the steep grade. More loose rocks clattered off the top of the boulder. Tori raked a hand through the mud beneath her, groping for a rock. The one her fingers closed on was pitifully small.

Then the noise stopped. "I don't see nothing," said the grabber with the low voice. There was more rustling and cracking as he withdrew to the top of the ravine. "See the mud there? Looks like a footprint to me."

The men seemed to be casting about like hounds on the level ground above the ravine's lip, twigs crackling beneath their clumsy weight.

"There's another one. Over here."

"Shit," the grabber with the whiny voice yelped. He sounded excited. "That's blood. I must've got her before. She's wounded. Look at all this. And you trying to tell me I missed my shot."

"Well, we're not supposed to kill her," came the deeper voice, tracking away from Tori and the ravine now. They were heading toward the stand of pines where the young man lay bleeding into the poison ivy. He was probably just about buried under the leaves by now. "How many times I gotta tell you that?" the grabber snapped. "Just enough to bring her down. You kill her, we got nothing to sell to the hitters."

"Yeah, yeah."

"I'm just saying, don't shoot till you're sure. And just go for the legs, remember?"

"Shh!"

Both men went quiet. Tori's ears strained.

A shot fractured the stillness. Tori jerked as if she were the one who'd been shot, her back scraping against rock. She cringed into the muddy shadows.

"Got her! Whoo!"

Above the ravine, footsteps charged through brush. Then: a moment of charged silence.

"Holy mother!" The deep voice. "I told you to wait till you were sure!"

"Like hell you did!" The thin voice was sharpened to a needle by panic. "Is he a hunter, or what?"

"He's a hitter, moron!"

The grabbers exploded away into the forest.

Tori held back, wondering if they were really gone. But they'd sounded genuinely panicked. That panic convinced her. Unfolding her cramped limbs, she eased out of the hiding space. She still clutched the rock as she dragged herself up the slope.

The stand of pines was all cool green shadows and the scent of rich people's Christmases.

Tori inched closer. The young man was still alive somehow, his breath a slow froth, but part of the top of his head had been blown away. Blood glistened on the dark matting of the forest floor. His eyes were glazed.

Tori crouched beside him. A kid. Her hands shook, wanting to do something. But there was nothing she could do. And if he really was a hitter, how long before somebody would be in here looking for him? Looking for her? As soon as the Glynn River guards got a look at those grabbers and their wild panic, there'd be all kinds of people tramping through here. She had to leave.

She grazed her fingers across the man's shoulder. As she touched him, his body went limp. His lips slackened like slashed tires, air whooshing through them, and his chest shuddered flat.

She snatched her hand away and staggered back. Jesus, he was just a kid.

Yeah, and he'd have killed you and been happy to pick up the paycheck. So cut the bullshit crying.

She glanced at the encircling trees, cocked her head. No indication anyone was coming yet. She dropped to her knees. The odor of blood was stronger now, overpowering the smell of pine needles. Did he have another gun on him?

Great. Another gun you won't know how to use.

"Oh, shut up," she told herself.

Too bad nanny school didn't include the handling of firearms in the curriculum, between how to burp a newborn and the best way to get mushed carrot stains out of overpriced linen-and-silk sailor suits. She rummaged through the cargo pockets on the hitter's camo pants. She pulled out three sticks of gum, a couple of hard butterscotch candies, a stick of beef jerky, a smashed comm that was sleeker and lighter than anything she remembered from ten years ago, a pair of sunglasses—also smashed—and a billfold.

No extra ammo in those big pockets. He'd probably been expecting to drop her with one shot from the rifle—before it fell a hundred feet out of a tree and got its barrel so bent and dinged that it was no longer usable.

He only carried twenty bucks in cash. Tori shoved it down her sweat-drenched bra. She paused over a business card.

Thomas Edgers
Regency Inc
Expert Marksman and Licensed Executioner

"Not anymore," Tori muttered, shoving the empty wallet and card back into his pocket. She shoved a butterscotch into her mouth, grateful for the rush of sugar, and pushed the rest of the edibles into the front pocket of her jeans. She thought briefly about taking his camo jacket, but much of the fabric was sodden with blood and it was way too hot for a coat anyway. By winter she might not need one.

The most vital thing was a weapon, and she couldn't find one. With a foot, she pushed aside the leaves surrounding Thomas Edgers' body. Poison ivy, and lots of it. She grimaced, imagining she already felt the prickle of a rash on her arms.

Nothing. If he'd had another gun or some other weapon, he must've dropped it.

She couldn't linger here any longer. There'd be another hitter. If not right away, then eventually. Maybe grabbers too, who knows? Maybe these guys had buddies. Buddies who were brighter and a lot more dangerous.

Tori stood. She listened. No voices, not yet, just the flap of a crow's wings overhead as it climbed a thin shaft of sunlight between the pines and disappeared from view.

Be nice to have wings. Fly out of here. Instead, Tori turned west and, on wobbly, exhausted legs, headed into denser forest.

« CHAPTER 6 »

MERLE EDGERS PASSED THROUGH private security at the edge
of the helipad and headed for the third pier of the Annapolis Four Winds
Marina. Most of the slips were empty on this weekday morning. Crappy
times for the boating industry, he thought. Hell, crappy times for almost
every industry except prisons, guns, liquor, and drugs.

He made his way toward Allied Corporation's behemoth *Liberty II*
surging at the far end of the pier. All 70-plus feet of the yacht gleamed
white in the brilliant morning. A flag with Allied's logo fluttered at the
bowsprit just beneath a mammoth stars-and-stripes. Looking up, Edgers
scowled at the bevies of lawyers, lobbyists, and consultants gathered at the
front of the main cabin, just behind a curved wall of glass that faced the
ship's bow.

He chafed against the sensation of being a little fish in a big pond, but
in the realm of privatized penitentiary management and prison industries,
Allied was the great white shark. Progressive Prison Systems, Edgers'
much newer, much smaller venture into that pond, wasn't a maneater . . .
yet. But today's gathering was another step toward that future.

He pulled out his comm and made one more quick check of his
messages. It was after nine o'clock and still no word from his nephew
Tommy since an early-morning message that he was heading to the release
area outside Glynn River.

"Merle!" A tall man with gleaming ebony skin leaned over the railing
of the upper deck. He wore a well-tailored jacket made from some deluxe
synthetic that moved with him, as supple as muscle. Jonathan Hessler:

hotshot lawyer, congressional insider, and rising lobbyist for the prison industries economic sector. Edgers' mood lifted. If this man could work a little legislative magic, then Edgers might just have a chance to turn PPS into a major market force.

"Hessler." Edgers puffed to the top of the stairs to join the man. "I wasn't sure you'd make it up from D.C."

"Hey, if it involves a boat and a body of water, I'm there."

Edgers glanced at Hessler's drink. "Where'd you get that?"

As soon as Hessler pointed to the glassed-in cabin, Edgers was on the move. Hessler followed him into the spacious reception area bordered on three sides by windows. The mirrored wall behind the bar churned with color, reflecting the bright red of women's dresses, the dark smears of suits. After a quick stop for a Bloody Mary, Edgers headed to the buffet.

Across the room, Allied's CEO held court.

Hessler positioned himself next to Edgers. "They want you to testify at the Congressional hearings," Hessler murmured. "Allied, Omni, all the prison industry people."

Edgers sliced a large section of poached egg with his fork. A tremor ran through the floor as the yacht moved into the bay. "Why me?"

"The company that has the cleanest nose should take the lead. At the moment, that's Progressive Prisons."

Edgers bit down on the egg. Spices exploded like shrapnel. "Jesus! That shit looked like paprika." A sour pain winced deep in his belly and he wished he'd remembered to bring his pills with him. For a second, he even contemplated holding off on the rest of his drink—but only for a second.

"As Progressive's CEO," Hessler continued, "you should be the one to testify."

Edgers grimaced and pushed his plate into the hands of a passing waiter.

When his comm buzzed, he grunted and glanced at the time again. It had better be Tommy reporting in. "Hold on a sec," he told Hessler. Retreating to an empty corner, he checked the caller and scowled. Then, arranging his face into a pleasant expression and steeling himself with a deep breath, he accepted the call and brought up the vid. "Senator Logan! Glad to hear from you."

The Senator frowned, her short ash-blonde bangs failing to hide the deep lines that cut across her forehead. "Mr. Edgers, I'm surprised that *we* haven't heard from *you* yet."

Edgers' smile relaxed into something almost genuine. Senator Logan's words might be sharp, but he could hear the anxiety she tried to keep tamped down. She was worried, maybe even a little—what? Afraid?

"I didn't want to bother you so early in the morning," he said. "Not until I had real news for you."

"It's almost 9:30," she said, her voice tight.

"Sometimes it takes a short while for our operatives to report back," he answered easily. "There's the—ah, *physical* element to contend with afterwards, you know."

"Oh."

Edgers smirked at how that phrase, *physical element*, subdued her. He wasn't surprised. She'd seemed squeamish during their initial meeting and it took forever to pin her down with a signature on a contract. No stomach for death. "Plus, there's paperwork. Bureaucracy. I'm sure you're well acquainted with *that*."

She finally answered. "Of course." She paused again. "So it's, well, done? Your, your operatives have talked to you?"

"Everything's under control," he soothed and wondered again where the hell Tommy was.

"So you *have* spoken with them?"

Jeez, did the woman ever stop? Edgers forcibly relaxed his jaw. "They've called into the office, yes. Everything's going smoothly. I'll let you know any developments."

He dropped his comm into his jacket pocket. He wouldn't be able to fend her off for long.

Hessler appeared at his elbow. "Problems with Regency?"

"We're not here to discuss the execution business." Edgers practically tossed his empty glass at a waiter. "Bring me another one, will you? Bloody Mary." He squinted at Hessler. "So nobody from Allied wants to testify?"

"The riots at that facility they run in Tallahassee haven't exactly burnished their reputation. We don't want to give any Congressmen a reason to grandstand or call for investigations. Not when we're so close."

"I've toured that prison," Edgers interjected. "The bastards in there don't know how good they've got it. They could be shut up in one of the shitholes run by the Feds."

"Two dozen inmates killed," Hessler said. "Amnesty International's over in Sweden yapping about human rights violations."

"Production's up double digits at some of our facilities," Edgers said furiously. "You'd think that would make an impression on those dumbass senators. Don't they want this country to manufacture anything?"

"All you have to do is nail home the fact that any state-run prison factory will cost the government a hell of a lot more money to run."

"Money the government doesn't have." Edgers whisked his fresh drink from the tray of the waiter who'd paused beside him. "And they make lousy products to boot. Who'd buy anything that came out of Sing Sing?"

"They pass this bill turning construction and management of all federal prisons over to private companies—"

"—and lifting all the remaining regs on prison labor," Edgers inserted.

"And lifting regulations," Hessler agreed, automatically switching into a smooth, lobbyist's tone. "There'll be no need to raise taxes again."

"Why the hell *should* the Feds want to horn in? If they want more money-sucking quagmires, why don't they just start another war someplace?" Edgers' comm buzzed. He let out an exasperated bark and headed to the doorway.

The *Liberty II* plowed a strong breeze as it followed the shoreline. The outdoor air felt warm and moist after the chill inside the cabin. "What's going on up there, Spence?" he snapped at his executive assistant on the screen. "You know how late it is? Where the hell's Tommy?"

Spencer was silent for too long.

"He's called in, hasn't he?" Edgers asked.

Spencer cleared his throat. "I hate to tell you this."

"What?" Edgers' stomach burned again, pain searing through its walls. "Aw, shit. Jennings got away."

"That's right."

"There's no way he should have missed a target like that. You let him know he's off the job. Off the payroll. I want to see him in my office. *Today.*"

Spencer waited a respectful moment. "Merle?"

Edgers squinted at the sun-shot water. "What? You have other news to screw up my day?"

"Tommy was involved in an incident."

Edgers' vision darkened. He thought of Whelk and Sergei's latest debacle. Just what the company needed, another black eye. "What kind of incident?"

"No collateral damage, that's not the problem. But he took a bullet."

"Who the hell was shooting?"

"There were some grabbers out there. Real rednecks."

Edgers absorbed this information. "So where's Jennings?"

"I already talked to some of the staff who've worked out there before. They had some ideas about where she might head once she made it into the woods, but everything's on hold until you decide who takes over the job."

"Crap." Edgers brooded, staring across the water at a glass-fronted mansion glinting from a high bluff. In the brilliant sunlight, the towering protective fence that encompassed the mansion on every side glittered. He was going have to call Senator Logan and tell her that things didn't—what? Pan out? She'd love hearing that.

His mind churned with possible scenarios to feed to the senator that would leave Regency blameless. If he had to give back that payment . . . well, he wasn't going to. He'd fix all of this up somehow.

"About Tommy . . ." Spencer ventured.

"Yeah?" Edgers said, distracted. He should call Logan right away. Get it over with.

"He's in bad shape, Merle."

"What, they have him in the hospital? Shit, what's he complaining about now? The kid's got the best private insurance. I should know. I pay through the nose for it."

"The bullet got him in the head. The doctor said that even if Tommy lives, he's—well, he's not going to come back from it."

Hessler emerged from the cabin and started toward him. Edgers held a hand up toward the lobbyist who nodded and stopped a dozen feet away, leaning against the railing. Edgers blew out his cheeks. Tommy: dressed in camo since his diaper days, bang-bang-banging the toy guns his nice Uncle Merle gave him every birthday. Tommy: who never did get to be much of a marksman, and was pretty much a doofus to boot.

What the hell had he been thinking, Edgers berated himself, trusting a job like this to Tommy? *A job like this*, he repeated, trying to soothe his anger at his own sloppiness. *An easy job. Even Tommy should've been able to handle it.*

Edgers hunched over the comm. "Who've we got open right now?"

"Hani's going to Brownsville. Matt's not back from Thailand. The only ones available right this second are Paige and Mike."

"Great. Just great." Edgers clenched his eyes shut. "Look, shoot Paige the specs. Tell those two to consult about . . . whatever those two consult about. Tell her she's got till noon to get back to me."

There was a pause as Spencer made notes.

"Ah, about Tommy," Edgers continued. "Send some flowers to the wife or something, okay? A nice note."

He trudged over to Hessler and slumped against the cabin's glass exterior. Heat seeped through the back of his jacket.

Hessler turned toward him, leaning back against the railing with his legs crossed casually at the ankle. His black socks had the gleam of silk. He waved away a waitress who offered a tray of wine glasses sparkling with zinfandel. "Trouble?"

"No." Edgers snatched a glass.

"Listen, Merle, about this bill."

"Yeah, yeah, it sounds great. I'll do the testimony thing. No problem."

Hessler floated one hand, fingers spread. "One thing."

"Jesus, what now?"

"We've had some—hints?—that some of our fine Congressmen would appreciate a few deposits before the vote."

"Deposits? Haven't we forked over enough cash already?" Edgers slung back the zinfandel. Shitty old ladies' drink. "Who're they, demanding anything? They don't have enough money to keep their prisons going the way they are. They need us."

"Nothing wrong with a little gratuity to help the deal go through."

"But—"

Hessler raised a finger. "They pass this bill and you could end up like one of those old-time robber barons. Rockefeller. Vanderbilt."

Edgers mulled over the image of himself ensconced at his own version of Biltmore. He blew out his lower lip. "I've been thinking of putting myself 100 percent into PPS anyway. Sell Regency off."

"You'd be rid of all those—what is it you call your hitters?"

"Divas? Prima donnas? Bloodsuckers?"

"Maybe get rid of a few ulcers too." Hessler put a hand on his shoulder. "Catch the wave now. Give a little. Reap the harvest."

The *Liberty II* circled back toward the marina. Smoothing his jacket, Hessler started toward the stairs to the lower deck. "It's your decision, Merle."

Edgers leaned his cheek against the glass. Inside the cabin, a couple of VPs from Southwest Security swayed earnestly around Allied's people.

He had to go back in there and hash out a plan for the hearings. But first, he'd better talk to Logan before she got word from an outside source. He gave his comm a sour look and switched to audio-only. No need for Logan to glimpse the Chesapeake behind him and think he was out gallivanting instead of taking care of business. Hessler was right about this line of work. Nothing but migraines. Give him a bunch of incarcerated worker-drones any day.

As he was about to initiate the connection, the comm buzzed. He closed his eyes and ground out a sigh. The call came from his Philadelphia office and he wondered what new tidings his assistant had.

"Spence," he said. "I don't think I want to hear it."

"Why, Merle. That isn't a very gracious greeting."

Edgers drew in his breath. There was no mistaking Geoffrey Whelk's voice; each word left a viscous trail in the air. Edgers thumbed on the video.

Whelk was huge, a monolith of flesh and multiple chins filling the screen. "Young Spencer's told me of the most unfortunate mishap involving your nephew Thomas. I wanted to express my sympathy. And offer a helping hand."

"I don't need any fucking help. Or sympathy."

"Now, Merle. You know I don't appreciate rough language. And I don't believe you mean to speak so hastily." The voice was a slug, oozing insistently forward. Even the brief laughter sounded moist and subterranean. "Though you *do* tend to be more a man of action than of deliberation."

It took an almost wrenching effort for Edgers to speak calmly. "I'm not interested in talking to you right now, Whelk."

"Oh, I think you are. We do go back a long way."

"Not so far."

"Oh, far enough that I know where you obtained the seed money for Regency."

Edgers stood, paralyzed. "All right."

"It would certainly be a pity if the authorities ever received documentation of your previous career. Imagine the headlines! The CEO of a prison industries corporation serving time in one of his own facilities."

"Okay."

"Slaving on a factory line with all the other ne'er-do-wells."

"All right!"

"And then there's the other matter."

Edgers stiffened. Every cell of his body went on the alert. "What other matter?"

"Some footage of your little . . . frolics, shall we call them? The hostess from the Wesley Steakhouse. Were you aware she was only 15?" Whelk's chins quivered. "And what might your long-suffering helpmate say if she were to learn of—"

"—I said, all right! Jesus."

"In any case," Whelk continued smoothly, "you have problems. And I can help you solve them."

Edgers cast aside the image of his wife studying a vid of what had happened in that hotel room with the Steakhouse girl. Damn it! He'd thought the girl looked younger than 18, but he'd been in too much of a hurry, hadn't been careful, hadn't checked anything out. He gave his head a hard shake and forced himself to focus.

"You're going to solve my problems?" he said. "Like the last time you 'solved my problems?' Why the hell did Sergei have to burn down half that lady's house?"

Whelk made a dismissive sound. "The woman was harboring an Executable. That's always a dangerous and foolish avocation. But you'll note that our quarry did not escape us."

Edgers hesitated.

"That's right." Whelk spoke like a teacher encouraging a particularly slow student. Edgers bristled, but stayed silent. "Now, why don't we have a nice chat about Miss Jennings?"

Edgers sagged against the glass; on the other side, mouths stretched and pursed in silent conversations. The breeze stiffened, working individual hairs loose from his ponytail, floating the strands across his face and in front of his eyes as if he were submerged in water.

He gripped the comm and listened.

« CHAPTER 7 »

SUNLIGHT DRILLED THROUGH the branches. The air was heavy and sodden, like a soaked towel.

At first, Tori tried to walk quietly, flinching as she blazed a far too noisy path through dense foliage. Twigs snapped underfoot. Leaves rustled against her arms and legs and against each other. She gripped a heavy stick in one hand, ready to club someone at an instant's notice, until her arms shook with fatigue and her hands were slick with sweat. Her gaze flicked from side to side, dodged to the branches overhead, grabbed a fast look behind. She probably looked like she was hyped up on Peel.

The heat was relentless. She was so thirsty her throat ached. Her heels scraped a miserable rhythm up and down against the cheap canvas of her shoes that left the skin raw and bleeding. The stick drooped in her right hand and dragged on the ground. She couldn't stop thinking about the hitter twitching and frothing to death in a pool of rusty pine needles and poison ivy. Thomas Edgers. She'd never imagined a hitter would be that young.

When she came to a creek, three feet wide and ankle-deep, she threw herself flat beside it and scooped handful after handful of tepid water into her mouth. The water tasted mossy and thick. Swarming with weird bacteria or germs, most likely. Probably give her a bad gut-ache or the runs, but not drinking wasn't really an option, not when her body already felt like she'd sweated a good portion of it out through her skin. When she couldn't drink any more, she raised herself onto her knees and splashed water over her face and throat. Drops cascaded onto her t-shirt, darkening the fabric.

She ran her fingertips down one side of her neck where splinters of bark from the bullet striking the tree had broken the skin. She'd been lucky. There were only a couple of the splinters and they were short. They didn't hurt much, just a quick stinging sensation when she touched the protruding ends. Her fingertips came away dotted with blood. She washed them in the creek and moved on.

She came to a road and peered out from within the last fringe of trees. Heat simmered above the cracked pavement in an oily mirage. A truck shuddered past. Tori shrank back. She watched the trees on the other side. What if a hitter stared back at her? The stick was useless, but she clutched it nevertheless.

The sunlight was too brilliant, the road too open. She crept deeper into the woods and headed south, following glimpses of pavement snatched through the trees.

But she couldn't stay in the woods forever. The sun was sinking, the sky turning to purple dusk. She'd been on the move all day, 14 or 15 hours, she calculated, with no food and little water. Her adrenaline was gone. She winced at every step as her shoes slid across the raw blisters on her heels. So when she saw, through the darkening trees, a sign by the road—

Wel ome to Granite, Pe n.
Estab. 1827
Pop. 40 2
Stay aw ile!

—she decided to take a chance.

Pinckney's convenience store, a flat-roofed box of a building, hunkered two hundred yards past the Granite sign. A pickup in front of the door looked decades old, its tires bald and its tailgate strapped into place with rope. A large spaniel waited patiently in the passenger seat.

Tori tucked her head down and scuttled around the side of the building. Detouring past a dumpster, she found a door decorated with a stenciled outline of a woman in a pert triangular skirt, the figure weathered down to scraps of white paint.

The knob flopped, broken, in her grasp. A stink of urine crowded against her as she stepped inside and almost slipped on the wet floor. She brushed a hand across wall tile that stank of mildew. Her fingers found the light switch. A bulb above the sink snapped on. Dried pink soap scabbed the mirror like day-glo snot. Tori leaned forward to examine herself. She looked bad, but not as completely lunatic as she'd expected. Thank the quick wash up in the creek for that.

She plucked out the small splinters from the side of her neck. Tearing a piece from the soggy roll of paper towels behind the sink, she soaked it and wiped her face and throat, ran it across her hair, raised her shirt to give her stomach a quick wash. A tick hung like a miniature bat from her armpit. She snorted with disgust, pinched it off, and re-checked herself in the mirror.

Better. Not great, and the clothes were ridiculously baggy and worn, but she didn't think anybody would immediately peg her as an E. Or an escapee.

Leaning against the sink, she pulled out the money. She imagined her dad's fingers folding these same bills, smoothing them. Her eyes stung.

A minute passed. She counted the bills. A hundred fifty, plus the twenty from the hitter's wallet. What if this was all her dad had had left? She couldn't bear the thought that he'd given her everything while he lay helpless in some pisshole public hospital.

She wanted to see him. Wanted it more than she'd ever wanted anything in her life.

She rubbed the money with her fingertips. A hundred seventy dollars. How many places even took cash these days? The number had been dwindling ten years ago before she'd disappeared into Glynn River. A lot of people had started adding finance to their ID chips and using that at stores instead of credit or debit cards. *Can't leave home without it* as the old American Express vid told everyone. *The ultimate in convenience.*

Still, there was always some kind of cash economy if you looked for it. It wouldn't take any time at all to run through $170, and then what? She couldn't work, not legally. Which left what? Hooking, drug slinging, peel muling, sweatshops?

Her breath got shaky. Refolding the bills, she stuffed a third of the money down her bra, another third in a shoe, and pushed the remainder back into her jeans pocket. She gave herself one final check in the mirror, tugged a bra strap into place, and punched the light off as she stepped out the door.

She rounded the front of the building. A bell jangled as she pushed inside the store. A skinny teenage boy glanced up from the register. "Hey."

His gaze dropped behind the counter where the voices of sports announcers buzzed.

Tori edged sideways past a man with a round gut and a graying, untrimmed beard who studied a rack of chips. He looked as innocuous as the clerk, but what *did* a hitter look like?

She continued toward the refrigerator cases at the back. Her gaze darted from red cans to purple plastic bottles to milk cartons.

Ten years. Ten years since she'd been allowed to make even a basic decision like what to drink. In Glynn River, the prisoners drank water, tea that tasted like water, or coffee that tasted like weak tea. The drinks came in crusty little plastic cups that slotted into the food tray. No one asked you what you wanted. You drank—and ate— whatever they gave you.

Yanking the door open, she closed her eyes and relished the cold air blasting across her face.

Milk? Chocolate milk? Lemonade? Soda? She found herself reaching for a water bottle while her other hand grasped a carton of grape juice. She glanced over her shoulder and the bearded man immediately looked away from her, his pudgy cheeks reddening. Tori pulled back behind shelves of cereal and peered across the tops of the boxes.

He could be a hitter. Maybe hitters disguised themselves as slumpy, flabby rednecks all the time. But her gut told her the guy was okay. Yeah, he'd been staring but his gaze had seemed curious and—crazy as it sounded—admiring. Not predatory.

"Hey, Ben, you got any doughnuts?" the man asked.

The cashier didn't look up. "Powdered sugar."

"You guys need to get some of the chocolate-covered ones, will you?" The man's beefy hands closed on a package of corn chips.

Calmer now, Tori headed up the back aisle. She stopped in front of packages of soap stacked on the top shelf and inhaled the clean, brisk scent. She checked the price and moved on.

As she stepped to the counter, the bearded man shuffled up behind her. He smelled like motor oil and stale peppermint. "You visiting here?" he asked.

On sudden impulse, Tori snatched a browning banana from a basket on the counter and set it beside the juice. "Not really." She busied herself with peeling a couple of small bills from the rest of her money. "You sell combs?" she asked. The cashier pointed at a small rack of toiletries.

"Toothbrush?" she asked, pushing a comb across the counter.

"I don't think so."

"You a tourist?" The bearded man pressed up alongside Tori and she flinched back. He didn't seem to notice as he dropped a jumble of cellophane and foil next to her selections. Tori stared down at a display of alcohol-laced chewing tobacco.

"Like there's anything to see around *here*," Ben muttered. The comb's price popped up on the reader.

"What, we got Clanahan Caverns." The man lifted his unruly eyebrows at Tori. "You ever been there?"

"No." Tori tried to sound bored.

"You're not much of a talker, are you?"

She snapped toward him. "What's there to talk about?"

His chin tucked down toward his chest. Hurt clouded his eyes. Tori raised a hand, let it waver in mid-air. "Sorry," she mumbled. "I *don't* talk much."

The man's face cleared. "That's okay." The counter wedged deeper into his gut as he pressed forward. "My name's Sam."

Tori gave a tight smile and added a sleeve of crackers and cheddar cheese to her purchases.

Ben squinted down behind the counter. "That's $19.68."

"Highway robbery," Sam observed. "You can go to the grocery up in Glynn River and get the same stuff for half that."

The boy rolled his eyes as he dropped the items into a small sack. "Not half."

Tori extended two tattered ten dollar bills.

Ben stared at the bills like they were some species of exotic insect. "Cash?"

"Yeah." Tori's hand began to tremble.

"You don't got a money link on your chip?" Ben craned over to look at her wrists.

Tori crossed her arms. "No."

"Well, that's okay. We can use the account number and the last five digits of your fed ID." Ben was already tapping at the monitor. "You want to scan your ID?"

Laughter threatened to burst from Tori's throat. He wouldn't look so bored, she thought, if she stuck her wrist under the scanner. The letter *E* sang through her head like something from a kindergarten tune: *A is for Apple, E is for Executable.*

"I'll just use cash, thanks." She set the money on the counter. "It's been sitting around the house forever. I figured I might as well use it."

"Hey, I hardly use the money link on my chip," Sam commiserated. He slid a debit card from his billfold. "Weirds me out a little." He tugged a ratty slip of paper out of the billfold. "I probably should though. Look at this. I can't even remember my passwords without it."

He pointed a sausage finger at the back of Tori's hand. Tiny pink bumps raised themselves from the skin. God only knew what she'd brushed against in the woods. "That poison ivy?"

Tori shrugged. Poison ivy didn't show up that fast, did it?

"You should get some Caladex for that," Sam continued. "Personally, I pour bleach on it first. Burns like hell, but keeps it from spreading. Now, if you've got money for prescription stuff, I hear there's some good—"

"Thanks," Tori cut him off.

"See, the thing is," Ben said, "I don't have any change. See that?" His hand floated toward a sign tacked to a shelf behind him: NO CASH. The sign was tiny; no wonder she hadn't seen it. Beside the sign, layers of dust dulled miniature bottles of scotch and tequila. "I mean, we can still take cash no matter what the sign says. But we can't give any change back. My boss decided it wasn't worth the hassle. It was all slingers and peelouts and skinwastes trying to steal what we kept in the drawer."

"Don't insult the lady," Sam bristled

Tori's eyes burned. "I don't need change," she told Ben. "If that works for you."

"I don't know . . ."

Tori tried to laugh. "It's not counterfeit."

"Oh, for God's sake, Ben." Sam grabbed the bills and pushed them into Ben's hands. "The lady's not a crook. You can tell that, just looking at her."

Sucking at his front teeth, Ben rang the money into the register. Tori nodded her thanks, took the sack, and started toward the door.

"Hey, Miss? Lady?" Sam called after her. "You need a ride somewhere?"

"My boyfriend's picking me up."

Sam nodded furiously. "Sure, sure, I understand."

Outside, Tori hurried to the shadows along one edge of the store and huddled there to devour the banana and gulp down the bottle of juice. She should probably go back into the woods, but she was still hungry and those two—Sam and the teenage kid—they hadn't seemed so bad. She couldn't stay in the woods forever, unless she wanted to starve to death.

The banana set her stomach clamoring for more food. She'd find a real meal, she decided, then hide back in the woods for at least tonight.

Slinking around the perimeter of the parking lot, she limped along the road into a neighborhood of shabby bungalows and then to downtown Granite, or what there was of one.

Most of the old downtown shops stood empty, 'for lease' signs askew in their windows. Someone had shattered the streetlights. Trash barrels on the corner beside what had once been a bank looked like they hadn't been emptied in weeks. Overflowing garbage disintegrated to a wet muck on the pavement.

A neon sign, *B Lodge Diner*, flickered above the door of a small restaurant. The place looked less like a traditional diner than a poorly-constructed cabin, with concrete mortaring the gaps between fake logs.

Tori swayed, light-headed. Her mind wouldn't focus, thoughts sliding over one another. Her stomach ached as the diner's smells resolved into onion rings, tacos, and coffee. Then she saw the sign perched in one of the windows:

CHIP OR CASH ONLY!
NO CREDIT CARD!

That made the decision easy. She flexed one foot, feeling the bump of folded money through her sock, then stepped with feigned indifference into the doorway.

« CHAPTER 8 »

PAIGE EISEN JAMMED THE FINGERS of one hand into a minute crevice and paused halfway up the three-foot-wide vertical crack in the massive rock. Letting her weight rest on a back foot, she tilted her head to study the terrain above her. Mike Renz was a good twenty feet higher, spidering his way up the rock face. Since Paige had accepted his spontaneous challenge to scale Rattler's Tooth free solo—climbing with zero protection—they carried no racks, no gear at all, just Mike's small pack stuffed with plastic bottles of OJ and water and a can of his favorite beer to celebrate the ascent.

Ten feet above Paige, the chimney into which she'd wedged herself narrowed and closed, like the top of a cathedral window. It was time to head sideways along the steep rock face. She examined it, picturing each move needed for the most efficient ascent. The coarse granite was still warm, but the dry desert breeze had cooled slightly with the approach of evening. She'd have a bit of a leap to get around the edge of the crack; she'd also have to trust the holds to stay firm. She didn't like it, didn't like losing that third point of contact with the rock and didn't like putting her weight on any hold without testing it first.

Didn't like having to trust something she couldn't control.

If she fell from here, it was a long drop. The kind that cracked bones clean in two, smashed in the skull.

A dark stairway. Donny Oxlade in a slow-motion, arm-waving plunge. His ridiculous high-pitched shriek cut off by the smack of his forehead against a metal baluster. Vertebrae crunched when he struck bottom. Paige's blood pounded behind her eyes, throbbed inside her ears. Nausea soured her sense of triumph.

"Hey, you doing okay?" Mike had stopped moving. He stared down at her.

Paige's concentration was lousy today. And free-climbing Rattler's Tooth was not the time and place to allow distractions to crowd her head. She closed her eyes. *Picture the move*, she commanded herself.

She opened her eyes. "Terrific!" she called back.

Even with Mike's eyes concealed behind mirrored sunglasses, Paige could tell he was frowning. It wasn't just the set of his mouth, it was the set of his shoulders, the poised tilt of his head, the stillness with which he watched her.

"You sure about that?" he asked.

In answer, Paige sprang sideways, her weight swinging around a protruding edge of rock. Her right foot landed on a solid two-inch ledge an instant after her left foot vacated it. She clenched her fingers into a hand jam. For a minute, her heart felt like one giant cramp in the middle of her chest. Breathing came hard.

She glanced down. A hundred and twenty feet below, a quartet of climbers goggled up at her. They looked as stolid and unmovable as the yuccas and Jerusalem thorns dotting the cracked dirt. Racks of carabiners and chocks glittered across the climbers' hips. Even from a distance, Paige could tell that the group was expensively equipped.

She eyed the blinding glint off their leather packs. Prada, probably. You had to have some serious cash just to enter the privatized national parks, much less buy a climbing license. Better to shell out the money than wade into the few federally-controlled parks that remained open. Knocked-over port-a-potties, empty potato chip bags and filthy tents where "vacationers" had obviously been squatting for months.

One of the men on the ground jerked a big thumbs-up at her. His approval didn't mean much to her as a climber—anybody just starting a climb this late in the day was either inexperienced or not too bright. Still, the sight of him filled Paige with a warm satisfaction. He was successful enough to be here, with plenty of fancy gear . . . and so was she, even if she'd left most of her gear in the trunk. All the years of effort had paid off. She hadn't busted her ass—getting scholarships, taking on the most challenging training, graduating summa from Army Intelligence College— just to fall back in with the grimy slack-jaws she'd been trapped with as a kid. She'd wanted out, and she'd made it out.

Paige took a breath and climbed.

She advanced steadily. Mike had 20 feet on her, but she didn't try to catch up by taking the same route since that would bring her right beneath him and directly in his path if he fell. She worked out a separate route and set off even farther to her left.

Almost 150 feet off the ground, Mike reached Hallelujah Ledge and leaned into it for a moment's rest before the final, easy ascent. Paige paused, hands jammed into crevices, and looked up at him. Mike's skin was deeply tanned, but chalk painted his hands dead-white, the pallor startling and aboriginal. He'd sweated through his gray t-shirt; the damp fabric showed the cut of the muscles beneath.

"Tricky one," he called down.

Paige caught an unusual thread in his voice—anxiety? Why? Because he thought she couldn't handle the free solo or because he was thinking of what his life would be like if something happened to her and she was no longer in it? Paige stared up at him another minute, trying to read his face, impossible with sunglasses concealing his eyes.

She wasn't used to anyone being particularly concerned about whether she was okay or not. "Are you worried about me?" she called back.

"You want me to be?" His tone was light, but he didn't smile.

No. Oh, hell. Yes.

Flustered, Paige returned her attention to the rock, focusing on how rough it felt against her palms. The smell of cedar cut through the scent of her own perspiration. The muscles in her arms strained, taking on her entire weight, as she mantled onto the three-inch-wide ledge. From above, Mike clapped, then pushed himself up from his own ledge and onto the rock face again.

Paige ascended the rest of her route swiftly, passing two bolt anchors as she swung herself onto the top of Rattler's Tooth.

Mike had the orange juice waiting. He snapped his own beer open and flicked the cap in a long arc off the cliff edge.

"I wish you wouldn't do that," Paige said.

Mike settled back onto his elbows and stared across the expanse between Rattler's Tooth and The Devils—an imposing array of cliffs and tumbled boulders. Jumping chollas twisted across the desert floor like contortionists. Mariposa blossoms flared bright orange. "Damn, that felt good," he said. "I miss climbing. I haven't even made it up to the Gunks since last fall."

"I went to Yosemite a couple months ago," Paige said.

"El Capitan?"

"The Nose and Salathe." She leaned forward to watch the other group's leader start up the rock. The lead's partner stood braced on the ground and fed out a line of rope.

Mike took a swallow of beer. "How was Portland? The job go okay?"

Crumpling the empty juice container, Paige handed it back to Mike. "Pack it in, pack it out."

"Some kind of acid, wasn't that what they wanted?"

She shut her eyes. The bloody froth bubbled from the man's throat. His eyes begged for mercy. Filthy rapist. Like she'd feel pity for him.

Deeper memories crawled out of her brain. Donny Oxlade slamming his fist through the flimsy kitchen wall. The other foster kids scattering outside to hide. Paige slowly stirring the pan of macaroni and cheese on the stove. *He's going to throw this boiling water in my face.*

He hadn't touched the pan, just looked at her, his face snake-thin, his eyes flat. He came treading into her room that night. He—

Mike touched her arm. Paige bolted stiffly upright.

"Hey." Mike pulled back, held both hands up, fingers spread. "Just me here. Mike."

Paige's face was hot. She had to get a handle on herself. She didn't want to remember, not unless she was killing some skinwaste like the E in Portland. Then remembering was okay because she didn't think about what Donny Oxlade did to her, but what she did to Donny Oxlade.

"Paige?" Mike's arm was a warm pressure against hers.

Paige deliberately relaxed. Turned on a bright smile. "How was San Pedro?"

Mike just watched her for a minute. Her gut clutched. She didn't want him to ask too many questions. Or, at least, she didn't want him to ask the wrong questions.

The moment passed. Mike took another swallow of beer. "Same old. No bonus. One crap payout. And it doesn't count toward annual incentives either." He pretended to bow from the waist. "Thank you, Merle Edgers." Mike finished the can and scooted closer. "I've been thinking about checking out the competition."

"Regency pays better."

"You sure?"

"I've already looked into it."

"Okay, Regency pays better." Mike sank back. "So why've you got that frown-thing going?"

Paige was relieved. Career, money, hobbies: all topics she could handle. "It's not just the question of money. It's getting so Merle's willing to sign up any job, no questions asked. He keeps trying to pawn off questionable—*very* questionable— cases on me." Paige massaged her hands, working the tightness out of the muscles. "I turn them down. Not that it makes much difference. Whelk and the others are only too happy to pick up the slack."

Shouting clamored below. Paige glanced down. The belayer hadn't paid out enough rope. The leader, stranded on a too-short leash, hollered.

"They'll be climbing in the dark at this rate." Mike probed into his pack and pulled out a bag of trail mix.

Paige held out a palm. Mike poured a generous heap of mix onto it. "Spencer called me this morning," she told him. She pinched a small portion of the granola while Mike upended the rest of the bag's contents into his mouth. He punched the bag flat and pinned it and the empty beer can under one foot.

"About what?" he asked.

"Clean up. The two of us, fifty-fifty. On a job I already turned down."

"Lucrative?"

"Definitely."

Mike dropped flat on his back. A needle of pure crimson cloud sliced down the center of each mirrored lens of his glasses. "Clean up. The E got away, huh? A Regency screw-up."

"Yeah. *Another* one."

"But lucrative," Mike said. "So we'll take it?"

Paige ticked a glance at him. She nervously swept her palms against each other, brushing them clean. "Merle wanted to know by noon."

"Noon? Today?"

"That's right."

Mike waved a hand at the setting sun. "Well, kiss that money goodbye then."

Paige glanced over at him again, trying to tell if Mike was genuinely upset that she'd kept the offer from him until now.

She made her voice easy, almost flippant. "Don't get worked up about it. Regency's overbooked and Merle has nothing but dregs. If we want to come onboard in a day or two, he'll make sure somebody gets reassigned to accommodate us."

"So who this lucrative E?"

"Remember the senator with the grandson that got poisoned? Logan? Family lived in Bryn Mawr?" It had been a huge story at the time. Paige hadn't been living in Pennsylvania yet, but she couldn't have avoided the trial news if she'd wanted to.

Mike's head rose an inch above the ground. "Yeah. It was the nanny, right?"

"Well, the nanny's fresh out of Glynn River. And she got away."

Pulling off the sunglasses, Mike met Paige's eyes. "The nanny poisoned a little kid, Paige. That's the kind of job you snap up, kiddie killers and rapists. Not to mention the pay scale. So what's the problem?"

"I don't like it," she answered. "Not from what I've seen of the specs. First of all, they stuck her with Stephenson for a lawyer."

"I've seen his name before."

"That's because his clients have a tendency to end up as E's."

Mike's fingers tapped against rock. "But they ran tests right? They knew for sure the kid was poisoned?"

"Antifreeze."

"Antifreeze. Homicide." Mike's hands opened, questioning.

"That's what the M.E.'s autopsy report concluded. But that same M.E. left Philly under a cloud a couple of years later."

"Okay, so she wasn't always the most competent. That doesn't mean she was wrong a hundred percent of the time."

"There were always questions cropping up about her, but she really stepped in it with the R.I.S.E. riots. Lots of bodies to examine after that whole fiasco. Civilians, cops, little kids. Her reports were a mess. Basically snuffed out the prosecutor's case and let cop-killers walk. The police weren't about to let her stick around after that. Word is she ended up in some dump around Johnstown." Paige frowned at the fire-rimmed clouds engulfing the sunset. "And Jennings . . ."

"Who?"

"The nanny, Mike. The nanny."

He shrugged. "Okay, what about her?"

"No history of problems. No mental health issues, at least none that were documented. Forget a criminal history. Even her vo-tech records are clean. Exemplary student. Excellent recommendations from the teachers in the program."

"Which was what? Nannying? You can get a degree in that?"

Paige shot him an annoyed look. "Early childhood development is what they call it."

Mike shrugged, offered up that slightly crooked grin that only annoyed her more because it always charmed her—even when she didn't want to be charmed. "Maybe she just realized she didn't like kids," he said.

Paige ignored the comment. "I'm just saying I'm not convinced."

Mike sighed. "And you know I'm not going to be convinced until you're convinced. Any idea when that might be?"

Scrambling to her feet as if she planned to start that instant, Paige said, "I need to track some people down."

Mike stood. He thrust the water bottle at her. "A little hydration before the climb down. Sorry it's Sierra, not Geneva."

Paige accepted the bottle, cocked an eyebrow at the label just the way she knew Mike expected her to do. "I've had worse, I suppose." Her remark brought out his smile again. Pleasure warmed her.

"Yeah? Where was that?" Mike drilled a stare at her. "Malaysia? Southern Philippines? Tibetchen? C'mon, Paige. Lighten up a little. Let me in."

No. Paige let a faint smile play at the corners of her mouth as she returned the bottle, but the pleasure she'd just felt a moment earlier seeped away She stepped farther from Mike, stood balanced at the edge of the rock. Almost 200 feet below, four climbers now flailed at the stone. "You always assume I've been to all these exotic places."

"Because you have. C'mon, look at me."

She turned. "You really think I have dark secrets?"

Mike moved closer. She could smell the perspiration drying on his skin. "I *know* you do," he said.

Paige pulled back. "Tell me one."

"I don't know. That's why they're called secrets. Come on, 'fess up."

Donnie Oxlade. The name trembled on her tongue. *Wire across the top of the staircase, four inches above the top step, just high enough to catch Oxlade's ankle, send him head-first down the stairs. Vertebrae snapping in the darkness of his house.*

"You've only known me how many years?" Mike asked.

Paige cocked an eyebrow again, but this time Mike didn't react to it. "You sure you want to bring up basic?" she teased. "You really want to remind me of what a pathetic maggot of a puke-green recruit you were?"

"I don't know. I kind of like remembering what a hardass, hardcore bitch of a D.I. you were."

"Toughened you up, that's for sure," Paige tossed back.

Mike wasn't deterred so easily. "Just one secret." His voice had darkened a shade and he wasn't smiling. "One thing you've never told anybody else."

Someone snapped rubber bands tight around her lungs. *I can't. I just . . . can't.* "Someday. Maybe." She shot a puckish grin she didn't feel. The grin felt like a stricken alien creature attached to her mouth. "If it's declassified."

A distant shout echoed below, a single drawn-out word that might have been *falling.*

Falling. Fallen. Oxlade's body bunched up like a heap of litter at the bottom of the stairs. His head jammed nearly backwards, face peeking up over the back of one shoulder. Eyes bald and blank in the shadows.

Mike took her hand and touched her fingers to a ridge that marked his left forearm. "We can compare scars."

Paige drew her hand free and extended her arms, palms up, to expose the delicate skin of her wrists and forearms. "Not a mark on me, Mike." *None that you can see.*

She couldn't bear the keenness of his gaze. She glanced away at the reddening sky, then prodded at Mike's trash with one foot. "We need to go. Pack it out." She started toward the trail on the other side of the rock.

"Too bad we can't rappel down," Mike grumbled, loping after her. "It'd be a lot faster."

"Well, we don't have any gear. And whose idea was that?" Loose rock scattered from beneath Paige's shoes as she sidestepped onto the steep pitch of the trail switchbacking down the north side of Rattler's Tooth. Steep was good. Steep required concentration.

The climb up had been dangerous, the path was down treacherous, but neither was nearly as threatening as revealing a secret.

« CHAPTER 9 »

AN EXPOSED PIPE SNAKING across the diner's ceiling dripped water into a murky puddle at Tori's feet. The music—a hard, grinding song—split into two competing strands, staccato words stabbing at electric sitars. Tori stopped short in the doorway.

Only three customers in the place, and none made her think *hitter*.

"You can sit yourself." A waitress drilled past, coffee pot throttled in one hand.

A counter ran along the back wall. A man in blue slacks and a white undershirt slumped over a plate, his elbows jabbing the countertop and his face swaying inches above his food. A tumbler of coppery liquid brimmed by one elbow.

A couple of young women occupied a booth at the front. One of the women leaned back, orange hair pixied in a dozen glittering barrettes, her gaze flicking at Tori and away. The second woman stared out the window. Her coarse blonde hair shimmered with a frost of pink glitter. Pink paste diamonds embedded in the skin shone along her hairline. Injection marks pitted the flesh of her neck.

"C'mon, honey." The waitress swung past Tori again. She was middle-aged, bony as a starving cat, and wore a maroon T-shirt that hung past her flat hips. "Wherever you want."

Head down, Tori headed for an inconspicuous table in a corner and sat with her back to the other customers. She hunched her shoulders, made herself as close to invisible as she could. The music rose to a jackhammer crescendo. Behind her, over the noise of the music, she could hear laughter shrilling from the women in the booth. Tori shifted in her chair, uncomfortable at not being able to see what was going on behind her. But she didn't want people staring her in the face, either.

"Special's on the board." The waitress snapped a menu down on the table and clunked a glass beside it. A fishy smell clung to the water. "Pay in advance. Money chip?" The waitress held out a scanner.

"Cash." Tori bit her lip. "Your sign said—"

"We *love* cash. In fact, you want to go out back later, that's cash only."

"Out—oh." Tori gave a quick nod that she understood. Out back, cash only. A different kind of diner. Drugs as the entree, with maybe a few hookers thrown in as sides. Tori self-consciously ran a hand over the razor-buzzed hair at the back of her neck. Did she look that bad? Like some kind of synth-head?

The waitress took the twenty dollars that Tori pulled from her pocket and waited. Tori reluctantly handed over a second bill. "I'll get your change. What're you having?"

Tori glanced over at the board. Open-faced turkey sandwich, mashed potatoes, green beans, hot roll. Saliva filled her mouth. She didn't need to look at the menu. "The special."

The waitress disappeared into the kitchen. Tori hunched deeper into her chair as a bell jangling over the door announced new customers. She turned her head enough to see the pair of men loping in from the doorway. They were both skinny, one with a stubbly, unshaven face and the other with cheeks that looked like he'd scraped them raw with a bad razorblade. The unshaven man wore jeans and an undershirt, his friend a greasy jumpsuit.

"You here to eat tonight?" the waitress asked the man in the jeans as she slung out from the kitchen.

The man shook his head. "Anybody in back yet?"

"A couple." The waitress clattered two plates of fries in front of the women in the booth. The blonde's head drooped onto her folded arms. The redhead shifted upright, offering the men a sidelong look.

The man in the jumpsuit stopped beside the booth. He toyed with one of the clips in the redhead's hair. Tori cringed in disgust, imagining those grimy fingers rubbing at her own hair, sliding along her jaw. She pressed her foot to the floor, felt the small square of money between the sole of her foot and the shoe. Not much cash, that was for sure. It wouldn't last long. Hell, in a few weeks she might be grateful for the attention of men like these.

Assuming she was still alive.

"These come out?" the man was asking the redhead. Tori peered around again.

"Depends."

The man tapped his other hand against a pocket at the front of his jumpsuit. "You want to come back with us?" he asked. "It's on me."

The redhead shrugged and clambered out of the booth, her feet pigeon-toed in rhinestoned stilettos. The man in the jumpsuit snaked out a hand and engulfed her around the waist, gripping her hard against his side.

"How 'bout you?" the man's friend asked the blonde. She didn't answer, or move her head.

"She's so nailed." The redhead laughed. "But she'll come later. She needs the money."

The man in the jeans made a sour face. "Wow. Thanks."

"Whatever." The redhead, pinned to the other man's ribs, clomped past.

The man in the jeans headed for Tori's table. Tori quickly turned forward again and fussed with the paper napkin dispenser. From the corner of her eye, she saw the faded denim and thin cotton of the second man's clothes. He stood beside Tori, waiting. She moved on from the napkins to the salt and pepper shakers, arranging them closer to her utensils.

The man cleared his throat. Tori darted a glance his direction. She held herself stiffly and wondered why he didn't get the message—*Get the hell away from me*—that pulsed from her skin. The man extended a hand, palm-up, like a seedy gentleman asking for a dance.

"I got paid today," he told her.

Tori stared at the tabletop.

"I got enough for both of us. If you want to go back there with me."

Tori didn't answer.

"Think you're some special shit, huh?" Fingers flicked at the back of Tori's neck. She held herself motionless, but her teeth clenched hard together. "Well, you're not. You look like crap. Your hair—and what's with your skin? You got fleas?" He spun away and followed his friend to a pleated plastic screen spread across a doorway at the back. When they pulled the screen aside, Tori glimpsed the purplish glow of blacklights. The man in the jumpsuit gave the redhead a push. The two men pressed after her.

Tori's stomach knotted. If some man shoved his hands under her shirt or down her jeans, she'd smash him on the head with a brick or a lamp. Drug-slinging seemed positively bright in comparison.

So why was she in here, spending precious money on a meal? She should be at the dumpster out back, eating for free.

A plate clattered onto the table. Tori jumped.

"Didn't mean to scare you," the waitress said.

Tori's smile was thin and weak. She fumbled at the utensils.

"You finish that water already? You want something else? We don't make anything fancy, but you can have vodka, scotch, rum, tequila, or gin straight up."

"No, thanks." She'd never had anything stronger than beer. A shot of something strong enough to obliterate fear was tempting, but her head was already muddy with exhaustion and nerves. And liquor was definitely too expensive.

A vein of fat glistened through pink slices of turkey. Gluey mashed potatoes lurked beneath coagulating gravy. After Glynn River's cafeteria, this was gourmet. Tori's appetite opened with raw force on the food. She'd devoured half the meal before the waitress reappeared with the water pitcher and Tori's change. The coins were so worn that Tori could barely make out the portraits of Washington and Reagan.

The waitress eyed Tori's plate. "Nobody's going to take it away from you, girl."

A retching noise strained from the booth at the front and the waitress whipped around. "Oh, no, you don't. Not on *my* shift."

The blonde leaned over the table. Her back heaved. The waitress yanked her from the booth. "You get out, right now."

The man at the counter swizzled his head in lopsided circles that matched the loopy music. "Hey, Britt, you need some help?" he slurred, dragging his hands up from the counter like they each weighed fifty pounds, then letting them flop into his lap.

The waitress dragged the blonde to the doorway and pushed her out to the sidewalk. Then she stumped to the counter and gripped the guard's shoulders. His glassy eyes swung toward her.

"You're as bad as she is. You'll be puking all over my mopped floor in a minute. Up. Up, up. Come on." She snatched a cap from the stool beside him and jammed it onto his head. Tori's mouth went dry.

It was a Glynn River cap. How many guards had she seen with that same cap plastered on their bristly heads while they kicked a prisoner or

61

beat somebody with a truncheon, or eyed the naked women in the showers? Now she realized that his blue slacks were uniform pants. He must have taken off the regulation blue uniform shirt when his shift ended.

Heart slamming against her ribs, Tori bent over her plate. How many of Glynn River's staff lived in this town?

"I'm 'kay," the guard said.

"You think so?" the waitress said. "Because I would've said you're a holy mess, that's what." The guard creaked around on the stool, mouth half open, flailing arms protesting the waitress's judgment. Tori didn't recognize him. His gaze dragged across her. He was either nailed or drunk.

"Jus' coffee now." The guard swiped one hand across his cheek, rouging his face with ketchup and steak sauce, and wobbled the stool back around until he could sag against the counter again

"Jesus H. Christ. All I got to say is, you throw up in here, it's you going to be pushing the mop." Jamming a stained towel under her waistband, the waitress stalked through the saloon doors to the kitchen.

Good time to get out of this place. Tori swung up from her chair and placed a couple of dollars on the table. She glanced at the kitchen, hesitated, took the money back. She paused again, the dollars caught between thumb and finger. She couldn't afford to keep bleeding money. But if she stiffed the waitress, that guaranteed the woman would remember her, and not happily either. Which would be bad news if a hitter came nosing around.

Tori slid the bills under the salt shaker.

The guard didn't look up as she slipped behind him to the door. Tori cringed as the jangling of the bell over the door announced her exit. Breathing shallowly, air stuck in her chest, she trotted to the opposite sidewalk.

She blundered through an alley, emerging between a boarded-over liquor store and an empty laundromat. Her legs ached to the bone. The cuts on her cheek and neck throbbed. She sank onto the cracked curb and blinked at the darkness. Night was probably the safest time to travel. She should leave Granite now.

She pressed her face against her hands. So tired. She had to sleep first. Not optional. Just for a couple of hours. Maybe find a deserted backyard or an empty lot.

Headlights burst from the darkness. Tori froze as the lights turned full on her. She scrambled to her feet and braced herself to sprint. The truck braked. A head thrust out the open window.

"Miss? That you?" The man sounded both surprised and pleased.

Tori couldn't decide whether to run or stay put.

"Remember me? Sam? From the gas station?" He turned his head to either side so Tori could examine his face in the faint illumination of the dash. "I don't want to stick my nose in your business, but if you don't mind me asking, what happened to your boyfriend?"

Tori's gut told her Sam was no hitter, no informer. *Like you have a clue,* she silently mocked herself. But she took a step forward. "He never showed."

"Son of a bitch! Excuse me, there."

"That's okay. It pretty much sums him up."

"He doesn't have a brain in his head, standing up a beautiful woman like you."

Tori touched her sweaty, rough-shorn hair. The guy couldn't be serious.

Sam leaned farther out the window. "You don't have any place to go?"

"I didn't see any motel."

"The closest motel's in Glynn River." He gave an awkward laugh. "The town, not the prison."

Tori turned away so he couldn't see her expression. "I'll be all right." She was so tired she could barely force herself into a shuffle. The truck nosed along beside her.

"Hey, you can stay at my house."

Tori glanced over. Sam's grin was big and sloppy. He nodded at the dog that had clambered across him and that now gazed out at Tori. "Anyway, Pretty Girl loves company."

"I don't think—"

The dog barked once. "See? She likes you."

Tori threw a glance at the abandoned stores and the squat, beetlish houses across the street. Her shoulders sagged. Outside, exposed, and still this close to Glynn River was no place to be. She crossed in front of the truck. Sam pushed the passenger door open and Tori clambered up into the seat.

"My boyfriend'll come for me tomorrow," she said, slicing a forbidding look in Sam's direction. She managed to shut the door as Pretty Girl bounded onto her lap. The dog's claws pressed at her thighs. "He's just late."

Sam worked his mouth. "Men are like that sometimes," he said. "Sons a—you know."

Tori thought of the man at the diner flicking his grimy fingers at her neck. "*People* are like that," she answered. Then she glanced at Sam. He watched the road, steering around potholes and trash.

"Maybe not everybody," Tori amended. She bit her lip and added, "But almost."

« CHAPTER 10 »

SAM'S HOUSE WAS AS BLOTCHY and untended as the man himself. Pretty Girl, frisking in and out of the shaggy front lawn, darted over to nose at Tori's hand every few seconds. Tori waited on the porch while Sam fumbled a key card into the reader beside the door. She jiggled one foot, part of her wanting to run before she had to decide whether she trusted Sam enough to go inside his house. The rest of her just wanted to crawl into a corner and sleep for the next 24 hours.

Sam slid the card half a dozen times through the reader before the lock released with a loud click. "Sorry about that," he muttered into his beard, head down, the knob disappearing beneath his beefy hand. "Sorry the place isn't cleaner." He dared a glance back at her, cleared his throat. "Usually, I'd, you know. Wash the dishes and stuff."

Tori eyed the fingers of paint peeling off the porch railing. Weeds exploded in the yard. But there was a bird feeder stuffed with seed hanging from a branch of the nearest tree and metal bowls of kibble and what appeared to be reasonably clean water on the step.

His hand still engulfing the door knob, Sam turned back. He watched Tori gently toe the water dish. "We got lots of stray cats around here," he explained. "Turns out squirrels like cat food too. And they all like a watering hole."

Pretty Girl dashed through the doorway. Sam shuffled after the dog, fumbling just inside for a light switch. *Hell, you already got in his truck*, Tori thought. *You trusted him that much.* She stepped into the house.

They were in the living room. A grubby couch strewn with dog hair and a pair of chairs swam in the murky urine glow of the overhead light. "Let me get some air in here." Sam shoved a window open and wedged an empty bottle into the gap. A warm, humid breeze filtered through the screen. It smelled like shaggy pines.

Sam lumbered into the adjacent kitchen. "You hungry?"

Surprised, Tori found she was. She'd had ten years of her stomach never being full and apparently one diner meal wasn't enough to make up for that. Her feet sank into ancient shag carpet as she followed him.

Faded wallpaper of palm trees and dancing pineapples peeled away from the kitchen walls. Bits of carrot peel and cracker crumbs flecked what was visible of the sink between leaning stacks of dirty dishes.

Sam opened a cabinet door and peered inside. He glanced over his shoulder at Tori. His face wrinkled into an apologetic smile. "Afraid you caught me without much in the pantry. Didn't get a chance to go to the grocery store today." He let the door thump shut while he scanned the counters. "Here!" He snagged a single apple from the windowsill above the sink, rubbed it with a stained dishtowel, and presented it to Tori.

"Thanks." She took it.

"I know it's not—"

"No, it's great, it's fine. Really." And compared to the occasional bruised, mushy apple that had appeared on her Glynn River food tray, this one was a beauty.

Sam swept up a spotted glass draining on the sideboard, filled it at the tap, and thrust it into Tori's other hand. He grimaced at the sink. "I know it looks like crap around here. My wife, well, ex-wife, she divorced me last year. I'm not real good at this housekeeping sh—stuff." His hands fidgeted against his thighs. He looked up at Tori, his face hopeful, the expression more like a boy's than a bulky middle-aged man's. "You want to watch holos or something? Thrill-stream's pretty good."

"I'm kind of tired," Tori answered gently.

"I'm sorry. God, what an idiot." He smacked his forehead. "It's been a rough day for you, with your boyfriend and everything." A mournful smile strained his face. "Sorry. You probably don't want to talk about him."

"Not really."

"Hey, I'm an idiot, I know." Sam backed from the kitchen into a short hallway. "The—uh—bathroom's right over there." His hands patted the air. "And that's my bedroom. But you can have it if you want." Tori caught a glimpse of fusty sheets. At least he wasn't pressing her to share a bed. She rubbed the shorn hair at the nape of her neck. Maybe it shouldn't be too much of a surprise, Sam's willingness to leave her alone. She wasn't much to look at.

"I got a spare room too," Sam added, pushing its door open. "My wife—I mean, my ex—slept in here the last couple of years." The narrow bed was neatly made, the spread tucked beneath the pillow like a bib under a chin. Tori wondered if the ex-wife had been the last one to make this bed.

"Guest room's fine with me." Tori followed Sam inside and set the apple and glass of water on a small nightstand.

"I think she might've left some pajamas." Sam shuffled to the dresser and dragged a couple of drawers open. "There's this. If you want it, I mean." He drew out a cotton nightshirt. Tori took it from him. The shirt hung to Tori's knees. "It'll fit you pretty good," Sam observed. His cheeks glowed pink. "Not that I'm trying to say anything—I mean—you know, hit on you, or anything."

Tori folded the nightshirt across the bed. "Thanks."

"Hey. Let me get the vids going, just in case. But you can keep it mute." A screen was set into the wall just above the foot of the bed. Sam snapped his fingers twice. Pretty Girl whined and sat at attention. "Shoot." He clapped his hands—hard—and the screen burst into color. Images played in three quadrants. In the fourth, newslines appeared and disappeared.

"Okay, then." Sam backed to the door. One foot fumbled directly into Pretty Girl's chest. The dog skittered to the hall. "Help yourself to anything in the kitchen." Sam fled to his own room and shut the door.

It was a relief to be alone although Tori wished Pretty Girl had stayed with her. Five steps took Tori across the room to the window. She lifted the blue-flowered curtains away from the glass and peered out. She couldn't see much in the darkness, just the bristly outlines of pines and the dark squares of other bungalows daubed along each side of the street. The room was stifling, but she didn't open the window. Instead, she checked that it was locked, then re-crossed the room to shut the door and check its lock as well. It had one, sturdy and shiny. New-looking. Probably added by the ex-wife.

Dropping cross-legged onto the bed, Tori faced the monitor. In prison, she'd had no access to news-streams. Occasional rumors floated among the inmates, but those rumors were usually about something happening on the inside: the warden's affair with one of the youngest guards; menu changes (always bad) in the cafeteria. The world outside Glynn River was a ten-year blank.

Headlines floated forward and dropped back to reveal holo-news, both words and images eventually disintegrating.

Leak Detected at BioZone 19

More Social Security Cuts Loom

Turkish Sector Massacre

Mercon Tests SkinRip Drug

L.A Peel Kingpin Sentenced

Her head ached. She hadn't seen vids in more than a decade and she couldn't filter out the frantic rush of it anymore. She was about to say 'off' when an ad, fizzing behind the entertainment bar, saw its opportunity and swooped out. Tori sucked in her breath. The glass-paneled chamber holding a single metal chair was so sharply three-dimensional that it seemed to float out above the dresser. Tori's hands shook as a pearly mist enveloped the chair.

Blood-red words stabbed the mist. WHEN THE COLD-BLOODED KILLER OF FOUR POLICE OFFICERS AND THREE FBI AGENTS FINALLY MEETS JUSTICE, THE BEST SEAT IN THE HOUSE IS IN *YOUR* HOUSE! An image of the condemned materialized in the chair. He glared straight at her. EXPERIENCE A KILLER'S RAMPAGE . . . AND WITNESS HIS DEATH. JULY 23RD, 8:00 EST, VID-STREAM SR2. The mist obscured all quadrants of the screen. The lettering turned elegant, royal-blue. Brought to you in part by Progressive Prison Solutions, Inc.

The mist contracted into a revolving cube. Classic movie scenes played on its six faces. Tori stared past them. She had to sit on her hands to stop their trembling. Had the condemned man really killed all those people? Or was he like her?

Cop-killers and terrorists, they were the ones who died in the chamber. That man was trapped. But if she could elude the hitters, stay out of their sights until—? She snorted, disgusted with herself. What, Senator Logan would drop the whole thing if the hitters failed and enough time passed? Months? Years? Right.

The thing was not to stay any place for too long.

She needed to get out of this town. Get away from Glynn River guards hanging out at the local diners.

Give yourself a little credit, she thought. She'd made it a day . . . almost a day. How many Executables could say that?

She turned off all the streams and sat down on the bed. She waited an hour. The house was silent. She unlocked the bedroom door. In the hallway, she paused outside Sam's closed door. Dual snores rose and fell on the other side.

She stole into the living room. She'd seen a comm in there, sitting lopsided on a stack of papers, the device ridiculously old-fashioned even to her, with a broken screen the size of a matchbox.

The only illumination came from a streetlight down the road; it cut through the half-closed blinds with a harsh light that reminded Tori of that last relentless light in solitary confinement. Cautiously, she turned the comm on.

"The time allotment for this billing cycle is 75 minutes. You have 52 minutes remaining. Thank you for using CBI." A woman's voice cut the air. Tori fumbled at the volume. "Number please."

Tori licked her lips. "Six-one-oh." She started slowly, then reeled off the rest of the digits with the ease of childhood memory. "Four-nine-five-three-three-one-two-six-eight-seven."

"That number is no longer in service."

Tori's hands were damp. She repeated the sequence of numbers. The recorded voice came again. "That number is no longer in service."

Tori lowered her face against her palms. Not in service. Because her father was in the hospital? Or dead? Or was it just that he didn't have enough money to pay the bill?

"Do you wish to make a call?" the voice asked. Tori raised her head and blinked at the shadows in the corner. The room smelled like Pretty Girl.

"New call," Tori said. She tried Mrs. Healy, their long-time next door neighbor, but that number was also out of service. She asked to be connected with the hospital nearest to her father's house, but the woman who answered refused to state whether Tori's father was or was not a patient. She tried another hospital, a little farther than the first. No one picked up and Tori was cut off halfway through her attempt to leave a message in a shaky voice.

She slumped back, let out a trembling breath. She could make for her dad's house. But isn't that where the hitters would expect her to go? Straight to her only remaining family? After what the minister said, she didn't have a lot of hope that her father would be there, waiting for her. Unless he was . . . and the hitters were waiting right there with him.

She pressed the back of her hand against her mouth.

Nothing you can do. Don't think about it.

Okay. So where?

Sarah. It was the only other name that came into her head.

They'd grown up on the same block, gone to the same crummy schools, counted themselves lucky when they both got into Vo-Tech's early child development program. Nanny-school is what it really was or, more accurately, glorified babysitter-training for poor teenagers with nothing much in their future.

They both worked hard and earned their certificates. Sarah got lucky. She went to a prominent surgeon's household where she took the night shift of bottles, dirty diapers, and two a.m. shrieks. Then Tori struck it even luckier. Tori was hired by a do-gooder senator to help out the senator's daughter, saddled with a colicky newborn.

Tori had never felt comfortable, had never taken one easy breath after she started that job. The gated neighborhood was a larger flowered prison, employers peering at you like you'd just stolen the silver, women dewy and fresh-faced in the mornings while the nannies were bleary from getting up three times during the night.

Tori and Sarah got each other through it all. Just knowing there was one other person to vent to when Tori's employer breezed into her room without knocking or made remarks to friends about Tori's 'unfortunate background' made the condescension bearable. Knowing that there was someone to spend free days with, talking and commiserating, gave her something to look forward to. She and Sarah would take over a shady bench in the manicured neighborhood park and drink wine coolers or hot chocolate that Tori surreptitiously made in the microwave in the downstairs kitchen that she wasn't supposed to use. With Sarah, every miserable incident was an off-kilter story that had them both laughing.

Now Tori sat quietly, recalling the string of numbers she'd memorized for Sarah years ago. She bent over the comm, paralyzed. Even if Sarah was still at this number and even if Sarah agreed to let her come—two very large ifs—Tori carried danger with her now like the smell of her own skin. Hitters might track her to Sarah's, and bring Tori's only friend right into the fight. Or the hitters might be there already, waiting for Tori to show up.

Do you really have a choice?

A door opened in the hallway. Something bumped. Tori shrank on herself, huddling around the lit yellow rectangle of the comm's screen like it was a match about to be blown out. Footsteps. She cringed. Sam might not appreciate her using his minutes. Or maybe she'd misjudged him entirely. He might have waited until the middle of the night to bring out his gun, or to unchain the front door for the hitters crowded on the sagging porch.

Another door creaked down the hallway, shut softly. The bathroom. Tori breathed easier, but stayed hunched where she was, closing her eyes as if that made her invisible in the shadows. The toilet flushed. Water struck the sink. Footsteps re-traced their route, from the bathroom to Sam's bedroom. A door shut.

Tori waited several minutes, quietly breathing the darkness in and out. Then she clenched her eyes shut—*let it work, let it work*—and prayed that the same sequence had followed Sara wherever she now lived.

Tori opened her eyes. "New call," she said and recited the number. Her breath snagged. The ID bar flashed an address in Arlington, Virginia. The vid square on the cracked screen stayed blank and she was suddenly glad of that.

"'Lo?" Drowsiness muffled the voice, but Tori recognized it instantly.

"Sarah?" She crossed her arms tightly, suddenly light-headed.

"Who . . . oh. . . oh, my God! Tori?" A fumbling noise. "Damn vid's not working."

Sarah really sounded like someone who'd just been woken up in the middle of the night and not remotely like someone frantic and terrified, trapped on a chair in the middle of a circle of hitters brandishing guns and other weapons, waiting for the E to call.

Tori took a breath, swallowed. "Vid's broken on this end."

"Oh, my God—Tori—-where are you? The ID says Sam Mantell. Who's he?"

"Just a friend." Tori grimaced, annoyed at the lie. Sarah was her best and oldest friend. So why did Tori feel like she couldn't just tell the truth?

There was a moment's silence. "You're not at Glynn River anymore?"

Tori rubbed a hand across her face. There was no reason Sarah should have remembered the exact release date. Ten years, for God's sake. It was only inside the prison that time slowed, each day a boulder to shoulder aside.

"No," Tori said, "Not as of six o'clock this morning."

More silence. "It was today? You mean, there weren't any hitters?"

71

"Oh, there were hitters. But I—" She felt more light-headed than ever, saying this aloud. "I got away."

Sarah laughed, the same light, delicious peal Tori remembered. If Sarah was on the screen, she'd have her hands raised together to her lips. A bright, crooked-toothed smile outlined in strawberry pink lipstick. Crinkles invading the blue eyeshadow sparkling on her eyelids.

"Oh, my God, Tori. You did it? You did it!" A squeak on the last word, then, hushed: "Geez, I didn't even know today was, you know, the day. I didn't see the news."

Tori waved off the apology, then remembered Sarah couldn't see her. "That's okay. Really. Hey—" Her heart practically clogged her throat. "Have you heard anything about my dad?"

"No. I mean, not since right after the trial. I never go back there now. My mom moved and there's no one else there I still want to talk to."

Tori sagged. She wanted to say: *what about my dad? All the times you hung out at our place? The summer you lived with us when your mom was dating that guy you hated so much? You really didn't want to talk to my dad after you left?*

Maybe Sarah sensed her thoughts because she said, "It's just . . .everything was awkward with your dad. After what happened to you."

Tori sat up straighter. She and Sarah were the same age, separated by only a month. Sarah had been a teenager at the time of the trial. What could you really expect a nineteen-year-old to do when all the crazy shit hit the fan?

"So . . ." Tori paused. Words weren't coming—which was ridiculous. This was *Sarah*. "You didn't stick around Bryn Mawr."

"Where? Oh, God, no. I left that job a couple of months after the—after you went away. Couldn't stand those people without you around. I worked for a couple of families in a really hoity toity neighborhood in Bucks County and then—hey! You don't know yet. I got married."

Tori blinked at the cracked, blank screen. Married? Well, of course. It's not like everybody else's lives stood still for a decade. Just hers.

"—a great guy, he manages a gas station."

She should be happy for her old friend, but instead Tori felt vaguely sick. Her heart climbed so high up her throat, it practically stuffed itself into her mouth. Even if Sarah didn't mind helping her, this husband might not be thrilled about it.

Tori had to know. "Sar, I need to ask a favor." *Just say it.* "You think I could crash with you?" She finished in a flurry: "Just for a day or two, I swear."

"Are you kidding?" Sarah asked and sickness instantly swam through Tori's veins. Shit. Alone. Alone. She was going to have to do this on her own for the rest of her life.

She almost didn't hear the rest of Sarah's words. "I can't wait to see you!"

Sarah's questions, directions—"You know the address? You got any money? Maybe the bus would be the best way."—fluttered around Tori who collapsed onto the shag carpet and wept soundlessly into its stink of dog fur and potato chip crumbs.

« CHAPTER 11 »

TORI WOKE AT DAWN. She was exhausted from the previous day, every muscle ached, and a poison ivy rash erupted in pink bumps down her left forearm. More sleep was definitely not happening.

Birds whistled from the yard. Tori pushed herself up from the bed and crossed to the window. Careful to stay out of view, she peered around one edge of the shade. Even this early, the morning steamed, green and lush. Robins and sparrows crowded the feeder and flitted down to a birdbath half-hidden in the shadow of the pines.

She imagined a hitter crouched at the very back of the shadows. She jerked back from the window and dropped the shade. A tremor ran through her.. She closed her eyes and gripped her hands together until they were still.

Hitters could be anywhere. Around the back corner of the house, in a neighbor's yard, in one of the cars parked down the block. The uncertainty of it, the impossibility of knowing, brought a sickly trickle of adrenaline through her body. Her feet twitched, ready to run.

She couldn't stay still. Sliding open the dresser drawers and opening the closet, she looked through the few clothes left behind by Sam's ex. There wasn't much, just a few oversized t-shirts, a pair of enormous sweatpants, and some mismatched socks.

Taking a blue t-shirt, she stole into the hallway. The house was quiet, the door to Sam's room shut. She went into the bathroom and locked the door. She wanted to take a long bath, let the grime soak off her and the hot water relax her muscles, but naked in a bathtub was not where she wanted to be if a hitter burst into the house.

She took a shower that was only a little longer than the ones at Glynn River. At least this shower was warm. The water set the rash on her arm to a murderous itching.

She dressed in the same underwear and jeans she'd worn the day before. Sam's ex-wife's t-shirt hung halfway down her thighs. It smelled like a hamster cage. A clean hamster cage, at least. She put on two of the ex's mismatched socks as well, a blue and a gray.

When she'd finished, she returned to the guest room and waited for Sam to wake up. She sat on her bed, her back straight and sneakered feet solidly on the floor. Sam's room was directly across the hall. She'd left the door to her own room wide open so she could keep an eye on his. Birds chittered outside the glass.

Her phone call to Sarah in the middle of the night still lit her with a thin, fragile hope. She wanted to be with Sarah, just sit and breathe in the presence of a friend. She also wanted to be out of Granite, far enough away that she'd never be recognized by an off duty Glynn River guard who might alert the execution company in exchange for a small gratuity. She worried that the money the pastor had palmed to her might not even buy a one-way bus ticket.

An hour passed. Sam's door across the hallway crept open. He scratched his beard and glanced down at his T-shirt and the gray sweat pants cut off at his knees. Behind him, Pretty Girl still sprawled across his unmade bed. His eyes shifted to the bathroom door. "Did you need to—you know, go in there?"

"I already used it."

"Great. Well. If you're done, I need to, uh . . ." Sam's skin blazed pink through his beard as he fumbled into the bathroom and shut the door.

Tori stayed where she was, glancing now and then at the shaded window. Sunlight seeped around the edges of the blind. If anyone was out there, she'd never make it out of Sam's yard.

When Sam emerged from the bathroom, he wore beige mechanics coveralls that stretched taut across his belly. Gold thread spelled SAM in cursive letters across the chest pocket. He detoured into his room and hunkered down to snare a pair of work boots from beneath the bed. Pretty Girl shifted to a fresh, cool part of the mattress, snorted out a noisy breath, and shut her eyes again.

"I've got some cereal," Sam told Tori, shifting from one socked foot to the other in the doorway to her room. The boots dangled from his hand like a pair of shot ducks.

"That'd be great." Which wasn't an exaggeration. Corn flakes, frosted flakes, toasted oats, whatever: compared to Glynn River's gluey oatmeal and charcoal toast, a simple bowl of cereal sounded downright amazing.

"I hope you don't mind—" Tori tugged at the ex's t-shirt. "I just wanted something clean."

"No. Geez. Glad they're doing somebody some good." Sam raised the hand with the boots. "Let me put these on and I'll get the cereal." He lowered himself onto an uncomfortable looking wooden chair standing sentry against the guest room wall just inside the door. He grunted, bending forward to cram his feet into the boots.

Tori glanced at the shabby room and felt bad about what she was going to request. But even a one-way ticket to Sarah's was sure to take a big chunk of her cash. So, yeah, she felt bad—but not as bad as she was going to feel about slinging or smuggling or selling herself when the cash ran out. Better to push off that situation until the last possible second.

"Can I ask you something?" she said.

Sam stopped tying his shoelaces. He twisted awkwardly at the waist, turning to look at her. Hope—for what, she wasn't sure—brightened his face.

His expression only made her feel worse, but she didn't stop. "I don't . . . well, what I mean is, I'm kind of low on money right now. I'm in— I've been in some trouble and I could really use . . ." She broke off. "I hate to ask."

Sam immediately hoisted himself upright and, untied laces ticking and scratching across the floor, barreled toward the kitchen. Confused by this unexpected burst of energy and decisiveness, Tori rose and stepped hesitantly along the hall to the living room.

Sam rushed back out of the kitchen a moment later clutching his billfold. "I only have a few bucks on me." He pulled out the money, then tugged a card from its pouch. "There's not a lot on this either. I know you said you don't have bank on your chip, but we could transfer this onto your card instead."

His generosity astonished her, made her feel the smallness, the meanness of the fear and doubt that cringed inside her. She wondered if he would be so generous if he knew who she was. Somehow, she thought he would be, but she just couldn't take the chance of telling him. Anyway, she'd be gone soon.

"I don't have a card either," she said.

Sam's eyes and mouth widened until he looked like a surprised jack-o-lantern. "You don't?"

She shook her head.

"Is it that boyfriend? He won't let you have one?"

Tori let him take her silence as a yes.

"Well, that's lousy. I mean, if you excuse me saying so." He extended the money card to Tori. "You can just have it."

"I can't take this."

Sam's face was solemn. "That's okay. You need it. Anyway, there's not much on it." He looked at the floor as if his lack of money shamed him. "I'll be all right. I got 15 hours pay coming to me. And I won't need the card. I'm getting bank added to my chip in a couple of days."

"I thought you said you didn't want that on your chip. That chips are creepy."

Sam rubbed one forearm as if somehow checking whether his chip had already been reprogrammed to handle all his financial transactions. "The bank said I have to. They're phasing the cards out. And the government doesn't like cash. Everybody trying to ditch out of their taxes." He dug out a scrap of paper and gave that to Tori as well. "Password."

"God . . . thanks." She pushed the card, the cash, and the paper into a pocket. "This is so nice of you." The words were inadequate. She swallowed thickly. Sam beamed.

"Is there a bus that comes through town?" she asked as gently as she could.

Sam's face dimmed. "Glynn River's got the only bus station around here."

So she'd have to go back. But only to the town, she reassured herself, not the prison. As if she'd sensed Tori's distress, Pretty Girl jumped down from Sam's bed and clicked down the hallway to lean against Tori's left leg. Tori bent to stroke the dog's satiny head.

Sam lowered himself onto the couch and worked his bootlaces tight. "So—uh—you figure he's not coming back? Your boyfriend?"

"No, I think he's pretty much history."

"Jerk," Sam muttered. "Sorry." He stumped up from the couch. "You know you can stay here as long as you want."

"I have a sister in New York." It seemed as safely anonymous as any place could be.

Sam rubbed at his beard. "Are you sure you don't want to stay?"

Tori's hand stopped moving on the dog's head. Pretty Girl whined and mouthed Tori's fingers. Tori gazed around the living room. The carpet exhaled the humid, canine odor of a kennel. Past the dusty window shades a skinny orange cat stalked invisible prey in the overgrown yard.

The shabbiness and the smells didn't matter. Hell, shabbiness and smells were a hundred steps up from Glynn River's kill floor. Part of her wanted to stay here. But she needed to keep moving. And she wanted to feel that relief again, that sense of belonging, that she'd felt when Sarah told her to come to her house.

Sam was watching her, his face bright again with hope. Tori's chest tightened. "I'm sorry," she said. "But I have to leave."

He only nodded, but the light went out of his face. "All right, then. Whenever you're ready."

The bus station in Glynn River was, if possible, even more decrepit than the downtown that ensnared it. Flecks of green and blue glass glimmered across the parking lot like rocks in the bottom of an aquarium. Tori's sneakers crunched as she climbed down from Sam's truck. She paused, leaning into the car. Her plastic bag swung from her fist. Sam had insisted on adding some candy bars and a couple of his ex-wife's shirts to the meager stash.

"I hope you're not late for work," Tori said. "Driving me all the way up here."

"There's no late. I just go and hang out, see if any jobs come up today. Anyway, Pretty Girl likes the drive."

Sam's face looked like it might crumple at any second, and Tori hastily said, "Well, it was really nice of you."

Sam swam toward her, his thick arms paddling across the taped upholstery. "Are you sure you don't want to stay?" His voice hitched. "Pretty Girl would sure like the company."

"Thanks for everything." Tori swung the passenger door shut. Tucking her head down, she hurried toward the station entrance. When she glanced back, Sam's truck hadn't moved. He and Pretty Girl both stared after her.

Inside the low-ceilinged station, a pair of men loitered outside the women's bathroom. One of the men had cratered skin that marked him as a survivor of a Pox-12 epidemic. Long, raised sores, shiny under protective ointment, striped the face and throat of his companion. SkinRip: One of the first mutations to show up after the biobombings. Nobody had managed to stop the terrorists and the crazies during the last decade, that was obvious. Tori wondered if the man came from Philly, how long ago his neighborhood had been fenced into a no-go zone, and how long the quarantine had lasted before the few survivors were released and the many dead bodies were trundled to the crematorium.

Tori skirted the men, feeling their stares follow her, and approached the one ticket dispenser that didn't have an out-of-order sign taped across it. She frowned at the readout. The machine wouldn't accept cash. A woman grappling with a toddler crowded behind her as Tori pressed Sam's money card into the dispenser.

"Stop with your *shit*," the woman snapped at the child. Tori fumbled with the scrap of paper bearing the access code.

The machine added highway transport and security and interstate fees to the fare. The muscles in Tori's neck hardened into knots as she waited to see if Sam's accounts held enough money to pay for a one-way ticket. Seconds later, the dispenser spat out both the card and a receipt. Tori snatched them into a pocket and stumbled away. She glanced toward the bathrooms. The Pox-12 survivor had stopped a young girl, maybe 16 or 17 years old.. He was leaning into her, touching her arm and smiling in an intimate way that might almost have been charming if the skin of his face weren't mutilated. The girl let him touch her.

A pimp? Recruiting some new product for his loyal customers?

Tori's hands shook. She'd sling drugs before she went to work in the Pox-12's line of business. Assuming she had a choice. Slinging and whoring went together like two strands of a rope, a fact she'd learned from assorted inmates in Glynn River.

She pressed her palms together hard, but that only made the trembling worse. She glanced at a clock on the wall. It was stuck at 5:02. She wondered if any guards from Glynn River came through here and if there were any more hitters from the execution company hanging around. Her best hope was that no one would suspect she might return to Glynn River after escaping it.

She stepped carefully across broken tiles to the station's front window and peered through the oily glass at a pawn shop and a taco stand butting up against a large granite obelisk across the street. She could just make out the largest words of the dedication near the top of the monument. It was a memorial to soldiers killed in Desert Sword. The engraved columns must be the names of the dead.

A barely intelligible voice crackled onto the intercom to announce Tori's bus. A woman took her receipt and nodded her through a metal detector.

Sam's truck was parked across the street. Suspicion jolted Tori's heart, just for a second, before she dismissed the ridiculous image of Sam-as-killer.

He was staring moonily past the rolled-down window, one beefy arm hooked around Pretty Girl's neck. He looked like he was going to cry. Climbing the tall steps onto the bus, Tori caught his eye and waved. He straightened, waved back.

The A/C on the bus was broken, the windows open. The only remaining seats were back near the bathroom which exuded a bleachy odor every time someone opened its door. The upholstery was a gray vinyl that stuck to the backs of her sweaty arms. Up front, a toddler shrieked.

The bus pulled out and rattled onto the winding two-lane highway. It was heaven to smell the woods and fields, to feel the wind pour over her skin, to stare at the remarkable colors of the wildflowers dotting the highway's edge with butter-yellow, violet, and carnation-pink. Nobody paid attention to her.

A couple of miles outside town, they passed the penitentiary.

She stared, fascinated by the place that had swallowed ten years of her life. She'd originally arrived at Glynn River after dark and had only glimpsed the exterior for a few brief seconds while guards shuttled her between the windowless van and the intake door.

She saw now that it was as dismal on the outside as it was inside: gray featureless walls ran on forever, barbed wire tumbleweeded on top of the perimeter fence, and cars in the parking lot sparked off green and red sunlight like the dead husks of giant beetles. She thought of the inmates who were working the kill line right now behind those walls, the prisoners cussing each other to shreds in jammed cells. Executables counting down last days in a sweat of terror.

She tasted blood in her mouth and realized she'd bitten her lower lip hard enough to break the skin.

Her gaze swept from the prison to the trees on the opposite side of the highway. She couldn't pinpoint now where she'd run into the woods, or where the gunshots had come from. The previous day was a sickly green blur of adrenaline and exhaustion.

She shook her head at the thick foliage. How the hell had she managed to get away? She should have been a body twisted on the ground, her skin torn by a dozen bullets. Instead, that young man—that hitter who looked like a teenager—had provided the body.

She strained her neck, staring back through the window until the prison disappeared from view. Then she slumped forward, her eyes closed, and massaged the headache that suddenly bit at her temples.

What did an execution company do when a hitter got killed instead of the Executable? Did they get extra pissed-off? Start looking for revenge instead of just doing a job?

Her pulse thumped so hard it made her jaw ache. She couldn't stop the questions careening through her head. How long would they look for her? How many times would they try to kill her, these people who must love killing more than just about anything?

Could she ever run far enough to get away from them?

« CHAPTER 12 »

BEN, THE TEENAGE CASHIER, didn't recognize the man who surveyed the interior of Pinckney's convenience mart from just inside the door. The man stood with his arms crossed and his stocky legs braced a foot apart. His cheeks had a coarse and brilliant ruddiness as if he'd used his razor to flay himself that morning, removing flesh along with the whiskers.

When the man strode to the counter in two quick steps, Ben floundered back automatically, bumbling into the crowded display shelves. Liquor bottles shivered and clinked.

The man leaned forward, hands splayed on the counter. White scars flecked the backs of his wrists and his knuckles. "You okay?" he said with a thick accent.

"Uh, yeah, I think so." Ben swallowed.

"Good!" The man's face cracked into a giddy smile. A gleeful light sparked his eyes. "We talk, then." One of his palms slapped the countertop as if he'd just told a joke.

Ben scratched at a ripe pimple above his Adam's apple. "Were you wanting something?"

The man smacked the counter again. "Yes!" Turning away, he busied himself with packages of doughnuts and breakfast buns. His back reminded Ben of an ape, squat and powerful, a bristle of hairs stabbing out from the nape of its neck. The man stank of a dark, musky cologne.

"These." The man pitched a pecan bar and a cinnamon doughnut on the counter. "And here." He waved his wrist across the scanner.

Ben's eyes flickered downward as he tried to study the read-out on the screen below with nonchalance. Sergei Chistyakov. Forty-two years old. First National Bank of Singapore account. The holo revolved, the Sergei it depicted beaming with an almost insane good cheer.

"Need my print?" Sergei said, his thumb popping up like a spring near Ben's face.

Ben flinched back. "That's okay." Somehow, Sergei's vigor and exuberance made the store, already cramped, shrink still more. Ben shoved the items into a sack and pushed it across the counter, hoping the man would just leave.

Forehead clenched, eyebrows drawn with something like sorrow, Sergei stared at Ben. "I tell you why I come here." Sergei sagged against the counter. He pulled out a comm, brought up a holo of a woman. "I look for my wife."

Ben blinked at the holo. He was pretty sure it was the woman who'd come in last night, the one Sam couldn't take his eyes off of. That woman had looked a lot like the holo, but her hair had been much shorter. Boy's hair, roughly chopped, and slick with sweat and grease. "She's your wife?"

"Ah! You saw her?"

Ben didn't answer.

"She left me. Left our kids. She has problems, you know." Sergei tapped one side of his head. "She runs away. She tries to kill herself." His chin jabbed toward the liquor bottles behind Ben. "Last time it was that. Vodka and pills." Sighing, Sergei bent his elbows against the countertop and buried his face in his hands. Light shivered off the white scalp visible beneath the thinning hair at his crown. "If she did it this time . . ." Sergei's voice was a rasp. "Killed herself . . ."

"I—I think I saw her," Ben said.

Sergei's head swung upright. "Yes? When?" The words bit at the dusty air and Ben thought of a dog's teeth snapping down hard.

"When?" the man demanded again.

Ben answered reluctantly even though he thought answers might make the man go away. "Last night."

"Early? Late?"

"It was just getting dark, I think."

"And she looked—" Sergei's left hand fanned open as he waited for Ben to finish the sentence.

"I don't know. She had poison ivy, or something. A rash. And she looked, well—just tired, I guess."

"She bought things?"

"Yeah." Jerking halfway around to point at the shelf of liquor bottles, Ben said, "But not any of that. Just, you know, regular stuff." He trailed off. "Snacks, like."

"Where did she go?"

Rolling out his lower lip, eyes searching the ceiling, Ben finally shrugged. "She didn't say." He didn't meet Sergei's gaze. Didn't want to.

"But which way she left?" Sergei's hands clenched in front of his chest, his index fingers protruding like a pair of misplaced horns.

"I don't know. I was busy talking to Sam."

"Yes?" Sergei surged across the counter. "Who is this Sam?"

Ben drew back. "Just a guy. They talked some."

"He liked her?"

"Well, yeah, I guess so. I mean . . ."

"I would never blame this Sam. My wife, she is pretty."

"I guess." Then, thinking he might have just insulted the man, Ben said in a rush, "I mean, she's too old for me."

To Ben's surprise, Sergei boomed into laughter. "So. This Sam. I could talk to him?"

"Well . . . yeah."

"What is his last name?"

"I just always call him Sam."

Sergei's eyes crinkled. He tucked his chin and gave Ben the look of a schoolteacher amused by the slightly naughty antics of a child.

"It's, um, Mantell," Ben said and immediately wished he'd lied.

"And Mr. Mantell would live where?" A glow lit Sergei's face as if a fire blazed just beneath his skin.

Ben couldn't stand to be around the guy another minute. Thrusting the bag closer to Sergei, Ben fumbled his way out through the narrow gap between the counter and the wall. "I'm supposed to check on some inventory," he mumbled. He stepped as widely as he could around Sergei and stumbled down a side aisle. Hunching behind a stack of water bottles, Ben strained to hear past the sound of the refrigerator's hum.

At last, he heard the crinkling noise of Sergei picking up the bag. "Well, I check a directory." The door swept open. "If I don't find this Sam, maybe I will be seeing you again!" Sergei called cheerfully.

The door shut. Ben peered out a wedge of window exposed between two jugs of laundry detergent. Outside, Sergei slid into a car and, champing on the pecan bar, steered around the craters in the parking lot.

Ben's hands fidgeted to his pimple again. His fingertips came away bloody. He hoped that Sergei never found his wife.

∞

Sergei broke the lock on the back door of Sam's house in less than ten seconds.

He paused in the kitchen to listen. The tap leaked, each drop echoing into the clogged-up basin.

Sergei swiftly crossed the dining room, the living room. He veered into the hall and paced toward the bathroom where he scrutinized the strands of hair that adhered to the damp countertop. He thought of the most recent images of Jennings. It was possible, at least, that the darker, finer strands—short as a prison haircut— might be hers.

He found similar strands on the pillow of a back bedroom. The room had the trim, dusty air of a space usually left undisturbed. Although the bed was made, a hollow at one edge wrinkled the quilt. The pillow bore a similar indentation and Sergei lowered a palm into its curve.

Standing upright again, he slapped his hands together with a noise as sharp as a detonation. Then he returned to the living room. He didn't sit, but stood beside the window, his stance relaxed and his face patient as he waited for Sam.

« CHAPTER 13 »

AT MOUNT CALVARY CEMETERY, Seth Krey parked on the far side of some trees so his family couldn't see him, and watched from a patch of dogwoods only thirty or forty feet away. A green-and-white striped canopy shaded both the freshly-dug grave and the pewter-colored casket waiting to descend into it.

Seth hadn't gone to the funeral. He hadn't been invited, of course, and he'd had too much respect for his mother's memory to risk a scene—hell, a fight—during the church service. The casket lid was shut now. He'd lost the opportunity to see his mother's face one last time. He bunched his hands into fists and swallowed down the loss.

The mourners clambered out of their cars and shuffled toward the grave, holding back a bit to allow the immediate family to get there first. Seth's father led the informal procession, looking much older than the last time Seth had glimpsed him a couple of years earlier. The old man stabbed along with a cane now. His hair was whiter, but still dense with cowlicks, his nose thick and pugnacious. He wore a double-breasted gray suit that Seth recognized from weddings, court dates, and police department funerals. His father drew himself proudly erect, his heavy shoulders thrown back, his gut pressing against the buttoned jacket.

Seth felt the familiar razor's edge of anger. It cut straight through his grief without providing even the relief of distraction.

Seth's older brothers stumped in their father's wake like middle-aged clones. They were all large men, bull-necked and florid, whose wives bobbed around them like delicate, crushable birds. Children scrambled in and out of the procession. They were Seth's nieces and nephews, but he didn't recognize half of them. He didn't even know some of their names.

His fists tightened. His hands were shaking. Jesus, he'd missed so much, but there was no way back even if he were willing to crawl.

Frank trudged along behind the others. He and Seth were only a year apart and they'd done everything together when they were growing up: football, target shooting, fishing. They'd even held the same lousy part-time jobs at the same lousy convenience stores and burger joints.

Three rows of folding chairs waited beside the grave. Seth's father shoved aside the helping arms offered by Seth's two oldest brothers, instead plodding alone beneath the awning. Family filled the chairs and other mourners ranged around the gravesite.

The priest was African, his accent dense. Seth took a few steps closer, grasped isolated words: *peace, paradise*. They failed to soothe. When he remembered his mother—how she'd been forced to make surreptitious calls to him, how he'd never even known she was ill—fury at his father and his dumb-ox brothers burned down to a dense, white coal.

Why shouldn't he be allowed to mourn for her? Would they deny him even that? More to the point, would he let them?

Seth stepped out from the trees. One of the little boys pointed. The adults, in quick succession, turned faces that were first curious, then startled. Seth's father crooked his head around like a bulldog on a scent. The old man's face boiled; veins knotted his forehead. Pitching out of his chair, he lurched from beneath the shelter. One shoulder knocked against a pole. The awning tilted. Shrieks and babbling swallowed up the priest's prayer.

Cane spearing the damp earth, Seth's father covered the distance between himself and his youngest son with surprising speed.

"Come on, Dad, leave it alone." Frank barreled up behind his father, who shook him off.

The mourners still squawked, fighting their way over fallen chairs and out from beneath the collapsed canvas, but between Seth and his father, silence flattened the afternoon.

Seth's father studied him, then carefully spat into the grass at Seth's feet. "You degrade your mother's memory. You degrade this family."

"I'm her son." Somehow Seth kept his voice level even though each word tried to choke him. "I have every right to be here."

"Right?" His father screwed up his face. "You don't have any right. You think we want to mix with cop-killers? Con-lovers? You think your mother could stomach a Judas any more than the rest of us?"

Seth glanced past his father's shoulder. A few of the mourners were straightening the tent poles, holding them erect. Others gathered in clumps, gazing with frank curiosity toward Seth and his dad. The priest attempted to continue the prayer, but no one seemed to be listening. Seth glimpsed the glint of the coffin lid and the hole gaping beside it. A similar black emptiness eroded his chest.

Frank charged up beside them both, his crisp white shirt stinking of too much cologne, his thick arm tightening around his father's shoulders. "Come on, Dad. Mom wouldn't like a scene. She'd tell you to let it go." He eased the man back toward the gravesite.

Seth's dad twisted around to glare at him. "She'd be telling *him* to get the hell lost."

"He'll get lost. Don't worry. He's on his way out of here right now." Frank gave the old man a firm push toward the others, then lumbered up to Seth.

"Come on, Seth, what're you doing?" Frank muttered. "You know you shouldn't be here." Frank's gaze twitched over to the gravesite where the priest continued to pray while a cluster of men stretched the canopy back into position.

Seth could only stare at his brother.

"Look, I went out on a limb, leaving you that message," Frank said. "No matter what kinds of problems we've got between us, I thought you deserved to know about Mom. But I sure as hell wasn't inviting you to the funeral."

Several of the younger children goggled at Seth.

"You threaten them with Uncle Seth when they don't behave?" Seth asked, nodding at the children. "Dad tell them I'm crazy, or something?"

"He just tells them the truth," Frank answered. "What happened. How you stood up for that lousy cop-killer."

"That is such bullsh—"

"You think anybody loves a whistleblower, Seth? You try to bring up your fellow officers on corruption charges, how do you think people are gonna take that?"

"They framed that guy, they—"

"It's not just that. Jesus, Seth, you just don't stop, do you?"

Seth bristled. "I'm not about to st—"

Frank cut him off, the way his big brothers always had. "Look, everybody knows you've got a problem."

Seth's blood rushed in a torrent, seeped a red film across his vision. "I don't have a—"

Frank cut him off again. "Christ, Seth, it's been how many years? Can you get off your high horse already?"

Seth didn't answer.

"Yeah. You know I'm right. And now—you're working as a Guardian?" Frank raised a hand, shutting off Seth's response. "Yeah, I know about that. Mom told me."

Seth frowned. He never should have told his mother. But she'd kept prying during that last phone call, sounding so sad and so worried about him—Seth, the only one of her five boys with no wife, no kids, no job, no life. So he'd broken the rule of silence and told her. Thinking—God, it embarrassed him to remember—that she'd be proud, just like she'd been proud of him years ago, always claiming he was her "special one."

And all his revelation had done was make her more worried, more unhappy, terrified some hitter was going to swat him down with a casual bullet.

Before he could say anything else, Frank pushed his face up to Seth's. "You Guardians are dupes, Seth. You act like hitters are the bad guys when all they're doing is wiping out scum that doesn't deserve to live in the first place. At least hitters aren't out there killing cops."

"No. They just kill E's. And Guardians."

Wheeling around, Seth strode back to the car and smashed down into the driver's seat. A white printout dangled from a slot at the center of the dash. Ripping it loose, he glanced at the message, crumpled the paper, and tossed it on the floor. He sank back and rubbed his hands over his face.

The car was a blast furnace, the A/C busted again. According to Bobby, one of his main contacts at the Guardian Network, "current donation levels" didn't allow for unnecessary repairs. So Seth sat with the windows down and stared through the leafy dogwood branches. The mourners, regrouped, stood beneath the awning again, their heads solemnly bowed.

Frank was right. He should leave. What the hell had he been thinking, coming here in the first place?

Seth had just pushed the ignition when his comm beeped. "Goddamnit," he muttered, grabbing the thing. Network. Kendall this time.

"Hey, how's it going? We've been trying to get in touch with you all morning." Kendall's cheerful voice burbled through the car. Grimacing, Seth turned the wheel to follow the road as it wound among headstones in the oldest part of the cemetery. "Busy?"

Seth pushed away the image of that black pit yawning into the earth. What his mother's waxy corpse must look like, hidden away in the coffin. "Kind of."

"Well, you want to get busier?"

On the day of his mother's funeral? Seth thought about it for a second. He had no home, no apartment of his own, just Network safehouses scattered across the region. No job to get fired from if he didn't show up. Nobody waiting for him. Sure as hell no post-funeral reception to attend later that day.

"Who's the client?" he asked, voice tight.

Now Bobby's voice came on, dour but efficient. "Her name's Jennings. They released her from Glynn River early yesterday."

When Seth hesitated, Bobby added, "She sounds like your kind of E, Seth. Really shabby treatment by the legal system."

"Shabby," Kendall echoed in the background.

"Innocent?" Seth clarified.

"Don't really know," Bobby responded. "But they handed her the worst public DA in the state. Didn't call a single witness on her behalf. Definitely didn't give her a fair shot."

"They never do," Kendall echoed.

Seth sagged in his seat. He was tired. Who was innocent? Who was guilty? Bobby was right about that: Who the hell knew?

"Well?" Bobby prodded. " 'Cause if you don't want it . . ."

Seth rubbed the back of a hand against his eyes. They stung, bleary and bloodshot.

"Why not?" He grabbed the wheel, gave the accelerator a reckless punch with his right foot. The car skidded across gravel, vibrated beneath the cemetery's arched gate. "Why the hell not?"

« CHAPTER 14 »

As Merle Edgers waited for the elevator, he pulled out his comm and instructed the valet service to bring his antique Alfa Romeo from the garage.

The afternoon smelled like hot tar. In the street, pylons blinking around an enormous crater formed a monstrous orange eye. A lopsided sedan, crippled by a second, unmarked crater and stripped by vandal-packs, sagged against the curb.

Edgers halted on the sidewalk. There was no sign of the kid or the car and he hated lingering outside. He imagined the kid joyriding in the beautifully refurbished, top-of-the-line sportscar. The vision fixed Edgers in place; anger foamed through him. Then a bulky figure shifted in his peripheral vision and he broke off his furious imaginings with a start. Downtown Philly was no place to daydream.

Right hand outthrust, Geoffrey Whelk pressed himself at Edgers. Whelk was pushing 300 pounds on his six-foot frame, and although his size was something of a joke around Regency, the jokes never seemed as funny in the man's presence.

"Where the hell did you come from, Geoff?" The perfunctory shake left Edgers' palm dripping. He flattened his fingers against his trousers and dried them surreptitiously.

"Sloppy, Merle," Whelk intoned. For a moment, Edgers thought the man was referring to the sopping handshake. "A man needs to pay attention to his surroundings down here."

Eyeing a withered man slumped under a one way sign at the intersection, Edgers had to nod. "I'm with you there."

"I hope you don't mind that I didn't call before popping over," Whelk said.

"No, no, this is great." Edgers glanced up and down the street. The valet could have driven to Camden and back by now. "Thing is, I was just leaving for lunch."

"What are you driving these days, Merle? Beamer? Benz?"

"Alfa Romeo."

"Ah, was it a gray convertible?"

Edgers slung around to face him. "Yeah, as a matter of fact, it is."

Whelk slapped him on the back so hard that Edgers stuttered forward a step. "I thought that was yours. I told the lad to take it back, that you'd be a little while yet." He swept an arm toward the skyscraper's glass doors. "Perhaps we should head up to your office to talk?"

"I have an appointment at two. I was just going for a quick lunch."

Whelk pondered. "Now that you mention it, I haven't eaten yet."

Edgers sighed. "Well, we can't take forever, that's all."

Whelk's left eyebrow rose. "Are there restaurants—*viable* restaurants—in this part of town?"

"There's a place where we can get a bagel sandwich."

"Enchanting."

As they made their way along the sidewalk, Edgers noticed a hitch in Whelk's gait. "You got a bum wheel there, Geoff?"

Pausing at the intersection, Whelk massaged down his right thigh to the knee. "I'm afraid most of this is arthritic."

"Gets us all. You think that would be a problem on a job?"

Whelk spat out a cough. "Merle, you know how I manage my people. I have others to do the running for me." He rolled off the curb. "In any event, my vision is still perfect, my mind is still clear, and I can still break a neck with a single twist."

A smell of acrid smoke fumed from an alley as the two men passed its mouth. Old wooden crates and skids burned in the alley's depths. At the next curb, Edgers looked down just in time to avoid stepping in a curled mound of feces. He did a sort of off-balance jig for a moment as he regained his footing.

"Let's assume those are canine, why don't we?" Whelk said.

"It's the bums," Edgers answered, keeping his head down to scan the sidewalk ahead of them. "The beggars. The peelouts. Seems like there's more of them every day."

Whelk studied the empty storefronts, the windows sealed with metal sheeting and thick, shatterproof laminates. "I'm surprised you haven't moved the office yet."

"Well, I've been looking at some properties out in the exurbs when I have time. Which is almost never."

"There's no reason to stay down here."

"I don't know." Edgers remembered when he was a kid, when sleek, downtown corporate offices still carried a certain prestige and credibility. Philadelphia had had plenty of problems even back then. Every big city did. But now? After the biochem bombings and job riots, the debt default and the depression that lengthened into an endless malaise? The office staff never set foot outside the building during the day. They parked in the secured garage, brought their lunch or ordered something in from a cluster of pizza and Mexican joints a few blocks away.

"I don't care what anybody says," Edgers said. "It still means something when you tell somebody you're from New York or LA or even Philadelphia. It's got more identity, more personality, than saying, "Hi, I'm from Shithorn, Nebraska.""

Pulling out a handkerchief, Whelk dabbed at his face. "And, of course, Shithorn, Nebraska is probably dying its own slow death."

"Yeah."

"And speaking of death, Merle—"

"Right. Right. You want to talk more about the job." Veering to a shop door, Edgers gripped the handle and tugged. When the door didn't budge, he tugged harder, then bent forward to squint through the glass. "Son of a bitch." The lights were off, the booths empty.

Whelk examined the darkened sign in the window. The words *The Bagelry* floated like black steam above the outline of a coffee mug. "It appears you've lost another portion of the tax base."

"Damn it." Spinning around, Edgers stalked back in the direction of the office. Hauling his comm out of his pocket, he buzzed the valet office. "I requested my car ten minutes ago. So could you get it the hell out front?" He jammed the device back in his pocket. "Look, Geoff, I'll push back my two o'clock. We'll drive somewhere, find someplace nice to eat outside the city. You parked in the garage?"

"I took a cab."

"Afraid your car'll get stolen in this part of town?"

"Of course. Now. The Jennings job, Merle? You've heard from Miss Eisen?"

Edgers let out an explosive breath. "Paige says she has to have more time to look into it."

"Which you refused, of course."

"Time's not exactly a luxury we have."

"No, not in a crisis such as this."

Edgers stopped dead. "Goddamnit it, Geoff, this isn't a crisis. It's a— a situation. That's all. Like a hundred other *situations* we've had before. I'll handle it."

Whelk swept Edgers ahead with a generous hand. "I would never mean to imply otherwise."

"Look," Edgers said, "what happened with you and Sergei in Ohio was bad news. Regency can't handle another debacle like that. You know how much our insurance premiums shot up because of your little incident?"

"I understand. Entirely."

Edgers stood, fixed. Another year, maybe two, and he'd be out of the execution business entirely and faced with nothing but the smooth, calm waters of prison manufacturing.

"You'd swear to me there wouldn't be any problems?" he probed. "No collateral damage. No liability issues. No bad PR crap. You'll keep Sergei on a tight rein. Sometimes I think he enjoys the, the bloody aspects a little too much, you know? Sadism is not what we're about. We're about clean hits and money in the bank."

Touching his fingertips to his chest, Whelk nodded gravely. "Now as I indicated yesterday, I already have people investigating."

"Right, right." Edgers set off again.

"I know how short-handed Regency is right now—"

"Okay!" Edgers interrupted. "So what've you got?"

"Murray and Slater already stopped by her father's old house. Which was a bit of a bust, I'm afraid—no sign of our quarry in those environs yet, and the man was so ill he was nearly catatonic. But we have stringers keeping watch in case Jennings shows up. At the moment they're checking into Jennings' old friends, favorite haunts and such. Sergei's sniffing about the Glynn River area. I am able to report that he has a promising lead. In short, we're in an excellent position to finish the job."

Edgers didn't have to consider for very long. "Okay, Geoff. It's yours."

"However, I do need to request a small advance for the assignment. Not much."

"How much not much are you talking about?"

"Fifty thousand. Cash would be preferable."

Edgers stared hard at Whelk a good minute. "I damned regret I ever started fronting you cash on a hit," Edgers muttered.

"Well, we appreciate it, Merle." Whelk's tone seemed not nearly grateful enough to Edgers. "Perhaps we could arrange the funds on our way to lunch."

They'd reached the alley again. Smoke uncoiled from it now, thick and dark. Edgers' eyes watered. Gray forms moved through the smoke. "Jesus, are they trying to burn themselves out of their own ratholes now?"

A breeze cleared the smoke for a moment, and Edgers gaped. There must have been twenty of them at least, the beggars and bums, shuffling toward him, their torn clothes fluttering around their gaunt bodies. Edgers blinked, his gaze scaling the alley walls as he tried to get his bearings. He had the crazy idea he'd been dropped into an old horror movie, one with hordes of shambling zombies.

Then the wind died, and the smoke thickened, concealing the beggars again.

Edgers surged into motion. "Get your butt in gear, Geoff."

Whelk billowed ahead, his limp considerably improved. "What is this?" he puffed. "Nineteenth-century Calcutta?"

They put a full block between themselves and the alley before Edgers glanced back. The vagrants were stumbling onto the sidewalk, spilling into the street. A small mob of them clumped in front of a slowed car, forced it to stop, then piled onto the hood.

The Alfa Romeo purred at the garage exit. From behind the wheel, the valet stared down the street with eyes like dessert plates.

Edgers flung the door open. "Out."

"What's going on down there?" The kid's voice rose to a squeak.

"Dawn of the Dead," Edgers said. Whelk was already lowering himself into the passenger seat.

The kid scrambled from the car and rushed back into the dark mouth of the garage. Edgers locked all the doors. The street was one-way, but he'd rather risk a head-on collision than have to plow through the skinwastes. And it wasn't like there was a lot of traffic, even in the middle of the day.

"Jesus," he said with disgust and blasted the acceleration. The beggars receded in the rearview mirror and Edgers let out a loud exhalation.

Geoff fussed at the seatbelt which fit tautly around his bulk. "You need to spend some quality time with your realtor."

"Jesus," Edgers muttered again, shaking his head, and turned onto another one-way street, heading with the sparse traffic this time. "Something's got to change."

"Absolutely. I agree. Carpet bombing the entire city might be a good start." Whelk settled back, his hands laced together across his belly. "And don't forget the bank."

« CHAPTER 15 »

TORI FELT BETTER—briefly—when the bus crossed into Virginia. But the closer the bus traveled to Arlington, the more she fidgeted on her sweat-sticky seat. Highway security tightened as they headed east and by the time they were twenty miles outside of D.C., the bus crawled in a single line of vehicles. Tori closed her eyes, pressed her fingers against the lids. The air oozing in through the open window was sluggish and hot against her face. Her mouth was a Sahara.

Arlington's bus station was a larger version of Glynn River's, decrepit rooms for skinwastes to drift and shamble through. Sarah had given Tori detailed directions from the station to her house four miles away and recommended taking a cab if she could find one. "We don't have a car," Sarah had explained. "Too expensive and we've got all the basics within walking distance. We're lucky."

Somehow, the phrase "walking distance" had given Tori the mental picture of a charming village from an old movie, with a tidy coffee shop, grocery, antique pharmacy and library set around a square of emerald grass. The reality of Arlington was gritty air and garbage rotting into slime in the gutters. She wasn't about to part with any more precious cash just to avoid a four-mile walk—hell, how many miles had she managed to stagger in the woods the previous day? She didn't even look for a cab.

Look like you belong. Look like you're not scared.

She squared her shoulders, jutted out her chin, and practically strutted along the sidewalk. There weren't as many people hanging around as she'd expected. A gaggle of pregnant teenage girls, and not one who looked older than fourteen. Drug slingers nodding off on front stoops.

The toxic decay of downtown gradually shifted into mere shabbiness. Ancient shotgun houses and apartment buildings with barred windows, cracked siding, and dangling gutters were replaced by small bungalows crouched in tiny, fenced yards.

Sarah's house looked exactly like its neighbors, except Sarah's was pale green with tidy forest green trim while the adjoining homes were scabby white. Anxiety flooded Tori as she loitered on the sidewalk and eyed Sarah's door. An odor of warm trash simmered from the uncollected trash cans jammed against the curb in front of each house.

She forced herself along the narrow concrete walkway and up the front steps and pressed the doorbell. The trill of it echoed inside the house. Tori half-turned, examining the length of the street. Sarah had obviously moved up when she'd married, but not too high. There was rust on the cars parked on the street and security bars welded across some of the first-floor windows.

She caught the sound of footsteps on the other side of the door and whipped around again, staring at the fake wood as if willing herself x-ray vision. The door, caught short by a chain lock, opened a couple of inches. The woman blinking at Tori was heavier than Tori remembered, but Tori instantly recognized the wide chestnut eyes and heart-shaped face.

Sarah winced and Tori self-consciously pushed a hand through her cropped hair.

"Oh, my God," Sarah exclaimed. "Tori! You really look . . . you look so different." Then Sarah was grinning. The chain clattered free and the door swung wide. "I can't believe it."

Sarah gripped her in a hug. Tori hugged her back, throat tight. "Thank you," Tori said, voice hoarse. They pulled apart.

Tori raised a hand to the cuts on her neck. "I look like hell."

"No, you look fine—I mean, my God, ten years in that place, and then everything else you went through." Sarah dropped back a step. She pressed her hands together, working the fingers rapidly against one another. "Come on in."

Tori glanced around. The objects in the tiny foyer—umbrella stand, coat rack, fake geranium in a stucco pot—seemed to rush toward her, then away. The coat rack and the geranium swayed...or maybe she did.

Sarah grabbed her hands, and the warmth suffused Tori's suddenly icy fingers. "Here, sit down."

Tori sank onto the bottom step of the narrow stairway to the second floor.

"Head between your knees, right?" Sarah pressed gently at the back of Tori's neck. Tori glanced up. Sarah flashed her a smile. "Just like we learned at vo-tech. Remember that crazy guy who taught first aid?"

Tori sucked in deep lungfuls of air until her head cleared. She stared up at Sarah. "I just can't believe I'm still alive."

Lines puckered Sarah's forehead. A shadow crossed her face. She sat beside Tori, put a hand lightly on Tori's elbow, then withdrew it.

"Listen . . . Tori . . . I have to tell you something."

An infant's cries squalled simultaneously from overhead and from a crackling monitor in a room off the foyer.

Tori stared at her friend. "You have a baby?"

"Justin." Sarah's smile reappeared. "I know. Seems pretty unbelievable, doesn't it?"

"No, I just . . . I guess I just never thought about it."

Sarah glanced up the stairs, then back to Tori. Her smile faded. "He's four months old. It took me forever to get pregnant."

The crying grew shriller.

"Listen," Sarah said. "I should tell you—"

"Sarah!" a man called from the second floor.

Sarah jumped up. "I'd better go check. David never heats the formula right."

Tori hesitated. "Can I help?"

"Oh, no!" Sarah answered immediately. "I've got it."

Uncertainty iced the pit of Tori's stomach.

Sarah turned halfway up the flight of stairs, tossed one more comment—quickly and with an unsettling chirpiness—over her shoulder: "Do you mind just staying there? For now?" Sarah turned away again and hurried to the second floor.

Tori's breath punched out of her lungs. She stared at the water stains that marred the wooden floor, at the empty coat rack lodged like a dead tree in one corner. Hushed voices crackled on the baby monitor. The man said: "—doesn't want to take the bottle."

"*No.*" Sarah's voice now, irritated. "Hold his head like *this.*"

More cries and then quiet.

David spoke again. "Who're you talking to down there?"

Sarah didn't answer. The monitor hummed. David broke the quiet. He was louder now. "It's not *her*, is it? She actually came here?"

Tori rose and stepped neatly into the side room, an office cheaply furnished with a flimsy desk, a single chair, and a floor lamp that hunched in one corner like a vulture.

"Please, David, just for one night," Sarah said. "She doesn't have anywhere to go."

"Let her go home. We're not her family."

"She can't go home. That's the first place they'll—" Sarah broke off, stumbling over her own words.

"Exactly," David answered. "And when they don't find her there, then what? What if they show up here?" Something—chair legs, Tori thought—screeched across the floor overhead.

Sarah's voice was so low it was barely audible: "Do you really think just one night . . .?"

Listening hard, hands tightened into fists, Tori stared out the window. An immense, old woman weeded a plot of marigolds in front of the house across the street. Next door to her, a thin man with dark blonde hair and a light, silvery stubble on his cheeks rested on the top step of a bungalow with a 'for rent' sign planted by the curb. He tugged at the long sleeves of his plain white shirt.

"I don't want her in this house," David said. "Not with Justin."

Sarah's voice came low and agitated. "I know."

"She killed a baby, for God's sake! And you want her around our son?"

"She was my friend." Sarah paused. "And she didn't kill anybody."

"Oh, you know that for a fact, do you?"

"Tori never would've done something like that." Pause. "Not on purpose."

Tori sagged. She stared blindly outside. The gardener limped around to the side of her house and out of view. The bungalow's steps were empty.

Tori tried to think about where to go next, what to do. Her mind stayed stubbornly blank.

"Just get her out. And don't give her any money. We can't afford it."

The harshness of David's tone drove Tori back into the foyer. She reached for the front door, but paused as footsteps thudded across the floor upstairs. A man came stabbing down the steps. Sarah hurried behind him, carrying the baby wrapped in a blanket.

David stopped in front of Tori. His burgundy-red boat shoes were dusty, one toe smudged black. Yellow blotches smeared his shirt where the baby had spit up. Tori forced her gaze up to meet his. He wore glasses on his narrow face, the gold frames thin and fussy. His pale blue stare was sharp and hard, stabbing through the lenses.

"I have to make one thing perfectly clear," he said.

"I'm sorry, Tor," Sarah blurted. "I was trying to tell you . . ."

Tori's tongue was a rusted hinge. "I'm leaving," she finally managed.

"We have to think of our son," David answered. "Sarah?" Sarah stared fixedly down at the baby's head, her mouth tightening in a quick, embarrassed smile.

Tori wanted to erase herself. Her chest felt hollowed-out, her heart banging away inside the emptiness. "It's okay." She reached forward, not quite touching Sarah's arm. "I wasn't going to stay." Her own smile felt as fake as Sarah's looked. "I need to find out how my dad's doing."

Sarah leaped on this with frantic nodding. "He's going to be so happy to see you, Tor. It'll be incredible."

"Good." David grasped the door knob. "Sounds like you need to be on your way then."

Something rapped at the decorative rectangle of frosted glass that framed one edge of the doorway. Tori and the others turned toward the sound.

A bang. The glass shattered. Pieces of it sprayed around their feet.

Tori realized first. She snapped into motion.

"Go!" She shoved Sarah and the baby into the office, and turned back to the foyer. David gaped at the debris shimmering on the floor. Tori careened past him. Behind her, another gunshot smashed more glass.

Tori sprinted for the stairs.

« CHAPTER 16 »

SARAH SCREAMED AS THE DOOR smashed open. Tori was two-thirds of the way up the stairs, feet scrabbling and slipping on the uncarpeted risers. Her heart slammed the walls of her chest.

A man's voice boomed: "Everybody on the floor! Now!"

From the top of the stairs, Tori just glimpsed two men burst into the foyer. She plunged down the narrow hallway that ran to the back of the second floor.

"Nobody move!"

David's voice was reedy, barely audible above the infant's shrieks and Sarah's sobbing. "Hey! you can't—"

"You, shut up!" the same booming voice interrupted.

Tori paused at each doorway, her gaze skimming the sparse furniture and the closet doors. More shouts rose from below and a thud, like something—or someone—thrown against a wall.

She darted into the master bedroom and almost tripped over a heaped laundry basket just inside the door. Steadying herself, she froze at the center of the room and listened. Footsteps treaded the stairs.

She instantly rejected the closet and, turning to the bed, snatched up the edge of the quilt. The bottom of the bedframe came within two inches of the carpet. She spun away from it. On top of the dresser lay a letter opener. She grabbed it and whipped toward the adjoining bathroom.

The bathroom was cramped. A shower stall with a clear door filled one corner. Towel-stuffed shelves crammed the linen closet. She turned to an old-fashioned wardrobe standing beside a window barely large enough to accommodate a toddler. Pennsylvania Dutch tulips decorated the wardrobe's front panels. Tori yanked at one of the doors. The interior was dark and hung with jumpers and oxford shirts.

Footsteps clocked the length of the hall.

The wardrobe was an obvious place, but there was no more time. No other choices. Tori tugged the wardrobe's door shut behind her and sank to a crouch, the letter opener clutched in one fist. Her eyes traced the faint lines of light edging the wardrobe's doors. A clean, sharp scent of laundry detergent bit the air.

Footsteps in the bedroom now. A skirt dangling against her face pressed warm and dry as a smothering hand across her mouth. In her mind, she followed the footsteps to the bedroom closet. Hangers rattled. She heard a fat billowing *whoomph* and understood that the man was tossing heaps of clothing onto the bed.

She'd brought killers to her best friend. To her friend's family. *I'm sorry, I'm sorry.*

Footsteps clipped across the tiled bathroom floor. Tori couldn't breathe. The shower door thumped open, then the door to the linen closet. The hitter positioned himself in front of the wardrobe.

Tears burned Tori's face. Her mouth gaped open, tongue sticky and dry. *Sorrysorrysorry*

She tensed her arms as if she would drive the weapon upward. But her body was frozen.

The wardrobe door eased open. Tori glimpsed the scrubby gray of the shower stall, a towel collapsed beneath the towel rack. The air in the room fluttered between pale evening green and shadow. Something moved on the other side of the opened wardrobe door. Black men's sneakers, the laces tightly drawn and tied into even bows, were just visible in the gap between the floor and the bottom of the door. They shifted and a man stepped into view. A harsh sob ripped through Tori's throat.

She lurched awkwardly up, pushed the dull blade toward the man's chest. He caught her wrists, wrenched her hand back until her fingers opened. It was the man from the bungalow steps. She met his eyes. They were calm and disinterested, dark against his pale skin. He smelled like deodorant: fresh cotton.

The man watched her as he pocketed the letter opener. When his hand emerged from his pocket, he held a pair of wooden grips connected by a gleaming silver wire. He took one of the grips in each hand and pulled the wire so taut that it hummed.

Tori shrank back, pinning blouses behind her. The blouses dragged loose from their hangers as she sank to the floor.

Her voice floated up from somewhere outside her body. "You won't hurt them, will you?"

She sensed her arms trembling, her legs collapsed and shaking, but all of that seemed to be happening at a distance.

The man's narrow face grew even more somber. He snapped the wire tight again. Tori watched, transfixed by the molten silver.

"Please," she said, the word flat and dead. The wire pressed lightly to her throat. Bit at her skin.

Color and motion flurried behind the hitter. At the same instant, the barrel of a handgun pressed into the hollow of the man's cheek.

"Easy now." A second man stood behind the hitter, smiling slightly, his eyes never losing their concentration and his grip on his gun steady. "Drop the wire. Hands on top of your head. Good."

Tori's hand rose to her throat. She stared at the men as if they were both unreal, holos projecting from a screen.

The man with the gun reached into the hitter's pockets and pulled out a pistol which he pushed under his own belt. "Now step over to the wall there."

Tori sagged in a corner of the wardrobe, watching. The hitter crossed to the opposite wall and pressed his face against it. "I have a license," the hitter said. "We have authorization to harvest this felon."

"And I'm staying the execution," the other man said. "Now, real gentle, back up with me and out this door." He kept the handgun trained on the hitter's skull. With a gesture, the man indicated Tori should follow.

She fell the first time she tried to get to her feet, her legs crumbling beneath her. She took a breath and tried again, managing to stumble behind the two men as they entered the hallway.

"You're that Krey guy," the hitter said. "Seth Krey. Son of a bitch."

Seth pushed the barrel closer to the hitter's temple. "And you're working for Geoff Whelk. Murray's tied up downstairs. Your turn next, Slater." Seth navigated the hitter down the stairs. Tori stumbled after them. She felt numb inside, like she'd already died.

Murray, a big, bulky man with dark hair as thick and greasy as fleece, curled on the entryway floor, his wrists trussed to his ankles with metal cuffs and attached chains. David stood guard. A shotgun trembled in his grip, but he managed to keep it trained on the bound man. In the office doorway, Sarah smothered the baby against her chest. She kept her face turned away from Tori. Regret flooded Tori. She never should have come here, never should have risked putting Sarah's family in danger. Now she'd lost her best friend. Her only friend.

Seth Krey pushed Slater down next to his partner and glanced at David. "I don't have any more restraints. Get some electrical cords and tie this guy up."

"*She's* the *E*," Murray grunted into the floorboards. "You oughta be tying *her* up."

"Get some duct tape too," Seth called after David. "Shut this guy up."

David reappeared with a neatly-looped extension cord and a roll of silver tape. Kneeling, he followed Seth's instructions, knotting the cord around Slater's ankles, then pulling it up around his wrists. The tape shook in David's hands as he pressed it over Murray's mouth.

"What are you, anyway?" David glanced back at Seth. "One of *them?*" Now David pressed tape over Slater's mouth. "Working for a different company?"

"I don't work for the execution companies." Seth stepped in front of Tori. "Ms. Jennings?" he said. "Tori?"

Her eyes wouldn't focus properly.

"Come on," Seth tried again. Tori felt the gentle pressure of his hand on her shoulder. "Tori, listen to me. I'm with the Guardian Network. You heard of it?" He brought his face close to Tori's and raised his hand from her shoulder to her chin, clasping her jaw between his thumb and fingers. "Tori, I need for you to come with me now. Everything's going to be okay."

She concentrated on his eyes, warm brown flecked with dark green. The directness of his gaze cut through the fog in her head, and she finally managed to rasp: "Where?"

Releasing her, he gave his head a quick shake. "You'll find out when we get there." He looked out the shattered front window. "We need to get going. No telling who else might show up." Tori took one step to follow, then stopped. She eyed the pistol gleaming at his belt and the handgun he held at his side.

He could drive her out to some woods or an old, abandoned barn. A basement. Someplace where he wouldn't even have to finish her off fast.

David pushed forward. The left lens of his glasses was broken, giving that eye a demented look. Color spewed into his face. He thrust his face at Tori. "Just get the hell out."

She searched past him for Sarah who still refused to look at her. "I'm so sorry—" Tori said. The words choked her.

"Come *on*," Seth insisted.

David fumbled away. "What about these guys?"

"Call your cops," Seth answered. "Hope you're paid up with the local squad."

"What about our *house?*"

"Write your congressman." Seth leaned into Tori, put his mouth near her ear. "I want you to stay as close to me as you can, okay?" A sense of unreality swept through Tori again. "We're going to that brown truck." His gaze flicked to the empty rectangle that had once housed the decorative glass. A dirt-colored hood and scuffed bumper were just visible at the curb. "Let's go."

Then they were outside. A scent of freshly-mown grass pressed at Tori. Her glances were frantic, looking for more hitters behind every tree, on each porch. Her feet kept tangling against each other.

Seth brandished a remote that clicked the doors open and flared the ignition.

"Come on," he coaxed her.

Tori froze beside the truck. Stood poised to spring away. Threw a despairing look at the barred windows of the houses around her, the scaly siding. Remembered Sam. Not everyone was a killer. She had to take a chance.

Tori dropped into the passenger seat. Seth smashed himself down behind the wheel.

"Get on the floor," he said. The tires crunched away from the curb. "Don't move till I tell you to."

Tori crouched, the back of her head pressed against the glove compartment and her hands gripping the seat's torn upholstery. The plastic was hot. Foam spilled through the rips. Every time Seth rounded a corner, Tori swayed and reached out to catch her balance.

She blotted at her damp face with the bottom of her shirt. Seth's glance ticked between mirrors, then at her. "You look like you're about to melt," he said.

A mechanism inside the door groaned, and the window shuddered halfway down. The air that rushed in was warm and humid, but Tori pressed her face into it.

She was still alive. Her mind could barely take in that simple fact.

"Couple more car changes. Just keep your head down." Seth had set the handgun on his lap, but now he laid the gun into a molded depression between the two front seats where the weapon was easily within Tori's reach.

She let out a long breath. Whatever the man was, he *wasn't* an executioner.

As if he knew her thoughts, Seth spun a grin at her. "Not a single bullet hole," he said, waving a hand at either the windshield or the hood, Tori wasn't sure which. Or maybe he was referring to the hand itself. "I'm taking that as a good luck sign."

Tori settled into her cramped space as best she could. She closed her eyes, opened her mouth, and tasted the wind that poured across her face. It tasted like freedom.

« CHAPTER 17 »

ONE THING TORI had already learned: an Executable never felt free for long.

As night fell, Seth kept to old rural routes, their concrete disintegrating at the edges, gravel washed into ditches. The old farm houses they passed were black monoliths set against the night, no lights in the windows and tractors abandoned in the fields like murdered livestock. The roads smoothed into blacktop whenever they approached the high barbed fences of giant industrial farms.

Tori was tired, but she couldn't sleep. Didn't dare to. She kept glancing off to each side, flipped down the mirror so she could watch the road behind them. Pointless, of course. Each time she glimpsed headlights, she jolted up, stiff and alert, but there was no way to know if the vehicle behind the lights held farmers or kids or killers.

They stopped once, at a falling-down barn, and switched cars. Tori went behind a heap of broken wooden beams to pee. Seth gave her privacy. When she climbed in the next car, an ancient blue hatchback, Seth's gun was no longer in view. But there was a bag of potato chips on the dash and a couple of packs of beef jerky.

"It's not much," Seth said. "But help yourself."

Tori ripped open the bag, pressed her face to the opening to smell potatoes and oil. "I haven't had a potato chip since I was 18."

"Not on the menu at Glynn River, huh?" Seth bumped the car down the tussocky drive and out onto a road that was only slightly less deteriorated.

"Not hardly." Tori tried not to cram handfuls of chips into her mouth. The saltiness on her tongue tasted incredible.

"So what was the menu? Bread and water?"

"And gruel." She popped another chip. "Damn, that's good." She extended the bag toward Seth. "Sorry, you want some?"

"Later."

Seth fell silent again. In the blue glow of the dash, his hands gripped the wheel hard, his knuckles glaring and bald. His face was tight, the muscles in his neck strained.

Fear jolted Tori. Half-chewed potato chips, suddenly flavorless, congealed against her tongue.

He had the gun. He'd pretended to be so casual with it in the first car to get her defenses down. But where was it now?

She shifted closer to the passenger door. She looked from the speedometer—60 mph—to the road's coarse surface racing past. If she jumped out now, she'd die. Plain and simple.

They were heading east again. Dull pink stained the horizon. They'd been headed the opposite direction an hour ago. Seth had been backtracking and changing directions all night.

Throwing off hitters? Toying with her?

She couldn't think any more. Exhaustion and headache gripped her.

Staring straight ahead, Seth said, "I just want to know one thing." He hesitated. "What happened with that kid?"

Tori's stomach dropped. Shit. This was all part of the hitters' deal, wasn't it? Part of a contract. Torture her with her memories of Robbie Cameron, get her sobbing and hysterical with grief and terror . . . *then* off the baby-killing bitch.

Her throat tightened—with fear, or anger, or both. Next time the car slowed, she'd do it. Jump

"I don't know," she answered.

"You don't know." Seth didn't so much as flick a look in her direction. "Okay. But you know you didn't do anything."

Memories shoved into her head, hulked there like a migraine. She pressed her hands against her face, covering her eyes. But she still saw the little boy's listless face, his slack arms and legs, smelled the sour milk soaking his bedclothes.

"I didn't do anything," she whispered. "He got sick all the time. They kept taking him to doctors, but the doctors didn't know anything. They just acted like they did." The pediatrician had prescribed special formulas, special diets, checked for allergies. "Sometimes it seemed like Robbie was getting better. A little. But he always ended up sick again."

Without really seeing anything, Tori stared straight ahead. Dawn bled out into the sky. She remembered waking at three a.m. in the nanny's quarters at the back of the Camerons' elegant brick home. The house had been silent except for the low rush of cool air from the vents. The quiet had gnawed at her. By the glow of a Mickey Mouse night light, she'd shuffled through the connecting door into the nursery.

Robbie wasn't breathing. His face was white, his mouth slack. His chest didn't move.

And she couldn't breathe either, stumbling down the dark hall to the Camerons' bedroom, fists slamming the door, shoving it open. She could still see Kelly Cameron's annoyed, sleep-smeared face sliced with shock and terror. And suspicion.

Doctors in x-care pronounced Robbie dead at 3:43 a.m. Police took Tori into custody that same day. The coroner's determination was antifreeze poisoning.

No one took Tori's side except her father and Sarah, both erased from her life the moment the jury found her guilty of an E-class felony. She could still smell the court-appointed attorney's cheap cologne, how it sweated from him like the stink of his own haplessness. She could still see the prosecutor's confident smile and the contempt on the faces of the jurors. The fury and desperation she'd felt then scalded her now.

Tori whipped around in her seat to face Seth. "I don't know what happened to him," she snapped, "but I sure as hell know I didn't put antifreeze in his bottle."

"Okay—okay—" Seth raised one hand from the wheel. "I'm just—"

Tori's voice shook. Her fingers scrabbled for the door handle. "If you're so damn sure I'm guilty, why don't you just stop the car now and do it?"

"Do what?" Seth's eyebrows cinched together and he held his free hand toward her gently like he was feeding birds from his palm.

"You're a hitter." She was breathing hard, her mouth open. "So just do your job."

The car jolted through a pothole. Swearing, Seth snapped his attention forward and slammed the wheel to the left to avoid a second hole that swallowed half the road.

His gaze flickered between Tori and the windshield. "You think I'm a hitter? I could've gotten killed back there getting you away from Murray and Slater—who *are* hitters, in case you didn't notice—and you think I'm the one plotting to kill you? Jesus." He shook his head. "Jesus," he repeated in a wondering tone. "I'm a guardian. Not a hitter."

Tori's face burned. She was surprised her cheeks didn't cast a glow into the early morning gloom, like a jack-o-lantern. God, she'd screwed up everything. But how was she supposed to know who to trust and who to run like hell from? "I didn't mean anything—"

She stopped. Watched, amazed. Seth was laughing. Oh, he'd pressed his lips together, trying to hold it back, but the laughter came simmering up and out. His shoulders shook. Crows' feet sprayed out from the corners of his eyes and his teeth shone pale white in the twilit morning. One of his teeth was a little crooked, raised higher than the teeth beside it.

"Well, Tori, I've got to say that was a new one. Hitter." His shoulders hitched with one last spasm of laughter.

Tori spread her hands across her thighs, stared down at them. "I am sorry." Her voice was quiet but steady. "I guess I'm—everything's so— confused. Crazy."

"That's okay."

She cut a sideways look at him. "What I should really be doing is figuring out how to say thank you."

"I guess you just did."

The sun was a blade of orange and yellow light knifing above the trees and the roofs of old farmhouses. It was nearly blinding, but Tori couldn't stop looking at it, taking in every gorgeous variation in color, the shimmer of silver-green on the trees. So many years without a sunrise. The clock on the dash read 5:45. At Glynn River the women would be on the kill floor already. Cracked concrete floors, sweating walls, the smell of blood instead of coffee or bacon.

She heard herself say: "You saved my life."

Seth's gaze shifted carefully between the road and the rearview mirror. He was, Tori realized, looking for anyone who might be following them. Her stomach curdled.

Seth sucked at his upper lip, gave her a half-smile. The beginning of a beard bristled along his jaw. "Well, sure. That's what the Network's all about."

He heaved the wheel and they were on gravel again, dust pluming up behind them. "Couple more minutes and we'll be there."

Tori, bewildered: "Where?"

Seth's half-smile became a grin. "Caracas."

« CHAPTER 18 »

THE CAR SHUDDERED to a stop at the rear of an old farmhouse ringed by neglected apple trees. Folding chairs littered the back porch; another seemed to float in the shaggy grass at the bottom of the steps. Strips of pale green showed through a peeling coat of white paint. Rusty water stains shadowed the downspouts.

"Come on," Seth told her. "Let's get inside."

The first room held an old couch and patched-over beanbag chairs. Nails staked ragged movie posters—old classics like *Bladerunner* and *Ferocity*—to the walls. Towers of dirty plates and glasses threatened to topple onto the floor.

"Caracas?" Tori asked, bewildered.

Seth maneuvered past her. "Otherwise known as sanctuary. At least until the hitters show up."

He veered into an office that had the advantage of card tables and a pair of computers that didn't look particularly advanced from those Tori remembered. A young man wearing jeans and sandals, his braided yellow hair dangling just past the neck of his T-shirt, sat slouched in front of a monitor. He jumped up, striking a finger at his screen as he moved. Blocks of text replaced the bright graphics of a game.

Bounding at Tori, he pumped her hand. "It's so great to meet you!"

Seth stepped between the two, forcing the man with the braid to finally drop Tori's hand. "Tori, this is Kendall." Seth nodded at a second man who lounged on a stuffed chair, its foam innards bleeding onto the floor. "And that's Bobby."

Bobby glanced up from his comm. "Hey." But he wasn't looking at her. He was scowling at Seth.

Grinning, Kendall stepped back to look at Tori. His teeth were small and white, like a child's. "You look good, Tori. Really good. A little tired maybe."

"Where's Jared?" Seth interrupted.

"Working the Post," Bobby said. He drank from a glass of iced tea, set the glass back on the floor, and dried his fingers on his brown cargo shorts. "The pick-up go okay?" His voice became an accusation. "We didn't hear from you."

Seth had one hand on the door frame like he was ready to push himself away from the room. "A couple of Regency's guys beat me there, but other than that . . ."

Tori remembered that long gleam of wire stretching toward her throat and shut her eyes.

"Hey, you all right?" Kendall asked her. "You want to sit?" He scooted an extra folding chair behind her.

"I'm okay," Tori said, but her legs felt flimsy. She sat.

Bobby's eyes fixed on Seth. "You didn't hurt anybody, did you?"

Seth made an exasperated noise, and Kendall drifted toward him. "Seth, we're *Guardians*. We're not about hurting people."

Bobby jabbed a finger at the gun still holstered against Seth's side. "You should get rid of that thing," he said.

Seth's right hand rested on the gun. "You want to do the next pick-up? Without any protection?"

"Look, Seth, nobody's criticizing you," Kendall interjected, his hands patting the air as if that would calm everyone.

"Something at Marrakesh with some aramid in it would've been nice," Seth said. "You know. Body armor? A nice Grapamid vest? You've heard of those things?"

Bobby shrugged. "Marrakesh should be stocked with it."

"*Should* be."

"Kendall takes care of the suppliers. You know that."

Kendall's braid wagged as he nodded energetically. "There's a couple of safehouses that don't have any right at this exact moment. I know that. We're restocking as soon as we get the funds. Donations have been down."

"You know we don't like guns in here," Bobby said. "You should take it outside."

Seth's hand hadn't budged from the gun. "Sure. And if any hitters show up, we'll just beat 'em off with your comm there."

Staring at the tiny screen of the device, Bobby waved Seth off with one arm.

"And, no," Seth added. "I didn't hurt anybody. A few bruises, that's it."

Without looking up, Bobby swiped the screen and reached for his iced tea again. The chink of ice cubes made Tori realize how thirsty she was. She pressed her parched tongue against her teeth. Her legs were a pair of logs. She contemplated just letting herself sink down to the floor, take a little rest. Nobody was looking at her. She could have been in another room. Another house. Hell, another state.

"You've got a route going?" Seth asked Bobby.

Bobby tapped his forehead. "In here."

"We're thinking she can go to Nebraska first," Kendall said.

Tori stared at him. They'd already decided this? Without a word to her? Before they'd even asked her if she wanted their help?

"Just temporarily," Kendall was saying. "And then up to—"

Bobby cut in. "Then some other places. Which we'll tell you when you need to know. And she doesn't ever need to know."

Tori jerked up from her chair. "Nebraska," she said. "What the hell?"

Kendall gaped at her. Bobby and Seth stared, Seth's gaze holding an instant longer than the others'. Then he turned deliberately to Bobby and said, "So. Endpoint where?"

Bobby drained the iced tea. "Toronto's no good anymore. There's a new place outside Vancouver, but we think it's been compromised."

"Hitters have snagged seven E's in Canada since the beginning of the year," Kendall broke in. "It's crazy."

Tori's gaze roamed between the men. Her mouth opened like she was going to speak, but she realized she had no idea what to say. They were deciding everything, assuming everything, but if they hadn't sent Seth to Arlington when they did, she'd be dead now. Her windpipe severed and blood and air leaking from her throat.

Weakness flooded her. She blinked, groping a hand at the wall behind her to balance herself.

Seth noticed at once. He loped to her. "Hey, you okay? Ken, get her some of that tea." Seth grasped Tori's shoulder, murmured, "C'mon. Sit down. You're exhausted."

114

Tori studied the shadows under Seth's eyes, the hollows of his cheeks, the stubble smearing his jaw. "And you're not?" She let him press her down onto the chair.

Kendall snagged up a plastic cup and a pitcher that stood sweating on the card table. Tea glugged into the cup. "Look, Seth" he burbled while he poured, "I'm not trying to be a downer. I'm totally optimistic about how everything's going to turn out for Tori. It's just that international isn't looking so great right now. You hear Regency just tracked down a guy in France?" He handed the cup to Tori and gave one braid a mournful tug. "But what are you going to do? Where are you going to go that corporations can't get to?"

"Yeah, that's optimistic all right." Seth shot a glance at Tori. "Can you shut this guy up?" he asked Bobby, who shrugged.

The tea was cool and surprisingly good. Tori downed half the cup, let the chill of the tea and the sharp minty edge of it rejuvenate her. She swallowed the rest of it and plunked the cup onto the floor under her chair. Ten years of being told what to do by guards every minute of every day had accustomed her to staying silent, letting the person with the uniform and the authority make all the decisions. Hell, just deciding what drink to buy at the gas station back in Granite seemed like a complex operation. But this was her life, her future. She wasn't behind bars anymore; she had to stop acting like she was.

Seth turned to Tori. "Come on, we'll find you some food and—"

Tori stood and planted herself in the middle of the floor. "Look. You don't have to talk around me. You don't have to try to protect me. I know how bad the odds are."

"I doubt it," Bobby muttered.

Tori rounded on him. "I know I'm damned lucky that I made it out of Glynn River to start with. I know I have to get out. You think I need to go to Timbuktu, okay, I'll probably go to Timbuktu."

Bobby opened his mouth. Tori raised a hand to silence him. "But there's one thing. I have to do one thing first." She stopped, took a breath. "My dad."

Kendall shook his head. "Oh, no, Tori, you can't see your dad. That would be such a bad idea, you just don't know."

"I *do* know."

"I hate to say it," Seth told her, "but the hippie's right."

"It's just . . ." Tori's arms were stiff at her sides, her fists burrowing at her thighs. Her eyes were suddenly wet. She blinked back tears and pushed down the knot in her throat.

Seth pressed so close to her that she could feel the warmth of his skin. "Why?"

"I know he was sick. Recently. I mean, really sick. He might even be—" She pushed the word out. "Dead."

Something flickered in Seth's eyes. He looked away.

"I just—" She struggled to finish. "I need to know." Her lungs burned like she'd just sprinted a mile.

Seth's hand closed gently on her shoulder. "Your dad's is the first place they'd expect you to go."

"But if he's sick! If he's dying—" Tori dropped her voice to a hoarse whisper. "I have to know."

Seth looked not just tired now, but haggard. "And you have to see him." Seth said this in almost a singsong tone, like he was imitating a hundred previous Executables who'd said the exact same thing.

Tori considered. "No. Actually."

Seth's eyebrows rose. "No?"

"If I knew how he was, where he was . . . if I could let him know I was alive. That would be enough." When she thought about never seeing her father again, her chest ached, as if her heart had sprouted claws that gouged her from the inside-out. "I could live with that. I think."

Seth studied her for a moment before turning to Bobby. "I'll go talk to Jared. See what he can ferret out."

Bobby nodded. "Knock yourself out. Just don't stick around too long."

Seth paused beside Tori. "Your only chance is to keep moving. Safehouse to safehouse. Never let yourself slow down too long. Never let down your guard."

"It's your best chance," Kendall said.

"Your *only* chance," Seth clarified. "Nobody should ever go back where they came from."

Tori digested this. She understood, on a rational level, that they were right. But emotionally, it was a lot harder to accept. "Not even if they're innocent." Bitterness tinged her voice.

"Oh, we only help the ones we think are innocent," Kendall said.

"Better P.R." Bobby's face was impassive. "Only way to get donors onboard. Even if some of us think the entire idea of capital punishment for *any*body is a crock."

"Yeah, well, some of us wouldn't *be* in the Network if we were helping killers," Seth told him, his voice bland as if they'd had this argument too many times already. Tori remembered his earlier question about what had happened to Robbie Cameron. "Keep drawing up a set of initial routings," he told Bobby and strode out of the room. Tori watched Seth disappear through another doorway at the far end of the hall.

"Hey, Tori." Kendall smiled comfortingly at her. "You want something to eat?"

What she really wanted was to meet this Jared guy that Seth seemed to think could pull out some news about her dad. "Maybe later," she said and slipped down the hall after Seth.

« CHAPTER 19 »

THE BASEMENT AIR TASTED of dank brick. Seth edged himself onto the one slice of tabletop not occupied by monitors and electronic devices. Jared looked up, nodded at something coming through the wireless listening device lodged in one ear. Red and yellow lights blinked and flickered. Seth studied images fleeing across a screen.

"You've stirred up a hornet's nest," Jared told him. "The traffic on here was nuts last night. You have any idea who you're up against this time?"

"Regency. Murray and Slater, at least." He really didn't want to think about it right now. He wanted a bed with some clean sheets and a fat pillow, and then he wanted to hightail it from the East coast, get Tori well enroute and away from the hitters.

This whole thing about her dad . . . he shouldn't be encouraging it. He should've just made a flat declaration: the Network makes the rules and if she didn't like it, she was welcome—free— to walk out of Caracas and keep herself alive if she could. He'd been too soft with her, too sympathetic. If his own mother hadn't just died . . . died without him knowing she was terminal, without a chance to see her one last time, he'd never have been so weak with Tori.

"How you doing with the encryption?" Seth asked.

"We haven't been able to get through all of it yet," Jared said. "Just enough to know you left 'em trussed up like a couple of Thanksgiving turkeys."

Seth exhaled and pushed his fingers through his hair. When he closed his eyes, he saw—not Regency's goons bound in electrical cords on a cheap foyer floor—but the poisonous red contortions of his father's face, and his brothers lumbering from beside the burial pit.

Jesus, he needed some sleep.

"How's the girl?" Jared asked.

A woman's voice—barely trembling—came from above them on the stairs: "The girl's okay. More or less."

Seth jolted around, one hand sliding to his holster. Tori was halfway down the steps, leaning out over the railing. Her face was white and drained, shadows pooled under her eyes. Her hair stuck up in a ragged hedge.

The tension went out of Seth's shoulders and his fingers relaxed away from the weapon. He hadn't heard a thing before she spoke. Sloppy. He was going to be useless until he got some rest. And stopped thinking about his family.

Jared half-rose from his chair, sank down again. "Hey. I'm Jared."

"Tori." She came down the rest of the stairs.

"Did you get fed up with those buffoons upstairs?" Jared asked.

"I think they're just . . ." Tori hesitated, glanced at Seth. "A little wired. They have a lot of questions. And a lot of plans."

Seth met her gaze. "Plans that'll help you stay alive," he said. Her eyes were dark brown, and softer than he expected. Between years slaving in a prison factory and a "freedom" that promised bullet wounds, burns, or exploded limbs . . . well, E's usually had eyes that already looked dead.

Electronic chirps fluttered the lights on one of the computers. Tori stared at the mess of electronic equipment. Seth watched her. The yellow panel lights sallowed her skin. She drew her arms across her chest, hunched her shoulders. She looked like a bedraggled animal run to ground.

Hell, he probably looked about the same, or worse.

"So this is the Post?" she asked.

Jared swung around to the monitors. "Listening Post, yeah. Where we try to intercept communications. From the execution companies, the hitters."

Tori bent to look, nudged closer to the apparatus as if a bunch of blinking lights and whirring fans were going to provide some kind of enlightenment. Seth closed his eyes. Saw the black pit, the ragged grass beating against the nearby headstones. His heart accelerated. A headache clamped his skull. He smelled the dirt, its damp, wormy odor.

Tori's voice sliced through his thoughts. "What were you saying before?" she asked Jared. "About who we're up against?"

Christ. She needed to know, but Seth didn't want to totally scare the piss out of her again. She needed a reprieve, no matter how brief. He slid off the edge of the table and caught her arm. "Hey, Tori, we could both use some sleep, something to eat. We can talk about this later."

Tori stepped neatly away from him. She planted her feet and squared her shoulders. "I want to know."

"No, you don't. Not on an empty stomach."

She didn't relent, just tilted that ridiculous cockatoo head at him like she was going to impale him on the spiky bits of hair if he didn't answer her questions.

She said, "You called those guys at the house Murray and Slater. You said they worked for—" She squinted, thinking. "Geoff Whelk?"

"Son of a bitch should be in prison." Anger flamed Seth's face. His skin burned. "His buddy Sergei too. That whole crew."

"Why?" Tori asked.

"You know guys like that, they never do time," Jared turned up his palms. "But you'd think Regency would be through with them."

Tori gnawed at her upper lip, but her gaze held steady. "Why?" she repeated. "Why should they be in prison?"

Maybe she deserved a straight answer. "Because they kill people." Seth's hand shot up to stop her interruption. "Yeah, it's legal, I know, I know. But they don't just kill people. They relish it. They don't usually choose something as simple and quick as a bullet in the brain."

"But—" Tori hesitated. Reflections of the yellow lights burst and died in her eyes. "But they're allowed to do that. To people like me."

"Yeah, that part's legal too." Seth shut his eyes for a second, pushing down the sudden rage that boiled up from his gut. "It's the collateral damage that's going to bring them down someday."

"Or maybe not," Jared inserted.

Tori's forehead wrinkled.

Seth reached to touch her arm. His hand paused an inch above her skin, fell away. "You know. Regular citizens. Non-E's. And their property. Geoff Whelk, Sergei Chistyakov, they tend to spread a lot of chaos."

Tori tilted her head, squinted at him. Then she nodded.

A faint chatter rose from Jared's earpiece. He pressed the device harder to his ear with one hand and listened intently.

Seth stared at the monitors. He was sick of blood. Sick of seeing it, talking about it, drowning in it in his dreams. But he could walk away whenever he chose. He wasn't an E. He sensed Tori trembling inches from him. He tightened his jaw. She needed the truth, not a lot of gauzy lies.

Shaking his head, Jared tugged the earpiece loose and glanced at Seth. "Did you hear about how Merle Edgers is testifying in front of Congress today?" he asked.

"About what? The screw-ups on his staff?"

Jared gave a lopsided smile. "They've got him there as an expert. On prisons."

"Who's Merle Edgers?" Tori asked.

Seth and Jared exchanged a glance. Tori stepped between them. Seth looked down at her hands. Yeah—still trembling, but she was gripping them together in an attempt to hide it.

"One of Regency's hitters?" she said.

"He's the owner," Seth told her.

Silence. Jared toyed with the earpiece.

"Doesn't sound like he's going to jail anytime soon," Tori ventured. Her mouth twitched into a quick smile. "Joke."

Jared gave a weak snort and returned to the chattering earpiece again.

Seth leaned into Tori. "Listen," he said. "Promise me one thing. We find out what the deal is with your dad." His brain flashed on Mount Calvary Cemetery again: headstones wallowing in the weeds, gleaming casket, the pit. "And whatever it is, he's okay, he's sick, he's dead—"

Tori flinched.

Seth rolled on, forcing himself to be merciless. "Whatever it is, we stay away from P.A. We head out."

The damp basement air swallowed Tori's whisper. "But if he's sick, he'll need me. There's nobody else."

Shit, he hated this, almost as much as the blood. Getting E's to understand—really   understand,   hammer-it-into-their-brain-like-a-railroad-spike understand—required a certain amount of cruelty.

"There's been nobody else for ten years," he said. "If he's sick, and you go back, you're going to end up dead and he'll still be alone. And if he's dead, there's no point." *Trust me on that last one.*

Tori's long exhalation was shaky. She shoved a hand through her hair. It bristled up, making her look fierce. "If he's dead, I wouldn't want to set foot in that state ever again anyway."

"And if he's sick . . . " Seth coaxed.

"Then I could go by myself."

"Like hell."

"I'd take the chance. For him."

Heartburn soured Seth's throat. He clenched his hands. Why hadn't Frank had the decency to let him know Mom was sick? One lousy call, one message, give Seth a chance to see Mom one last time.

"You okay?" Tori asked.

He'd squeezed his eyes shut without realizing it. He opened them, stared at Tori.

"As your Guardian," he said, "I'm not willing to let you take that chance."

Tori looked stricken.

Seth's jaw softened. Maybe he was getting too old for this Guardian business, too sentimental. But damn it, to have talked one more time with his mom, heard her gentle lullaby voice just one more time, held her papery hands.

"Let's just hope they find out he's okay or he's dead," he told Tori. "Because if we end up in Pennsylvania . . ."

What the hell are you even saying, screamed some rational portion of his brain. Tori looked as astonished as he felt.

"If we end up there," he finished, "the easy part of this trip is over."

« CHAPTER 20 »

"OH, YES," Sergei Chistyakov said, working the lid off a foot-high metal drum. "Seth Krey, he is with her. Slater, Murray, they tell me this." The lid clanged onto the floor of the van. "I think I will get—how do you say it?—one stone, but two birds?"

Whelk, just outside, swayed back from the van's rear doors, both flung wide to admit the maximum amount of daylight to the vehicle's interior. "Perhaps you might want to cushion that?" He nodded at the lid still vibrating against the hard vinyl mat.

Sergei rapped a gloved knuckle against the side of the drum. "This T-12, very stable. You must have a detonator. Or there is, what?" He extended his curved hands above his head, then brought them gently together like a mushroom cloud moving in reverse, diminishing. "Nothing."

Whelk wallowed back one more step. "You're sure?"

Putting his hands against opposite sides of the drum, Sergei tilted the container to the left, then back to the right. "You see?" He funneled a small amount of the feathery powder into a second container that held a maroon clay-like substance, then worked the powder into the clay. "Be prepared always, this is good, yes? Ahh." Sergei molded the blended clay into a rough brick. He raised the brick on one palm like a headwaiter carrying a platter of blue-ribbon filets. "The compression. The fragmentation. Enough T-12, we bring down bridges, buildings—"

"Tori Jennings. That's what we're after. Not bridges. Just Jennings."

Sergei showed his teeth. "Oh, yes."

"The family hasn't specified a preferred method."

Finishing a second brick, Sergei loaded it next to the first inside an empty drum. "I have mine," he said. "Preferences."

As Sergei pressed a third brick into shape, Whelk dropped a black satchel inside the van. "Two thousand dollars," Whelk said. "And three dozen peel caps. That should be more than sufficient to bribe our little drug fiends." He leaned against one of the open doors. The hinges groaned. "You may not need to offer the monetary compensation at all, Sergei. I have yet to see the peelout who could turn away from a single cap." His head swiveled toward Sergei. "You didn't learn anything useful from that man?" Whelk squinted at the white clouds streaking across the sky. He snapped his fingers twice. "In Granite?"

"Sam Mantell." Sergei contentedly added another pair of bricks to his stash. He held up a thumb and forefinger half an inch apart. "Only a bit."

"And?"

"She had lied to him. She said she would go to her sister. In New York."

"Tori Jennings doesn't have a sister."

Sergei ticked his head to one side to signal his agreement. "So, New York, no. Arlington, I do not see she will go there again. So *where?*"

Whelk hefted himself away from the door. "A string of safehouses, cross-country," he said. "As per usual."

"Maybe." Sergei was humming, an old Rolling Stones song Whelk couldn't quite name.

"We've picked up some tidbits about a possible Network hotspot in Virginia, one in Wilmington." Whelk heaved his enormous shoulders in a shrug. "She might loiter around the Philadelphia area. Her father lives there, I believe."

Sergei whipped his head up, flung a grin at Whelk. "He *lived* in Philadelphia. The father."

"Ah. I detect a past tense."

Sergei's grin remained fierce, his eyes uncomprehending.

Whelk gusted out a sigh as oversized as his barrel chest. "The old man's dead?"

"Oh. Yes." Sergei worked the lid back onto the drum of explosive. "I went myself to check. The girl was not there. No one there. Just the rats and the roaches. Having a party." He snapped another grin.

"Perhaps the gentleman moved to a nattier residence?"

"A what? No." Two solid thumps on the lid with a fist and Sergei shoved the drum to a back corner of the van. "His neighbor, she shared the sad news with us. Dead, burned, gone." The Russian swept his fingertips close to his mouth and pretended to blow ash from them, like petals from a flower.

"No notice from a funeral home, I assume?"

"No. This man, he was poor. Dirt. The house, it had nothing."

"Except the roaches and rats, yes." Whelk stroked his multiple chins. "And the Social Security death index is only years out of date. I wonder if Miss Jennings knows this tragic bit of news."

"Only if she has been to the place and talks with the neighbor herself."

"I'll wager she plans to. Eventually."

Sergei shrugged, pushed out his thick lower lip. "We have people watching. No worry."

"And in the meantime—"

Sergei stripped off his gloves, picked up the satchel, and rooted through it. "I send Murray out. And Slater. With this. "

"Be sure they show off the holos," Whelk said. "We were able to acquire some excellent images from a helpful guard at Glynn River. Taken from security footage shortly before her release. It's all right if Murray and Slater want to distribute a cap or two to grease the rails, so to speak. But no one gets the motherlode until we have Jennings sighted. And, preferably, harvested as well. If then."

"No worry, Geoff," Sergei repeated and sprang down from the van, the soles of his shoes smacking the blacktop.

Whelk humped along after Sergei toward the back door of the house. It opened directly to the kitchen. "Seth Krey," Whelk mused. "That man should be dead by now. Connelly shot him in the leg in Detroit, remember? Simpson forced his car off the road. And yet?" Whelk cast a gimlet eye at the bread crumbs on the table drowning themselves in a puddle of spilled vodka. "Here he is again." Whelk's gaze hardened. "He would have had us doing time, Sergei. Federal time. Plucking maggots out of hospital sheets in one of Merle's industrial laundries. Signing up to burn our lungs out in pharmaceutical experiments for the sake of a few months shaved off our sentences."

Whelk twisted around to eye the Russian. "And why? So he could feel *good* about himself? Pat himself on the back because he was the last honest cop, standing up for justice against the big, bad hitters? As if anyone— least of all the police—cared about a little incidental damage."

Pushing the faucet to full blast, Sergei turned his hands palms-up beneath the pounding water. Steam turned his skin pink. "Damage," he said, grinning and tugging at his soapy fingers.

Whelk settled his over-sized rump against the counter's edge. "The minute he tried to bring charges against us when we were just doing our job, trying to fulfill our contracts—all sanctioned, all legal—that was the minute I knew he was due for elimination, whether he was a cop or not. I can't say I was surprised when he turned all "Truth, Justice, and the American Way" about that Mahmoud guy, wailing that the poor copkiller was framed. And what did it get the poor sap? Booted off the force. Shunned by kith and kin, from what I hear."

"And then he turns Guardian."

"Yes. So he can continue to play Mr. Integrity, Mr. Holier-Than-Thou, this time trying to save E scum instead of copkiller trash. You know, Sergei, it rather makes me want to put a hand in."

"Then you better put that hand in fast." Sergei snapped a towel from a rack behind the sink. "Or I will have him dead before you get the chance."

« CHAPTER 21 »

FROWNING, PAIGE CLIMBED the three busted wooden steps that ascended to the shotgun house in North Philly. Block wooden letters—LAW OFFICE—were nailed, lopsided, above the door. A single fern littered the top step with brown, brittle leaves.

She knocked, striking the scabby wood hard and then jerking her knuckles back as if germs swarmed in the splinters and peeling paint. God, people were slobs. Sloppy, lazy, useless, vicious slobs.

Her gaze clicked to the window. The blinds were bent as if a cat had clawed at them. The nearest edge of the blinds twitched. She rapped her knuckles against the windowpane. The blinds convulsed.

"Mr. Stephenson." She leaned in close to the door. It was warped; gaps swelled between it and the frame. "I left a message requesting an appointment at two."

Finally, the door edged open. The man who hunched in the entry couldn't have stood much over five-foot tall, a good half-dozen inches shorter than Paige. He gave Paige a cringing, upward look. Tiny globes of sweat fattened around the roots of his receding hairline.

"I don't think I can help you." His voice was as pallid and thin as the rest of him.

Paige knifed past him into the office.

"Now, wait—" Stephenson scuffed backward through a chaos of papers and envelopes heaped on the yellowed linoleum floor. "I can't help you," he repeated, folding himself onto a chair behind a card table.

"But I think maybe you can."

His eyes briefly shut. "Your message said it involved a criminal case?"

"Tori Jennings."

Stephenson blanched.

"You remember her," Paige said.

The lawyer's head wobbled 'no.' "I do wills," he insisted. "Divorces. Landlord problems."

"Mr. Stephenson," Paige said. "I'll call you Lou."

"For bail you need to go see Al Ramirez down the street. Or there's Jo Stein, down by the—"

"I already have a will, I'm not married, and I don't need bail money."

"Oh." A drop of sweat ambled down Stephenson's forehead and nested like a fish egg in his left eyebrow. His fingertips tapped against his mouth. The shiny cuffs of his shirt drew back from his raised hands, exposing wrists bruised eggplant-purple.

"No criminal cases these days, Lou?" Paige leaned forward, her palms pressed flat against the tabletop. "Why not?"

His gaze swam away from Paige. "Too much stress."

The evasiveness, the slack-off "don't-ask-me" irresponsibility reminded Paige of too many social workers, too many foster parents. The fury in her belly vibrated to a higher pitch. "Or too much work?" she asked.

Stephenson rubbed at the scalp exposed along his hairline. "I have another appointment I have to prepare for."

"Somebody's already stopped by, haven't they?" Paige picked up a pen, jabbed it at Stephenson's wrists. "Who was it?"

"Nobody! I swear."

"Who?"

Stephenson's gaze crawled to the tabletop. "I don't know." His voice was a sandpaper whisper.

"A big pale guy, bloated, looks like a huge amphibian that crawled up from a cave?"

Stephenson's mouth sniveled to one side. His yellow tie quivered.

"How about this, then? Compact, muscular, Russian, eyebrows like roadkill?"

Stephenson refused to answer. Which was an answer, Paige thought. Whelk and his goons were on the job; it didn't matter which particular goon had shown up here. "He told you not to talk about Jennings to anybody else," she said. Whelk wouldn't want any grabbers tracking Jennings down before his squad did. "Otherwise," she mused, "he said he'd beat you up? Torture you? Kill you?"

Three swift jerks of Stephenson's head, like a rod snapping up and down as a fish nabs the bait.

"Well, I know those guys. If they said it, they meant it."

Stephenson's eyes were huge. He swayed on the chair like he might pass out.

"However, I'm afraid my partner and I might have the same response to a *lack* of cooperation on your part."

"Partner?" Stephenson wheezed.

"Outside," she said. A lie. Mike was probably shopping for that new rifle sight he'd been talking about. And waiting for her to call? Hell, probably not. Probably asking some gorgeous neighbor at his gated condo complex over for a beer. Expensive German beer.

She shoved in close to Stephenson. Wanted to smash his blubbering face, watch the bastard disintegrate. "Tell me what you remember about the Jennings case."

"It's been a long time," Stephenson whined.

Paige thumbed her comm, tossed the device onto the table. Video of a courtroom played across the screen. In the video, a younger Stephenson with more hair droned at a collection of jurors who looked bored and tired, like students trapped in a late afternoon class with the school's dullest teacher. The judge looked positively drugged. Only Tori—white-faced, dark hair falling out of a loose ponytail—looked awake. Wary. No, terrified, her gaze sliding from the judge to the jurors to Stephenson, her fingers cramped around each other.

"You didn't call *any*one to testify on Jennings' behalf," Paige remarked.

Stephenson stared at the screen.

"You compiled a list of potential witnesses," Paige snapped.

Silence.

Paige snatched a knife out of her bag, slammed the six-inch blade into the table.

Stephenson jerked back. He wobbled in his chair, nearly toppled over. His eyelids skinned back until the whites of his eyes were enormous.

Paige was trembling, sweat starting under her arms. *Damn it, control yourself,* she thought. She yanked the blade free and held the weapon drawn back. Ready to strike. "I said," she repeated slowly, "you compiled a fucking list of witnesses."

"I . . . I guess so. I mean, I must have."

"So why didn't you call any of them?"

"She was guilty anyway." Stephenson's whine grew more nasal.

"She confessed to you?"

"She didn't need to." A sheet of paper stuck to his damp hand. He shook the paper loose. Closed his eyes. "Lemme think here. I've got to think."

Paige snorted. "Are you capable of that?"

Stephenson opened his eyes. They watered worse than before, gumming up at the corners. "Okay. That's right. The tests the M.E. ran, they were conclusive."

"Were they?" The hilt burned Paige's palm. She was quivering like a sick dog. She had to get control of herself. She swallowed down her anger.

"It was Dr. Bannock. I remember. She never mentioned any doubts."

Stephenson must have noticed that Paige was shaking and decided she wasn't as terrifying as Whelk and his goons. He was starting to sound too comfortable.

"There weren't even any other suspects," he went on. "Jennings looked guilty. She acted guilty."

"Ahh. Lawyerly intuition, then."

Stephenson's gaze slid past her again toward the door. "I have another appointment."

Paige sprang at him, crowded up against his side. The blade pressed at his throat. Danced in time with the wild pulsing of his carotid artery.

Sweat flooded Stephenson's face again. He stank like a dirty locker room.

"What I'm really interested in, Lou, is any records you have on the Jennings trial and on your own stellar performance in that courtroom."

"They already took everything I could find," he whined.

Paige glanced through a half-open door leading to a second room in the back. Papers and folders and envelopes buried the space. An ancient printer squatted in the chaos, disassembled, its innards spread across the floor. "You have electronic copies," she said.

"A lot of those files never got converted over," the lawyer bleated. "It got all screwed up. My secretary was a joke."

"Not just your secretary. Where's your comm?"

"Those guys took it."

Paige shoved a notepad and a pen in front of the lawyer and stood just behind his left shoulder, the blade now poised at the nape of his neck.

"I want your notes," she said and nodded at the notepad. "Anything that might have struck a competent attorney as having any importance.

Witnesses and experts you never subpoenaed. Conflicts in stories. Theories you never bothered to check out." She briefly lifted one hand. "I'll wait."

Stephenson stared at the blank pad and slowly began to write while Paige scooped up random piles of papers and folders from the havoc of the back room and brought them into the front office. She checked the lawyer's progress. Sloppy loops of script filled only the first half dozen lines of his notepaper.

"I think you'll want to do a little better than that," Paige said.

Stephenson redoubled his grip on the pen. Paige, rooting through the miscellaneous papers, noted misspelled terms: *amicus curae*; *faciendem*; the idiot couldn't even spell *Cinncinatti* or *Albiny*. She dropped the untidy stack on the floor and fetched a second heap, and a third. Probate tussles; ludicrous personal injury suits; requests for filing extensions.

The lawyer shifted his thighs on his chair, the wood squeaking as if his rump squashed a dozen mice beneath it. Paige's gaze snapped to him.

"I'll take a look at that now." She reached for the pad, tore off the top sheet, and scanned the writing. He'd covered less than half the paper with anemic notations. "Pretty sparse."

The loose skin at Stephenson's throat bobbled. "I told you it's been a long time."

Paige ran through the information. Bannock was the M.E. on the case. She'd left Philly "under a cloud." One of the things she'd wanted to ask Stephenson about anyway. Paige gave Stephenson a sharp look. "What is that?" she asked. "A c*loud*?"

"I don't know. I just heard she got forced out."

"You realize," Paige said, scrutinizing the next couple of lines, "that I already know that there was a trial? Astonishing, but I'm even aware that Jennings was sentenced as an Executable."

"I don't remember much," Stephenson complained.

Paige stopped at the final words: *Dr. Karen? Kathy? Sheldon? Simon? Shapiro? Kept bugging me about testifying. Something Syndome? Prob. wanted her name in the news.*

Paige snapped the paper down on the table and jabbed a finger at the variations on the name. "Who is she? This doctor?"

Paige caught the lawyer's scuttling, sidelong look of guilt. He froze as she rounded on him, knife out, fingers resting on her holstered gun.

"I don't know! She said it might have been something else, not antifreeze."

"And you ignored her?"

Stephenson managed to shrink farther back. He blinked. "I guess it must not have seemed worthwhile."

"Or not worth the effort."

"They always gave me the lousy cases, the ones nobody could win."

Paige took up the paper again and dropped it into a shredder. "Kathy Sheldon?" she said. "Karen Shapiro?"

"It was—uh—no—Kyra, I think. Yeah. Kyra. Or maybe Kayla?"

"What about the last name?"

He shook his head hopelessly and eyed the knife.

"Where did she work?

"I don't remember." Stephenson's hands were all over the place: fidgeting in his lap, tapping at the peeling surface of the table, rubbing at his scalp. "She was here. In the city." Wrinkles clutched his forehead. "I just can't place it."

It doesn't matter, Paige calmed herself. The man was a moron. A negligent, complacent moron, but that didn't matter. Tracking down a researcher like this Sheldon or Shapiro or whatever her name was would be simple enough, especially if she'd stayed in the region.

Paige tucked her knife away. "I doubt I'll be talking to you again," she said. Stephenson puffed out a breath, visibly relaxed. Paige pinned him in place with a look. "But those new friends of yours? They always mine the same turf, over and over."

She left Stephenson slumped at his desk, his face green and slick. Pausing on the porch, she wondered how far ahead Whelk and his squad were. And why she couldn't just let it drop, like Mike suggested. Jennings might be guilty.

But you know you don't believe that.

"It's not my problem," she muttered. Behind her, from the other side of the door, a deadbolt slammed home and a chain clanked into place.

Paige crossed her arms hard over her chest. Remembered the shiny gold doorknob that her foster dad had installed on her bedroom door after he'd removed the one that locked. The foster mom had stared dumbly. Paige's caseworker had remarked, "Goodness, a man is allowed to do some home maintenance, isn't he?" And left Paige to whatever came next.

Protect the guilty. Sacrifice the innocent.

Paige bent, scooped up a chunk of broken concrete from beside the steps. Straightening, she smashed the concrete through the front window of Stephenson's office.

Silence inside. The stillness of a terrified rabbit.

She smiled, imagining his queasy face, his churning gut. Then she brushed her palms against each other and hurried to the car.

« CHAPTER 22 »

WREN WAS BLASTED. Shit-faced blasted on the last hit of peel she'd borrowed from Owen's stash last night.

Blasted was good. It gave the world a satiny texture. It cut away the stink of the trash heap where she and a dozen others picked through slimy lettuce leaves, filthy diapers, and sticky plastic bottles, looking for something to sell.

Plastic bags rattled in the wind. The noise sounded a mile away. She crouched in the muck and watched her hands slide through it, plucking up bits of fabric and glass, smashed milk jugs. She'd found a watch once, a good one. Got forty bucks for it. If she could find something good today, sell it, buy more peel and maybe some tamales for dinner, chain up with Owen that night . . . it would be about as perfect a day as she could imagine. She wanted to push her face into the crook of Owen's neck, nuzzle the warm muscle. Fall into a sleep soft as snowflakes.

"Hey! Wren!"

She heard the name, but it took a minute for her to recognize it as her own.

"Wren! Get your skank-ass down here!"

She blinked through the dust simmering at the bottom of the heap. Two men stared up at her. The tall, bulky guy jabbed a finger in her direction like he wanted to blot her out. The smaller man pressed a wadded shirt against his nose and mouth.

Wren stared. She knew them, she just wasn't quite sure, at the moment, who they were. Memories oozed through her head.

"*Wren!*" the tall man shouted again.

She glided down the heap in slow motion. The sultry air was water and she swam her arms through it.

"Great," the short guy said, briefly pulling the cloth away from his face. "She's totally fucked-up."

"She usually is." The tall guy whipped his hand in a *come here!* gesture.

Disquiet slunk through Wren's calm. Her feet turned from feathers into weights. She was wading through garbage now, slipping and skidding down the steepest part of the slope. Crows erupted from a heap of tire treads beside her.

She stumbled to a halt in front of the men. The skin of her face stung as if it were just coming alive. A spidery sensation jittered her intestines. The morning's hit was fading—fast—the way it always did with cheap peel. The world sharpened to a razor-edge that cut her eyes.

Something jolted against her, sent her staggering. Her hands smacked down in a goo that squelched like hot yogurt. She squinted up.

Jeddy quivered in the spot where she'd just been standing. His stringy biceps quaked. He clutched a stained canvas bag lumpy with whatever sellables he'd picked from the trash that day. Moron skinwaste. Trying to shove his way in, get all the money, all the peel caps. Wren staggered to her feet.

"You fuck-ups ready for a job?" the tall guy said. Murray. The name finally clicked in Wren's brain.

The shorter guy—Slater, that was it—added, "We got a couple of people we want you to keep an eye out for. The usual spots."

"The safehouses?" Jeddy kept squeezing his eyes shut hard and then popping them open again. Wren crammed herself beside him, almost fell over. Fuck him if he thought he was going to swipe all the prizes here. She'd been helping out with the Guardians' safehouses longer than him.

"Yep, safehouses," Slater answered. Snapping open his comm, he thumbed up a holo. A woman's image circled, three-dimensional, from the unit. She looked sallow and thin, the tendons in her neck whip-lean. Her cropped brown hair stuck up at the crown. Her eyes made Wren think of that old-time movie star—the skinny bitch?—yeah, Audrey Hepburn. This woman had eyes like that: big, round, the color of a melting brown crayon. Like you could hurt her real easy. But the lowered chin and the set mouth said otherwise.

"Tori Jennings," Slater said. "An E from Glynn River. You seen her?"

Jeddy pinched dead skin from his lips, his fingers jerking thin and quick. "Guardians aren't letting me in anymore."

Triumph burned through Wren. Jeddy must've fucked up. Well, more for her then. She pushed against him like he was trash to be shoved into a corner. When he protested—"Hey!"— she scraped a look up and down his face.

Murray shifted forward, his barrel chest pushing at Jeddy's scrawny frame. "You screw up? You tell the Guardians about working for us?"

Jeddy's hands rose. "I don't know anything. I swear—"

"You people are the most worthless, pathetic . . ." Murray hawked and spat. Saliva oozed a dark trail through the dust on Jeddy's cheek.

Slater turned the holo toward Wren. "What about you? Seen her in any of the safehouses yet?"

But Jeddy rattled in front of her. His head was popping on his neck. "They're gonna let me back in the Network! I swear. They said this was just till I got into rehab, got my shit together. You know, a little more together."

"Bullshit." Murray pushed Jeddy aside smoothly as sliding a chair away from a table. "They know you're a peelout. They're not giving you any second chance. Shit, I don't know why they give you ex-cons a first chance."

Jeddy tried to worm closer. "I was just in for nothing. Siphoning gas. And I didn't even do it. It was my friend."

"Yeah, well." Murray paused, then rammed him so hard that Jeddy flew off his feet and landed in a glitter of broken glass. Jeddy squealed, revolving on hands and knees, plucking at his bleeding palms. "Get the hell out of here."

Jeddy limped a dozen paces off, stood watching from beside the scavenged bones of a dishwasher, like a cast-out wolf hoping the pack will take him in again.

"Now," Murray announced, wheeling around. "*You.*" He grabbed Wren's upper arm, pulled her off balance. She fell to one knee. He jerked her upright again. Her shoulder burned. "You seen this woman, you sorry-ass peelfreak?"

Tears sliced her eyes. She wagged her head.

"The Guardians cutting you out these days too?" Murray shook her arm back and forth like a piece of rope.

The peel had burned out of Wren's system. She could feel everything now. A power saw was cutting her skull into ragged strips. "I'm still in."

She had access to two safe houses. Safe rooms. All she had to do was keep them stocked and in return she got food, a little cash. Kendall had no idea about the peel. As far as he knew, her veins were clean and she was 100% rehabilitated from crime after a single foray into identity theft.

"You seen her?" Murray asked again.

Wren squinted at the holo. "Unh-unh."

Murray dropped Wren's arm and gave her a light shove that knocked her off-balance once more.

"We need you to be our eyes and ears," Slater instructed. "Keep a look out for her. And this guy. Seth Krey."

"Man, I'd like another crack at him," Murray said.

Slater continued. "They may be together. Maybe not. You see either one of them, you contact us. *Immediately.* The faster we hear about it, the faster you get paid. And the more you get paid. Here." Slater pulled out the plastic bag Sergei had passed on to him from Whelk.

Wren quivered, instantly on the alert. The red capsules gleamed through the plastic bag. They practically winked at her.

"This is just a taste, you understand?" Slater said. "A small taste of what you could get. To show you how much we value our stringers." He flapped a decrepit twenty dollar bill and dropped a single peel-cap into her palm. She clenched her fingers tightly around the capsule. "You be our eyes, okay? The places where you go."

"The shitholes, you mean," Murray muttered, turning away, squinting up at the trash heap's summit. "The dumps and the outhouses and the garbage cans where you people like to hang out."

Wren's face grew wobbly. She wanted to cry. She always wanted to cry after the peel wore off. "I'm a person, you know?" she whispered.

"What's that?" Murray inclined one ear toward her.

"I'm a person." Her hand, still clutching the capsule, cramped itself into the fortress of an armpit.

"Could've fooled me," Murray said. "Come on." He smacked Slater on the back. "Let's get out of here. Before we choke on the fumes."

"Remember," Slater called back. Wren touched her wet cheeks with her free hand. "Tori Jennings. Seth Krey." Slater held up a single peel-cap pinched between two fingers. Its red shell caught the sun. He flicked it at Wren. It flew past her and disappeared into the garbage-strewn ground.

Wren dropped to her knees. She scrabbled at the trash, digging her fingers into the slime.

"There's a lot more where that came from," Slater called. "If you come through for us."

Wren barely heard him. She had her face inches from the mucous-covered ground, her eyes twitching like grasshoppers, desperate for a glint of red. She didn't look up. And when Jeddy crawled up beside her, his fingers stabbing and sliding through ooze of trash, she just dug harder and faster.

« CHAPTER 23 »

BLUE SHADOWS DARKENED the windows. Tori pushed herself up from the lumpy mattress. The sun was down, a half moon rising through the branches of the apple trees. She'd slept for hours, but she still felt sluggish. From somewhere down on the first floor rose applause and measured speech punctured by outbursts of Kendall's reedy, outraged voice.

As she tugged at her sleep-crumpled shirt and combed a hand through her hair, she searched for a clock. The walls were bare; likewise, the old-fashioned school desk shoved into one corner. Stretching, Tori padded across the wooden floor into the hall.

A half-dozen rooms opened off the corridor. She peeked into each, curious about what a safehouse would look like, what its rooms might contain. But the rooms were nearly empty, holding little more than beds or cots, a scuffed chest of drawers, a lamp.

The last room before the stairs was different. It looked like some sort of library. Tori stepped onto the threadbare braided rug at its center and examined books so yellowed they might have been a century old. Lots of names she didn't recognize—Mills, Bentham, Sartre, Orwell, Kerouac—as well as a smattering of novels with spaceships and tentacled aliens careening across the covers and ratty paperbacks with the words *death penalty* or *capital punishment* in their titles. Several three-ring binders stood in a row along the back edge of a table. Someone had left two binders out. The red binder was closed, a printed card—*Regency*—taped to its cover. A second, yellow binder lay open.

Tori bent to study the exposed sheets. She drew back with a sharp exhalation, unsure what she was really seeing.

With one hand she fumbled at a small table lamp. The burst of light revealed the details of each photograph: a face crosshatched with razor cuts; a drowned body, the bloated face purple-gray; a throat slit back to the vertebrae. Unable to breathe, Tori turned the page. The plastic film was slippery and cool beneath her fingers.

Gunshot wounds, arrows, some sort of chemical burn. She stopped at the full-page photograph of a woman who could have been her age. Strips of leather bound the woman's wrists and ankles. She'd probably been Spanish, maybe Asian, a knot of hair like a sleek black tassel against her blood-soaked throat. The nearly continuous bruises covering her exposed flesh had turned her skin murky green.

A buzzing filled Tori's head. Her stomach clenched.

"Aren't you supposed to be getting some sleep?"

Tori whipped around. Seth watched her from the hall. His gaze slid to the photograph. He started forward, brushing a hand reassuringly across Tori's shoulder as he passed her.

"If you were looking for a good book to curl up with," he said, closing the binder, "you won't find it here."

Now Tori could see a card on the front of the yellow binder. It was labeled *Regency* as well. However, a second card affixed beneath the first added the name *Whelk*. Seth pushed the binders back into place with the others.

Tori fell back a step. She was trembling. "So that's Regency?"

"That's Whelk. And his buddy Sergei Chistyakov. Regency hires them for the uglier jobs." He gave Tori a slow, careful look like he wasn't sure how much to tell her. "And sometimes they're just given the leeway to do it how they want."

"It's sick," she said.

"No argument on that one."

Tori sagged against the table. All the terror she'd felt before her release from Glynn River sweated from her pores again. She might have been luckier if they'd gunned her down the second she stepped off prison grounds. The photographs surged into her mind. Better a gun than that. She wanted to vomit.

"But you've . . . you've faced them before?" she finally said.

"Yeah."

"And you managed."

Seth's glance cut sideways.

"Right?" Tori pleaded.

"I've managed. Sure."

Tori hesitated. "And the people you were guarding?"

Anger and sadness passed across Seth's face. Tori wished she hadn't asked. "I did better by some than by others," he muttered.

"Are any of these . . ." The room swooned, breathless and hot. Tori slid a finger across the spine of the *Whelk* binder. "Did you know any of them? I mean, did you guard them?"

Seth's mouth turned bitter. "Do we really need to talk about this? Look. Let's just say, I've seen what Whelk can do when he's on his game."

Tori touched the back of Seth's hand. "Did he ever hurt *you*?"

Seth pulled away from her. "That's not important."

"But—"

"What's important is that we keep moving, screw up his plans." Seth pulled out his comm and called up a series of holos and short biographies. "Regency's boys." He flicked past an attractive woman with blonde, chin-length hair and chilled eyes. "And girls." He stopped at another image. "That's Whelk. In his younger days. He looks like he just graduated from thug school there. Maybe twenty, twenty-five years ago. He's what? Almost fifty now."

Tori examined the face. It was puffy and damp, the eyes cunning, the hair already thinning across the top of the scalp. Whelk held an enormous cigar in one hand. In the background stood a trio of men in tuxedoes and a woman in a long black dress. The woman held—

"A violin?" Tori said.

"Geoffrey Whelk, patron of the arts."

"You're kidding me."

"That's him, all right. Whelk the pompous asshole."

Tori shook her head wonderingly and leaned closer. "It's his eyes. He looks cruel."

"Well, yeah, he's got cruel down pat. But otherwise, he's changed a lot. He's a lumbering hulk of what he used to be." Seth snapped off the holos and pocketed the comm. "He's killed a lot of people. A lot of good people. Not just Executables. He's killed Guardians too. Avery, Chen—" Seth broke off, motioning toward a series of framed photographs on the wall. "Some of our best." A thin wire of anger pulled his words taut. Flicking off the lamp, he turned and headed for the door.

Tori paused before the photographs. They showed ordinary-looking men—and a couple of women—wearing jeans or sweats, sitting at kitchen tables or leaning against cars, drinking a beer, grinning, laughing. She turned away.

Seth waited for her. Downstairs, Kendall yapped something that sounded like *bastard*. Seth lifted his gaze to the ceiling, let out his breath, and gave a sheepish smile. He held out one hand, motioning Tori closer. The braided rug was rough and knobby under her feet. In the twilit hall, Seth's dark hair looked almost black. A crisp scent of soap clung to his skin. His hand tensed around her fingers. "We'll get through this, okay?" His hand was calloused, warm.

Tori met his eyes. "Why are you doing this?"

Seth put on a smile, twitched his shoulders like he didn't quite understand. "Doing what?"

"Guarding people. When you know you'll have guys like Whelk coming after you."

He glanced away from her, then looked back and widened his smile. "Everybody needs a hobby."

He released her hand and turned toward the stairs.

Tori wanted to press him, to push past his flippant non-answer. Instead she said, "Hey, were you guys watching vids?"

He hesitated. "Nothing very entertaining."

She caught up with him. "Mind if I come watch?"

"Ahh, it's nothing, it's—"

"That Edgers guy you were talking about earlier? Testifying?" Tori couldn't help smiling at the gloomy surprise on Seth's face. "Yeah, I remember. And yes, I want to see what he looks like, this guy who wants me dead." A tremor betrayed the bravado of her words. The images of Whelk's prey revolved in her mind. She brought her chin up. "I want to see if he's as ugly as Whelk."

This time Seth met her smile with a spontaneous grin of his own. "Not possible." He swept an arm toward the staircase and stood back to give Tori room to pass.

Bobby and Kendall had ranged themselves in front of a screen in what passed for a living room. Tori looked past them to the monitor. Captioning identified the man on the screen as Merle Edgers, CEO of Progressive Prison Systems & Regency Enterprises.

Edgers' bulk filled two-thirds of the space. Microphones bristled up from the table at which he sat. Notes formed a neat sheaf beneath his meaty hands, but he didn't refer to them. Instead, his attention focused on the Congressional representatives before him.

"Not very many," Seth commented, leaning against the doorframe. "Go ahead, Tori. Have a seat." She lowered herself onto a ripped footstool in front of the couch where Bobby and Kendall hunched.

"Left," Kendall said, and the visual shifted that direction to reveal rows of mostly empty seats.

Bobby snorted. "Guess the rest of our fine representatives have already been bought off."

Tori leaned forward, studying Edgers. He looked like a well-fed, surprisingly manicured hippie. He wasn't old, but his face had a puffiness to it and a ruddy tint that Tori recognized from the drunks who'd slopped around her neighborhood when she was a kid.

Edgers' well-tailored suit moved easily with his arms as he gesticulated. "Ladies and gentlemen, are we now *trying* to weaken the very business people who are struggling to bring jobs back to American shores?"

"Unbelievable," Kendall squawked. "Oh, you want a job? Sure. All you have to do is get yourself tossed in the can."

A congresswoman wearing a red-white-and-blue scarf knotted around her throat half-rose from her chair. Her head swiveled to the right, searching out a camera. "What about Tallahassee? Twenty-four inmates died in the rioting in Allied's facility." A pair of congressmen flanking her cut annoyed, sideways glances in her direction.

Tori stared, riveted. Twenty-four inmates, dead in a riot? She'd never heard a whiff of that news inside Glynn River.

"A tragedy, absolutely." Edgers' head shagged from side to side. "A tragedy that could have been averted if Allied hadn't been crippled by so many unnecessary regulations."

"*Bull*shit," Kendall practically squeaked.

Edgers rumbled on. "Allied was forced to install inferior security systems, forced to staff the facility with 80% public employees. Undertrained, underequipped, poorly-motivated public employees. If the government had let Allied bring in their own staff? With decent pay, solid benefits, excellent—"

"Decent pay?" the congresswoman interrupted. "Are you seriously suggesting—"

"PPS has a prison in my district," a congressman beside her drawled. "Unemployment in that city's dropped eight points. Those people are damn grateful to have jobs. Glad to have *those* jobs."

Tori pictured the Glynn River guards, with their stunners and Hellhounds. Were they grateful for the work? Some of them had obviously enjoyed bullying and tormenting the inmates, but even more of the guards had seemed dead-bored, marking time.

"We're not evil, you know," Edgers said. "Sure, we want to make a profit. But we also know that our facilities are better and safer for the inmates than your state-run prisons, safer for the staff, and can bring real economic uplift to a struggling community." Edgers raised his hands and let them drop six inches to the tabletop. "But the regulations are killing us."

"What regulations?" Kendall interjected. "There's hardly any *now*."

"And what's going to bring manufacturing jobs back home?" Edgers gave the congresswoman a stern look. "We have to start somewhere. There are plants overseas using nothing but penal labor. They're crammed in barracks like sardines, like something out of Auschwitz, and nobody gives a rat's—nobody cares if they ever see the light of day again."

"Sounds familiar," Tori murmured. Seth shifted in the doorway. She glanced at him. He was watching her instead of the screen. Tori's right hand rubbed at her opposite palm, tracing the freshest cuts.

"But I'm an optimist," Edgers said. "I believe if we restart industries here at home, we can get people at least *thinking* 'Made in America' again" A smile, touched with gravity, creased his face. "Frankly, by rolling back these antiquated laws, you're ultimately giving all the workers of America hope."

"Jee-sus Christ!" Kendall flung a cushion at the screen which tumbled sideways. Edgers' image broke into static and the sound sputtered out.

Bobby deposited his bowl on the floor with a clunk. "Way to go, Einstein." He squatted beside the monitor and tried to shift it upright again.

Kendall stood. "Jeez, sorry, I just get worked up."

"You just get crazy, you mean. Aw, crap, look at this." The monitor lolled sideways again. "Help me lift it."

Kendall and Bobby carried the monitor into the kitchen. Tori winced at the sound of the monitor thudding onto the table.

"Jeez, be careful will you?" Bobby snapped.

"It slipped," Kendall said.

Seth still slouched in the doorway. "Looks like the entertainment's over for now," he told Tori.

Tori stared at the purple-black sky outside the window. She and Seth were a pair of ghosts reflected in the glass. Somebody could be stalking out from the apple trees, creeping toward this window, automatic rifle in hand. Tori's hands itched. If she had a gun herself, maybe she wouldn't feel so helpless.

"So, what did you think of him?" Seth asked. "Merle Edgers?"

"He doesn't have that—that sadistic look." Tori gestured in the direction of the library upstairs. "Not like that Whelk guy. Edgers is just . . . just a businessman, I guess." She returned Seth's gaze. "So he owns prison factories too?"

Seth nodded. "Progressive Prison Systems. Regency's going to be a bit player next to PPS in his empire. Hell, it already is."

For a moment, a stink of blood and bleach suffused the air. Automated blades whisked beneath a roaring tumble of conveyor belts. Tori pressed her calloused fingers against the numb scar tissue crisscrossing her forearms. She didn't want to remember.

"You all right?" Seth's gaze dropped to Tori's arms. She immediately clasped her hands behind her back, like a soldier told to stand at ease.

She felt anything but easy. "Sure."

Seth leaned forward to grip her arm. He turned it toward the light. "They worked you in one of his factories?"

Tori jerked her arm away. "I don't know if it was his or not."

"Doing what?"

She crossed her arms again, turning the ruined inner flesh against her ribs. "Meat packing. Poultry." She gusted out a nervous laugh. "They've got some crazy-ass claws."

A grin broke up Seth's somberness. She noticed again the missing chip off one of his incisors that added a down-to-earth affability to his smile.

His grin faded. "It must've been terrible. Doing that kind of work. Being locked up." *All of it*, he gestured, waving a hand.

"The worst thing," Tori said quietly, rubbing her arms, "was feeling so helpless all the time. So out of control." She hooked Seth's gaze with her own. "I want to learn how to shoot." She kept her voice low. "Bobby and Kendall don't seem to like guns much, but . . ."

Seth watched with sharpened interest. "But you need lessons in the fine art of saving your ass."

"I don't want everybody to feel like they have to protect me all the time. I want to protect myself."

Seth's lower lip puffed out as he considered the request. "It's not the usual way the Network deals with things. Bobby and Kendall would have one massive coronary about it, but—yeah. Why not? You're on."

"Great," Tori said, although her nerves quivered at the thought of pointing a gun dead-on at somebody and pulling the trigger. "Can we start in the morning?"

"Hell, no. Let's start right now."

She gestured at the dark windows. "But—"

"Target shooting in the morning. But you can start learning your weapon tonight. The parts, how to load it, unload it, clean it. Come on."

Two steps up, he paused, looked over his shoulder. "Just don't tell the guys. They'd drum me out of the Network. And then what am I going to do with myself?"

He said it lightly, but Tori had a feeling the question wasn't really a joke.

She padded up the stairs behind him. As she passed the room where the binders crouched in the dark with their pictures of tortured corpses, she extended her thumb and index finger and pulled off a single, silent shot.

« CHAPTER 24 »

THE NEXT MORNING Seth retrieved a pair of targets from the old-fashioned storm cellar at the rear of the house.

"You take these," he said, pushing a paper sack and the case for the gun she'd studied the previous night into Tori's hands. She clutched the guncase's skinny handle. Her palms started to sweat. Last night, handling the gun had made her feel more relieved than nervous. She was learning to protect herself and that was the important thing. Today, minutes from actually firing the gun, she was nervous that she might screw up, accidentally hit something—or someone—she didn't intend to shoot. She frowned at the case swinging against her thigh and wondered how much a gun this small kicked.

Following Seth past the apple trees and into the field beyond, Tori set the case and the sack on the ground. Seth strode out into wet, knee-high weeds glittering in the sunlight. He propped both targets upright, the first at a distance of about 30 feet, and the second another 25 or 30 feet beyond that. Each target was a rough-edged wooden rectangle, the height of a man. Seth tacked sheets of paper onto the targets with human forms outlined on them in thick black lines.

He waded back through the weeds and, kneeling, snapped open the case. He handed the gun up to Tori. She took it cautiously. He'd told her the night before that this particular gun was called a Jackal; it was compact, but lethal.

"It's not loaded," he reminded her now, showing her the box of ammunition in his hand. "And I've got the silencer engaged. Help keep Bobby out of our hair."

He dug one foot at the ground, dragged a line through the dirt. "Okay, step up here." Tori followed him hesitantly. He leaned into her, demonstrating. "Like that. See? The slide pulls back. There's the clip. Good. You're loaded."

Tori nearly dropped the second clip Seth pushed into her free hand.

"Put it in your pocket." He gestured at the borrowed shirt hanging loose over her tee-shirt. The shirt belonged to Kendall, its provenance clear from the threadbare pink-and-yellow weave, the lank and buttonless cuffs.

"I bet you grew up with guns," Tori said, wishing he wouldn't stare so intently at each clumsy movement she made. The gun felt awkward in her grip, like a block of cool wood. She averted her eyes from the outline of the human body on the target.

"Yeah, my dad took me and my brothers target-shooting. Hunting too when I was really young. But the licenses and the land fees and the kill taxes got so high, we couldn't afford it."

He arranged himself beside her, just behind the line. "Okay. Tell me. Is the safety on or off?"

"On."

"So you're not going to accidentally kill me, okay?"

Tori shoved a hand back through her hair. "Do I really look that nervous?"

"You bet." He grinned at her, but the smile vanished as his attention returned to the Jackal. He took it from her. "Now, put your arms out like this." He turned to face the nearer target and demonstrated. "Line your sight up. Remember, the gun is a natural extension of your hand. It should feel like it's a part of your body." Tori noticed with envy that he looked entirely at ease with the weapon. "Flip the safety. Take a deep breath. Let your shoulders settle. Pull the trigger back." Tori winced, expecting an explosion, but the silencer turned the blast into a muffled *thwump*.

"Yep, he's dead," Seth observed. "Left side of the forehead. Go ahead. Check it out."

Tori headed for the target. Her fingers smoothed the torn paper. Seth had the location right. She walked back to the firing line.

"You can go for the head or the neck," Seth said.

"What about the chest?" The silhouette's torso looked like a much easier target than its head or neck.

"Only if you know for a fact they're not wearing any Grapamid."

Tori squinted at him. "That's the body armor you were talking about."

"Yeah. It's pretty tough stuff. Most hitters'll be wearing at least a tunic or a vest, maybe even a full shirt under their regular shirt."

"Bullets won't go through it?"

"Not usually. Sometimes the seams are little weaker. And if it's a tunic or one of the vests, you might slide a bullet through the armpit, but I wouldn't chance it." He tapped his forehead. "Head or neck. You're right-handed." A statement, not a question.

"Yeah." Tori nudged her toes up to the line. The gun didn't feel anything like an extension of her body. It was heavy and lumbering in her grasp. Seth came around behind her, adjusted the angle of her body and repositioned her right arm. The adjustments did make the gun feel more natural.

"Okay, bring that left arm up." Seth's hands were firm on her upper arms, helping her line up the shot. When she glanced back at him, he met her eyes briefly, flushed and stepped aside. "All right, you're good to go."

Tori faced the target again. She tried to turn the human outline into an abstract shape. No head, just a bulge at the top. No neck, just a skinny bit. The upper left corner of paper flapped whenever the breeze caught it.

She squeezed her eyes shut and pulled the trigger. Opening her eyes, she took an eager step forward.

"Wait a minute," Seth called out. "Get the safety back in place. Keep it pointed down and away. Good." He headed about twenty feet into the weeds and thumped his foot a couple of times against the ground. "Right about here." He strode back to the firing line.

Tori stared at him. Okay, she'd had her eyes shut, but she had lined the shot up first. "Are you sure?"

"I saw the dirt fly up."

"Great." She shuffled back into position. If she couldn't do better than that, she might as well hand herself over to any hitters who showed up.

"You're not going to hit anything with your eyes closed, Tori. Except maybe me." Seth went behind her, helped her line up the shot again. "Eyes open, deep breath, Whelk's in front of you. Empty the clip at him."

She fired until the trigger clicked with a sound like teeth snapping at the air.

"Okay," Seth told her. "Clip's out. See where the slide is? You know you're out of ammo. Put the safety on." He squeezed her shoulder. "You did a hell of a lot better this go round."

"Really?" She sounded like a five-year-old, she thought, and gave her head a shake.

Seth went out to check the target. He squinted back at her. "You got a kill."

The word sent a strange coldness through her. He said it so casually.

"One kill, one flesh wound," Seth clarified, tapping the corresponding locations on the target. One round had cut cleanly through the center of the target's throat and a second had clipped the left forearm. Dumb luck, she knew.

Seth tapped the gun. "With a Jackal, you're pretty close range. Thirty, forty feet away. The most important thing is you've got to be ready to shoot." His eyes fixed on her. "You've got to be ready to kill to save your own life."

The images of Whelk's victims slammed, one after another, in front of Tori's eyes. She let out a hiss of breath, swayed, suddenly dizzy.

Seth's hand closed on her arm. "Let's take a break. We've got time."

"No, we don't." Tori shoved off from him, then planted her feet on the line and reloaded.

She shot her way through a dozen clips.

"Better," Seth finally pronounced. "Definitely better." He took the targets down and propped them against the trunk of an apple tree. Tori studied him. Maybe he was just being nice. Trying to be encouraging. But, no . . . she stepped up to examine the targets. The bulletholes were erratic—tearing off paper fingers and ears, stinging an elbow, hissing across a scalp. Maybe not lethal, but better than kicking up dirt.

Seth shut the Jackal in its case, set the case next to the targets, and picked up the paper sack.

"Couple sandwiches." He settled onto the remains of a fallen tree, the trunk lodged horizontally in the overgrown grass. Tori boosted herself up beside him. Her feet didn't quite reach the ground and she swung them forward and back. The morning was clear, the breeze hot.

"What kind?" She took the wrapped sandwich Seth offered.

"Cheese, lettuce, mayo. And the cheese smells kind of strong. Sorry, there isn't a lot of choice in Kendall's kitchen." He plowed through his own sandwich with a lumberjack's voracity.

Tori wasn't far behind him. She sucked a dollop of mayonnaise from one of her fingers, wiped her hands on the paper sack, and noticed Seth watching her.

"Hey, I missed breakfast, remember?" she said.

"Kendall's finest turnip and potato omelets." Seth grimaced. "You were smart, sleeping late."

Tori thought about how she'd jolted awake at five o'clock that morning and stared at the ceiling for an hour before she was able to fall back to sleep. "I worked seven days a week in Glynn River. Twelve hour shifts. And when I wasn't working, there was so much noise it was hard to sleep. This is luxury." She shook her head. "Ten years. There's a lot I could tell you about that place."

"So tell me."

"You don't really want—"

"Yeah. I do."

Tori stared straight ahead at the meadow. The sun burnished the weeds to a painful brilliance.

"It was meat-packing. Chickens. We killed them, cut them up, packaged them. People got hurt. It happened all the time." She put a hand to the side of her head. "The noise was incredible. There's still this ringing in my ears that never quite goes away." She paused to flatten the paper sack across her lap, smoothing the creases with her fingers.

"What about your down-time?"

"Down-time?" She laughed. "You mean, in the cell? They crammed us in. The cells had four bunks, but there were people on the floor too. You'd try to sleep or you'd just sit or . . . well, not much." She crumpled the sack into a tight ball. "Jesus, you know what I would have done for a vid? Or a book or a news-stream?"

"And I'd just as soon never see another news-stream," Seth muttered. "It's all lies, anyway."

Tori looked at him, surprised. He suddenly sounded bitter, lead weights hanging from his voice.

"Okay," he continued, "so they had you overworked, overcrowded. Cut your arms to pieces. Screwed up your ears. What else?"

Tori hesitated. Too many memories swarmed around her.

"A couple of months after I got in," she finally said, "one of the women in my cell went nuts, stabbed a girl. Killed her." Through her shirt, Tori rubbed the scar that crossed her ribs.

Seth's gaze flicked to Tori's hand. "She got you too," he said.

"But I was lucky. It wasn't deep. And then when they let me out, I got lucky too. I was sure I was dead. " She paused. "And then you."

Seth shifted position, crossed his arms. "Let's see how things end up before you start counting yourself too lucky."

Tori's pulse jumped at her throat. "Did they find out anything about my dad?"

Seth shook his head. "But Jared's still looking." He stared thoughtfully at the puffball clouds sliding overhead. "Kendall showed me some of the reports on your case. Court records, media accounts."

Tori's muscles tightened, the way they always did when the past came up. "Yeah?" She couldn't look at him.

"We don't protect just anybody, you know. We pick our cases."

Tori yanked a leaf from a vine encircling the trunk. Her fingernails pressed crescents into its green flesh. "What do you mean?"

"There's some low-lifes that anybody who looks can tell what they are. But a lot of others . . . So much corruption. I saw it when I was a cop. Police buy-offs, tainted evidence, screwed-up lab work, bottom-barrel lawyers."

Tori shredded the leaf into ragged strips, watched them flutter to the ground.

"So what happened to that child?" Seth's voice was gentle.

Tori slid down from the trunk, let her back lean against it. She stubbed the toes of her sneakers at the dirt. "It's just that I'm not sure. I mean, *I* didn't do anything, but Robbie was my responsibility. I fed him. I took care of him. So how'd that poison get into his blood?" She shut her eyes against the vision of the infant's slack face and glazed eyes.

"You have a guess?"

Now her throat got so tight she was practically whispering. "No. There was nobody. They ran all kinds of tests. He was always sick. We were constantly taking him to the doctor. But they never found anything. After he died, the coroner said it was antifreeze poisoning."

She practically flung herself around to face Seth. Her voice shook, but with anger now. "They said I was jealous because they're rich and they had a big house, a secured neighborhood—you know, everything I didn't have—and I took it out on Robbie."

Seth reached one hand toward her cheek, but drew it back before he touched her. Tori suddenly wanted to grab his wrist and bury her face against his palm.

"What about your lawyer?" Seth said. "Stephenson, wasn't it?"

"Yeah."

"He never exactly had a great reputation."

Tori waved that away. "But I still don't know what happened. I go over it in my head, over and over and over, and I don't know who would have done that to him. Or could have." Her eyes blurred.

Now Seth did touch her, tucking short wisps of hair back from her forehead. "You may just have to live with it. Never knowing."

"I hate not knowing."

"Sometimes you've just got to move on. The Camerons have another kid now, did you know that? The grandmother's in Washington doing the usual fuck-all that senators do."

"I just wish—"

"Move on, Tori. Trust me on this. I know."

She wondered again why he was doing this, running around the country playing guardian to a bunch of felons. Innocent felons, maybe. Felons with crappy lawyers for sure, but still felons.

"You said you were a cop—" she started.

Somebody shouted from inside the house. The back door banged open. Jared sprinted at them, zigzagging among the apple trees.

Tori stared, not understanding at first, but Seth was already in motion, snatching up the gun case.

"How close?" he asked Jared.

"Close enough."

Bobby charged out of the door, Kendall flapping after him. Bobby shooed at the car with both hands like it was an overgrown chicken. "Go!" he shouted to Seth and Tori. "Now."

Seth and Tori threw themselves into the car. Tori twisted in her seat to look out the back window. The house shrank to a cool blur among green shadows. She swiped her fingers to her eyes. It was too soon. Couldn't she get one more day—Jesus, just one!—within those sturdy farmhouse walls.

At the end of the private road, Seth cast a quick glance in each direction. In a field to the left, a tractor threw up dust. To the right, there was nothing but straight gravel road and stubbled fields.

"Good thing we didn't put off your shooting lesson." He slung the wheel to the right.

"Yeah." The word squeezed past a rock in Tori's throat. She pressed her fingertips against the gun case Seth had flung between the front seats. "Good thing."

« CHAPTER 25 »

"THEY STILL FILLING UP your paycard?" Wren's boyfriend, Owen Richter, asked as they ducked into a net spot a few blocks from the dump.

"It's on my chip." Wren crept one of her hands around Owen's wrist. Unlike hers, it had no small, telltale bump where an ID chip had been injected. Owen always insisted that he wanted to keep everything "underground, black market." Wren ran her fingers along his skinny forearm. Needle marks flecked the inside of his elbow like bird tracks in wet cement.

The net spot was crowded and dark, the windows so grimy that people out on the sidewalk were gray blurs sliding past the glass. The drinkslinger behind the counter shouted across the room: "You got an account?"

Wren jigged her head up and down. She fell onto the cold metal chair in front of an available screen. The woman at the next station pinched her mouth tight as if she'd tasted something sour. Or smelled something rank.

Wren tugged at her grimy blouse. It was several sizes too large for her bony frame. She hadn't had the chance to wash the blouse or her equally filthy jeans for a couple of weeks. She wondered if the trash dump's stink clung to her. She was so used to garbage, she couldn't smell it anymore.

Owen shoved a hand at her, smacking her shoulder. "Get me a beer." He flung an order at the drinkslinger. "One Kinelley." Grabbing Wren's hand, he slid her wrist over the reader to pay for it. The reader blipped green, gave out three quick beeps.

Wren gnawed at her already raw bottom lip. Kinelley was an expensive brand. "Okay, but see, Owen, they don't put a whole lot on my account. Not enough for a lot of drinks, okay?"

Owen gripped both of her wrists now, his iron fists threatening to crush bone. He twisted, leaning down so that his eyes were two inches from her own. His face looked like one giant muscle straining against itself.

"But I didn't order a lot of drinks, did I?" he said.

Wren shrank into the billows of her filthy shirt and nodded, over and over. "Okay, it's okay, Owen, I wasn't trying to say—"

"Aahh." He simultaneously released his grip and shoved. One of Wren's hands smacked the horizontal screen.

The drinkslinger was beside them, beer bottle sweating in his hand. "Hey, you break the screen, you pay for it." The man thumped the bottle down onto the tabletop and turned away.

For an awful moment, Wren thought Owen was going to jump the guy, leap on his back and start slashing. She'd seen him do it before. But Owen stayed where he was, quivering like a dog, his stare tracking the drinktender back to the bar.

"It's okay," Wren soothed. "It's okay. He's just an asshole. Why don't you sit down, baby? You can have my chair."

Owen flicked away the offer. He stepped around to the opposite side of the table, out of range of the pinpoint camera staring from the bottom of the screen and hurled himself into an empty chair.

"Go ahead," he snapped. "Get on the damn thing already."

Wren hurried, tapping the top edge of the screen and swiping her wrist across the reader again. The machine was shit. It took her a half dozen tries before the system recognized her account and logged her in.

She sat. The chair was off-balance, stumping from side to side whenever Wren shifted her weight. She could feel Owen's legs under the table, his knees pushed up against hers, his feet jiggling like a puppet's. He kept looking around and she involuntarily followed his gaze to the water-stained ceiling, the murky mirror behind the drinkslinger, the flickering exit sign pointing toward the bathrooms. Owen snagged up the beer, drained two-thirds of it at one go.

She'd better get her messages quick, before he had time to order another round. She hadn't been joking about the money in her account. Besides, she didn't want him drunk. Booze, pot, crack: they all increased his hunger for peel. She didn't want him searching his stash. When he found out there was peel missing, when he figured out who'd swiped it, he'd—

"One more of those," Owen barked at the drinkslinger. He swallowed the rest of his current beer like he was swallowing liquid money.

Trembling, Wren looked at the screen. She let out her breath, relieved. There was a picture of Kendall. A vid message queued. That meant work and work meant money and money meant peel.

Kendall was the only member of the Guardian Network she had contact with, the only one who shared his face and his name with her. Trusted her. She sometimes thought she would probably be in love with him if she wasn't already Owen's.

She tapped the message. A three-dimensional image practically obliterated the screen that housed it. Wren snatched up the earpiece from the tray at the edge of the table and jammed it into place.

"Real-time?" Owen asked.

"Message," she said.

Owen came back around the table, grabbed the other earpiece and crammed it into his ear.

"Hey, how're you doing?" Kendall's voice emerged with perfect, reedy clarity.

"Who's the asshole?" Owen asked, jabbing at the holo.

"Kendall," Wren said. "I told you about him, remember? He's a nice guy."

Kendall's forehead furrowed with concern. "Hey, I hope you're doing okay, Wren. We're so proud of you, staying out of trouble."

Owen snorted. "Asshole."

Wren tasted blood. She touched her lip. She'd gnawed the flesh open and bloody.

On the vid, Kendall glanced at the closed door behind him. "We trust you," he said.

"Mistake number one," Owen cracked.

Tears bit at Wren's eyes. She hunched closer to Kendall's image.

"Okay, so here's the thing," Kendall continued. "We need resupply at several locations. Your usual stops, Tampico and Sydney. And we have some new ones for you."

Wren reached toward the image as if she could actually touch Kendall. They were giving her more responsibility. They trusted her. For a moment, she managed not to feel like a failure.

Kendall went on: "Marrakesh, Delhi, uh wait a sec." He consulted a scrap of paper in one hand. "San Salvador and Naples. That's four new ones. You've done a good job." Kendall grinned and gave her a thumbs-up. "We need you to work pretty fast. Looks like we'll have a patron coming up your way any time now."

"A patron?" Owen said. "What the hell's that?"

"An E," Wren whispered, shifting closer to the holo. Owen leaned in too. Breathed out beer fumes.

"Okay, so you go to Tampico at six on Friday morning. You'll find the new locations and IDs there. It's all the usual procedure for each place, okay?" Kendall nodded happily. "We're counting on you, Wren. Great. So have a fantastic time, huh? And thanks for everything you do." A final encouraging nod and Kendall's image froze.

Wren flushed, proud. More safehouses, more money. The day may have started in the garbage dump, but it was on the upswing. Turning, she nuzzled one cheek against Owen's neck. He didn't move.

"I love how you smell," she murmured. Like gasoline. Bacon. Smoke.

"So," Owen said, "new assignments, huh? You're the big shot?"

"Oh, Owen. They'll give me extra money. Four more places." Four. She couldn't believe it. Four times the money. And if they put it on her chip tomorrow, she might be able to replace Owen's peel before he realized any was missing. And buy a little extra. Her own stash.

Owen pulled away. "I didn't hear him say anything about more money."

Wren nodded eagerly. "Oh, they will though. Just like I got more when they gave me Sydney." She stumbled up, her hands swooping at him. "Don't be mad, baby," she crooned. "We'll be okay."

Owen suddenly grinned at her, his teeth nubby and brown. He let her cling to him. She kneaded his arm, fingers, the ridged veins and tight muscle.

"I'm not mad," he said. "Why should I be mad when there's an E coming to town?"

Wren tilted her head to one side, squinted at him. "Yeah," she said. "An E means money. Because I've got to check all the places. I don't ever see the E though."

"This time you will." Still grinning, Owen reached for his second beer, downed it.

Wren just blinked at him. Her brain felt so fuzzy all the time, like she had cotton wadded in her skull.

Owen breathed a fresh blast of beer-stink at her. "Me and my guys, we're gonna grab this one. And you're gonna help us."

Wren blinked again.

"And we'll sell 'em back to the hitters," Owen said. His legs were getting jittery again, and his fingers tapped against his thighs. "Get some real cash."

Wren nodded, stroked his arm, gazed up at him. The thin beard at the point of Owen's chin quivered. He was jerking his head around now too, like he was caught in the very beginning of a seizure. He got this way sometimes, where he couldn't hold still.

"And you'll love me?" Wren could barely whisper the question, her gaze fixed on him.

"Yeah, sure." Owen pulled away, headed out the door.

Wren flurried after him. "Wait for me!"

He did. Stopped dead on the crumbling sidewalk and turned back, waited for her to catch up. She surged against him, suddenly feeling warm and sleek and cherished as a cat. "I love you," she said.

"Yeah," Owen answered. "So show me, where's this Tampico place?"

She kissed his neck until it was damp. "Can't that wait a little while?"

"That Kendall asshole said to go there Friday morning."

"Yeah?" She licked his earlobe.

"Today's Friday."

Wren froze. "Shit. It is?"

"So let's go." Owen shrugged her off. "Or you're gonna fuck this thing up before we even get started."

« CHAPTER 26 »

AGAINST SETH'S BETTER JUDGMENT—Tori knew because he voiced his opinion several times en route— they crossed into Philadelphia that evening. The car skimmed up to intersections and glided through without stopping.

"Peel slingers," he muttered, jerking his head at a pair of emaciated women shuffling from the curb, their left hands raised, their fingers clawed and scraping the air as if they were tearing the skin off some invisible beast. Frozen in her seat, Tori stared at them as if witnessing her future self.

She didn't know this exact part of the city, but it looked about as derelict as where she'd grown up. She fought against the impatience straining her muscles, an impatience that urged her to forget caution and safehouses and what the hitters might be up to and just rush immediately to her dad's house. It was maddening to be within the limits of the same city where he lived and to still keep her distance.

If he was even here now. If he was alive.

Tori hunched her shoulders and blankly watched the decayed buildings slide past.

In an alley, Seth unlocked a tall wooden gate that opened onto a muddy lot. The fence surrounding the lot, like the gate, stood at least ten-feet high. He parked between an open jeep and a rusted-out taxi with four flat tires.

The windowless steel door at the rear of the building reminded Tori of Glynn River. The bulb above it flickered and buzzed.

"Damn thing's still on the blink." Seth scowled up at the light. He reached into his pocket and brought out a curved strip of flexible plastic. He molded the strip over his right thumb and pressed it to the door's security reader. From somewhere inside came a heavy *chunck*. Seizing the handle, Seth pushed the door open.

It automatically locked behind them. "Back here." He led Tori past the stairs to an unmarked door and unlocked it. "We try to stick with ground floors. More ways out." He paused, reaching inside. "Of course, that means more ways in, too." An overhead light flared. "Welcome to Sydney."

He crossed the living room and another light burst on. Tori followed him into the makeshift bedroom where cots were shoved up against three walls, with a vid-screen fixed against the fourth. In one corner, blankets and a couple of T-shirts lay crumpled on a chair.

Seth leaned inside the bathroom and flipped the light there as well, illuminating chipped gray tiles, warped ceiling panels, and grout sprouting black mold. The toilet tank fizzed.

"I hate to tell you this, but this is one of the nicer ones." He crossed back to the living room, headed past a lumpy couch, a metal folding chair, a card table. "Anyway, we won't be here long." In the galley kitchen, he peered through the refrigerator's transparent door. "Terrific. Brown cheese and a black banana. That looks kind of liquefied, actually. You hungry?"

Tori was—she felt light-headed—but she wasn't about to complain. "I'm okay. It's not like being at your own place, is it?"

"I don't have one. I'm on jobs for the Network almost all the time." Seth yanked at the freezer door. Cloudy air swirled past him. "Nothing but ice. Great. Network's doing its usual bang-up job with supplies."

He headed back to the bathroom. "There's a towel," he said, leaning out of the bathroom doorway. "One. I think it's clean, pretty much. And some soap. The shower worked the other time I was here." He glanced down at his jeans, still dirty from target practice. "You want it first?"

"You go ahead."

He nodded appreciatively. "Eat whatever you want. If you can stomach it." Plucking up one of the crumpled T-shirts, he waved it at the cots. "Take whichever one you want. It's okay to have vids on. Just keep the volume way down." He glanced at the blinds drawn over the bedroom's sole window. "Get me if you hear anything. I'll keep this with me." He took the gun into the bathroom with him and shut the door. A moment later pipes whined and banged, and water thudded against the shower stall.

Sounds came through the window: shouts, singing, a siren. The noises made Tori jumpy, made her imagine hitters congregating on the street, planning their assault.

Screw that.

"On." Vids snapped into motion on the screen. Tori sank onto a cot. The bathroom door didn't fit into its frame and steam seeped through the gaps, intensifying the apartment's already uncomfortable humidity. She worked her sneakers free and let them drop to the floor. She was exhausted, but on edge. She couldn't imagine falling asleep.

The vids split into four streams, a barrage of mutating images. "Sequence." She stared at the flow of visuals: basketball, porn, mil-news, porn again.

The image passed before her brain registered and identified it. "Back one."

She'd seen executions. Everybody had. She remembered commentators speaking in low tones, black hoods draped over the convicts' faces, somber music.

Executions had changed.

The execution chamber was metallic and spartan, its surfaces designed for easy cleaning. Tori raised the volume just enough to hear that the condemned had killed a policeman, and that they were going to test some new chemdust weapon on him. "The weapon's first trial with a human subject," murmured the reporter.

When a quartet of guards brought the convict in, the man was already sagging. Tori leaned forward, her arms tight across her abdomen. Her gut ached. Her face went rigid.

The stream split, simultaneously tracking the witnesses, the family, and the prisoner as guards lowered him into a chair and tightened straps around his calves, arms, throat, and forehead.

"Jesus, Tori, what're you doing, watching that?"

Tori jerked her head toward Seth who strode from the bathroom, issuing the command as he moved: "Stream up." The execution chamber disappeared, replaced by a pair of shirtless men barbecuing.

"It was always lethal injection before," Tori said, her voice hoarse.

Seth planted himself between her and the screen. He wore a fresh T-shirt and the same jeans he'd had on earlier. A damp towel hung around his neck. "These things are sideshows. Anyway, the prison industries have

162

a hand in a lot of different pots. They've been using executions to try out chemical weapons and weird biowarfare stuff for years."

"I'd heard something like that at Glynn River," Tori said.

"They even let a Riker's loose on one poor guy. Wanted to check out a new venom, but it ripped out his throat before the guards got things under control. I mean, he was terrorist, but Jesus. There's talk they're going to send the E's this direction too. More profit using them as lab rats than hunting them down. " He grimaced. "Sorry. I need to shut up."

Tori swallowed noisily. Saliva ticked in her throat. She glanced past Seth at the screen. Part of her wanted to flick the vid back to the execution. "What gets me," she said, "is that it's happening now. We're here. Breathing. Sitting. Taking a shower. And at the same time . . ." She turned her hands up, a gesture of helplessness. The slowly healing gash on her palm blared bright-pink.

Seth slung his towel over the back of the chair and sat beside Tori. The cot sagged under their combined weight. His bare arm brushed against hers, his skin cool and damp.

"Here's the thing, Tori." He held her chin between his fingers and turned her head until she met his gaze. His eyes were a warm brown, the color of deer skin. "It's going to happen no matter what we do. Whether you watch it or not. So why watch it?"

Tori didn't speak. Seth leaned back against the wall. "Off." The screen blackened. "There's something else, isn't there?"

Tori shut her eyes. She didn't want to say what was in her head. Didn't even want to think it. "I keep imagining my dad." She opened her eyes. Her glance shivered across Seth. "That he's gone."

"You don't know that."

"I just have a feeling."

"Feelings are bullshit." He lowered his head. "Sorry. But all that, that intuition kind of stuff, it's bullshit. You know what I was doing when I found out my mom was dead? I was scrambling up a pan of eggs. Not a clue." He clenched his hands around his knees, massaging bone. His expression was raw.

"Has it been a long time?"

"A week. Almost."

"Oh, my God." Tori wrestled upright. "You shouldn't even be here. You should be with your family."

"I don't think so."

"But they must need you."

"Not really," Seth snapped. Tori flinched. Seth rubbed a hand across his face. "Sorry," he said. "Sorry. It's just—we've had some differences."

"Okay." She wasn't going to ask any more about it, but after a minute Seth continued. "I stood up for a guy. Alleged cop-killer, but I'm pretty damn sure he wasn't. That didn't exactly go over well."

"No," Tori said. "I guess it wouldn't."

"And then—" Seth raised a hand, let it drop into his lap. "I basically got my dad screwed out of a promotion for—oh, ten years or so. I didn't mean to, but that's how things shook out."

"Because of the cop-killer thing?"

Seth sighed. "No. This was a whole other deal. This guy in high school. Randy Close. He was the son of the police chief. You know, just my dad's boss. He also happened to be a world-class dick." Seth paused. He tilted his head back, screwed his eyes shut. "I beat the crap out of him."

Tori digested this a moment. "Did he need to get the crap beat out of him?"

Seth opened his eyes, regarded her with surprise. "Yeah. Yeah, he did. He was a bully. I mean, he and some of the guys, they tormented this one kid in particular." Seth's face tightened again, like he was in pain. "Kyle. Worked him over, day after day. Until one day . . ." He stopped.

"Are you okay?" Tori asked. "You look sick."

"Until one day, Kyle hanged himself."

"Jesus."

"In one of the classrooms. So, yeah. Randy Close deserved to get the shit beat out of him. But I killed Dad's chance for a promotion until after Chief Close retired. So that didn't exactly sit well with the family either. They always claimed it wasn't really Randy's fault. Anybody who'd kill themselves was already sick in the head."

"I call bullshit on that one," Tori said.

"Yeah."

They sat a moment without speaking.

"They didn't want me at my mom's funeral," Seth finally told her.

Tori didn't know what to say to that. "What was your mom like?"

Seth pressed a hand against his eyes like he was shielding them from intense light. "She was the kind of person who you know is always going to be behind you. In the end, no matter what's happened, no matter what other people think of you." He paused, lowered his hand. "I was her favorite." He shot Tori an almost embarrassed smile. "She would never have said it. But everybody knew. I was the last one. A surprise."

"The baby?"

"Yeah. My brothers . . ." His hand spiked upward in sudden agitation.

"How many do you have?"

"Four. They're real hard-working, hard-living types, like my dad. Tight. They'll work for the same outfit till they die."

"What do they do?"

"Cops."

"All of them?" Tori saw the curt faces of the policemen who'd arrested her. She could still feel the rough hands gripping her arms and then the cool bite of the handcuffs.

"All of them," Seth answered. "Going to work, raising their kids, that's all they ever wanted to do."

Tori traced the healing cut on her palm. The lips of the cut had come together in a pebbled seam. The skin there prickled and itched. "So what happened to you and your family?"

"Falling out. Office politics."

"Hey, you don't want to talk about it, I understand."

"No. No, it's not a big deal." Seth flashed a rueful grin. "Okay, I guess it is a big deal. To me." He bent forward, sighed. "Okay, so there was a guy charged with homicide-one. Killed an officer, one of my dad's buddies. They'd worked together for 25 years. But there was so much wrong with that investigation. Planted evidence, coerced testimony. They roughed the guy's confession out of him. The LPF didn't appreciate me making a stink about it. My *dad* didn't appreciate it."

Tori shook her head. "LPF?"

"Liberty Police Force."

Tori hadn't heard of it, but that was no surprise. Philadelphia was still a big city. Ten years ago, it had had any number of private police firms, each covering the subscribers in a particular part of the city.

"And your brothers?" she asked.

"Fell right into line with Dad. Frank, at least he can talk to me every once in awhile without spitting at me."

Seth pushed himself up from the cot. "You getting hungry yet?"

Tori put out a hand to stop him. Maybe he wanted to change the subject, but she didn't. "So what happened?"

Seth's shoulders dropped. "What do you think? The guy was convicted. He was a cop-killer so he got death."

Tori was already shaking her head. "No. I meant, what happened to you?"

Seth sank down beside her again. He poised at the metal edge of the cot like he was about to spring back up again. "I stayed with LPF. Not for long. I wasn't exactly a favorite with the guys by that point."

"You quit?"

"More or less."

"I'm sorry."

He shrugged, tapped one foot against the grimy linoleum. "I didn't like working there anyway. It drove me crazy, standing around the office while somebody's screaming on a comm about a rapist in their house. And all of us just sitting there, drinking bad coffee because that address hadn't paid up their PF subscription." He stared at—through—the opposite wall. His hands were fists. "Listening to some woman barricaded in her bedroom, screaming, scared out of her mind, begging us to help her . . ."

"But that isn't your fault."

"Don't be so sure of that." Seth shoved himself onto his feet again. He paced to the kitchen. Cabinets flung open, slammed shut.

Tori hesitated, then followed him. Seth was leaning over the counter, grimacing at a stain in the formica like it was about to swell up and swallow him.

Tori watched him for a minute, then went efficiently and quietly from cabinet to empty cabinet. In the space under the sink, she struck gold.

"Look."

Seth turned his head. His face was strained, his eyes bloodshot.

Tori held the bottle toward him. Cut glass shrouded in dust. Tequila. "I just wish to hell we had some margarita mix."

Seconds passed. Seth took the bottle. He blew dust from around the screw cap and cut a glance at Tori. "Straight up?"

"Sounds good to me." She was relieved when Seth hooked a smile in her direction.

"No glasses," he noted.

"Who needs glasses?"

Seth's smile broadened. "Right." He unscrewed the cap, flicked it onto the counter, and extended the bottle to Tori. "Ladies first."

Tori had never been much of a drinker, just a beer now and then with her dad or a cheap vodka and OJ with Sarah when they both got an occasional night off nanny-duty. But right now, in this run-down apartment, with that Whelk goon and God only knew who else tracking her and Seth, the fumes rising from the bottle's neck smelled sharp and alluring.

She raised the bottle, took a gulp, coughed.

Seth laughed. "That good, huh?"

Tori took another swallow. Almost at once, the warmth of it pressed through her veins, relaxing her arms and legs and the tensed muscles that held her neck and skull in a deathgrip.

"Yeah." She gave the bottle to Seth. "It is that good."

They downed three or four fingers each before Seth replaced the cap and put the bottle back on its grimy shelf. Tori would have been happy to have drunk herself into oblivion, let the rest of the day pass as a blank. Forget everything for a few hours.

Seth was more realistic, or more responsible although he didn't look any happier than Tori as he swung the cabinet door shut. He looked exhausted, his eyes red and lines carved around the corners of his mouth. Guilt cut through Tori: everything he'd been through with his family, with his mother's death . . . and now her.

"Can't let our wits get too dull," he added. "Well, duller, in my case."

He went to the other room, returned with the gun which he extended to her.

"Why?" she asked. Rising panic shredded her alcoholic calm. "What about you?"

"You keep this handy while I'm gone. Use it if you have to." Seth dropped a box of cartridges on the table. "You remember how to reload?"

He was leaving?

Tori stared at him. She'd made it out of Glynn River alone. She'd faced all this once already by herself.

She couldn't do it again.

« CHAPTER 27 »

"TORI."

Seth seemed to understand her panic because he dropped a hand briefly onto her shoulder. "I'm just going out for supplies."

"But—"

"Normally, I wouldn't. It's supposed to be Kendall's responsibility. Keep track of our people, assign locations, make sure contacts get supplies in place. But who's making sure he gets *his* job done? I checked for Grapamid too."

Tori steadied herself. "Nothing?"

"Not a stitch."

The gun lay flat on Tori's palm, like a rodent stiff with rigor mortis. "But don't you want to take it with you?" she asked.

"I'll be okay." Seth set a signal dome on the table beside the cartridges. "Look, I've got my comm. If I hear anything that indicates trouble, I'll activate this." He tapped the dome. "It should flash and sound an alarm. You take the gun and the ammo and get the hell out. Get to the subway at 30th Street Station. I'll meet you there. You know it?"

Tori nodded. She remembered what 30th Street had been like a dozen years earlier: the train station dead, the subway terminal still running, but given over to the homeless.

"It's one of the few subway stops that still functions," Seth told her. "The abandoned ones, they're pretty scary. And whatever you do, don't actually get on any of the trains. Bad news." He opened the door, moved into the hallway, stopped. He regarded Tori with a level gaze. "I wouldn't just leave you, you know that, right? Now. Lock the door ."

Seth's footsteps receded along the corridor. The heavy exterior door scraped open and banged shut.

Tori returned to the table and ran a finger down the gun's length. The metal was cool and so smooth it was silky. Leaving it, she wandered into the bedroom where she switched from one music stream to another, jumping from chop shop to piledrive to golden rap. She muted the music, sank onto a cot, and curled up. It might be a good idea to get some rest while she could.

The building's exterior door rushed open, fell shut. Tori froze in place. She listened for Seth's footsteps.

At first, she heard nothing. She told herself it was someone who lived in one of the other apartments, but in her head she saw Geoffrey Whelk and Sergei Chistyakov slipping along the edges of the corridor, their backs pressed to the walls.

Light footsteps skittered right outside the apartment door.

Whoever was out there wasn't Seth and wasn't just another resident.

Tori swiped up the gun and took aim at the door. The barrel swam, a gray blur jumping and sinking at the center of her vision. The deadbolt tumbled. Whoever it was had security ID and a key. Seth's ID and key? If they'd caught him, she'd—

"Hey?" A fusty head poked around the doorframe. Tori struggled to keep the gun in her sweaty grip. "I'm Network." The door pressed wider. The woman lifted one hand, showed the plastic sack dangling from her fist. "Bringing supplies."

The woman's bony frame was smothered by a long-sleeved black shirt and jungle camouflage pants. A film of dirt made the woman's skin as colorless as the two rubberbanded clumps of hair that sagged at either side of her head like failed horns.

She looked too pathetic to be a hitter. Nothing like those healthy, confident killers pictured in Regency's binder.

The woman squinted at her. "Who're *you*?"

"That's a good question. Who are *you*?"

"Wren."

"Nobody said anything about you."

Wren rubbed at a rash pimpling the back of her hand. "I take supplies different places. For the Network." Her head drifted vaguely in the direction of the sack. "It's food. You can look."

Tori nicked her head at the table. "You can put it there."

Wren shuffled to the table and let the sack fall open beside the signal-dome.

A loaf of bread, fat at one end and squashed at the other; slimy parsley; crushed oyster crackers; a warty cucumber; a bunch of bananas, already brown.

Tori held the gun down by her thigh. God, she was hungry. She reached for the bread. Dry, but edible.

Her heart tripped in the quiet. She stood in the middle of the room, trying to convince herself there was nothing to be afraid of. Wren was with the Network. It made sense. *Somebody* had to resupply the safehouses, move the cars around, make the IDs and the fake fingerprints.

Of course, Wren looked like some sort of pharm-freak.

So the Network hired peel-heads? Did that make sense? She'd smelled weed wafting from Kendall's room back at the Virginia safehouse, but weed was a long way from peel or X-gold or rapture.

She casually finished chewing her mouthful of bread, then just as casually asked, "Who'd you talk to? With the Network?"

Wren's face blossomed into a smile, showing gray, uneven teeth. "Kendall." Then she winced, like she'd bitten the inside of her cheek. "I'm not supposed to know his name. Don't tell anybody I know it, okay?" A tremor skittered, spider-like, along her jaw. "Please?"

Tori couldn't help feeling sorry for the woman. "I won't. I promise."

"I need these jobs," Wren rushed on. "And I don't want to get Kendall in trouble. He's so nice. He's the one that got them to take a chance on me."

Wren kept scrunching up her eyes, like somebody was about punch her. Tori had seen women like that in Glynn River, women so scared and cringing that they were painful to look at.

Tori kept her voice soft. Gentle. "It's okay. I'm not telling anybody anything." Except Seth, she added silently.

Wren blinked up at her. She was small, a good four or five inches shorter than Tori. "Are you the E they were talking about?"

Tori's muscles tensed. "Who was talking?"

"Kendall. That's why he wanted all the places stocked up. He said there was a new E coming to town."

Just how much did Kendall run his mouth anyway? Wasn't the Network supposed to at least try to keep things secret?

Wren tilted her head to one side. With her scrawny neck and the sharply-cut bones of her face and the timid slant of her head, she resembled the bird she was named for. "It's just, I never actually met one of you," she said. "The places are always empty when I'm stocking them."

"Sorry to ruin your streak." Tori finished off another hunk of bread. She brushed crumbs from her hands. Wren still regarded her with the same curious, almost wistful expression.

"Were you . . . were you scared?" Wren whispered. "When they let you out?"

"Hell, yeah."

"You got away." Admiration intensified Wren's whisper.

Tori spread her arms from her sides, cast a glance down the length of her body. "Looks that way."

She wasn't used to admiration, not in Glynn River, not when she was a nanny or a student in Philly's rat-trap schools. The only admiration she remembered was from her dad, telling her she was smart and pretty and good. His love was the single good thing she'd always been able to count on.

Wren dropped onto one of the plastic chairs around the kitchen table. She sagged there, her head bowed and her hands covering her face. Tori watched her in silence, let a couple of minutes slide by. A tremor quivered from Wren's head down her arms and legs.

Panic rose from Tori's gut. Was she coming down off peel, or something? What if she had some kind of seizure?

"Come on, Seth," Tori muttered through tight teeth. She leaned over Wren. "You want some water? You okay?"

Wren finally swung her head up. The motion appeared to take enormous effort, like hoisting a bowling ball. She wasn't crying, but her eyes were wet and pink. Her skin was nearly gray. "I wish I could be like you."

Tori startled into laughter. "Are you kidding?"

Wren, still trembling, gripped Tori with a gaze that was so wretched and lonely that Tori sank down onto the adjacent chair.

"Wren. I'm an E. Remember? A felon? People want to kill me?"

Wren let out a sigh that further deflated her already limp body. "But you're brave. And you got away."

"If I'd really got away, I wouldn't be in this room talking to you right now."

Wren looked away, her gaze flitting from the table to the barred windows to the dingy little galley kitchen. "Maybe nobody ever gets away."

Tori's lungs went momentarily flat. "That's not what some of the Network guys say."

Wren raised one hand in a listless half-gesture of dismissal. "Oh. You mean the E's." She closed her eyes.

Tori's glance flicked to the door. How long was Seth going to take? "You sure you don't want some water?" she tried again. "You need to lie down?"

Somehow that last suggestion instead brought Wren to her feet. "Oh, shit. I've got four more places to go to this morning." Her eyes grew wild. Anxiety pinched her face. "I can't lose these. We need the money. Owen's gonna be so mad if I screw up."

Wren flung herself past Tori. She seemed to have forgotten Tori's existence. "Can't lose it," she mewled desperately over and over, dragging open the door and scurrying down the hall. "Can't lose it."

Tori shut and locked the door. She hurried to the window, lifted the blinds a bare inch away from the smeared glass. Wren—still talking to herself—scurried across the street and wobbled around the corner out of view. A young man—drug slinger, she slotted him automatically, remembering the slingers around her childhood home—loitered at the corner. He was skinny under his white wifebeater. He had a comm out. His mouth moved in a silent torrent. He pocketed the comm and moved toward the front steps of Tori's building.

It might not mean anything. Tori tried to convince herself, but her body insisted otherwise, shooting adrenaline until her veins burned. Her brain jolted her back to the wardrobe in Sarah's house, the wire glinting toward her throat.

Sydney didn't feel like a safehouse. It felt like a trap.

Tori grabbed an ankle holster from the gun case, strapped it into position, and shoved the gun into it. She slipped out the door.

In the hallway outside the apartment, she hesitated. Pipes clanked in the walls. She stepped to the exterior door at the back of the building and pressed her palms flat against it as if there might be a fire on the other side.

With sudden decision, she gripped the handle and flung herself outside.

A stink of trash and burning rubber singed the air. Ducking out to the alley, she glanced left and right. Both directions seemed equally empty and equally ominous.

She'd try to put a block or two between her and safehouse, slide into another alley or a doorway or some other cranny, and watch for Seth.

She jogged down the alley to the street, turned left, and hurried to the intersection where she had a view of the front of the apartment building. The slinger in the undershirt hunched over the door handle and prodded at the security reader.

Maybe not a slinger, then.

Tori ducked back behind the side of the nearest building. She glanced frantically around, her stomach dropping at the idea that there might be other hitters working with this guy.

"Ugly bastard, isn't he?" A man's voice, speaking into her ear.

Tori jerked around, her breath gone.

Seth touched her arm, steadied her. She breathed again. "Don't *do* that," she whispered.

Seth's gaze dropped to Tori's calf. She understood, and bent to unstrap the holster and gun. She handed both to him. He tightened the holster around his own leg, but gripped the gun. Leaning forward, he squinted around the corner. Tori leaned out beside him until she could see the front of the safehouse again. The building's steps were empty.

"Must've gone around the other side," Seth muttered. An Asian man in a torn shirt strolled out from the recessed entryway of another building down the block. He eyed them, flicked his glance away. Maybe another slinger. Maybe not.

"Come on." Seth jerked Tori into motion. "Just keep going," His arm was like a leash, taut and insistent, that gripped Tori and pulled her along.

They walked half a dozen blocks. Seth cut into a small park. Someone had hacked at the U in the sign—*HULL PARK*—and painted a ragged *E* across it. The few trees were scrawny. Broken glass glinted in a sandbox and the chains of swings twisted around the top bar of a swing set like hardened intestines. An empty bottle balanced at the top of the slide as if it meant to hurl itself to the bottom.

"We've got a tail," Seth remarked. Tori automatically started to turn her head. "No," Seth told her. "Keep going." They sheered out of the park, across the street, then made another quick turn into an empty parking lot.

"Whelk?" Tori whispered. The sweat on her back seemed to freeze; her shirt was plastered against her skin.

Seth shook his head. "That slinger," he said.

"So now it's not just hitters we've got to worry about? It's slingers and muggers too?"

"Muggers'll kill you just as dead." Seth reached for the gun. "Hell, he might be a grabber."

He led Tori past *McCarthy's Pawn-o-Rama*. Glass crunched under their shoes. Seth pulled her into a narrow strip of overgrown weeds between the rear of the pawnshop and a wooden fence. "Get behind me," he told her.

He extended the gun, aiming at the corner of the building they'd just rounded. The barrel quivered like a hunting dog poised to see what prey might suddenly appear.

« CHAPTER 28 »

FOOTSTEPS CRUNCHED the gravel and glass littering the pavement at the side of the pawnshop. The corner of the shop concealed whoever was making the sounds. Tori's breath snared in her lungs.

Beside her, Seth tensed, then hurtled around the corner.

For one terrifying instant, Tori couldn't see him. Off-balance, she stumbled forward.

The first thing she saw was his gun flashing downward, metal glinting in sunlight. Its butt struck bone with a solid crunch.

A man dropped to his knees.

"Shit—*Christ*—" The man wrapped his arms around his head and rocked back and forth on the gravel. Blood threaded his slick black hair.

Seth trained the gun on him. "Get up."

"Jesus, you broke my fucking head."

Seth pressed the sole of one boot against the man's tailbone until he staggered to his feet, his head swaying and his eyes a watery pink. Tori recognized the Asian guy they'd seen across from the safehouse.

Seth motioned for Tori to go to the end of the fence and check the alley that ran along its other side. "Is it clear?" he asked.

She was shaking as she edged around the last, leaning slat of splintered wood.

The alley was a low-walled chute barely wide enough for a car. Midway down, a dumpster hunched, the garbage that protruded from its mouth rippling and sliding as rats scrambled through the rancid heap.

Tori ducked back. "Nobody."

Seth shoved the Asian guy ahead of him, gun jammed between the man's shoulderblades. With his head lowered, the slinger was shorter than Tori. Beneath his t-shirt, his chest was concave.

"You a grabber?" Seth guided him into the alley.

"I'm just running my business, man."

"Uh-huh. Got a cute little mom 'n pop store on the corner?"

"Gotta sell my shit somewhere."

"So you're just a slinger. Come on. Who're you with? You're not fat enough to be with the big boys." Seth pressed him toward the dumpster.

Tori trailed them. Her fingers worked at her palms, biting into the damaged skin. A stink like old milk and sewage boiled the air.

Garbage rustled as rats fled through cracks in the wall behind the dumpster or plunged deeper into the trash. Seth jammed the man against the front of the dumpster. Shoved him hard. "*Who?*"

The slinger muttered and ground his forehead against the metal.

Seth snugged the gun against the nape of the slinger's neck and patted the man's torso with the flat of his free hand. "Where's your protector at?" Seth crouched to pat down the man's legs.

"New York." The slinger's voice spasmed as hard as his body.

"That right?" Seth's hands rounded the man's ankles. The slinger tried to jerk his right foot away.

Tori moved closer. "Maybe he really is just a slinger," she said quietly.

Seth ignored her. Shoving the man's pants leg up to the knee, Seth yanked down a grimy tube sock. A row of peel-caps was taped to the man's shin. A plastic box, no bigger than a pencil sharpener, gleamed against his hairless calf. A small red light blinked at the top of the box.

Tori glanced, confused, from the blinking device to Seth. A signal box of some sort, she realized. And judging from Seth's grim expression, that wasn't good.

"Hey, it ain't nothing," the man protested.

"Goddamn grabbers." Seth yanked on the plastic cuff until the device popped loose and fell to the ground. He ground it into the gravel with his heel. "Who've you got coming? How many?"

"I told you, nobody . . ." Sweat greased the slinger's face.

Seth spared a brief glance at Tori. "Tori, I want you to climb up there." A jerk of his chin indicated the cinderblock wall rising behind the dumpster. "They'll be here any minute." Seth kicked the sprung components of the signal box into a small plastic and metallic shower.

"Who?" Tori asked, frozen where she stood. Her chest ached. She wondered if it was physically possible for a heart to explode.

"More grabbers," Seth answered. "Take you to Regency, collect a nice ransom, and leave you to Whelk's tender mercies. Now climb up there."

The tightness of his face silenced Tori's objections.

"Then go up the fire escape," Seth continued. "You can get up to the roof from there. See it?"

Tori gaped at the metal rungs that climbed to the building's broken gutter five stories above the street.

"Move!" Seth ordered.

Tori snapped into motion. She clambered up the side of the dumpster, her sneakers scrabbling against the metal, her hands gripping the steel bars fixed along the rim. The metal was slippery, slicked with grease and rotting lettuce leaves and carrot peelings. The lid had two halves, both slung back. Tori hauled one of them shut and crawled onto its flat surface.

She glanced back.

Seth had tightened his grip on the gun, was prodding the slinger . . . no, Tori corrected herself. The grabber.

"You're gonna do a little dumpster diving," Seth said.

Two men slipped into the alley, one at either end.

"Seth!" Tori warned.

Seth glanced up, then down the alley. The gun stayed steady in his grip, and his gaze clocked back to the Asian man. "Grabbers, Tori." Seth's voice grew quiet. "Get up there. Onto the wall. Go."

The two newcomers edged closer. Both looked as skinny and strung-out as their Asian companion. One of the grabbers held a pistol in front of him. The other man, with yellow-tinged skin and a wispy goatee, struggled to restrain a dog on a chainlink leash. Tori's heart shot into an adrenaline-laced gallop.

The animal's teeth ground together like serrated blades. Its shoulders massed, bulky as a piece of furniture, the muscles knotting and popping beneath short black fur. Its back was even with the man's waist. Its ears were black flaps, one ripped askew and healed at a sharp angle to the flat expanse of its skull.

A Hellhound. Riker's Doberman. At least at Glynn River the guards always had the dogs under quivering, but strict control. Seeing a Riker's on the street, pulling against the minimal weight of some scrawny, dragged-out skinwaste, was worse. A lot worse.

Tori lunged up from the half-lid of the dumpster, hurling herself at the top of the wall, her hands and forearms scraping like grappling hooks at the rough blocks. Her arms burned with fresh abrasions. As her sneakers scrambled for purchase, the grabber's pistol exploded.

"Go!" Seth yelled from below. Shoes digging and clawing at the cinderblocks, Tori worked her legs to the top of the wall.

"I got him, Owen!" someone shouted and there was another blast, this one so close that Tori's entire body flinched, contracting on itself like a pupil in sudden light.

Her gaze swiveled to the grabber who'd had the pistol. He kneeled with his shins flat to the ground and his bent torso rocking, screams chuffing out of his throat in quick, dry bursts. His pistol glittered a dozen feet away from him and blood smeared his hands when he raised them from his thigh. Tori realized that the shot had come from Seth's gun, not the grabber's.

The Hellhound surged free. Metal clanked against concrete.

"Seth!" Tori screamed.

The dog burst down the alley, the chain dragging behind it, iron links flung into the air as the leash popped up from crevices in the pavement. The dog's haunches drove forward like pistons. In the shadow cast by the surrounding buildings, its eyes snapped virulent yellow.

"Tori! Take it!" Seth held the gun in one cocked-back hand. The gun curved into the air, tumbling in an arc above the dumpster. Tori snatched at it. He'd pushed the safety into place and she fumbled it off, twisting the barrel toward the sprinting dog.

Seth gripped the top of the dumpster and pulled himself toward the lip of it. The sour-sharp tang of her own fear smothered Tori's nostrils. They'd never practiced shooting at moving targets and now she had no time to think about what she was doing. The snub barrel of the gun traced the frenzied streak of canine muscle and teeth.

The dog sprang airborne as it hurtled at Seth. Tori's index finger convulsed. The gun's explosion jerked her entire arm.

The animal clamped its jaws around Seth's left boot, its teeth disappearing into the leather like knives into fudge. Its heavy bulk dragged Seth toward the pavement. He smashed at the dog's sides with his fists, his hands a fury against its ribs. The Asian grabber staggered half-a-dozen steps away and watched, his hollow chest bellowing in and out.

Tori straightened the gun in front of her, shutting one eye as she took aim.

She shot again. Again. At first she thought she'd only managed to hit the side of the dumpster. The bullet blasted steel. The noise that drilled out from the collision was cold and enormous, vibrating through the alley like a shockwave. The Riker's let out a twisted yelp and raised a hind foot several inches above the ground. The paw dangled loosely, connected to the rest of the leg by threads of skin. Bone protruding from the end of the leg was jagged at its tip like a broken stalk of celery.

The dog's jaws widened momentarily and Seth yanked his foot free. His drawn-back lips exposed a rigor of teeth pressed together with brute determination. He hauled himself over the dumpster's lip as the dog twisted around to sniff at the shredded mess of its leg. Its nose wrinkled and its intact ear stiffened as if the scent of its own blood had reminded it of the kill.

The massive head turned back. The yellow eyes shifted, following Seth's progress as he heaved himself to the top of the wall where he collapsed beside Tori. He left a trail of blood, thick crimson globs.

A growl burred the dog's throat and its head swung sideways. The yellow eyes fixed on the Asian who was edging away, his feet sliding backward across the uneven concrete.

The growl ascended to a snarl and the dog took off, slamming into the man with a force that knocked him against the opposite wall. The man's hands were a flurry of brown and pink. The dog lunged for the throat. Blood plumed into the air.

It took Tori four more shots to kill the dog. The Asian grabber, sprawled beneath its body, didn't move. At one end of the alley, the dog's keeper hurtled back toward the street. At the other end, the grabber with the thigh wound was hobbling out of sight. After a moment's silence, rats' feet scurried against cardboard and plastic and the first rodents twitched their way out of hiding and padded toward the bodies.

Tori laid the back of one hand across Seth's forehead. Pain screwed itself into his face. The sweat that coated his skin was clammy and hot. She bent to look at his leg and gently drew back an edge of damaged fabric. She grimaced at the wound, then stiffened her face, trying to hide her reaction. Her hands hovered just above his skin.

"It'll be okay," she said with a confidence she didn't feel. "We just need to get it cleaned out, find some bandages."

Seth pushed himself upright. "What we've got to do is get out of here."

Tori stared at his foot. The leather upper of his boot was punctured and stabbed, the sole torn entirely free. The holster was gone. His jeans were ripped from knee to ankle. The skin around his ankle frothed, blood mixed with the remnants of the Riker's saliva.

Tori shot a worried look at Seth's face. His eyes were half-closed and an almost green tinge swelled across his cheeks. She leaned toward Seth's chest to listen to his breathing. He wavered upright again.

"We've got to get moving again," he repeated and although his voice was still weak, his words came more distinctly.

"Seth, your leg . . ."

"I'll make it."

She kept one hand gripped around the gun. With the other, she grasped Seth's arm, helping to support his weight as he limped to the fire escape ladder that rose to the roof. He sucked in his breath and paused each time his injured foot touched down on one of the rungs. Tori glanced down. Rats flowed over the dead man and the Hellhound like a living stream.

Seth reached the top rung. The edge of the roof was three feet above it. Seconds passed. Seth's arms strained and both of his feet—even the damaged one—pushed hard against the side of the building as he struggled. Tori's stomach dropped with a sickening hollow sensation—no way she could carry or drag him—but then he was over and she could breathe again.

He reached down. His hands tightened around hers. She clambered over, hunching beside him on the rooftop. They were both panting. Sweat poured off Seth's face, dripped from his chin. He still gripped her hands.

"Where do we go?" Tori said. A hush clung to her words.

"I'll show you," Seth muttered. Tori tensed. He looked awful, like he was going to collapse before he went much farther. If he did collapse, she had no idea where any of the other safe houses were. They'd have nowhere to go, no place to hide.

Seth finally released her. He turned away, hobbling across glittering squares of tar paper that covered the rooftop. The paper burned through the cheap soles of Tori's shoes. A stack of cages, mesh torn and doors missing, stood against a silver utility pipe. Brown and gray feathers, caught in the wire of the cages, shivered with each hot breeze that puffed across the roof. From one of the cages a pigeon's skull stared, tilted atop a scattering of tiny bones.

Tori flinched away from the remains and followed Seth, setting her feet into the sketchy red prints he left behind.

« CHAPTER 29 »

THIS SAFEHOUSE—this safe *room*, nicknamed Singapore according to Seth—smothered Tori with the same claustrophobia as the Glynn River suicide watch cell. The cheap paneling, walnut-brown and flimsy as cardboard, devoured the light that managed to slink around the doorframe and the edges of a sheet tacked over the small window. A low-wattage teller's lamp hunched like a vulture on the chipped floor tiles.

There was no bed, not even a cot or mattress, just a heap of tattered blankets. Seth sprawled on the floor, Tori crouching beside him.

"I'm going to rinse this out again." Tori held the balled-up wad of Seth's shirt close to his face to show him, but his eyes were closed. That was probably a good thing since Tori couldn't stop her hands from shaking. "Cool you off." *Try to*, she didn't say.

Seth was covered in sweat, his hair drenched. Heat poured off his skin. Tori averted her eyes from his leg. The glimpses she'd caught of torn flesh brought her to the jittering edge of panic. Blood saturated the ripped denim around his calf and smeared the floor in long streaks where he'd crawled across the tiles.

In the cramped hallway bathroom, Tori bent over the sink and splashed water on her face. She was grateful there was no mirror. She held the shirt under the tap until the water ran clear, wrung it out, and hurried back to Singapore. Hunkering beside Seth, she wiped his face, pressing the cool cloth against his closed eyelids.

"I'm going to try to do a little better job cleaning your leg now." She kept her voice low, trying to make herself sound calm. But the words quivered. Her fingertips whispered above the dirt-smeared edges of the wound. Using the damp shirt, she wiped at an inch of fluted skin. Seth grimaced and sucked air hard across his teeth.

Tori's hand froze in place. "All right?"

Seth swallowed. "Yeah."

Tori's hand pressed into gentle motion again, dabbing at the grime and crusted blood. The bite marks were deep, but there weren't many of them. Hellhounds preferred ripping away chunks of flesh. Tori winced every time Seth clenched his face with pain. She was hurting him and, for all she knew, making the wound worse, disturbing it with unsanitized cloth and water teeming with God-knows-what. Why the hell wasn't Singapore stocked with some kind of first aid kit? Kendall's fault? That Wren girl?

She kept swabbing at the torn flesh. It probably didn't matter. Bandages and disinfectant weren't going to do much against a Riker's bite. But she still wished she had them.

Seth opened his eyes. Smoothing the anxiety from her face, Tori smiled and kept working at the wound. "You know," she said, "Sydney was the Ritz compared to this place."

Seth jerked his foot away as the wet cloth probed deeper. Tori sank back onto her heels. This really was pointless without the right supplies.

"I'll go find some bandages," she said. "Medicine." She wondered if her remaining cash would be enough to buy antibiotics of some kind. Not that antibiotics were likely work against any poisons in the dog's saliva. Riker's antivenom was what she really needed. It was sure to be way out of her budget if she could even find someone slinging it.

Seth shook his head violently, then immediately gritted his teeth. Tori watched a wave of pain move across his face.

"Seth, it's going to get infected." *It probably already is.* "You need a doctor."

Seth touched the back of Tori's hand. "You're doing fine," he muttered. His hand dropped to his chest. "I'm feeling better."

Tori curled one side of her mouth. "Better than what?"

"Better than having a Riker's latched onto my leg."

"I'm serious, Seth. You need help."

"In the morning. Let things cool down out there."

Tori shook her head in frustration even though part of her—a cowardly part—snatched at the idea of staying put.

"God knows how many grabbers are after you," Seth added. "And Riker's isn't going to kill me tonight. Doesn't work that fast." As if that

183

were the final pronouncement on the subject, his face cleared and his eyes closed.

Tori stared. The tendons at the back of her neck gripped and bunched, starting a dull ache that stretched around to her forehead. "Seems like it's working pretty damn fast to me." She was going to cry. "Shit." She pushed the back of her hand against her mouth.

Without another word, she lowered herself beside him, pressing against his side. His arm drew in around her. She crushed her face against his neck and pushed her hand into the dark V of hair that narrowed from his chest down to his jeans. His skin was damp, the hair wet with sweat.

"I promise I'll get you through this." Seth rested his chin on the crown of Tori's head. "Avery Jackson, Gary Cavalieri." Seth's breath was warm. "Best Guardians we ever had."

Had. The ache in Tori's head sharpened to a razor's edge. Something close to panic twisted inside her. She imagined the Riker's venom sliding through Seth's veins, eating at his lungs, creeping toward his brain. Seth's fingers slid over her face, smoothed her hair.

She remembered the rumors she'd heard in Glynn River about women in the infirmary after a Hellhound attack: screaming, hallucinating, puking up their lungs.

If Seth died because she'd agreed to let him protect her . . . if any of the Network people died because of her . . . "I can contact Bobby or Jared or whoever you want me to. Get some help."

Seth's lips barely moved: "And tell them I screwed up?"

Tori raised her head. "You didn't screw up!"

"Look at us. You don't call this screwing up? I never should've left you alone at Sydney. My fault."

Tori drew herself up on one elbow. "Seth."

"Aw, shit," he mumbled. "Maybe you should comm Bobby. See if he's got a different guardian he can send. It's just—damn. I never lost one before."

He was shaking now, skin clammy, like he was freezing. He pulled her closer, like a blanket that could warm him. In the murky light, his face was gray.

"I don't want you hurt." Tori didn't say what she actually thought: *I don't want you to die.*

Seth dismissed her concern with an exhausted flicker of fingers. "Get what I deserve."

"You don't deserve this."

His shoulders rose, a barely-conscious shrug, and then he was asleep. Or maybe he'd passed out. His breath came raspy and short. Listening to it made Tori uneasy. Her own breathing was shallow, trapped high in her chest. She smelled blood and beneath it, a sour odor of Riker's fur.

Slowly she worked her way out from beneath the warmth and weight of Seth's arm. She crept to the opposite wall and stayed there, frozen into an awkward half-crouch, staring at the darkness webbing the corners of the room.

It could happen easily enough. As long as he was trying to protect her, he could die. The injury he'd suffered that day was sufficient proof. And, Tori told herself, it was too much. Her cheek burned against the wall. Seth's breathing made her think of a stick, dry and brittle and ready to snap.

He was like those other guardians they all talked about, Avery and the rest. She understood that now. Seth would take bullets, jump off a roof, take bullets. Let the venom work until he thought it was safe—safe for *her*—to venture out of Singapore.

The only way she could protect him was to make sure that he had no one to guard.

But before she could do that, she had to find Riker's antivenom. He needed help and he needed it tonight.

Who had antivenom? She fought to clear the panic from her head. Hospitals, sure, but Unihealth hospitals never had enough basic supplies. She doubted many of them kept Riker's antivenom stocked. And a private practice would be impossibly expensive.

So who else? Gangs. A slinger might have the right connections. But she could hand over all her money and get antivenom cut with sugar water or formaldehyde or vinegar for all she'd know about it. Slingers always cut the pure product with something cheaper.

Which left what? Mafia. Military.

Police.

Seth's father. His brothers. Tori sat up straight, trying to remember what Seth had told her. They didn't get along, they didn't speak, except . . . except for his brother Frank. Frank still talked to Seth. He wouldn't let Seth die, would he? His own brother?

Tori crept back across the floor until she hunched next to Seth. Heat flung itself from his skin. She touched his chest. It was slick, the hair matted with sweat. She eased the comm out from his jeans pocket, then carried it out to the hallway and into the murky little bathroom where she closed the door, fastened the lock, and prepared to make a call.

« CHAPTER 30 »

PAIGE AND MIKE didn't need their forged security badges to get past the front desk of Greensford Public Hospital. The facility, set on the decayed Main Street of a long-defunct steel town in central Pennsylvania, was equally atrophied. The floors were sticky, the overhead lights gray with dust. Paige glimpsed patients through half-open doors. They were a half-dozen to a room, bare legs sprawled akimbo on stained sheets. The air was swampy.

"Remind me not to let my insurance lapse," Mike said.

Paige sucked her upper lip between her teeth. "Assuming you can still afford it with the kinds of jobs Merle's been tossing us lately."

Mike let her precede him onto an elevator. "Where are we going?"

Paige punched a button. The elevator groaned and shuddered. "Basement," she said although 'hell' might have been a better answer.

The door slid open. They slipped out into an empty hallway.

The odors of preservative chemicals overwhelmed a desperate quantity of bleach. The corridor stretched low-ceilinged, lights flickering and buzzing above empty gurneys and an abandoned IV stand.

Mike made a face, twisted his head to one side. "God. I hate the smell of formaldehyde." He pressed closer to Paige. "You do remember that Whelk's already taken over the Jennings job? He's probably already finished processing her. We could walk out of here right now. I'll buy you a milkshake somewhere." He raised an eyebrow. "Margarita-flavored."

Paige shook him away with an exasperated toss of her head. She didn't drink, not after witnessing her foster dad's alternating stupors and rages.

Mike was always needling her about the teetotalism. He was annoying as hell, but she'd have missed the teasing if he'd stopped.

Paige halted in front of a heavy door with a narrow horizontal window set into it. The tinted glass obscured the form of a body on a table and, hunched over it, a short woman in a lab coat.

As Paige opened the door, the doctor's head swung up from her work. She was barely five feet tall, with coarse ash-blonde hair that flipped up at her shoulders. Her lab coat engulfed her body. Yellow and red fluids streaked her surgical gloves and smeared the scalpel gripped between her fingers.

"Dr. Bannock?" Paige advanced on the steel table.

"Only authorized staff is allowed in here."

Paige had already snapped out a badge.

"Did you check in with Security?" Dr. Bannock scowled at the badge. "I'm in the middle of an autopsy here."

"You don't say."

Mike snorted. Paige cut a look at him. He settled back, leaning against a wall and crossing his arms.

Paige glanced at the body on the table. A clean slice curved from one shoulder, slid down around the bottoms of both breasts, and ascended to the other shoulder. A flap of skin, folded back, exposed ribs which the doctor had only begun to cut free. She'd seen worse.

"If there's any criminal issue with this patient, no one's informed *me* about it," the doctor said and dropped the blade onto a tray. She didn't look at Paige or Mike, as if ignoring them, disrespecting them, would cause them to vanish.

Paige's jaw tightened. *Keep your voice steady*, she ordered herself. No getting all pissed off because the woman wasn't taking her seriously. "I'm here to talk to you about an older case. An infant. Robert Cameron."

Bannock's hands stopped moving for a moment. "My report is on file with the Philadelphia coroner's office."

"So you remember it, then."

Bannock's chin rose. "I remember every case I've worked on."

"And no second thoughts? No doubt?"

"No." Peeling off her gloves, the doctor tossed them into a plastic bin fixed to one wall, stepped to a sink, and scrubbed her hands. She returned to the exam table, stood over it like a soldier determined to hold a position, and balled her hands against her hips. Taking possession of the table's opposite side, Paige pressed her palms flat to the slick metal, her fingertips an inch away from the mottled cellulite that dimpled the corpse's hip.

She hated lies. Hated them almost as much as she hated smug incompetence.

"There isn't a possibility that your conclusions could have been . . ." Paige lifted an eyebrow. "Wrong?"

"I stand behind my work."

"Even after they drummed you out of the big city?"

Dr. Bannock's head shot up, the muscles in her neck quivering as if defensive frills of reptilian skin might erupt at any moment. "I chose to leave Philadelphia."

Paige surveyed the room. "For this?"

"It's the same work I've always done."

Paige leaned her elbows against the edge of the table and cupped her chin in one hand. Cartilage and veins splayed below her. She ignored them. "But it isn't like the old days, is it?" she mused. "Homicide squads requesting reports. Lawyers waiting for your verdict. Juries lapping up your testimony. Everybody ready to accept whatever you told them because you're the scientist."

"Okay." Dr. Bannock pushed herself away from the table. "That's it."

Mike stepped smoothly between her and the door.

The doctor bristled. "What do you think you're doing?"

"Just giving you two a chance to have a conversation."

Dr. Bannock's face paled. "I don't have to talk to you. I'm a professional. A respected professional. Do you know how many exams I've done? Do you know how many trials I've testified at? I don't have to defend my work to you."

"So why are you?" Paige asked.

Dr. Bannock's mouth opened and shut. Paige wheeled a chair around. "Why don't you sit down, Joyce?" she said. "I just want to ask you a couple of questions."

Mike pushed the chair up against the backs of the doctor's knees. Dr. Bannock perched at the edge of the seat. "The Cameron autopsy was a long time ago."

"But you said you remember it." Paige settled against the table. The cadaver's belly quivered.

Dr. Bannock's voice regained confidence. "That particular one was a simple conclusion." Her fingernails, blunt and colorless, drummed against the armrests.

"Antifreeze," Paige prompted.

"Yes. Of course. The tests came back positive. My physical observations left no doubt." Paige scrutinized Dr. Bannock's face until the doctor squinted and bunched up her mouth. "The blood samples showed a high level of ethylene glycol." Dr. Bannock's clipped her words. "That's consistent with poisoning. Specifically, antifreeze."

Mike spoke from the doorway. "How do you know the tests were run accurately?"

Paige raised her eyebrows at him. Mike? Helping her look into a case? He tossed her a grin.

"We used two labs at that time," Bannock said. "Running multiple samples. One at McNair, one with Ulana Corp. There was no reason to doubt their results."

"Maybe the samples were contaminated before they even got to the labs?" Paige suggested.

The edges of Dr. Bannock's face hardened. Despite her petite size and the cutesy flip of her hairstyle, she suddenly looked her age. Fifty-seven. Paige had looked it up. "Those samples were drawn, sealed, and shipped under my supervision," the doctor said. "There was no contamination."

"I'm not implying the contamination was deliberate. But maybe an accident?"

"Absolutely not. And in any case, there were crystals in the brain and several internal organs. Calcium oxalate. Even the formula bottle had traces of the poison in it. And who gave that infant his feedings? The nanny."

"Tori Jennings," prompted Paige.

"Jennings. That's right. That was her name. A girl like that—she had no business being a nanny. Certainly not for a senator's family."

"No?" Paige heard the keen edge of her voice. How many times had she heard "a girl like that?" *Foster kids, they're all trouble. Not their fault, but they're messed up. Broken. Kids like that aren't going to do anything but shoot synth and breed a bunch of skinwaste brats.*

Paige shook herself, a light motion like the skin of a horse rippling beneath a fly. Mike was frowning at her. Bannock was still talking.

"I saw her at the trial when I testified. She came from nothing. I remember her dad sitting there in the courtroom, wearing a bowling shirt that was about ten sizes too big for him. Couldn't bother with a suit, I guess." The doctor's eyes focused on some invisible point in the air. "I don't remember her mother."

"Her mother died when Jennings was six," Paige said. "They lived right next to a contaminated zone. Lung cancer, spread to the brain. The dad had cancer too."

"Well, all I know is Jennings had no business being in charge of children. And I do fault the Camerons for that." Dr. Bannock stood. "You have the transcripts and the autopsy report? Maybe you ought to study them a little more thoroughly." She snapped on fresh gloves. "You can find your way out?"

"So there were no other possibilities?" Paige said. "Nothing else it could have been?"

Dr. Bannock's shrug barely raised her shoulders. "People always drum up all sorts of idle speculation. I prefer to rely on scientific findings."

"What about the rumors?" Paige glided closer to the woman.

Picking up a pair of forceps, Dr. Bannock examined them in the light before exchanging them for a larger pair. Looking down at the partially-dismantled ribcage, she waved the forceps at Paige and, with her other hand, plucked up a lethal-looking blade. "We're done."

"So you didn't leave the coroner's office in Philadelphia under fire?"

The forceps gripped the edge of the long incision. "I don't deal in gossip and innuendo."

Paige showed her palms. "So why did you leave the city, Joyce?"

The doctor's lips thinned at the sound of her first name. "Why does anyone leave?"

A sort of glee threaded Paige's body, buzzed her with energy. She loved pressing these smug sons of bitches, knocking a little anxiety into their lives. "They've made some mistakes on the job. Things have been swept under the carpet for too long. They're facing pressure to get out. R.I.S.E. started some riots that got a lot of people killed and the autopsies weren't quite up to snuff."

The overhead light leached the blood from Dr. Bannock's face, the color from her hair. "Philadelphia was turning into a pit. *That's* why I left."

Mike's voice floated over. "You've gotta give her that."

Paige waved him off. "So the R.I.S.E. trials had nothing to do with it?"

The doctor bent over the cadaver, her hands working furiously now, disengaging another rib, exposing an expanse of slick, gray tissue underneath. The blade slipped from her fingers and punctured an organ. Forceps clanged onto the tray.

191

"The initial results were correct. The rest of it was just politics." The doctor flicked on a recording system and glowered down at the corpse. "Continuing, 1:14 p.m. The layer of adipose along the primary incision is 5.2 centimeters thick. The muscles at the anterior of the abdominal cavity show signs of severe atrophy. There is thick fluid gathered beneath the sternum—"

Paige motioned Mike from the room. The door swung shut, amputating Dr. Bannock's dictation.

Paige stumped into the elevator, stabbed the button.

"Well, that was kind of a bust," Mike ventured as the elevator heaved itself up to ground level.

"She was butchering that woman in there."

Mike snorted. "Well, autopsy, butchering . . ."

Paige shot him an annoyed look. "She was using the wrong instruments half the time. And what the hell was that U-cut? Why wasn't she using a xiphoid incision?" Paige traced the pattern along her own body, her fingers pressed close together to mimic a blade's flat, honed surface. "What century is this? That was totally half-assed."

They emerged into a lobby that doubled as a waiting room: peeling walls, a fallen ceiling tile that exposed bundles of wire ten feet overhead, a coffee pot gummy with the remains of a long-ago brew, people slumped on busted sofas.

"Look at this place," Paige said. "If you're a person with a big ego, if you enjoy power, you don't leave the job she had and come to a place like this. Not unless somebody gives you a shove."

Mike put a shoulder to the automatic door which was struggling to open on its own and put on his sunglasses. "Okay," he said amiably. He was using his 'calm down' voice.

"I'm not upset," Paige snapped.

"Of course not."

She stopped on the sidewalk in front of the building. The midday sun turned the concrete into a griddle. Heat burned through the soles of her sandals.

"Look," she said, "you don't have to be a part of this, okay?" She was horrified to hear a hitch in her voice.

Mike paused beside her and pushed his sunglasses up on his head. He gave her a look that was becoming all too familiar: eyes narrow, gaze sharp with scrutiny, like he was trying to see past her skin and right into her thoughts. He raised his hand and ran his fingers along her jaw. His fingertips were calloused. Paige stood perfectly still at his touch.

"It's okay, "Mike said. "I'm in. On one condition."

"What?" Paige's voice was steady, she noticed with relief. Well, steadier.

"You let me buy you that milkshake. And it can be as vanilla as you want."

« CHAPTER 31 »

THE SUBWAY STATION was nearly empty; even the attendant's booth with its bullet-proof window and steel bars stood abandoned. Tori swallowed hard and fingered Seth's gun tucked beneath her waistband. The shape of the gun was obvious beneath the fabric of her shirt. She was glad she had the gun, and glad that anyone approaching her would know she had it.

Metal gates barricaded the escalator to the platform, forcing the few customers to the stairs. Hot air poured up from the station's bowels. Tori eased down the steps to the south-bound platform that Frank Krey had specified. The tunnel was a claustrophobic cave, its walls black. The platform itself was ulcerated with the blanket-and-cardboard pallets of the homeless.

Tori waited near the bottom of the stairs. It seemed wise to stay as close to the exit as possible. She kept the wall to her back so no one could sneak up on her from behind.

A train screeched, its headlights drilling through the gloom. It had only three cars, and they shuddered as they dragged to a stop. The doors slid open and Tori instinctively drew back. Frank Krey hadn't given her any description of himself beyond "I'm wearing a red shirt." Young voices rang off broken tiles. Gangbangers? Muggers? Vandal-packs? A few teenagers lunged out of the last car. They never gave Tori a look, just galloped across the beggars dozing on the platform and plunged up the stairs.

A man in a red plaid shirt partially buttoned over a white undershirt stumped out from the middle car. Despite his square-shaped bulk, Tori knew immediately that this was Frank. He was a bull-necked, florid version of Seth, with the same height, the same dark hair and long, sensitive mouth. His gaze locked on Tori. She tilted her head down, the barest nod. He paced toward her, avoiding the bodies littered across the platform, and stopped an arm's length away from her.

Now Tori could see how his eyes resembled Seth's too, the same warm brown flecked with green. Her throat tightened at the memory of Seth as she'd left him: sweating and delirious, his eyes turned to matted slits.

Without a word, Frank pulled a slim plastic case from beneath the red shirt. Opening the case, he tilted it so Tori caught the glint of light on six sealed syringes fixed side-by-side like miniature pool cues in a rack.

"One injection a day for six days." Frank snapped the case shut. "There's voice instructions with it." He held the case out. When Tori reached to take it from him, he tightened his grip on it long enough to add, "He misses one injection, he's in big trouble." Tori nodded that she understood and Frank relinquished the medicine. "That Network of yours can't give you any anti-venom?" he asked. "Pretty useless."

It was hard to disagree with that. "They try," Tori said.

"They?" Frank shoved closer, his face inches from hers. He seemed to draw the oxygen away; Tori was suffocating. "You're one of his cons, aren't you?"

She wouldn't be drawn in. "Thank you. For this."

Frank's gaze sliced down her torso. "He lets you carry a gun around? Jesus, he's really gone over the edge."

Tori took a backwards step toward the stairs. Frank grabbed at her. His hand bit hard into her arm. Tori stopped, gasping at the pain.

"Look," Frank said. "I'm doing this for my mom's sake. You think I want to face her someday up in Heaven, whatever, and hear her ask why I didn't save her precious Seth's life?"

Tori stood frozen, quivering slightly like an animal trapped in a sudden blaze of light.

Frank let out a long breath and dropped her arm. He chewed at his bottom lip, rocked his weight to the balls of his feet and back. "Sorry about that. Grabbing you." He turned his head, stared down the dark tunnel. Far away, something metallic screamed. "So. How bad is he?"

"Pretty bad."

"Yeah?"

"I think . . ." Tori took a breath. Her eyes stung. She held up the case. "Without this, he could die."

"Serve him right," Frank said, but without conviction. "Always flattering himself he's some kind of do-gooder." He swung around to examine Tori. She made herself stand straighter. The man's stare was withering. "Helping a bunch of felons," Frank said. "I'll never understand how he got from Kyle Martin to a bunch of baby rapists and wife killers." His gaze sharpened. Tori sweated and blinked like she stood under a klieg light. "So what are you?" he spat.

"Innocent. That's what I am."

Memories immediately flung themselves at her: Robbie, pale and listless; Robbie, not breathing; the prosecutor's finger stabbing at Tori's face: "*So how, Ms. Jennings, do you suggest that the antifreeze ended up in the child's bottle?*"

Frank snorted outright at her declaration of innocence. "You must've killed somebody. Or you wouldn't be an E."

"Thanks for the medicine," Tori snapped and spun away.

Her foot caught on a pile of rags. The sharp-sweet stink of nico-hash billowed up from a grimy body. She was halfway up the stairs when Frank grabbed her arm again.

She rounded on him. "Look, I said thank you. Twice." She shook the case of antivenom at him. "I'm a killer and a skinwaste, right? So what do you want from me?"

Frank looked down, scraped the bottom of his sneaker back and forth on the step. When he looked up again, his eyes were so exactly like Seth's that Tori sank back against the grimy wall.

"I want you to not get my little brother killed. That's all."

Tori couldn't speak. She'd almost gotten Seth killed by the Hellhound—and that was assuming the antivenom fixed him up—but the hitters chasing her were just as likely to kill Seth tomorrow or the next day or next week.

Frank jammed his hand into a pants pocket. He pulled something out, hidden in his fist. Then he glanced up and down the stairs, waited for a middle-aged man clutching a trash bag to toil his way down to the platform.

Frank grunted and opened his fist. He pushed the clutch of tightly folded bills at Tori.

She stared. "What for?"

"Leave Seth alone. Okay? Take the money, use it for whatever—hire yourself a coyote, get yourself a room at a flophouse, I don't care. Just leave him the hell out of it. Can you do that?"

He was only echoing the terrifying thought that had seeped into Tori's mind already. Leave Seth out of it. Leave Bobby and Kendall and that girl Wren and all the Network people out of it.

Face it alone. Die alone.

Frank loomed over her. "You say you're innocent. Okay. So you don't have any deaths on your conscience. Not yet. Why don't you keep it that way?"

Mute, Tori allowed him to press the cash into one of her palms.

"All right, then." Frank heaved himself back towards the platform.

Tori lifted her head. "Hey."

Frank stopped and turned.

Tori asked: "How do you know I won't go blow it on synth and then head right back to him?"

"I don't."

Tori descended two steps until her face was level with his. "So why are you even trying?"

"For my—"

"Mom?" Eyebrow raised skeptically, Tori said the word at the same instant Frank did.

Frank paused. He let out a grunting sort of laugh. A corner of his mouth lifted, reminding Tori, again, of Seth. "Yeah. That's right."

Tori leaned closer, pressing. "You so sure that's really the reason?"

Frank's mouth tautened, a length of tough cord. "Well, it isn't for the sake of Seth's sorry, E-loving ass."

The words hung in the air, ate it like acid. All humor was gone. The man looked like a boulder now, with a face carved from rock.

Tori raised one hand. It wavered between them. "Hey," she said softly. Another train was smashing through the tunnel. Warm air blasted up from the platform "Who was Kyle Martin?"

Brakes screeched.

She didn't think Frank was going to answer, but then his mouth moved, reluctant lips in a stone face. "Just a kid. Sad sack. Got stomped on by the other kids at school. Usual story."

The doors on the subway cars juddered open. Frank's gaze ticked toward the train. His mouth worked like he was trying to chew something hard and indigestible. "Some guys beat him up pretty bad. Seth was there. Got in a couple licks himself."

"Seth?" The subway din receded as Tori tried to picture it. A younger Seth doing—what? Punching another kid in the gut? Head-butting? What?

"It wasn't really a whole hell of a lot," Frank said. He was half-turned, staring off at something invisible. "Seth didn't do anything but give a couple of kicks once they'd pulled the guy down. Pretty feeble."

Tori tried to visualize this. How weak did a kick need to be to qualify as feeble in Frank Key's mind?

Frank helpfully cleared up that question. "Didn't break the guy's ribs, or nothing. But the kid got his revenge. Hung himself in one of the classrooms a few days later. Seth's the one who walked in on it."

Tori's hand pressed against her mouth. "Jesus."

"Yeah, well, he's been a screwed-up pain-in-the-ass ever since. Never will forgive himself. I think he'd actually like to get shot to pieces guarding one of you people."

Tori imagined legs dangling, fibrous rope, the stink of the body's last urine puddled on the tile floor. Was that really the reason Seth was a Guardian? To work off some sort of penance? Because he thought he deserved execution himself and fending off hitters was a good way to get it?

Tori's gaze met Frank's. She lowered her hand. "I promise you," she said. "He won't get killed guarding me."

"Better not." Frank stumped down the steps and onto the last car just before the doors shut. The train shuddered into darkness.

Tori crammed the money down her pants. It nestled beside the gun. She clutched the box of anti-venom to her side and vaulted up to the street.

The summer dusk was thick and hot as blood. She waded stubbornly through it, head down and one arm in front of her, trying to hurry, but the air resisted movement, like rows of hanging corpses.

« CHAPTER 32 »

TORI'S FINGERS SKIMMED the heat off Seth's face like skin from a pan of warm milk. Sweat dripped from his hair. It glittered in the low wattage light cast by the lamp beside him on the floor.

"Seth?" She brushed her fingertips across his arm. He flinched away, never opening his eyes. His mouth was slack, a thin opening for breath that barely seemed to raise his chest.

Tori examined Seth's leg. The dog had gouged parallel gashes that started at the top of the foot and extended a good eight inches up the calf. The gashes were scarlet and inflamed, sunk deep into the flesh. The skin surrounding the wounds was bruised purple. Pencil-thin streaks, violet and crimson, extended runners out from the swollen skin.

"Seth, I'm going to give you a shot, okay? Antivenom."

She hunched, a syringe in one hand, and listened to the recorded instructions one more time. At least she didn't have to get the needle into a vein; she just needed to inject the antivenom beneath the skin. Taking a breath, she steadied her hand, sank the needle into the meat of Seth's calf muscle, and pushed the plunger home.

Seth didn't react. That scared Tori more than anything else had. Her hands were shaking again. She clicked the used syringe back into the case and settled cross-legged beside Seth. She kept one hand on his shoulder, the other intertwined with his fingers. Heat poured from his flesh into hers.

All night she sat beside him, both of them sweating in the dark. He muttered once, nonsense words that made her tighten her grip on his hand.

Early morning light glowed pink around the window shade when Seth opened his eyes. His face was white, stubble flecking his jaw like grit. He tried to shift his injured leg, and hissed with pain.

Tori stroked his face. "Hey." Did he even know who she was? She smoothed his wet hair. "I got the medicine." Her voice wobbled. "You need another shot tonight, about seven o'clock, and then four more. Four more days. One shot every evening" She picked up a cup of water, lifted Seth's head, and tilted the cup to his dry lips. "Come on, Seth. You need to drink."

He looked at her then, and seemed to recognize her. His lips parted. She tipped the bottom of the cup higher. "There. Are you hungry?"

He managed to turn his head to one side. His hands gripped into weak fists, but that couldn't stop their trembling. He looked like he might pass out at any second. Tori set the cup on the floor and lowered his head again. "Rest," she said.

It was just as well if he didn't want to eat. She didn't have many options to offer, no broth or soft-boiled eggs or toast. All she'd found in the room were three tins of Vienna sausage and an opened box of saltines. She'd devoured a sleeve of crackers and half-a-dozen sausages during the night

The cash Frank had given her sweated against her skin. She had to leave—Frank was right—but she couldn't yet, not until she trusted that Seth could handle the injections himself.

And she didn't want to leave. Didn't want to be alone, suffer alone, die alone. Didn't want to face the truth: She would never see Seth again.

He slept all day. Tori bathed his face and neck, rubbed his fingers. He was still feverish at nightfall, the wound fiercely purple, but his breathing turned deep and regular.

When she gave him the second injection, he winced and sucked in his breath as the needle slipped beneath his skin. It was a good sign, she thought, that he was reacting to pain now.

He looked right at her. "Tori."

She nearly sobbed with relief. She stroked his face, the stubble catching at her fingertips. "You're back," she said, grinning, the room wavery and her eyes wet.

Seth lay awake another hour, watching Tori as she bathed his face with a wet cloth, then cleaned the stale sweat from his throat, arms and chest.

"You're so beautiful," he muttered and closed his eyes.

Tori stared at him. Her ragged nails touched her oily crop of hair. No one had told her she was beautiful in so long. Her father used to say it all the time: "You're beautiful, you're smart, you're good"—a whole litany of wonderful qualities. He'd even, sometimes, made her believe it.

She kneeled, brought her face close to Seth's. "You are too," she whispered. She kissed his forehead, his rough cheek, his mouth. She closed her eyes and pressed her face into the curve of his neck. She stayed like that for a long time and fell asleep to the rhythm of his breath.

When she woke, his arm was around her. She carefully, reluctantly, pulled herself away. She refilled the water cup and set it near him, along with an open can of sausages and a new sleeve of crackers. She took his comm into the hall and shut the door while she recorded more instructions about when and how to take the remaining injections.

"I have to leave, Seth," she finished. "Seeing you get hurt like this . . . it's too close. I don't think I could stand it, if you got hurt again or—or even—and if I had to live with that." Her face was hot and pink. "I could— I could care too much," she blurted. "For you."

She paused.

"And your brother? Frank? He doesn't hate you. He worries about you. He loves you."

And I think maybe I do too. The words skidded to a stop midway up her throat.

She returned to the room and hesitated, the comm in her hand. A thin ache cut through her. She closed her eyes and leaned against the wall. If she let him help her, if she could get out of the country, if Seth would come with her . . .

She shook herself. There was no safe country, no magical place. Not for her. And no safety for Seth as long as he was with her.

Crouching, she placed the gun and the comm beside the open syringe case and set the comm to *alert* and *repeat*. Her message should wake him well before time for the next injection, but she thought—looking at the color gradually seeping back into his face, listening to his easier breaths— that he would wake up on his own long before then.

She allowed herself a moment's relief, a quick, wordless instant of thanks. She touched his forehead, checked the money still stashed against her hip, then slipped out the door.

In the hallway, just before she stepped outside, fear assaulted her, twisting like a screw in her bowels. Her hands rose in front of her chest, palms out, as if she could push away a terrifying loneliness. She couldn't, and she stepped out the door anyway.

« CHAPTER 33 »

STEPHENSON'S LAW OFFICE looked marginally less seedy in the dark. The streetlights in both directions along this block had been shattered which was fine with Paige. She liked the shadows.

She edged around the side of the converted shotgun house, picking her way through weeds and vines. Considering the state of the 'landscaping,' the grounds were probably choked with poison ivy. She'd worn black jeans and a long-sleeved black t-shirt for camouflage, but they doubled nicely as protection against the small wilderness surrounding the office.

"Pathetic," she muttered, and peered through the window beside the back door. Dirt crusted the glass. An equally filthy bit of sheer curtain hung motionless across the windowpanes.

The back room was dark. Papers and folders were mounded like untidy black Everests on the floor. Paige drew back, checked around the window and door for any indication of security. She felt confident that Stephenson wasn't the type to invest money in that sort of thing, but maybe he'd tried to get his act together after meeting Whelk and his buddies. Frankly, she doubted whether the man was intelligent enough to figure out the instructions for an alarm system.

Time to take a chance.

Paige shoved at the door. It was locked. The window didn't budge. Hell, the thing was probably painted shut. She shook her head. Why *not* make the whole place as much like a dumpy little prison cell as possible?

She'd already surveyed the surrounding houses. About half of them appeared to be abandoned; the other half sagged behind barred windows and unrestrained vegetation. She had a filed-down Allen wrench and a pick in the black satchel slung across her back, but saw no need to bother finessing the lock. The residents of this particular neighborhood were stone-cold poor. No way were they forking out money to buy protection from whichever private police force happened to cover this area . . . that is, if all the police companies hadn't completely pulled out of this neck of the woods and left its residents unable to buy coverage at any price.

And anyway, as Mike would so elegantly put it: "None of these poor fucks is going to get off their ass, short of a nuclear bomb hitting their house." Paige smiled, imagining Mike's voice.

She clicked on the small flashlight at her belt, trained the light across the door, gave it a gentle push with the flat of one hand. The door, she guessed, was probably solid core, but had no metal cladding, no obvious reinforcement. The thing looked about as weak and timid as the man who owned it.

She turned sideways to the door, test-aimed the sole of her right foot so it tapped just beneath the knob. Keeping that leg slightly bent, she pulled it back to gather force, then struck at the door with maximum momentum.

The trim around the door cracked.

Without pausing, she kicked the door again. A deep fissure split the trim. She reached for the knob, pushed, nodded with satisfaction at the broken latch. She swung the door open and slipped inside, pulling the door closed behind her in the same motion.

The stench struck her like a fist in the face.

Paige flung an arm up, her elbow smothering her nose and mouth. She breathed shallowly through the cotton of her sleeve.

Jesus, what a stink. Impossible not to recognize the reek of rotting carcass. The smell was the same whether it was deer or raccoon or human. There wasn't much doubt about which of those waited in the front room.

Gun extended, she edged through the back office, paused at the door to the front. There was no sound at all, not even the hum of air moving through ductwork. Not a surprise. The office was stagnant, the air so humid that she was instantly coated in sweat. Outdoors, in the distance, an engine throbbed.

She passed through the doorway and saw him at once, a dark mound heaped into the chair behind the desk, as lumpy and featureless as the piles of papers she'd just walked past.

The room was clear, no indication of any intruders. Paige moved closer, let the flashlight's beam settle on the man. He was slumped forward, his thick buttocks pressed deep into the chair, his belly wedged against the desk, keeping his entire body fixed in place. Strands of gray hair glowed like oiled wires. Beneath the sparse hair, freckles dotted his scalp. At such close range, he stank of the piss and excrement that stained his pants and blotched the chair's upholstery.

"Okay, big boy. Let's take a look at you." Paige slid a hand, already sheathed in a latex glove, beneath the man's chin. The fatty wattle of skin felt cool and dry. She raised his head into the light and recognized Stephenson's doughy features. His mouth was pinched, wrinkles set hard in his forehead and around his eyes as if they'd been screwed into place. He looked as anxious in death as he had when he was alive.

Paige moved around the corpse, checking for any signs of injury, any indication that Whelk or his men had paid a return visit. She saw nothing. So what was it then? He'd certainly looked unhealthy the last time she saw him. The sight of Sergei booming through that front door again might have been enough to instantaneously drop Stephenson with a heart attack or stroke.

Or maybe it was just too many cheeseburgers and onion rings.

Either way, Paige was pleased. The man had been useless as a source of information anyway and now she could take her time going through the chaos of paperwork piled around these rooms. If Whelk or Sergei had recently made a return visit, she wouldn't have to concern herself with them popping back in again.

And Stephenson deserved a little hellfire and damnation vacation in whatever circle of the Inferno was reserved for lazy-ass, slack-jawed, shit-for-brains attorneys.

The only negative was the stench, but she could live with that.

Sliding open the desk drawers, she ferried the folders they housed to the other room. When she'd emptied Stephenson's desk, she returned to the back, shut the door between the two rooms, opened the window (which, to her surprise, was *not* painted shut), switched on a light, and settled cross-legged onto the floor to work. She kept her gun close at hand—just in case.

Five hours later, she dropped yet another folder onto the floor and watched in disgust as useless scraps of paper slid from it. She pulled her hands through her hair, gazed at the mess surrounding her. She'd searched through file after file, most unlabeled, and discovered more papers beneath the furniture and stacked on the toilet tank in the tiny bathroom. Skimming the crazy quilt contents of each file cabinet drawer had given her a piercing headache.

At least she was getting more accustomed to the smell.

Her comm buzzed. Mike's face squinted from the screen. A wooden headboard rose behind him. In low lamp light, stubble glinted across his cheeks and onto his throat.

"You know the sun's about to come up?" he said.

Paige rubbed her eyes, stifled a yawn. "I know. I'm almost done."

"Listen. Come over here. I'll make you some amazing waffles. Blueberry."

She might be more acclimated to the stench, but not so much so that she could even think about food. "Maybe."

"Definitely."

The screen went dark. Paige realized she was smiling at the comm. She jammed it back against her hip and snagged the next folder. One more cabinet to go and then, yeah, maybe she would head over to Mike's. Maybe blueberry waffles would even sound good by then.

Her hand froze when she saw the name scrawled on the file label: Victoria Jennings. The sad sack had filed it under V—misfiled it actually, between the surnames Vinton and Voorhees.

Paige slapped through the contents of the folder: ancient phone messages and receipts, completely unconnected to the Jennings case. She let them drop to the floor.

She yanked out a sheet of paper that was torn in half, lengthwise. Unbelievable. A lawyer keeping ripped-up pages? What the hell had he used the other half for anyway? Kleenex? She smoothed the paper and bent over to read it:

> stent with antifreeze poisoning as Dr. Bannock
> psy report bears this out.
> SE Syndrome is also a possible culprit.
> esearcher into such disorders in the
> atal and neonatal populations.
> value to your defense effort.

eater depth or discuss a courtroom appearance.

Sincerely,

Kayla Simmons, M.D., Ph.D.

The letterhead was from the University of Pennsylvania.

Paige wasn't tired any more. She scoured the rest of the folder and those remaining in the cabinet. Nothing mentioned Dr. Simmons.

She tucked the half-sheet of paper into her satchel, palmed the gun.

"Stephenson." She tossed the name through the closed door to his office. There was no way she was going to open it and let the full stench of that body billow around her. "You may just have helped after all. Asshole."

She went out the back, rounded the house, hurtling through the weeds without a second thought about poison ivy. Mike wasn't going to be too thrilled about heading over to Penn first thing—he was probably hoping the law office was a bust and they could just forget about Jennings and agree to take a different job. But that was okay.

Paige would make sure to exclaim over a couple of his blueberry waffles before she told him what she'd found.

« CHAPTER 34 »

TORI STOPPED AT a street corner and stood there, crabbed her arms around herself, trying to figure out what to do. She estimated that she'd been walking for at least half an hour, putting distance between herself and Seth. Her body felt weak, her brain numbed by exhaustion, sadness, and fear.

She didn't recognize the neighborhood, and the tilting street sign above her was indecipherable beneath black graffiti. Neon blared down the next block. Red lights raced along lottery pits and announced rooms available at quarter-hour rates. Tori glanced sideways at the whores and Scars loitering along the curb.

"Wan' a room, hon?" one of the Scars called. He snaked his split tongue from his mouth and caressed the metal studs that outlined his lips.

A light-headed sensation rushed through Tori. Before her trial, she'd shared a cell at the Detention Center with a pair of Scars. They were young, with knobby ceramic horns bulging from their foreheads. She'd always assumed they were convicted of whatever they'd been charged with and sent to an actual prison. She didn't know how other prisons operated, but Glynn River did not look kindly on body mods. At Glynn River, horns were excised and split tongues crudely stitched together.

She briefly considered disappearing into one of those quarter-hour rooms for the entire night, but decided against it not only to save money, but because whoever ran those seedy hotels could easily send someone into Tori's room to rob and rape her. A room could be a trap as well as a haven.

She veered left at the corner to avoid the neon blaze and its inhabitants. This cross street was nearly empty, decayed apartment buildings on one side and a small park on the other. The sparse trees clawed the night like emaciated muggers. The park didn't look much safer than the streets or alleys, but it *was* darker—which could be a danger or an advantage. She might be able to conceal herself well enough that she could get some rest.

Beneath the park's rusted-out gateway, she hesitated. She thought of Seth and the memory of him steadied her, somehow. She had to keep her head clear. Focus on first things: sleep, food, water. Get past her fear. Get past images of Seth pale and unconscious on the safehouse floor.

Tori carefully moved a dozen paces into the park. Then, from the darkness, a woman slurred: "Ah, fuck. The pond."

Tori froze. She knew that voice.

Seconds later, Wren swayed out from the shadows and nearly fell into her.

"Hey?" Wren's features struggled against each other. "I know you?"

Wren's companions staggered up behind her. The man had his shoes off and was wringing out his socks. The woman stank of beer. Wren's face tilted close enough that Tori could see the hectic red suffusing her cheeks, the blistered rash crawling down her neck. Wren's left hand wobbled forward until it brushed across Tori's hair. She didn't seem to notice how Tori drew back.

"Ye-ah." The word seeped from Wren's mouth. "I saw you at that place." She tried to snap her fingers, but the tips slid soundlessly across one another. "Sydney?"

Tori dropped back a step, and wondered if anyone in the Network knew how loose Wren's tongue was—or just how many drugs she swallowed.

The man grabbed Tori's hand with wet, wormy fingers. "What you got?" he said.

Tori jerked her hand free. "Sorry. I'm clean out right now."

"Shit. Everybody's out." The man tottered past. The drunk woman slung herself after him.

Wren's face swam up at Tori's. "You still staying there? Sydney?"

"No."

Wren considered this, one hand picking at her rash. Her fingertips came away bloody. "You staying anywhere?"

Tori weighed a response. Wren's slack face and cloudy eyes didn't seem capable of harboring plots and betrayals, but Tori was wary. "Here and there. What about you? You living here in the park?"

Wren rolled her eyes upward, the gesture grotesque in slow-motion. "Nobody *lives* here." She stared over Tori's shoulder. Her mouth drooped open. A line of saliva glimmered between her upper and lower lip like a strand of spiderweb. "Where's your Guardian?" she slurred.

There was no point denying that she'd had a Guardian, that she was—in fact—an Executable. Not when Wren had seen her in a Network safe house. "We're going to catch up with each other later," Tori said.

"He nice to you?"

Tori lifted her shoulders, confused by the question. "I guess. Sure."

"He love you?"

Tori's shrug turned awkward, off-balance when she remembered what Seth had told her: *You're so beautiful.* "No."

Wren's eyes glistened. "He's good to you. I can tell. Shit, he's a Guardian. He'd die for you."

"I'm not sure that counts as love, exactly."

Wren's bony fingers plucked at Tori's sleeve. She was skinny and bereft as an orphan, flat-chested and small-hipped as a ten-year-old. "It's love," she said. Tears quivered in her rabbity lashes. "My guy loves me too. He just won't say it."

"I think a lot of guys don't like to," Tori answered, wondering what the hell she knew about men anyway and why she was standing in a run-down park in North Philly discussing romance.

Wren smiled a gray grin. "Yeah, that's it. They hate saying it." She stroked Tori's arm, patted at Tori's hair. "You got a place to stay?"

"I was kind of looking, actually."

"I know a place," Wren said. "If you got some money."

"Not much."

"Well, Mom don't charge much. She'll feed you too." With one last scratch to her rash, Wren drifted to the sidewalk. She looked back. "You coming?"

Tori shot a glance at the dismal park and another at the neon signs pulsing back at the intersection. Turning away from both, she cautiously followed Wren.

The smells of smoke, cooked cabbage and weed pressed like a solid wall of stink in the streets nearest the encampment. The encampment revealed itself gradually as the women approached, the jumble of tents, boxes, and wooden crates assembling themselves into a precarious village. Clotheslines slumped between the hovels, pale ropes and clothespins crisscrossing the night like strands of long-dead Christmas lights. Above, an enclosed highway bridge formed a dense concrete sky.

"Mom?" Pushing aside the blanket that covered the doorway, Wren leaned into a tent. "I got one needs a place."

Light from a rusted camping lantern flickered against the canvas walls. A boy hunkered by the entrance and stared out at Tori. He looked about five years-old, his white-blonde hair brush-cut to expose an even whiter scalp.

Wren disappeared inside. Tori waited, her arms crossed, hands rubbing her elbows. She kept a sidelong watch on a fire smoldering in a big metal trashcan three tents away, and on the men hunched around it to cook.

A moment later, Wren waved from the entrance. "It's okay. You can come in."

The tent's interior reeked of moldy canvas and cooked beans. Tori blinked against the smoke that oiled the air. But the dirt floor was neatly swept. Folded blankets made a rough skyscraper in one corner.

A woman pushed herself up from the ground with a grunt. Her smile bared broken front teeth. "Wren tell you about the money?" she said. Her voice was smoke-scratched. "Fifteen bucks. It's cheaper than any motel, but I can't afford to run a charity house here."

Tori slipped a couple of bills from one of her shoes.

The woman extended her hand from the too-long sleeve of a faded pink blouse. She took the money, counted it. "You got almost enough for two nights, but I'd need five more."

Tori raised her palms and lied. "I don't have it. But I'll get it tomorrow."

Wren slipped around Tori, muttered to the woman: "I gotta have my cut. Tonight."

The woman closed her fingers around the money, hiding it against her palm. She scrutinized Tori. "We'll work it out. Before tomorrow night." The woman motioned at the blankets. "You can use one. I know. It's like a sauna in here already."

Tori took one from the center of the stack, wanting one that hadn't been too freshly used. The blanket was thin, but smooth and almost cool. She held it up, searched for signs of bedbugs, lice. That was one point in Glynn River's favor. They made sure everybody got a regular delousing and sprayed the bunks down with a foul-smelling insecticide every couple of weeks. The poison probably took years off the prisoners' lives, not necessarily a bad thing.

The boy sat crossed-legged opposite Tori and stared at her with watchful blue eyes.

Tori dropped to her knees and tried to smile at him. "This your boy?" she asked the woman.

The woman let out a sputtering laugh and roughed one hand across her gray hair. "That's nice of you, but I know how old I look. He's my grandson. I watch him sometimes for my daughter. She's got a man, not the kind who wants any kids underfoot. They got a tent down closer to the water." The woman bent over a stewpot warming on a hotplate. The air inside the tent blazed up several more unbearable degrees.

The boy had already lost interest in Tori. He shoved his head against the ground, his elbows jutting out as he attempted a wobbly headstand. His legs wavered toward the canvas overhead. His grandmother was lifting the pot from the heated coils. "Cut that out," she snapped. "You'll knock the whole damn thing down."

The woman pulled brown mugs from a shoebox, handed one to Tori.

"What about me, Mom?" Wren whined.

Mom continued to ladle stew into Tori's mug. Scant bits of meat mixed with the carrot and potato. The gravy was thin and was so heavily specked with pepper that Tori's nose twitched.

"Mom!" Wren grabbed an empty mug and thrust it at the woman.

The older woman's mouth soured, but after filling two other mugs, she grudgingly poured the last of the stew into Wren's cup. It was half empty. The woman jabbed a bent spoon into Wren's hand. "That's all you get till you're paid up." Wren squinched up her mouth like she was going to protest.

"Unh-uh." The woman raised a finger.

Wren sank back.

The old woman settled between Tori and the boy and let out a deep sigh.

The meat was tough, the vegetables near-mush, and the broth made Tori sweat even more. She imagined each individual grain of pepper stinging the roof of her mouth. But she was hungry and she devoured the food in quick, scraping mouthfuls.

Wren fidgeted, letting spoonfuls glop back into her mug. Her feet jiggled and her glance kept twitching to the door flap.

The silence lengthened. "Are you really Wren's mom?" Tori finally asked.

"Nah. Everybody calls me Mom. You might as well too." The woman put her spoon to her mouth and sucked at the broth. "Wren's from out Ohio somewhere."

"Detroit," Wren said.

Mom shrugged. "She never gets it real clear." Mom's spoon scraped at the bottom of her mug. "I've got one son in Johnstown. The other one got himself shot in a fight at another camp, over off Passayunk."

"I'm sorry." Tori turned her empty mug awkwardly in her hands and wished for seconds.

Mom's face didn't change. "His fault. Slinger."

Gathering the mugs and spoons, she put them in a milk crate with a black-specked sponge and a bottle of soap.

The boy sprang up and took the crate from her. "Right to the pump," Mom told him, "and come back as soon as you're done. No messing around. No talking to anybody."

The boy was gone before she'd finished with her warnings. The air that entered when he pulled aside the flap was sultry, but carried just enough of a breeze to momentarily relieve the swampiness of the tent's interior. Wren pulled her damp shirt away from her chest and back, and slipped out past the flap too.

Tori clambered up, unsure if she should follow Wren or stay put. She pushed one hand back from her forehead. The roots of her hair were soaked. She assumed she stank although she couldn't really tell, what with all the odors packing the tent. "So there's a tap around here?"

"One. And some people get water from the river, but there's other people going to bathroom in it. So I don't really recommend that." Mom unbuttoned her shirt. She wore a camisole beneath, white polyester worn dingy gray and darkened with sweat. Folding the shirt, she laid it on a small stack of clothes in a cardboard box.

"Just the one tap?" Tori asked

"Just the one."

Tori pictured the tents and makeshift huts. How many people were squatting here? Three hundred? Four hundred? No wonder they ended up using the river. She became uncomfortably aware of her own bladder. "What about a bathroom?"

Mom snorted.

"Outhouse, I mean," Tori amended.

Mom just laughed, snapped open a blanket and spread it across the dirt. Knees popping, she lowered herself onto the blanket and lay flat on her back. "You got a gun on you? A knife?"

Tori thought about the gun she'd left with Seth. His absence dug hard into her chest, like spurs against the ribs of a horse. "No."

"I got this knife." Mom pulled it out from beneath the folds of her skirt. "Anybody comes in here, they're going to get an eyeful of this. For real, in the eye. I got a suggestion for you. You find yourself some kind of weapon fast as you can. Keep it by you. Especially at night." Mom closed her eyes.

The stifling air, the claustrophobia, the other woman's rasping breath: it reminded Tori of the penitentiary. She shrank into the safety of her own crossed arms.

All these rooms and hiding places and safehouses, all these spaces felt like another string of prison cells. Despair dragged at her. She would be in some form of Glynn River for the rest of her life, however long—or short—that was.

"I did have one question for you." Mom suddenly propped herself up on her side. "Just how're you planning to get more money? See, I don't like people fighting about money. There's enough ugliness. That's why I'm bringing it up now."

The money Frank Krey had given Tori sweated against the sole of her left sneaker. She wasn't going to be here long enough to waste another dollar on Mom's accommodations.

"You know of any jobs?" Tori asked.

"Just make sure you stay away from the men here, any come up to you saying they have a proposition. They'll get you whoring or slinging before you know what you're doing. Whoring, more likely." Mom squinted at her. "You don't use, do you?"

"No."

"Didn't think so." Pause. "You should try the work vans." Mom stabbed a hand in the direction of one of the tent corners. "You go over early to the front of the camp, get there by dawn, and places that need workers'll have vans waiting."

"Need workers for what?" Tori stared at the canvas roof sagging four feet overhead. She could see the flurry of talons again, feel the swipe of chicken claws slicing her arms. She'd had enough meat-processing to last a lifetime. She prayed that the cash she already had would be enough to pay a coyote to get her safely out of Philly, maybe across the Canadian or Mexican border.

"Different places," Mom answered. "A lot of the time, it's those Black Swan people looking for workers for their factory across town. Over off Olney and Broad."

Tori jerked her head up. Olney and Broad? That was only a half-dozen blocks from her dad's house.

Mom was still talking, but Tori only half-listened. Yeah, she had to find a coyote, had to get out of Philly, out of Pennsylvania—soon—but maybe she could use a work van to get to her old house. It would be a lot faster and safer than trying to go by foot or subway, even if the old neighborhood station was still open. It would only take a minute to check the doors and windows, see if Dad was there and if he was okay. If she just knew he was all right, that would be enough. Then she would be able to bear leaving.

"The pay's no great shakes," Mom finished, "but it's better than making money on your back."

The blanket flung away from the entrance. Mom's grandson shoved inside the tent and dropped the crate with a clatter. The smells of the camp trailed after him: smoke, gasoline, garbage stewed to a fine reek by the summer heat.

Mom eyed the washed dishes with suspicion. "That was pretty quick."

The boy nodded.

"You didn't wash 'em in the river, did you?"

The boy shook his head. Mom squinted at him a minute, then announced, "Bed. I gotta get up early. This girl too."

"I'm going to wash up," Tori said and bolted from the tent.

Campstoves and fires in barrels spotted the darkness, casting uncertain light on the humps of tents and the jagged roofs of sheet-metal huts. The streetlights on the encampment's perimeter were smashed or burned out. Tori squinted up at the underside of the enormous overpass. It was easy—too easy—to imagine it fracturing, giant slabs flattening the squatters camped beneath. Especially since large chunks of it already appeared to be held in place by wire cages.

She turned to the problem at hand. Where was she going to find a coyote?

Tori hesitated. The canvas of Mom's tent exhaled damply against her back. Even from three tents away, the flames billowing from the nearest barrel coated her body with a fresh layer of sweat.

It wasn't going to be as easy as looking for a drug slinger, something she'd watched other kids do plenty of times in her old neighborhood. Coyotes moved people across the borders in and out of the U.S. for different reasons, but she was going to have to lie about why she wanted to leave. How many coyotes would want to transport an Executable with hitters on her tail? Hell, coyotes would probably just grab and turn her over to the killers for a nice fee. At best, they'd demand a sum she'd never be able to afford.

Maybe the coyotes would be hanging around the slingers. Two-for-one deals.

Her mouth curled, like she'd heard a bad joke. She pushed away from the tent, picking her way past the rubbish littering the encampment's crude paths, and headed for the perimeter. That's likely where the slingers would be, in the territory between the tent city and the streets, visible and available to all potential customers.

At the stacks of broken crates and strewn garbage that marked the entrance to the camp, she stopped. Fifty yards down the street, a single streetlight fizzed, on the verge of going out. The windows of the buildings on the opposite side were dark, abandoned. An occasional figure, pale black against the even blacker night, flitted from the narrow passages between buildings or appeared and vanished behind the junkyard cars lodged against the gutters.

She was going to get killed out there. Maybe with a nice rape thrown in as a bonus.

A hand brushed her arm.

Tori jerked back, spun around, blood charging her veins.

"Hey, so you like Mom's?" Wren reached forward again, stroked Tori's elbow.

For a second, Tori couldn't speak; she was choking on her own breath. Then she exhaled, wagged her head at the girl.

"You okay?" Wren's face shriveled into a worried frown.

"Yeah. Yeah, you just surprised me."

Tori tried to step away, but Wren only pressed in closer, gripping Tori's elbow now. Wren's hand was feverish and wet, her fingers like stripes of moist flame against Tori's skin. "Did I help?" Wren pleaded. "Finding you a place?"

"Sure." Tori resisted the urge to shake the girl off.

Wren's voice cracked. "I really try. To help. To be good."

Tremors quaked through Wren's hands, shivered into Tori's arm. Tori recognized those shakes. Wren needed her next hit. Synth, probably.

Tori kept her tone gentle. "I know you try."

"Owen thinks I'm shit." Wren suddenly let out a sob so high-pitched and long it was nearly a wail.

Tori glanced around, searching doorways and flat-tired cars. "Shh! It's okay."

"I took some of his stash. He's gonna kill me."

"He's not going to kill you," Tori said, thinking he probably would. Shit, was that somebody crouched between those two cars? Probably pulling out a knife, getting ready to slam across the street and cut their throats.

Wren plucked at her arm again. "You sure you don't got a cap you could give me? Maybe two?"

"Sorry."

"What do you need? I got a bucket at Mom's. I can get water for you. I don't mind carrying it for you. Whiskey too. I know a guy. Sneakers. Joints."

Wren was bartering for caps Tori didn't even have. Tori shifted her weight, feeling the folded rectangle of money against the sole of her foot. Money could buy a coyote's services. Money could buy caps. Which could buy Wren's knowledge—if she had any.

"What I need," Tori said, "is a coyote."

Wren nodded spastically, not looking at all surprised. "Okay. Okay."

"You know somebody?"

Still nodding, Wren said, "Yeah, but where do you want to go?"

An image of Seth flashed into Tori's head. Seth at the Virginia safe house, his hair damp from the shower curling black against the back of his neck. The fresh smell of soap on his skin.

"It doesn't matter," she said, and believed it. Mexico, Guatemala, Haiti—hell—Antarctica. Seth wouldn't be in any of them. Neither would her father. "Just out of the country."

Wren stared at her. Seconds ticked past. Tori cleared her throat. Did the girl have a clue, or not? "Do you know anybody who can do that?" Tori finally nudged.

Wren held out a trembling hand, palm up. Grime filled the creases that cut across it.

Now Tori understood. "I'll get the cap first. Then you take me to meet the coyote."

Wren's shoulders dropped. She smiled, obviously relieved, but anxiety bit at the edges of that smile. "Can you get it now?" she asked.

"Yeah, just—look over there. Don't look at me."

Without questioning, Wren stared at a busted-up concrete block where a woman huddled over a cigarette. Tori slipped into the shadows pooled beneath a shattered streetlight and behind a heap of shredded and smoldering truck tires, disappearing just long enough to fish some cash from her shoe.

She gradually shifted closer to a young teenage boy loitering by the opposite curb. The exchange of cash for synth caps was swift, discreet, and nearly wordless.

Tori returned to Wren, showed her one palm. The cap gleamed like a yellow eye, staring from the center of Tori's hand. Wren reached for it.

Tori closed her fingers around the capsule. "No. After you find me the coyote."

Wren shuddered. Her mouth worked. "Don't know if I can wait."

"Well, you're going to have to." If she let Wren have a cap now, the girl would be a boneless, nodding heap in the gutter in five minutes.

With a jerk of one claw, Wren motioned Tori to follow. They cut through the encampment, weaving between sagging tents and huts built from trash bags spread over crates. People crowded around a single faucet spewing water from a knee-high pipe. The ground was black slime, slippery and steaming. The stink clogged Tori's mouth, made her gag.

Water and sewage flowed out the back of the encampment, like excrement from a rectum. One red vinyl tent—across the front of which someone had helpfully written the words 'Shit House'—lurked there, but from what Tori could see, people were as likely to be squatting outside the tent as in it.

Wren tugged her past the ramshackle latrine and out from beneath the overpasses. A weedy space, half as big as a football field, spread out where buildings had been razed. Chunks of concrete still littered the weeds like giant gray hailstones, with rust-gnawed vans scattered among them.

People were living in the vans. The rear doors on some of the vehicles were slung open. Blankets and dirty carpet remnants softened the interior walls and floors. Babies crawled among piles of clothes and dishes. Older kids played tag, darting behind stripped-out cars and junked washing machines.

An ancient camper with flat tires lodged at the very back of the lot. Vicious-looking wire crisscrossed the windows. Two broken concrete blocks served as stairs. Wren stood at the bottom of these steps. Her quivering arms were crossed and her gaze jerked between the camper door and the jeans pocket where Tori had stuffed the cap.

"The coyote's here?" Tori asked.

Wren nodded. Tori dug out the cap. Wren shoved a palm out, ready to receive it. Tori let the cap drop.

Wren shoved it in her mouth and swallowed. Within seconds, the muscles of her face relaxed, her shoulders loosened. "All right," she murmured. "All right."

Tori stared up at the camper door. Maybe Wren was feeling more relaxed now, but Tori's body felt like one giant muscle cramp. A headache crawled from the back of her neck up over the top of her skull.

"So, what do we do?" she said. "Just knock?"

Wren glided around to the windshield. A sheet covered it on the inside. Wren took up a heavy stick leaning against the fender and struck the stick four times against the glass. She hummed in time with the rhythm. Balancing the stick in its former position, she slipped next to Tori.

The camper door opened. Whoever opened it was invisible behind the door. The sweet, sickening stink of weed rolled over Tori. She strained to see what was inside the camper before she actually committed herself to entering, but little was visible besides a threadbare Persian carpet draped across the opposite wall and another flung over the front seats. Lamplight glowed yellow from somewhere in the camper's depths.

Wren's breath grazed hot against Tori's back. "It's all right," Wren murmured again, and leaned a cheek into the hollow between Tori's shoulderblades.

"It better be." Tori strode up the steps and through the doorway.

When she rounded its edge, a gun jammed into her side. Tori jerked away.

"Hands up against that wall," a man said. The muzzle guided Tori to a cheap particle board partition. She put her hands flat against it and stood motionless while the man patted her down from neck to ankles. A wave of the gun indicated she was to move deeper into the van. Her palms left damp prints on the partition. Behind her, Wren was being searched in the same way, then pushed forward. The guard planted himself next to the shut door.

Tori blinked in the golden light floating upwards from near her ankles. A trio of table lamps stood on the floor, encircling yet another scrappy-looking Persian carpet. Faded pillows, silky and beaded and dripping with torn fringe were heaped in the corners. An enormous joint smoked in a rhinestone-crusted ashtray.

It was like some crazy person's idea of a harem, Tori thought, staring.

In the center of it sat a woman with the clean hands and clipped nails of an accountant and the sharp bony face of a 19th century convict. A much younger man lounged beside her. He picked up the joint and touched it to his mouth, pursed his lips and blew out a long eel of smoke.

The woman didn't gesture for Tori to sit. Her gaze clicked to Wren who swayed, drifty and eyes half-closed, beside Tori. "I take it you've found a cap?" The woman's voice was as sharp as her face. She studied Tori again. "And you? Not peel, no. You're a mess, but not that kind of mess."

No sense putting things off, Tori's father had always told her. Best to be up front.

"I'm looking for a coyote," she said.

The woman's expression didn't change. "To go where?"

Tori swallowed, uncomfortable. *Make a decision. Sound like there's a place for you somewhere. For God's sake, don't sound like an Executable.*

"Guatemala," Tori answered. What the hell did she know about Guatemala? Just that a bunkie at Glynn River had grandparents who'd come from there and they'd talked about the country's beautiful birds. "Mexico would be far enough. I can go the rest of the way myself."

"What's in Guatemala?"

"A friend. And a job."

"You speak Spanish?"

"A little." You couldn't very well be in Glynn River without picking up a few words.

The woman's gaze cut across Tori's cropped hair. "You come straight out of the crib?" she asked.

Be up front. As much as you can be. "Glynn River."

The woman's axe-blade eyebrows sliced upward. "Felon."

"Yeah." Tori straightened her stance. "Slinging. That's why I can't go across the border legally."

"Are you afraid they're going to haul you back in for something else? Is that why you want to leave?"

"No. It's just . . . my family's gone." The words—not too far from a lie and maybe not a lie at all—caught in Tori's throat and her next words stumbled over them. "I don't have anybody left to stick around for." Voice about to break. Eyes hot and watery. She tightened her fists. *Christ, get a grip.* "And I'm tired of this place."

Something—understanding, maybe—passed beneath the woman's carefully stiff face. "Who the hell isn't?" She nodded and pulled out a comm, tapped at it. "Mexico. We get you past the border, that's it. It's far as we go."

Tori was surprised to realize that she felt no relief. But how did you know that the coyote was for real? That you weren't a sheep about to get fleeced and killed and dumped in a ditch?

"Fine," she answered. "When?"

The woman put up a hand. The young man lounging beside her laughed, short bursts of smoke rising from his lips to the ceiling and dispersing there like fog breaking apart. "Money first," he drawled.

Gaze still fixed on Tori, the woman ran her fingers down the young man's leg. "Yes," she said briskly, "the fee."

Tori lungs might have been encased in iron, but she nodded. "I've got it."

"With you?"

Tori shot the woman a look of disdain. "Yeah, I always carry large amounts of cash on me." Tori was suddenly, acutely aware of the way the folded squares of money in her shoe and under her bra pressed against her skin.

"But you can access it quickly," the woman said. "Cash only."

"None of that's a problem," Tori answered.

The woman paused. "Four thousand."

Tori had already counted Frank's 'donation.' That, along with the money from her father and Sam, was barely three thousand. Sweat dripped through her hair. The reek of weed made her queasy. "Two and a half."

The woman shook her head, smiling. "Save the bargaining for Guatemala. I hear they like it there."

"Two and a half," Tori insisted.

"Four."

"Are you kidding?" Tori said. "You offering some sort of warranty with that? A guarantee?"

"No guarantees in this line of business."

"Two and three quarters or screw it."

"Three and a quarter."

"All right then."

The woman started to nod.

"Screw it." Tori spun away. "And while you're at it, you ought to air this place out. It stinks worse than Glynn River."

The man who'd frisked them for weapons stepped solidly between Tori and the door. He glanced over her shoulder to where the woman sat, gestured for Tori to turn back.

"Two and three quarters," the woman said. "The van will be at Torresdale and Margaret. Tomorrow night, 10 pm."

Tori, mute, nodded and turned back to the door. Wren wafted along behind.

It was a relief to be outside, breathing in the hot, gritty air.

Wren smiled beatifically at her. "I helped you, didn't I?"

Tori gulped a deep breath, looked at Wren's hopeful face. "Yeah," she answered, wondering if she'd just struck a brilliant deal or just gotten fleeced like the saddest lamb in the world's most gullible flock. At least she had enough to cover the coyote's fee, but it sure wouldn't leave her much.

Wren stroked Tori's hand, gazed at her with soft, warm eyes like she was about to bestow an act of worship or a grand compliment on Tori.

"Hey," Wren murmured, "you got another cap?"

« CHAPTER 35 »

SETH WOKE TO THE SOUND of Tori's voice. He didn't understand the words at first, didn't even try. Her voice, quiet and earnest, was a rope he grasped at. It pulled him from blackness into pain, then into the world again.

He opened his eyes.

Sunlight burned around the window frame. Squinting, he tried to sit up. His leg felt like it was exploding. He fell back against the floor and tried to hold back a flood of nausea. Darkness spun around him. He breathed shallowly, mouth jutting open, and waited for the motion to stop.

Tori stopped speaking. Another voice replaced hers, a woman who sounded like a newscaster, her voice buffed, clean, and encouraging. She was instructing someone about an antivenom agent, about sterile packaging and syringes and the necessity of rest.

Seth coughed up phlegm that sat like coffee sludge on his tongue. He swallowed down the bitter taste.

"Tori?" he said.

The room went quiet.

"Tor?" He struggled to prop himself up. His leg throbbed and sweated like an engine. A stained t-shirt—he recognized it as his own—encircled the calf and ankle in a makeshift bandage. The exposed skin just above and below the bandage looked ominously dark.

He could remember the alley and the Hellhound and the instant its teeth sank into his calf. Everything after that was gone, wiped out of his head like none of it had ever happened, except for a single moment: Tori leaning over him, her dark gaze intent on his face.

"Tori!" His tongue was thick and rusty. Where was she? He looked around the drab room. The door and window were shut, the shade pulled. Something close to panic rose in his belly and he thrust himself onto his feet.

The floor slipped under him; the walls flew apart. His hands swung out, brushing against something cool and hard. He grabbed at it and found himself half-bent over an ancient radiator. Clinging to it, he wheezed like an old man.

He stared down at an open can of Vienna sausages near his feet. The ends of the sausages were pink and crumpled like crude belly buttons, the fluid that enveloped them oily and thick. The sight heaved his stomach.

He turned quickly away from the food, spied his comm which was also on the floor. A blinking green light indicated that it held a message. A white plastic box next to the comm was open, displaying a series of wrapped syringes.

Syringes? What the hell? The Network could barely keep the safe houses supplied with stale crackers. Medical supplies were definitely not in the picture. And these were medical, not street.

He limped to the comm and stooped to pick it up. Fire engulfed his leg. He sucked in his breath, paused. Two of the syringes were used. Four more waited. Where the hell had Tori gotten them? How many times had she left this room?

Christ, he was supposed to the one doing the protecting, not sending her out to face the likes of Sergei.

"Message one," he croaked. He licked at his lips. They were cracked, the lower lip split right down the middle, cutting the stale taste in his mouth with a bright hit of blood.

Tori's holo opened in front of him. Her face was pale, eyes hollow. She'd recorded herself in the hallway outside the room and she kept looking over her shoulder at the dark stairs to the second floor like she expected a lunatic with an axe to come screaming down them.

"I'm sorry," she said. "I'm sorry."

A cold wave struck Seth, blasting to his bones. Then the cold swept away, replaced by sopping heat. He let his head slump against his hands. He was shaking and feverish.

"I'm not going to let you get killed," Tori's image said.

Seth kept his head bowed, sweated into his hands. Agony ground up his damaged leg. Failure swamped his mind. Humiliation.

"Please don't look for me. Just keep yourself safe."

Yeah, like Avery would've let any of his E's slip away. Like Chen would've just said: *Sure, okay, you take on the killers alone and I'll just hang out in the safe house.*

Nausea surged. Seth clenched his face, his skull like hardening iron. He squeezed his eyes shut. Lights cracked against the lids.

He could smell it again, the smell of chalk and paper, metal desks. Excrement. Two skinny legs dangling, as motionless as the hot Indian summer afternoon. Sneakered feet made two grimy white ovals in mid-air, the toe of one shoe only an inch above Mr. Scicolone's desk.

And Seth, stunned and gawking, frozen at the edge of the room. A failure then. A failure now.

"Just make sure you follow the directions and take the shots," Tori said.

Seth raised his head, stared at her rueful face. Her anxious, beautiful face.

"I just wish there were some painkillers. You're going to have to tough it out." A quick, pressed smile that wasn't really a smile. "Both of us, huh?" She raised a hand in an aborted wave. The long gash she'd suffered working at Glynn River puckered across the middle of her palm.

"I'm going to miss you," she said, ducked her head, raised it again. Gaze warm like honey.

She didn't reveal where she'd secured the injections or how she'd paid for them. Her image disappeared.

"Message delete, save, reply, share?" the comm inquired.

"Shit."

The voice glided from the comm again: "You options are delete. Save. Repl—"

"Shut up!" he snapped and thumbed the device to silent.

Did Tori really think he wanted to be protected? Did she believe he was going to leave her to face Regency? Leave her at all?

He straightened—too swiftly—staggered, righted himself. He found the shirt he'd been wearing over the t-shirt air-dried and stiff, folded in a corner. She'd tried to wash it. One boot, leaning against the wall, was intact. The sole was partially torn from the other. A blood-stained sock, rinsed but still blotchy pink, flopped from the mouth of the damaged boot. The left leg of his jeans flapped around his bandaged calf, the denim ripped along one seam.

He crouched to pick up the shirt. His gun, security IDs, and false prints tumbled from inside its folds. So she didn't even have a weapon. They'd flay her alive.

He dressed slowly, resisting the urge to hurry, stopping every few seconds as fresh pain pulsed through his leg. His hands were damp and the shirt buttons slipped through his fingers. Working his injured foot into the sock and boot almost made him pass out. He tore a strip of cloth from the shirt-tail and used it to strap the sole of his left boot into place. He sagged against a wall and tried not to think about how he was going to walk farther than the door.

"Eat," he muttered.

He raised the can of sausages to his nose, twisted his head away. Then he pulled the sausages out one by one and forced the wet skin and clammy meat down his throat. As he drank the cup of water Tori had left for him, the instructional message on the box of syringes clicked on. The voice told him, again, how to administer the injections. A counter inside the lid indicated the message was set to repeat every twenty minutes. How many times had he slept through it already?

"All right, lady, all right." Unwrapping a syringe, he held the needle to his thigh and sank the plunger. He barely felt the needle's bite beneath the agony raging through his lower leg.

Rubbing a hand across his rough jaw and greasy hair, he tried to figure out where the hell Tori would have gone.

« CHAPTER 36 »

JUST AS MOM HAD SAID, the work vans were there in the morning, stationed in front of the squatters' camp. One van boasted Cygnet Corporation's black swan logo on its side. Tori recognized the swan for two reasons. She'd seen it on industrial-sized containers of solvents and cleansers at Glynn River. In fact, the one time she'd accidentally spattered a little detergent on herself, it had bored through her jumpsuit like termites through old wood.

The other reason she knew the logo was because Cygnet operated a plant just a few blocks from her dad's house, on the edge of the North Philly no-go zone. She'd grown up smelling Cygnet stink and wiping the grit of Cygnet smoke out of her eyes.

Head down and determined, she pushed her way through the gray-faced mob waiting for the van's door to open. When it did, she shoved her way up the steps, past the driver and a pair of security guards who held stunners at the ready. An ID reader glowed on a post beside the gear shift, but no one volunteered—or was forced—to swipe a wrist into its wedge of blue light.

But that laxity would surely change when they reached the plant. Good thing she didn't plan on reaching it. The last thing she needed was guards looking at her funny and asking questions.

The van weaved around cratered sections of pavement, juddered straight through the smaller potholes. No one spoke. The passengers looked limp and exhausted, their bodies jouncing every time the van hit a bump or crevice. Tori kept her head down, taking quick sideways glances at the buildings they passed, one crumbling block of rowhouses after another. Boards covered the doors at the old Lasalle University campus, closed down as long as she could remember. The windows had been boarded over as well, but many of those boards had been pried or broken off and the glass smashed. Squatters, Tori assumed.

She waited as the last of the university buildings slid past, and squalid rowhouses reappeared. When the van jerked to a full stop to avoid a stalled car, she saw her chance and flung herself into the aisle. Immediately, the guards' stunners tracked her.

"Sick!" she gasped at the driver through clenched teeth and held her gut. "I need out. Now!" She stumbled down two steps to the door, banged her palms against it. "C'mon!"

"Don't throw up in here, don't throw up!" The driver slammed a lever and the door crashed open. "I gotta work in this thing all day."

Tori leaped down to the sidewalk. She crouched there, her head bent and her face inches from the hot concrete, until she heard the door thud shut and the van lurch away.

She started walking. No need to gawk like some kind of lost tourist. This was home turf. She knew exactly where she was going, she just didn't know what she was going to find there. Her fingernails cut welts that stared out like bloody eyes from her palms. She couldn't stop herself from picturing her father's dead body curled on the kitchen floor, slumped on the living room couch, livid and bloated in the rusty bathtub.

Ten years wasn't so long in this part of town. It was shabbier and sadder than she remembered, but even in her most nostalgic memories of childhood, the place was pretty damned shabby. Weeds bearded the cracked gutters. Plastic bags flapped against the fences. The few businesses that used to dot the area were mostly gone. Signs remained, creaking above the sidewalks or dark behind busted window blinds, advertising vanished bars, a bakery, a carneceria. The health clinic was still open, and burgeoning, patients spilling in an untidy line down the front steps. The air still smelled astringent and chemical.

She turned the corner, hurried alongside the ten-foot metal fence that ran along the edge of the no-go zone. The fence extended the length of the block, crossed the adjoining intersections, and continued. Razor wire coiled like tumbleweed across its top. The rowhouses inside the evacuated area were crumbling, cars abandoned.

The biocontamination bomb exploded when she was five, set by radical leftists or radical rightists or Al Qaeda. No one ever knew for sure.

The military made everyone leave the immediate zone and installed the fence and a bunch of warning signs, but fences and razor wire hardly qualified as magic barriers. The contamination couldn't really be contained. It only killed about ten percent of the infected. The survivors staggered on, with their scarred faces and bad lungs, lucky if they managed to avoid cancer or pneumonia a few years down the road.

Tori's mom had been one of the survivors, but not for long. Cancer gnawed at her lungs, decided it was still hungry, and proceeded to chew up her brain.

All their neighbors who could leave did. Tori's dad refused. Part of the problem was money. The government was broke so there wasn't any aid if your house was outside the official boundaries of the zone, not even if you were only a block away. Insurance didn't pan out either, not with the policy's 'acts of terrorism, acts of war' clause. There was no point putting the house on the market when there was no way it would sell.

And it was the last place Tori's mother lived, the place that held the most memories of her.

Those memories, for Tori's father, were mostly good and she knew he wanted to stay there so he could hang on to them more intensely. But the strongest memory Tori had of her mother in that house was her mom hunched over at the edge of the bed coughing ferociously, each cough ending with the wet splat of mucous in a plastic cup.

She reached the alley, passed it with a long look. From this short distance, she could see that the tiny yard at the back of her father's house sweated like a jungle, luxuriant weeds glistening in the morning light. The shed's roof had collapsed. Wilderness had reclaimed the backyards of the adjacent houses and broken glass fanged the windows.

Dread was a blue flame igniting Tori's fear. Panic blazed up like paper in fire.

She rounded the corner to the street. The row of shotgun houses looked just as desolate from the front, the tiny fenced yards drowning in weeds and trash. A few more minutes, a quick look inside: that was probably all she was going to need, she realized, stomach sinking. Then she faced the long walk back to get to the corner where the coyote was supposed to be waiting. She had the better part of probably fifteen hours to make it there; she suspected she'd need all of it.

Tori loitered on the sidewalk in front of her dad's house. No boards on the windows. A couple of panes were broken out of the living room window, but that was pretty mild damage compared to the adjacent houses.

Hope slivered through her fear. Maybe, just maybe, he was still here. She glanced around, knowing that she must look furtive. If any hitters had the place staked out, they gave no obvious sign of their presence.

Insects shimmered above a waterfall of vines cascading over the chainlink fence. The gate hung from one hinge, the latch missing. Tori pushed it aside and stepped through to the yard. The air hummed and buzzed.

Gathering her nerve, Tori crossed the narrow porch and twisted the doorknob. It was locked. She put her face to the glass. The front window was surprisingly clean, but sheer green curtains—the same ones they'd had forever—obscured her view of the living room.

No lights, just a dim rectangle of a room about to be swallowed by the black mouth of the kitchen doorway behind it. The same old couch hulked against the west wall, but the bulky coffee table they'd always joked about barking their shins on was gone. No chairs, no lamps.

Fear swarmed her. Maybe he'd just sold most of the furniture. God knows he could use the money.

But she didn't believe it.

Behind her, the gate smashed open again, rushing through the weeds. Tori jolted around.

A boy, maybe ten years old, stopped just inside the yard. Two more boys about the same age stared from the sidewalk. A much younger girl dragged a filthy jump rope down the middle of the street. They all wore dirty t-shirts, faded shorts, flipflops, and—other than the girl—had faces that were much too sharp and eager for children.

Tori found herself wishing she had a weapon, then shook her head as if that could shake the thought away. But, Jesus, they were kids. You'd think they could smile or laugh or just act a little shy.

She took a couple of steps nearer to the boy at the gate. "Yeah?" she asked. "You need something?"

The boy's stare moved from point to point down her face: her eyes, nose, mouth, jaw. The intensity of his examination carried an almost physical weight.

She realized he was trying to identify her. Comparing her to a picture he'd seen. Why? Because he'd seen something on a newstream about her release? Or because somebody had hired him as a lookout?

Her throat went dry. She stepped casually closer to him. Closer to the gate.

The little girl had reached the sidewalk. She stuck one end of the jump rope down the back of her shorts, making a long tail.

Tori glanced up and down the street. Nobody else. No adults.

She cleared her throat, made her voice casual. "You live over there?" Nodding at the house directly opposite.

The boy at the gate cocked his head, his gaze never leaving her face. "You used to live here."

"No. I'm Mr. Jennings' niece." Ridiculous, the desperate sense that she had to explain her presence to a bunch of kids. She smiled. "I just stopped by to check on him."

The little girl stopped prancing, let her tail droop to the concrete. "He falled down. There." She pointed at a spot on the sidewalk just outside the gate.

Tori skin went icy. "The man who lived in this house? Are you sure?"

The girl nodded.

"When?"

The girl pushed her lips out, fish-like, and reflected. "The day before the day before today."

Tori shut her eyes. Two days? Ten years in Glynn River and she'd missed him by two days? Her eyes snapped open and she advanced on the gate. "What do you mean, he fell down?" Then she froze, paralyzed. Fell down? What if hitters had shot him? What if Tori hadn't even come here and she'd still killed him?

Motion at the corner of her eye. The boy in the yard had a comm out—one that gleamed brand-new—and was swiping his fingers across its face. He glanced up at her and the greed shining in his face told Tori all she needed to know. Terror shredded her throat.

The kid had just told the hitters where she was.

« CHAPTER 37 »

SETH SLUMPED THOUGH the security checks at the back of the apartment building where Sydney was located. He thought about the call he was about to make. His jaw tightened until it ached almost as intensely as his leg.

He'd already slipped his last few bucks to the small-timers who inhabited the edges of the Network. The exchanges had bought him lousy information. He'd been to 30th Street Station and scoured the area around what he now thought of as 'Riker's Alley,' with a foray through Hull Park that almost got him jumped. The idlers hanging around the squatters' camps in the area scattered like Seth still carried the stink of cop on his skin.

Wasted hours. And it would take hours more to hike to her dad's house, make sure she wasn't trying to hide out there. Might as well stand in a spotlight as show up at that place. No question that hitters would have that house watched. It would help if Bobby could find him a car. To be honest, he didn't think he could walk much farther today. His leg was killing him and he felt too exhausted to think straight.

He saw at once that somebody else from the Network had been inside Sydney. Water puddled on the bathroom floor. Rumpled sheets filled one corner of the bedroom. Tori? Not likely. She didn't have the security, the ID. He paused, remembering how fragile and solitary she'd looked with the ghostly light of an execution vid flickering on her upturned face.

Limping to the front room again, Seth eased himself onto a chair. Pain drove an expertly-turned knife into his ankle. "Connect 18286651449168," he said into his comm. He rubbed a hand along his scratchy jaw. "Visual off."

A moment later, Bobby's sigh gusted from the device, clipping off at the end as if he couldn't spare the time for anything more. "Okay, Seth, let me guess," he started in at once. "You need *another* car?"

"Well, yeah, I could use one."

"This is getting to be a bad habit. You're careless. You just expect—"

"It's Tori." Seth's voice dropped like a dead-weight.

In the background, Kendall worried and yipped like a terrier. "Oh, my God, they got her?" Kendall asked. "Seth? Can you put the screen on?"

Seth squared his feet against the floor. Fresh agony flamed out from the wound. The comm's tiny panel blazed into color. Bobby's face filled two thirds of it. In the space behind him, Kendall's head bobbed in and out of view, his yellow braid flopping onto one shoulder. Seth recognized the workroom at the back of Caracas.

"Jesus, you look terrible," Bobby said.

Seth ignored the appraisal. He didn't care how bad he looked or how sick he was. What he cared about was how he'd screwed up. Left Tori on her own. He squeezed his eyes shut and confessed. "Okay, here's the thing. She's gone. She ran off. I haven't found her yet."

Kendall instantly set up a droning lamentation. "Shit, that is so bad, I can't believe she'd do that. Not to you, Seth, not to—"

"Our best Guardian?" Bobby interrupted. "What *did* happen, Seth? Why would she just leave? Did you do something to set her off?"

"We—hell, we ran into some trouble two—" Seth realized he had no idea what day it was, or how much time had passed since the Riker's attack "—three days ago." Slumping, he dragged his fingers down the length of his face. Exhaustion heaved against him.

"I hope to God you didn't shoot some innocent bystander," Bobby said.

"There were grabbers. They had a Hellhound with them."

Kendall's head swiveled between Bobby and the screen. "Aww, Seth, you didn't shoot the dog, did you?"

"Actually," Seth answered, "Tori did."

Bobby's hands slammed down. "Now you're passing out firearms to our clients?"

"She did a fair job with it."

"How do you think it makes us look to people outside?" Bobby said. "I try to get people to donate, help the cause here, and they see our Guardians running around shooting off guns, as out of control as the hitters. And now the E's are popping off rounds? Yeah, that's really going to win us a ton of support." Bobby's mouth thinned until it resembled a length of fishing line sunk into the lower part of his face. "All right. The question is, what to do now?"

"And you want to know what the answer is?" Seth replied. "I'm going to keep looking for her. And you're going to pull every resource you can from our contacts to help me."

"You aren't the only Guardian protecting a client at the moment, you know. Although you *are* the only one who's inspired their client to disappear." Bobby paused. "Congratulations."

When Seth flinched, Bobby's satisfied smirk filled the screen. "Well, when you do find her," Bobby said, "I mean, if you find her, you get her out of Philly pronto. She's got no more reason to stick around."

Seth was a little slow on the uptake. Then understanding blazed. "Oh. Oh, shit."

"Yeah, her dad. Jared said it just popped up on the death index."

Kendall swam forward. "He died yesterday. Poor girl, that sucks being so clo—"

"Natural causes?" Seth interrupted.

Bobby reconquered the screen. "Unknown causes."

Seth's headache sharpened. Tori probably didn't even know yet, unless she'd already gone to her father's house.

In which case, she was probably—

He clenched his eyes shut against the pain in his head. He'd told her not to go there, not yet and not alone.

He pictured her. Alone, most definitely. Afraid. No money, no place to stay, just wanting to get it over with, find out about her dad once and for all so she could get the hell out of Pennsylvania, out of the whole godforsaken United States. And, mingled with all that emotion, the possibility that, if her father was alive, she could grip his hands, hug him, grin into his grinning face, breathe in his existence after ten years of nothing?

What would he do, Seth asked himself, if he were the E and there was any chance his mother was alive and waiting for him?

He'd go to her. In a second.

Damn it. He realized now that he should've gone to her dad's place to look for her first thing. His brain was just so murky right now. He didn't know if it was the toxins or the injection. Or maybe the injections he'd likely missed at this point.

He realized Bobby and Kendall were talking to him from the comm.

"Seth," Bobby said. "Hey, Seth!"

"You okay, man?" Kendall added.

"Off," Seth snapped. The screen and sound went dead. The comm buzzed almost immediately: Bobby trying to reconnect.

Seth ignored it.

∞

"He's not going to pick up." Bobby stuffed the comm in his pocket. "Looks like he's in some real trouble. It killed him to admit it."

"Yeah, he looked kind of funny." Kendall reached down to pick at a ragged toenail. His toes extended a quarter inch past the end of each well-worn sandal.

"If by 'funny,' you mean 'terrible'." Bobby's eyes turned heavenward. "Well, he probably doesn't want any help, but if he needs it, he needs it. I'm not going to let Tori Jennings slip through the cracks because Seth—well, did whatever he did that made her ditch him. And I'm sick of his guns." Bobby thrust his chair back from the table. "You need to pack anything?"

Kendall lowered his foot to the floor. "Pack?"

"Just let me tell Jared what's up and we'll get out of here." Bobby grabbed some mem-cubes on his way out of the office.

"Where are we going?" Kendall called after him.

Bobby's footsteps thudded down the stairs to the Listening Post. His answer echoed from the walls: "Philly."

« CHAPTER 38 »

PAIGE ARRIVED AT the University of Pennsylvania building that housed Kayla Simmons' office a little before three in the afternoon. She flashed her chip under the reader at the front desk while the guard checked the appointments log. He grunted and nodded her through the lobby. One elevator bore an 'out of order' sign; the other, supposedly functional, failed to arrive.

She took the stairs which were grimy and dim, every other lightbulb missing. Paige couldn't keep her gaze from flitting ahead, then behind her. She disliked dark stairways.

The door to Dr. Simmons' office was wedged open with a long-outdated *Physicians' Guide to Pharmacology.* Memos and printouts of assorted sizes, taped to the back of the door, fluttered in the breeze of an oscillating fan.

Paige took one step into the office. The fan ground noisily back and forth. The woman sitting at the desk with her back to the doorway obviously heard nothing. Good thing Simmons wasn't an E. She'd be dead on the floor right now.

"Dr. Simmons?"

The woman jerked, whipped around in her chair.

"Paige Connor," Paige said. "We have an appointment?"

Simmons stared at her. "I only have a few minutes."

Seconds passed. Paige didn't move.

Dr. Simmons flushed. She pushed back the hairs that had pulled loose from her tortoiseshell barrette. "I'm sorry," she said and gave Paige a chagrined smile. "My experience talking to reporters has been pretty limited, but it's never been exactly what you'd call wonderful." She gestured at a second chair. "Please."

The chair, an old wooden one, wobbled beneath Paige. "I really don't consider myself a reporter."

"But you write books? That's what you said in your message."

"I'd call myself a researcher. I've never worked in the news media, journalism, any of that."

Dr. Simmons closed her eyes briefly and leaned into the breeze from the fan. It rippled the red paisley blouse she wore. "All right, then." She rubbed at her temples with both hands. "Your book. You said in your message that it's about the Cameron incident?"

"That's going to be a section." Paige leaned closer. "It was a fascinating case."

"Was it?"

Paige made her smile warm, a touch rueful. "I suppose you develop a different perspective when you're actually involved."

"*Involved* is a bit of an overstatement."

"You testified—"

"Not at the trial. I talked to the girl's—what was her name?"

"Jennings," Paige prompted.

"I talked to her lawyer. Very briefly. It was . . . oh, I don't remember what he called it. Fact-finding consultation. Something like that."

"And he never called you to testify at the trial?"

Dr. Simmons sagged in her chair. "He never contacted me again."

"Did you think Jennings would be convicted?"

"Given the M.E.'s report? And who the victim was? Absolutely." Simmons' eyes turned distant. "But I'd done what I could." The muscles in her face strained and she pressed forward. "Defending her was the lawyer's job, not mine. If he didn't want to listen to what I had to say . . ." She spread her arms. "My work takes too much concentration. And I'd had some health problems at the time. I decided I couldn't be a crusader anymore."

"Anymore?" Paige cocked her head to one side.

"I used to help out with Clear Conscience. I don't know if you remember them. They investigated some of the shoddier Executables cases back in the beginning. Hopeless, of course."

Paige squinted off to one side like she was trying to remember something. "It morphed into the Guardian Network, didn't it?"

"Eventually. When it became clear that there was no fighting the verdicts. That girl—Jennings—that was the last Clear Conscience project I was involved with. And like I said, even that was minimal."

Paige warmed her smile several more degrees. "So there must not have been any solid evidence that Jennings was innocent."

Dr. Simmons tugged at a single thread hanging from her shirt cuff. She looked directly at Paige. "It'll make a chapter of your book either way."

Paige ducked her head, blushed like she'd been found out. "I know it sounds crass, but frankly, if she's innocent, it makes a better hook." Paige leaned close, her voice intense. "That doesn't mean I don't care about seeing justice come through in the end. I'm spending a lot of time studying the cases I'm planning to use. It's not like I can just drop it after I've written my piece and never think about the people again."

Dr. Simmons' mouth softened. "No. No, of course not."

Paige decided to try surprise. "Did you know that Tori Jennings has been released?"

The doctor fidgeted, tugging her shirt collar away from her throat. Pushing herself up from the chair, she wandered to the single, dirt-streaked window. She touched the leaves of a fern hanging in the murky sunlight. "Has it been that long?" she said. "Was she—what happened to her?"

"She made it past the hitters and some third-rate grabbers on the scene. She's alive, for now. At least, that's what my sources indicate."

The doctor picked up a plastic water bottle from the windowsill and sprayed the fern's wilted leaves. "Spoken like a true journalist."

"Sorry about that." Paige waited a moment. "You thought it might be SE Syndrome that killed the little boy."

"SE?" The doctor looked puzzled. "Oh. You mean, DSE." Simmons returned to her desk. "DSE seemed like a possibility. The symptoms were consistent with either interpretation." She ticked them off on her fingers. "Vomiting, lethargy, failure to thrive, underweight, a build-up of acids in the body. Impaired respiration."

"Did you do any genetic testing?"

"I wasn't invited to. The test at that time was hardly conclusive anyway. DSE was a new disorder, one of the mutations that we saw after the first dirty bombs. Rare then and rare now."

"So the test's improved?" Paige said. "Could you run it now?"

"If the police had samples. If they stored them adequately. I'd have my doubts about that."

Sitting back, Paige reflected on this. "Is there a cure?"

"No. But it can be managed with quite a bit of effort on the part of the parents."

Paige thought of the Camerons' young daughter. "Would it be passed on to more than one child in the family?"

"A lot of the 'dirty' permutations still aren't thoroughly understood." The doctor pressed her fingertips together, raised them to her lips. "There's no question with DSE that seemingly healthy parents can pass it to their children, but there's still a certain amount of mystery. Not every child they have will necessarily suffer from the syndrome."

Paige met her eyes with a clear and steady gaze. "My understanding is that Scott and Kelly Cameron have another child. A girl, Emily. An infant."

The doctor's hands concealed her mouth, but not her dismay. "Do you know how old the child is? Specifically."

Fifty-two days to be precise. Paige said, "Very young. I think the pediatrician works out of Penn."

Simmons hesitated. "I'm only checking this for the child's sake." She tapped several times at the screen in her desk. The expression on her face changed from curiosity to concern to worry. "Not quite two months."

Paige didn't allow herself to sound eager. "Anything unusual in the history?"

Dr. Simmons shook her head. "This is all confidential. I shouldn't even be looking at it. I'm not the attending physician."

"But she's been sick?"

The doctor's silence served as an affirmation. "May thirteenth, failure to thrive," she finally muttered. "June second, lethargy. June fourteenth, vomiting. Diarrhea." She shook her head again. "They pumped her full of antibiotics, hydrated her intravenously, prescribed an expensive formula."

"No tests?"

"Quite a number. But not for DSE." She jigged a pen between her right thumb and forefinger. "She *should* be tested. I wonder if her parents have any idea . . ." The pen stopped.

"Dr. Simmons, did you think Tori Jennings was innocent?" Paige already knew how the woman would answer.

The doctor rubbed her temples again. "I suspected . . ." She broke off, regrouped, met Paige's eyes. "I did think there was a good chance of it. Yes."

"What about the ethylene glycol in Robbie's blood?"

"DSE elevates certain compounds in the serum. There's one compound in particular that I could imagine a technician, especially with

239

the equipment and tests they had back then, mistaking for ethylene glycol. And the sterilization process for the equipment they used to take the samples in the first place could explain trace readings."

"And the crystals in his brain?" Paige asked, genuinely curious. Bannock's report had played up that crystallization.

"Not just the brain. The crystallization—calcium oxalate—appeared in other organs too."

"Could something besides antifreeze cause that?"

Dr. Simmons leaned her head back and contemplated the ceiling tiles. "If they thought she'd poisoned the baby with antifreeze, they might have tried to treat it with ethanol. A drip. That could have had a crystallizing effect." Simmons laid the pen carefully on the desk. "I don't have contacts at the police department. I'd need to submit a formal request to reopen the case. Which you know they won't do."

"What about testing the daughter? Emily? If *she* comes up positive . . ."

"She *should* be tested," the doctor repeated. "But what about the parents?" She sank back. "I saw them after I came out of my interview with Jennings' lawyer. They said some pretty terrible things to me. Equated me with a murderer, for starters. In their minds it was antifreeze poisoning. Case closed. They aren't going to want to hear from me."

The fan hummed in the quiet. "What about the grandmother?" Paige asked. "The senator?" She remembered something Merle Edgers had said about Senator Logan: that it had taken forever to get her to sign the paperwork for the hit. Almost as if the senator had a conscience. Or doubts.

"We need parental consent," Simmons insisted.

"What if we don't worry too much about the formalities?"

Simmons let out a gust of nervous laughter and shook her head. Opening a drawer, she pulled out a stack of rubber-banded papers. "Look, I really have a lot of work to do." Falling silent, she dropped the papers onto the desk and watched as a loose sheet swirled ceilingward in the fan's breeze. "Do you really think Tori Jennings is even alive?" she asked.

Paige thought of Edgers again, this time with disdain . . . sending those cretins Whelk and Sergei on the job. How many innocents would Paige have killed if she'd just accepted his assurances that the E's were always guilty? Edgers would have made a murderer of her. Multiple times, most likely.

"She's already been out for four days," Paige said. "That's longer than 99% make it if they have an execution company on their tail. She's pushing her luck. If we're going to move out, we have to do it *now*."

Mouth pursed with curiosity, Dr. Simmons scrutinized her. "Move out? Were you in the military?"

Paige gave her a smooth smile that revealed nothing. "Confidential," she said, exaggerating the word, turning it into a joke.

Simmons' scrutiny intensified, then she made her decision. "We'll try the parents first," she said. "Although we can't tell them I was rooting around in their family's medical records." She glanced up at Paige. "So. Who gets the privilege of talking to them?"

Paige pushed the comm across the desk. "You're the doctor. And doctors always get more respect than writers. Don't you think?"

« CHAPTER 39 »

EVEN BEFORE the van appeared, Tori knew the hitters were coming for her.

It didn't take them long.

She'd got a small head start on the kids, took off down the street while the one boy was still on his comm, no doubt reporting her to Regency's squad. She sprinted. A vicious sidestitch clutched her left ribs. Over the pounding of her footsteps on concrete and the regular explosions of her heart, she heard the boys behind her, the slap of their sneakers and their excited, childish voices.

She cut down half a dozen alleys, hooked a right onto the street. She stopped, bent forward. Air smashed in and out of her lungs. The cramp in her side tightened itself into a screaming knot.

Her gaze fretted from one battered old rowhouse to the next. The buildings pressed together, side-by-side, no space between them. No dark wedge a person could slip into like a mouse to hide. Across the street from the rowhouses, the no-go-zone's high fence and razor wire loomed.

The boys' shouts echoed from the alley. They were too damn close. Probably had the commvid going, sharing everything they saw with the hitters. And they were about to see Tori.

She bolted for the fence, searched the metal with frantic hands. There'd been a way through this section years ago, she was sure of it. She'd gone through it once, on a dare, although she'd barely penetrated the zone itself which was sizeable, four or five square miles, at least.

A girl she'd known who'd lived above the laundromat had gone in on a dare too, and had never come back. After that, most of the kids left the place alone even long after the military guard had pulled up stakes.

A clipped wire cut her finger. She slipped sideways through a gash in the fence and darted deeper into the zone. Ducking behind a crumbling brick wall, she inched herself higher until she could peer over the top.

A white van appeared from around the corner. It nosed slowly half a block and drew to the curb. The front doors of the van swung wide. A man with a thick, powerful build thrust himself onto the street.

Tori recognized Sergei from the photographs in the binder at Bobby and Kendall's place. A particularly vicious-looking rifle extended from Sergei's right hand, grotesquely elongating that arm. He paced the sidewalk, throwing his body into each step. He tilted his head back as he scrutinized the buildings and studied the hazard signs bolted to the no-go zone's fence.

Another minute and the boys came drumming out of the closest alley. They stopped and fell silent when the rifle swung their direction. The barrel looped the air, urging the boys nearer.

They came forward, clustering around the boy with the comm, growing bolder when Sergei love-tapped them with his gigantic grin. He bent down to their height, flung his free hand around as he talked to them. At one point, he jabbed a finger at the zone. The boy with the comm shrugged.

Sergei said something more, pointed again.

The boy spoke, shrugged one more time.

Sergei slapped him. The hitter's palm cracked against the boy's cheek with such vicious speed that, in her hiding place, Tori flinched.

Sergei retreated to the van. The rifle snouted out from the still-open door, tracking back and forth along the fence. Tori sweated behind the wall. Maybe he didn't know for certain where she'd gone, but he seemed damned suspicious of the zone. A minute passed, then another.

The boys huddled in the middle of the street. Fear strained their faces, making them all look the same: drawn foreheads, open mouths, caved-in shoulders, searching eyes.

They stood there until, from the van's window, Sergei's rifle lowered on them. The barrel nudged in the direction of the zone. The boys hesitated. Sergei aimed the rifle just above their heads. He pulled off a shot.

The boys skidded to the fence and poured themselves, one after another, through the gash in the wire.

"Shit," Tori muttered. Her pulse threatened to lacerate her arteries.

The van crouched where it was, like a dangerous animal ready to spring, until the boys were through the fence. Tori's last glimpse of the vehicle, before she slunk down behind the wall and edged away, was the van grinding down the street again. Sergei, she realized, was going to patrol the area immediately around her dad's house. The boys were going to be his little snitches again, reporting back if they found her in the zone.

And God only knew how many more spies and goons Sergei was—right this second—ordering to haul ass to this part of town. Spread out the net.

Tori hunkered behind a row of rusting dumpsters for a minute. The kids were being quiet now which wasn't good. She liked it a lot better when they were whooping and laughing and she could pinpoint where they were and how far away.

She angled off into a second alley. The broken-down buildings lining it obliterated all view of the fence, of Sergei's van, of the outside world. Her throat ached for water. Sweat simmered from her neck and back.

Tori tilted her head back and squinted past the jagged roofs jutting along the abandoned street. The sky had a flat, implacably blue cast that promised nothing but more unbearable heat. Her shoes rubbed through her damp socks, raising blisters at the back of each heel.

Tears scraped across her eyes. She believed what that little girl with the jump rope had said about Dad. Jesus, what had it been? Heart attack? Stroke? If he hadn't fallen dead on the spot, the public hospital would almost certainly have finished the job. Anyway, he was almost 70 years old. A disposable age. Nobody was likely to make much of an effort to bring him around.

Her nose was running. She gave it a vicious swipe with the back of her hand, then gave the same to each eye. She couldn't think about this. Now yet.

She picked her way around a smashed dresser and charred rectangles on the cement where someone had torched the drawers. A refrigerator lay toppled on its back; wire snared the handle like a cheap bracelet on a bony wrist. The windows of all the buildings looked ruptured, exploded, leaving only an occasional long tooth of glass dangling from the otherwise empty frame. The air smelled like burlap soaked in a harsh cleaning detergent.

Nothing looked familiar from her one teenaged foray the place.

There had to be other makeshift exits through the perimeter fence. She just didn't know where they were. First thing, was to put some distance between herself and the boys, distance between herself and the streets where Sergei roamed in his van.

Then she could follow the fence until she found a way out. She could even climb the damn thing if there was a spot where the razor wire at the top was missing.

She trudged along the street. Her blisters sang raw against her shoes. Shells of sap vials crunched underfoot. Along one stoop, rusted hypodermic needles lay scattered like bloody teeth extracted from a robot. Tori glanced inside the doorway at the top of the steps and saw, at the back, a person huddled against the wall. The squatter hunched, wrapped in an olive-drab army blanket that concealed any indication of age or sex. The sight of the blanket just made Tori sweat harder.

A dog limped out of a doorway and watched Tori with yellow eyes. A growl vibrated through the silent heat. When Tori didn't move, the dog sidled along close to the buildings, its filthy fur brushing against the cheap, false-front brick facing. Its dugs swung like half-a-dozen sacks strapped around its belly.

Tori pushed herself into motion again. If there were people and animals alive in this place, then there had to be water somewhere. Her head swiveled, her eyes searching.

Someone screamed.

Tori froze, mid-step.

Not someone. A child. A boy, she thought.

The buildings exhaled, were silent. Then the screams sang out again from somewhere behind her.

Not her problem. *Not* her problem.

She pushed her legs into motion, ground out half a dozen steps as if it were a mile. Then, swearing at herself, she stopped, spun around and headed back the way she'd come.

« CHAPTER 40 »

"I THOUGHT you'd be happy," Wren said and snuggled harder against Owen. They sat on a splintery bench in Hull Park. Not doing a damn thing. "You can do your grab. We'll make enough to buy a whole suitcase of caps, huh?"

"You saw her?" Owen spoke with difficulty. The hollows of his cheeks quivered. His gaze meandered away, his eyes out of focus.

"I told you. I took her to Mom's tent. Tori's gonna be there again tonight."

"Tori? You her friend, or something?"

Wren's own vision blurred. She held herself still, fighting the panic that sizzled her blood. A hot wave of nausea made her whole body tremble.

Owen had more stash. She knew it. "I just need one cap for now," she said. "Just one, sweetie. So I can think straight."

"You never think straight," he said. But he was wrong.

Wren was proud of the plan she'd come up with. Tell Owen that Tori was going to be at Mom's tonight when she was really going to be meeting the coyote. Wren wouldn't play Judas, but Owen didn't have to know that. Tori was one of the only people who'd ever looked at Wren like she was more than shit. Tori would be safe from the grabbers, and Owen would be so happy that Wren could give him information about Tori that he'd reward her—right now—with a cap from his stash. Maybe even two.

Except that he hadn't given her anything. Yet.

And something fierce and dark waited at the end of her plan. After the grabbers showed at Mom's tent and Tori never did appear: What would Owen do then?

She'd tell him—well, something. Worry about that when it happened. Right now, she needed the cap.

She blinked until Owen's features slid into focus, clutched his arm. His skin was as damp as her own, his head quivering. She recognized the desperate need that swarmed like ravenous beetles just beneath his skin. It matched her own. Peel. The cap from Tori was long gone and Wren couldn't hold out much longer. She'd gone an entire day without it once, but that had almost killed her.

She crawled onto Owen's lap. "We're gonna have plenty. You can get a lot of money for her," she coaxed.

Owen twisted beneath her. "We gotta get things together. Get ready."

Wren saw her chance. "It's gonna be so good. Aren't you so glad I found her for us? But right now, sweetie, I just need a little advance, one little—"

Owen jangled onto his feet, the sudden movement crashing Wren down onto cement. Her knees struck hard. She gazed without interest at the abrasions and oozing blood. She felt nothing except the hunger splintering her veins. Peel: now.

"After we've got the E," Owen said. "After we've got the money for the E." He scrabbled in one of his pockets and came trembling out with a single peel-cap. Wren stared at the capsule, scarlet and shiny as a well-waxed sportscar. She swallowed, imagining the slickness of the coating as the capsule glided to the back of her throat, and then the spreading calm, a plush warmth expanding through her body, stripping her skin, opening her nerves to the sunlight.

Her hand trembled toward it. Owen shoved her away, harder than before. "This one's mine," he said.

"I need it. Owen." Her words emerged as a thin mewling.

"After we've got the payoff. Until then, baby, kindly fuck off." Owen tongued the capsule. His head slung back; his eyes almost closed. His left hand glided with the easy bliss of a hawk riding an updraft.

Wren shook so hard she barely stayed on her feet . "No. Fuck *you*, Owen. Fuck *you*." His eyes were silver slits, crocodilian, barely shifting as she staggered past.

He used to say he loved her! Used to say he'd marry her, as soon as they got a little money together. He never said shit anymore. Tori had a guardian who'd die for her. And what did Wren have?

She emptied her guts against a wall. The stink of vomit mingled with the smell of the hot bricks. One cap would make the nausea go away. One cap would make everything okay.

She remembered the sleek cap those two men, the hitters, had given her at the garbage dump, how it had dissolved on her tongue like cream and sugar. More where that came from, they'd promised.

She could feed the hitters some lies, maybe even the same story she'd fed Owen, the same lie about Tori returning to Mom's tent tonight.

And let them feed her some caps.

At first she thought she'd lost the card with their contact number and her hand shook harder than ever, her fingers fumbling in her pockets. When she finally pulled the card free, bits of gluey lint came with it, darkening her already grimy nails until they looked like the claws of some nocturnal beast.

She staggered out of the park. She'd find a friend—well, find somebody she knew, anybody with a comm—call the hitters, get enough caps to carry her for days. Hell, weeks.

And meet up with Tori at the coyote's van tonight. No grabbers, no hitters, just Wren, alone, to say goodbye.

If the hitters paid cash as well as caps, then maybe she'd even get in the van with Tori. Run clean away, forever and ever. Be with a real friend for a change.

It was a thought so warm, so soothing, that she forgot her hunger for peel. For about five seconds.

« CHAPTER 41 »

THE GUARDS AT the entrance to the secured neighborhood where Senator Logan lived ran a level-three security scan on both Dr. Simmons and Paige before allowing them through the electrified main gate. The entrance looked like it had been lifted from an old English estate: gray stone walls, cascading red and pink roses, a massive and elaborately wrought black gate. Even the guards' shelter might have doubled as a porter's or gamekeeper's lodge.

Paige drove along neighborhood streets that curved cool and dark through the shade of enormous oaks and maples. In the passenger seat, Dr. Simmons studied her comm and made an occasional comment about the current state of DSE research.

"This is the one," Paige remarked, pulling into the circular drive of a large house every bit as elegant and English as the front gates. A home oil delivery truck was already parked near the house. All the rich people had powerful home generators for backup during the brownouts and blackouts that happened frequently, especially during the summer. Paige thought of the generator in the basement of her own house. Satisfaction warmed her. She'd done all right for a foster kid. More than all right.

Dr. Simmons let out a nervous laugh and tucked her comm in her briefcase. "I'm amazed she's willing to talk to us at all. I really butchered that call to her daughter."

Paige shut off the engine, leaving the windows cracked in the heat. Birds whistled from the oaks congregating on the front lawn. "Don't be hard on yourself. I think we both had a pretty good idea how Robbie's mom would react."

"Still. You'd think a mother would be more concerned about her child—her living child— than about getting revenge."

"Justice, I suppose she'd called it," Paige answered. "Not revenge."

"Still."

"So we do what we have to do."

Dr. Simmons turned to stare at Paige. "We don't *have* to do anything. Actually."

Paige kept silent. Even in the shade, the car was already getting hot. Perspiration pricked at her back and she unstuck herself from the seat.

Dr. Simmons frowned at the windshield. "The senator isn't the child's legal guardian," she fretted. "I'd never be able to justify it to the board, you know. None of this. And honestly, I can't imagine the senator's going to listen to us, any more than her daughter." Her glance flicked sideways at Paige. "Although maybe she'll be able to refrain from calling me a monster and a shill for Jennings. Maybe."

Paige swung her door open, but didn't make a move to climb out. Finally, she observed, "Emily could die, just like the other one."

Simmons hesitated. Then she shoved her own door wide, picked up her briefcase, and slid out.

They advanced in silence to the front door. The polished black surface reflected their faces back at them as they waited for someone to answer the bell. Paige looked smoothly confident, expression calm, sleek hair tucked behind her ears. Dr. Simmons' hair frizzed out from the tortoiseshell clip and a red spaghetti stain marked her shirt just below the collar, but she looked far calmer than Paige expected. The doctor looked determined to see this through.

The door opened. The woman behind it was small and Spanish, with a crown of coiled black hair as large as her head.

Paige deferred to Dr. Simmons who leaned forward and said, "Dr. Kayla Simmons and Paige Connor. We have an appointment with the Senator."

The woman nodded and, a moment later, they were crossing the foyer's cool floor, the gray marble streaked with white like thin ridges of frost. The women stepped through a pair of French doors that opened onto a study.

"Please." The housekeeper gestured the visitors onto a cherry-wood settee upholstered with pale blue velvet. She pulled back the heavy draperies drawn, Paige presumed, to protect the antique furnishings from sunlight. "Please, you wait," the housekeeper said before withdrawing into the foyer. "Senator Logan come soon. I bring coffee."

Paige had barely set her bag on the Persian rug and crossed her legs before heels tapped across the marble foyer and the door opened again. Senator Logan did not pause as she entered the room; she advanced on the settee, halted directly before Paige and Dr. Simmons, and said, "Which one of you called my daughter earlier today? She was very upset. Distraught."

The senator's hair was an apricot confection, sprayed hard as fondant. She was whip-thin and square-shouldered in a boxy raspberry suit, her face scribbled over with fine wrinkles.

Simmons shifted uncomfortably on the stone-hard cushion. "I'm Dr. Kayla Simmons. I did talk to your daughter, but only—"

The senator wagged a finger. "Wait. You're not a pediatrician?"

Simmons sat up straighter. "I never said I was. But I am a doctor and my research concerns genetic diseases that manifest themselves in the neonatal population. I've focused on just a couple of these diseases, but there's one in particular I'd hoped to discuss with your daughter. The symptoms may interest you. Lethargy. Bouts of vomiting, diarrhea. Dehydration. Fevers that are never really explained."

Senator Logan became very still. She frowned at her spidery hands and turned the heavy diamond ring on her wedding finger slightly, repositioning it. Then she let out her breath. "If you're wanting to discuss funding issues, you'll need to make an appointment with my office. Although I have to warn you, it's very unlikely in this budget climate."

Paige uncrossed her legs. "Actually," she said, "we were hoping to talk with you about Emily."

The senator raised her head sharply at the name. She looked wary. "My granddaughter?"

"Yes. And Robert," Dr. Simmons added. Paige tried not to wince, watching the senator's face harden at the mention of her long-dead grandson. "It's important, or we wouldn't have troubled you. Or your daughter."

"Important to whom?" Senator Logan asked. "Tori Jennings?"

Paige touched Dr. Simmons' arm. The doctor slid her a puzzled look. Paige rose and said, "Important for Emily. More important for her than you can imagine."

The senator regarded Paige with cool eyes, her jaw frozen. For just an instant, Paige might have been a skinny, scraped-knee foster kid again. She prodded herself out of those feelings of desolate inferiority by letting her thoughts touch on her comfortable house, the attractive furnishings, the investments. And, yes, the generator that she owned . . . just like all the rich people in this neighborhood.

Paige smoothed her voice and met Senator Logan's eyes. "Emily's been sick, hasn't she?"

The senator stared back as if riveted in place, one bony hand hovering at her throat. She didn't look nearly so certain of herself anymore. The air of superiority and outrage dropped from her like a cloak falling to the floor.

Paige quieted her voice and intensified her look of compassion, a compassion she was surprised to find herself actually feeling for this woman. One grandkid dead, another seemingly on its way out...bad times, no matter how rich or important you were.

Simmons sat forward. "Senator, I'm not the child's doctor, but I have reason to understand that she's had any number of medical difficulties already. Complications that may seem small at times, may seem unrelated, but probably aren't."

The senator closed her eyes and gripped the armrest of the chair behind her as if she felt dizzy.

"You know there's something wrong," Paige insisted.

Senator Logan raised her chin. "My granddaughter is in the care of the finest pediatrician in the city."

Someone tapped at the door from the foyer. The housekeeper, balancing a tray of china cups and a silver coffee pot, peered into the drawing room.

"Not now, Elaina," the senator snapped, waving one hand dismissively. Then her face sagged, and her shoulders, and she added, "I'm sorry, Elaina. We're just . . . we're in the middle of something."

The housekeeper silently withdrew.

Paige picked up the thread. "And what has the finest pediatrician told you? Not to worry? Emily's going to be fine?"

Dr. Simmons added, "And you don't believe them."

"Of course I—what makes you think—?" The senator's indignation dissipated as quickly as it had flared. She looked down at her hands. Her fingers pushed together, forming an acute steeple. "I'm not sure what I think, if you want me to be perfectly frank." She raised her eyes. "There. Are you happy now?"

Dr. Simmons touched the woman's wrist. There was no mistaking the physician's sincerity or her concern. "I'd like to test Emily for DSE Syndrome."

"I've never heard of it."

"It's rare," Dr. Simmons replied. "Extremely rare."

"And it's genetic?"

Dr. Simmons nodded and gently withdrew her hand. "It's an autosomal recessive trait, but it's very likely that neither you nor your husband—"

"Ex-husband."

"—are carriers, or your son-in-law's parents for that matter. DSE didn't exist until after the first dirty bombs. It's one of the whole crop of new congenital defects that sprang up afterward. Your daughter—Kelly?— grew up in the Philadelphia area? And her husband?"

"New York," the senator answered.

Paige's comm vibrated against her hip. Probably Mike, wondering when she was going to wrap things up so they could meet up for the salmon and asparagus he'd promised to grill for her that afternoon. She knew he still thought she was a little crazy—"touched," was how he put it, teasing her—wasting all this time on something that wasn't going to bring in so much as a dollar. *But I guess that's one of those quirks I kind of like about you, Eisen*, he'd told her last time they'd talked.

The comm stopped twitching in her pocket and Paige hauled her attention back to the exchange continuing in front of her.

Dr. Simmons was tapping her fingertips together in front of her lips. "Philadelphia. New York. No matter what precautions were taken, it's certainly possible that Kelly and Scott were exposed to mutating agents years ago. Maybe even in the womb. I'm afraid there are still a lot of dark spaces in our knowledge of DSE. Of all these mutations."

Senator Logan's fear was obvious now, in her bloodless face and the desperate stare she fixed on Simmons. "And what about Emily?"

"Your granddaughter's clinical presentation, as I understand it, correlates with the expected symptoms. Asymptomatic at birth and for a period of two or three weeks thereafter. Correct? Then the symptoms I mentioned before. The lethargy, the GI issues, random fevers. I'm afraid that if it is DSE and Emily receives no treatment, the next stages will be a lot more serious."

The senator finally broke her gaze away. She stepped to one of the built-in bookcases and ran her hand across a row of leather spines. Paige kept her face smooth. Seriously, did this lady think the shelves of fancy leather books impressed anyone?

"What do you mean, serious?" Senator Logan asked.

"Respiratory distress. Hypotonia. Hepatomegaly. Seizures. Coma."

"There's something else," Paige interjected before Senator Logan could respond to the doctor's litany of misery. "Dr. Simmons' research shows that your grandson's symptoms were the same. Entirely consistent with DSE."

The senator's gaze flickered between the two women. "So this *is* about Tori Jennings."

"Only tangentially," Dr. Simmons reassured her. "Our primary concern is the child who can still be saved. Certainly, the existence of correlative symptoms in two siblings greatly increases the odds that there's a genetic disorder at work here." The doctor stepped toward the bookcase—and the senator. Paige held back, sensing that Dr. Simmons was the one Logan trusted. Sunlight glinted off the volumes' gilt lettering in blinding shots of gold. The smell of burnished leather rolled from the shelves.

"For the child's sake, Senator," Dr. Simmons said. "Please allow us to run tests."

The senator barely hesitated. "Where would you run them?"

"Well, the top labs will do the specific chromosomal markups that should give us a definitive answer. But that takes time. DSE makes very subtle rearrangements involving information on up to nine different chromosomes. It's not an easy diagnosis to make. I'm not surprised if your pediatrician missed it."

The senator stared into the distance. Paige could guess what she saw: convulsions, coma, a tiny coffin. "I don't want to wait," Senator Logan said and raised a hand involuntarily to her mouth. Her lips twitched and her hand was unsteady.

They had her. Paige stayed silent, careful not to interfere, not to give Logan any reason to suspect this was as much about Jennings as it was about the baby.

"We can run a quicker test at MyrexLab," Simmons told her. "It's only a 45 minute drive from here. The results aren't as definitive, but sufficient for a preliminary diagnosis."

"Is it painful? The testing?"

Simmons gave her a reassuring smile. "We'll just have to take a blood sample. Very simple."

"And we'll know—today?"

"That's right. It'll take a couple of hours, but that can't be helped. With DSE, there are deficiencies in specific enzymatic activities. The lab can test Emily's blood for those enzymes. If they're not present, or only found in a very low concentration, we'll be able to make a pretty good guess about what's going on. They can also check for the buildup of compounds that normal enzymes would be able to break down." Simmons touched the senator's shoulder. "And then we can do something to help her."

Senator Logan nodded and led them to the foyer. "MyrexLabs," she said, keeping her voice hushed. "My daughter was so upset about your call that she had to get out of the house. Emily's at home with the nanny. It's nearby. I'll get the child and meet you at the lab."

She led them outside. A mingled scent of cut-grass and roses simmered above the front steps. "My driver is also a bodyguard," she added, her voice a warning. Letting them know she wasn't an easy mark, in case that's what they were thinking. "Licensed to carry arms. Trained to use lethal force."

Paige forced herself not to smile at that.

"And I will have to run your credentials again."

"Oh, absolutely," Dr. Simmons assured her. "I understand."

"So I'll be a little behind you."

The senator stayed there, just outside the door, watching them as they followed the stone path to the drive. Paige and Simmons climbed into the car. Before Paige flicked the car into motion, she glanced back at the house. The black door gleamed. The roses swelled and tumbled.

The senator was gone.

"You got her," Paige told Dr. Simmons with admiration and a little envy. It seemed so pleasant, how the doctor could just be herself, say what she really thought, not worry about what emotion her face might be projecting. No masks. No hiding anything. Just freedom. And she'd still achieved her objective.

"Well, we'll see," Simmons answered, smiling and poking at some papers in her briefcase. "I hope she turns up. With Emily. The bodyguard, lethal force I could do without."

Paige pondered this. "Yeah. Me too." In her pocket, the comm vibrated. She started to reach for it, stopped herself. She'd call Mike back later.

She wheeled the car under the archway of branches that covered the street. "Me too," she murmured again, and wondered if she was going soft.

« CHAPTER 42 »

AFTER ENCOUNTERING the locks at the back of the apartment building, Sergei sent Murray trotting back to the car.

"Stupid bitch forgot the security," Murray told Slater who twitched a stylus above a crossword on the dashboard screen. Murray leaned in across the back seat where Wren, the Guardian Network's very own stool pigeon, practically floated above the upholstery.

Murray had only given her one cap in exchange for the location of the safehouse she'd called Sydney. She swore she'd seen Jennings there early that morning. Damned if the scrawny bitch hadn't dry-swallowed the cap about a millisecond after it dropped into her hand. Now she was drifting in a peel-fog and was about as useless as a one-legged dog.

"C'mon!" he ordered. When Wren didn't move, he shoved her hard. "You better look for it," he added. "Now. Lock code. Keycard. Fingerprint."

Slater glanced up from his crossword. "Good luck with that." He smirked and returned to the puzzle. Slater always drew the easy jobs, that smug bastard.

Wren still didn't respond. Murray jammed his hand into each of her pockets, bringing up the false fingerpad and the keycard immediately. The lock codes were scribbled on a scrap of paper that he dragged from a cargo pocket just above her knee. "First floor, last door on the left," he said. "Right?" Wren grinned vacantly at the seatback in front of her.

"Freak." Murray slammed the door.

Just outside the building, Sergei took control of the items. He worked the fingerprint against the reader. For a moment, nothing happened. "Come on," Sergei crooned. When the green light glowed, he tossed Murray a look that was almost giddy. It was an expression Murray never got quite used to.

The last door down the first floor hallway looked just like all the others: blotched, heavy, and thoroughly unwelcoming. Sergei pressed an ear to the door. *Nothing*, he mouthed at Murray who aligned himself with the frame, readied his gun, and waited as Sergei jabbed the card into a slot beside the handle.

The lock sprang free and Murray kicked the door wide.

Twilight slicing through blinds striped a skinny guy with a short sand-colored braid who lounged on the sofa, his sandals dangling from his toes. "Hey," he said in mild protest and sat up.

A second man catapulted from the table at the back of the room. Murray stabbed his gun forward, the metal glinting in the tigerish light, and the man stopped halfway to the door. "That's right," Murray said, stepping closer. "You just stay put."

Sergei let the door fall shut. The skinny man with the braid gestured at it. "Hey, what're you trying to do?"

Tripping lightly to him, Sergei drew the muzzle of his pistol like a tender finger across the skinny man's throat. "What do you think?"

The skinny man glanced helplessly across to his friend. "Bobby?"

Bobby's face went bloodless, eyes wild. Murray could see the panic inside the guy, building up like carbonation in a shaken pop bottle. He also saw recognition, of Sergei at least.

"We don't have anything valuable," Bobby jabbered. Trying to play it as a simple burglary even though he had to know that wouldn't cut ice with Sergei. "You can take whatever you want, okay? But there's really nothing."

The man with the braid sat up straighter. "Hey, if you're just hungry, you need food, we don't mind sharing."

Sergei leaned his head to one side and drew the gun back just above his shoulder. The barrel slammed down. Twice. A third time. The man with the braid groaned and slid from the couch to the floor. Red flecks glittered in his pale hair.

"Sounded to me like something cracked," Murray observed, keeping his own weapon trained on Bobby.

Stooping to examine the man on the floor, Sergei offered Murray a solemn look. "And it was not the gun, my friend. Not the gun."

∞

Kendall opened his eyes. At first, everything around him was murky and confused, forms moving like fish at the bottom of a deep pond. The back of his head throbbed and he tasted blood. He blinked hard, but his vision remained blurred. When he tried to move his arms, something cut into his skin. The same biting cords secured his calves to the chair legs.

"Bob . . ." he croaked. His throat was parched, his tongue swollen.

A dark shape across from him shifted. "Just keep your mouth shut, Kendall." Bobby's whisper was fierce. "Don't start anything, whatever the hell you do."

Kendall worked his neck from side-to-side. He squeezed his eyes shut, imagining an orange-sized lump at the back of his skull. When he opened his eyes, his vision had cleared. Opposite him sat Bobby, trussed into a chair.

"What—" Kendall began, but he couldn't even formulate the question, what with the headache clawing his skull apart and the fear busily slicing a pit somewhere in the general area of his belly, and the way Bobby ignored him to stare at the two men crossing back and forth in the exposed galley kitchen.

The shorter man strode from cabinets to drawers, opening them, smacking them shut. The taller hung back from the activity, his hands matted with hair thick as a gorilla's as they gripped the edge of the counter.

The shorter man flipped a switch on a metal box on the countertop, then picked up a knife and inserted the blade into the box until the sound of metal grinding against stone shrilled through the apartment.

The pit in Kendall's gut suddenly ballooned, endlessly deep. He had the brief, queasy sensation that all his organs were slowly sliding into that pit.

The tall man released his grip on the counter and edged toward the living room. "Hey, Serg?" He waited for a pause in the grinding noise. "Sergei? I'm gonna head back out to the car, check in with Slater. Find something to eat."

"Get over here, Murray," Sergei barked, lighting a burner on the stove and holding what looked like a long blade into the blue flames. "Get that bag. Take it all out."

"Come on, man," Murray whined. "I didn't get any lunch *or* dinner." Nevertheless, he carried the bag to the table and removed its contents.

"That, put that on the chair," Sergei instructed and Murray lowered some sort of car battery or something onto the empty seat. Wires, their red and yellow plastic coverings peeled back to expose glinting copper, spiraled up from the box.

Bobby licked the corner of his mouth. Kendall, shocked, saw the trickle of blood on his friend's lower lip.

"You see what they're going to do to us?" Bobby's voice quivered. All his muscles were twitching and snapping, out of control.

"But we're not Executables," Kendall whispered, denying what his eyes witnessed. Denying the pain throbbing in his head. It was a mistake. This was against the law. They had to understand that. "They don't have any right to touch us."

"What are you *doing*?" Sergei burst out.

Kendall jerked against the cords. Bobby swallowed noisily, like he was trying to force a desiccated rodent down his throat. Sergei was craning his neck to watch Murray's progress. Frowning, Murray plucked at a pair of wires. He picked up the battery and revolved the entire knotted mass in front of his face as if that would help him solve the mystery.

"Here. You take this." Sergei raised the knife from the burner, extended it toward Murray, and nodded. "This—maybe—you can handle."

Murray practically dropped the battery onto the table. He raised his hands and backed away. "Sergei. Seriously, you want me to drop these guys, I'll do it. No problem. You know that. But this kind of crazy shit . . ." Murray sidestepped the table and started toward the door.

"Murray." Sergei's tone stopped him. "You cut out now, you go, I tell Geoff. I tell Merle. I tell every person in this work. No job. No check. The—what is it?—the blacklist for you." Sergei extended the knife toward Murray who kept his hands balled at his sides.

"Aren't you gonna give'em a chance to talk before you start with this shit?" Murray said.

"Ah! But do they tell us true things, or not true?" Sergei asked. He lowered the blade once more to the burner. "This will make sure."

"I don't think it works like that," Murray mumbled. He slumped his shoulders and shuffled back to the kitchen.

"Good." Sergei pressed the knife handle into Murray's grasp.

The name—Sergei—finally penetrated the clamor in Kendall's skull. Sergei was a bastard, sure, cold-blooded, and sometimes there was some property damage, but he only killed the E's. And the very occasional

Guardian. Kendall rifled through his memory for everything he'd ever seen on the Russian. Sergei tortured E.s' Killed E's. Had done the same to Guardians. But not to people like Kendall or Bobby. He just needed to be reminded of who they were, what this situation was.

"Sergei?" Kendall called out. "Sergei Chistyakov?"

"No, Kendall!" Bobby struggled against the cords pinning him to his chair.

Sergei's head snapped up. He snatched up the last empty chair and, with it, bounded over to Kendall and Bobby in three strides. He plunked the chair down backward and dropped onto it, resting an arm along the back.

"You know me, friend?" he asked, a black eyebrow arching upward. Kendall gaped at the inward twist of the man's front teeth. A tremor quivered through his gut.

He tried to smile. "I'm Kendall. I'm with the Network."

"Ah, a Guardian," Sergei piped, tossing a playful glance at Bobby who shrank against his chair. "Both Guardians? Fantastic." He nestled his chin against his arm and gazed across at Kendall. "You see, I need information. Things a Guardian knows."

"But we're not really Guardians," Bobby said.

Sergei twisted sideways to look at him. "No?"

"Not Guardians like *you* probably think of Guardians," Kendall said. "We're more like administrators." Again he attempted a smile, but couldn't quite manage it. "It's not very glamorous."

"Glamorous?" Sergei raised his hand, let it fall. "Well, glamorous, it is for the vid stars." Sergei smiled so ferociously that Kendall's bladder loosened.

"You're going to have to let us go. It's the law." Kendall knew he was babbling, but he couldn't stop himself. "Technically, you're trespassing. I guess you thought you had a legal right to enter, but there's no Executable here, just us. But it's not your fault if you didn't realize that. I mean, we're not going to press charges or anything."

"You know?" Sergei answered. "You are right." Relief flared through Kendall. Sergei continued: "It is *not* my fault." He gestured grandly toward Murray. "I ask my comrade and he told me we can do these things. He should know. He used to be a policeman!" Sergei paused. "How is the knife, Murray?" Murray raised the blade and lowered it again, dipping the point into the flames. "Ah. Better leave that and help me over here, yes?"

Murray trudged over.

"See, here's the thing," Kendall said. He could feel something rising inside him, something dark and bristling with fear. He spoke too fast. "You survived in Russia. You should understand better than anybody."

"Understand, my friend?"

"What happens when a government goes totally crazy."

Sergei swept Murray closer. "Our government, it is crazy?"

"It's not *my* government," Kendall said. "It's not your government either."

Sergei put a hand to his heart. "I am a citizen now, yes."

"Well . . ." Kendall stopped in confusion. "The whole country's gone haywire." He couldn't think. Pain plowed his head like a newly-sharpened harrow.

Sergei pulled a pair of rubber gloves from the bag. Sliding them onto his hands, he snapped the fingers into place with a sound like gum popping. Next, he withdrew a set of brass knuckles which he tossed to Murray.

"Ah, Russia," Sergei said. "Do you know, my father, he was a soldier for Russia. Chistyakovs go back far, Soviet army. The old men, they knew tradition. Old ways." Still watching Kendall, Sergei ticked a finger at Murray. "Yes. And they would have, what? *Enjoyed* you. Yes." Sergei's eyes hardened and, in that split second, the excruciating ache smashed at Kendall's skull until lights flared at the perimeter of his vision.

"Murray." Sergei gave a light nod.

Murray gripped Kendall's forearms. The chair rose several inches before Murray let it jolt to the floor. Murray's right hand struck out and split Kendall's cheek. Kendall tasted blood, warm and bright. A pebble floated on his tongue. It took him a moment to understand that it was a tooth.

Another nod, and Murray strode behind Bobby. His left hand closed on Bobby's throat, his right on the back of Bobby's neck. Bobby's eyes bulged and his mouth gaped. His face darkened from flush to purple, like a skinned grape.

Kendall was too stunned to do anything but stare. And shrink into his bonds, praying the Russian would somehow forget Kendall was even there.

Murray eased his grip. Bobby hacked and sputtered, his head lolling toward one shoulder.

"Please," Sergei told Murray with a be-my-guest sweep of his hand. Cranking his arm back, Murray buried a punch deep into Bobby's gut.

Bobby slumped forward, wheezing. Murray raised shaggy eyebrows at Sergei who said, "Oh, do not stop now, no." Murray grabbed an ear and twisted it hard. Bobby screamed. "None of that, now." Sergei tore off a fresh swatch of duct tape and plastered it across Bobby's mouth.

Please. The word dissolved in Kendall's mouth and he went numb as Sergei ducked back to the kitchen to retrieve the knife. Blade in hand, Sergei stopped to survey Bobby who drooped against the cords. Sergei cuffed him lightly. Two fingers slipped to Bobby's chin to thrust his head upright. "No sleep *now*, my friend. You would miss the excitement." He dragged the chair holding the battery closer to Kendall.

Murray shifted toward the door. "That kid'll tell you anything now," he said.

Sergei's gaze snapped to Kendall. "Is this true?"

Pins and needles pricked Kendall's face. He was going to pass out. "Whatever you want to know," he heard himself jabbering. "Anything you want. I'll tell you anything. Just stop. Please . . ."

Sergei tutted.

"Just ask me," Kendall flailed. "What're the questions? It's not fair, you have to ask questions."

"You disappoint me." Sergei sighed. "The Chechyans, the Pakistanis, the Israelis, they understood the silence, yes?" Sergei slapped a strip of duct tape across the bottom half of Kendall's face. Kendall desperately sucked air through his nose which was suddenly, bizarrely, clogged with snot. He realized then that he was crying.

Still clutching the knife, Sergei pushed Murray to the apartment door and shoved it open. "My father, my grandfather, they would not be so proud of you either," he told Murray.

"Yeah, well . . ."

"Okay," Sergei interrupted. "Handle this. You go back out to that girl. You and Slater, you see what else she knows."

Murray's gaze flickered toward Kendall.

Kendall jerked against his bindings, tried to walk the chair across the floor toward Murray and the doorway.

"I swear, Sergei," Murray said, turning into the corridor. "I understand about doing a job. But this, I just don't get it."

"And you never will." With a nod, Sergei slipped back inside the apartment and let the door thud shut with a bang that struck Kendall's heart like a bullet.

« CHAPTER 43 »

TORI EDGED UP on the building the screams had come from. There was no sound now except the incongruously cheerful tinkling of windchimes over the doorway.

The building stood two stories tall. The screams—she thought—had come from the second floor which, at this point, might harbor anything from abandoned storage space to old offices to empty apartments. The ground floor had once housed a restaurant.

Tori peered through one of the restaurant's broken windows. Tufts of foam spilled from the seats of the half-dozen booths lining the walls. Wasps' nests frilled the ceiling. A counter near the back was covered in debris where a portion of the ceiling had collapsed.

Tori gave the street behind her a hard look. The man draped in the army blanket still slept. Otherwise, the block was empty. It looked empty, at any rate. Adrenaline snapping along her nerves, she eased herself through the doorway.

The first order of business was to find a weapon. There wasn't going to be a semi-automatic lying around, but there had to be something she could use to defend herself. A butcher knife, maybe, or a cleaver. Was that too much to ask of a former restaurant?

Her heart rate escalated She rounded one end of the counter in a sudden rush, hoping to surprise anyone who might be crouching there. But the space was empty.

She pushed herself through to the kitchen. The grimy light seeping through a window at the rear showed metal countertops and dented appliances coated with grime. She searched the drawers and cabinets. Not a single knife—not even a 2-inch paring knife—remained. The few utensils that still littered the room were random and useless: a buttery-soft rubber spatula, a plastic colander, a brillo pad. She picked up the last—*I could scrub somebody to death*—and dropped it again.

She found an old broom in a tiny utility closet. A greasy film covered the handle. She hefted it, holding it backwards to thrust the wooden handle forward like a bayonet. She'd rather have a gun or a length of metal pipe, but a 5-foot wooden stick was better than empty hands.

A single scream shattered the quiet.

Tori's head snapped back. Her gaze roved the water-stained ceiling tiles. No question, the scream had come from the second floor.

And it was definitely a kid.

Shit. She'd bet, a hundred to one, that it was one of the boys who'd followed her into the zone. She wondered if the kid's commvid was shooting a livefeed back to Sergei. Who didn't seem like the type to ride to the rescue.

Tori swallowed fear like black tar thickening in her throat. What was she even doing here? She should be crossing the no-go zone, searching for a way out. Trying to get back to the coyote by ten p.m.

She couldn't leave.

Gripping the broom with both hands, she held it angled in front of her chest like a pugilist's stick. The stairway was narrow, tucked behind the kitchen. A tall window—smashed, of course—filled one wall of the landing, spraying light up the steps and along the second floor hallway.

The hallway was short. Only four doorways radiated from it, two on each side. Poised at the top of the stairs, Tori listened. Now she could hear the voices coming from the last room on the right. Well, one voice, a man muttering "Shut up, shut up," over and over. In the same room, a ragged, childish sobbing threatened to spiral into noisy hysteria.

And almost as loud as the crying was the jagged, harsh breathing of pure terror. It came from a different room, from behind the first door on the left which was closed and, Tori now saw, padlocked. The guts of a smashed comm scattered a trail down the corridor.

Understanding clicked. She knew, as if she could see through the cheap wooden door, that at least one of the boys who'd been chasing her was trapped in there. Waiting for the man to take him across to the other room.

Her stomach turned. In an instant, she forgot why the boys were in the zone in the first place, didn't care.

She stepped along the hallway, lowering each foot slowly to minimize any creaking from the floorboards.

The door to the second room on the right stood wide. A skinny man, naked from the waist down, hovered above a boy curled on a pallet of dirty blankets. The boy's wrists were tied together.

"Shut up, shut up, shut up," the man kept saying in a mechanical, lifeless voice. His shoulderblades jabbed again and again at the back of his thin t-shirt as he ground forward and back.

Rage and disgust poured pure energy through Tori's limbs. In that instant, she saw every guard who'd ever raped an inmate, every prisoner she'd seen clubbed or beaten, smashed and cut in the factory machinery.

She sprang across the room. The broom's wooden handle cracked against the man's skull before he'd even turned halfway toward her. He crumpled to the floor. Tori smashed the stick across his upturned face, over and over, heard the crunch of teeth breaking. Blood spurted from his nose. But his chest, she noted vaguely, moved. He was still breathing.

Kneeling, she reached one hand for the boy. He stared at her, eyes straining in their sockets, then at the red-smeared broom Tori clutched in her other hand. Snot dripped from his nose onto his upper lip.

He was the boy the others had grouped around. The one Sergei had slapped. The one who'd taken the lead in snitching on Tori's whereabouts.

Tori allowed herself the briefest glance at the rest of him. Naked, but no sign of blood on his skin. No semen. Apparently the man hadn't made it quite that far before she'd barged in.

There was a small heap of clothing by the boy's feet and, near that, a carving knife with a healthy-looking blade. Tori dropped the broom and picked up the knife.

"Hold out your hands," she said quietly.

The boy eyed her.

She dug at the man's ribs with her foot. His body moved limply with each scuff and kick.

"Seriously?" Tori asked the kid. "You think I'm going to hurt you? If I wanted to hurt you, I'd have just sat back and let this guy do his bit."

Slowly, the boy extended his arms.

"Hold still," Tori said. The blade was as sharp as it looked. It cut easily through the thin cable binding the boy's wrists. As soon as he was free, he snatched at his clothes. Tori turned away while he dressed.

"What about your friends?" she asked, back to him. "You know where the key to the lock is?"

She waited, her breath shallow, ears sharp as she listened to the boy zip his pants, pull on his shoes. Still, she kept her back to him. Her muscles tensed. She had the knife in one hand and the broomstick by her feet, but part of her expected the boy to suddenly throw himself at her, attack her. Or maybe he'd just sprint past her, down the stairs, and out of the building. Get the hell out of the zone, with or without his buddies.

His footsteps scuffed across the floor. He stood at her elbow. Tori half-turned. The boy held a pair of ragged pants between two fingers. The unconscious creep's pants, Tori realized. The boy looked like he wanted to throw up. Instead, he thrust the pants at her.

"The pocket," he said. She was surprised by how clear his voice sounded. Tough little s.o.b, she thought, and gingerly explored the pants pockets.

"Bingo." She held up a small gray key. "Let's get your friends. They've gotta be wondering what the hell's going on."

The boy nodded. Tori gave him the broom. She kept the knife and key.

From the hallway, she looked back. The boy had stayed behind. He raised the broom handle high overhead and smashed it down with all his wiry strength against the man's side. Ribs cracked in the silence.

The boy followed Tori to the door to the locked room. Utter silence on the other side of the door.

"Your comm's busted," Tori observed, pushing the key home.

" 's okay," the boy said.

Tori twisted the key, pulled the padlock free. She glanced over her shoulder at the boy. "Okay because you aren't planning to run to Sergei and tell him you saw me?"

The boy looked down, sheepish. "I'm not telling him nothing."

"Okay. Thanks." Tori pulled the padlock free. "What's your name, anyway?"

"Mateo."

Tori pulled the door wide.

The other two boys huddled in the far corner of the room.

"You can come out." Tori took a step back. Left them a path into the hallway. They didn't budge, just stared. She followed their gaze, realized with a startled laugh that they were looking at the blade she gripped in her right hand.

She dropped farther back, swept Mateo forward with a sweeping gesture. "You tell them. They'll listen to you."

He hurried to them. While he told them what had happened, Tori leaned her head back against the corridor wall and closed her eyes. Exhaustion swept through her. Her legs trembled. Memories of her dad rushed into her head. Tears pressed from her eyes. She tried to stop them, couldn't, and gave in.

When she opened her eyes, all three boys stood in the hall. They hung back, watching her with worried frowns like her tears alarmed them. Like she was an unpredictable creature, possibly violent.

Mateo said simply, "We owe you."

Tori wiped her face with her hands. She smelled like blood and bacon fat. "So," she said. "Where are you going from here?"

"I just wanna go home," the smallest boy said.

"You and me both," Tori answered. She thought of the old house, the empty rooms, her father gone. Her throat closed.

Mateo said, alarmed, "You can't go back there."

"I know that. Trust me, I know." She paused. "You really think you owe me?"

All three nodded at once, energetically, their eyes wide and sincere.

"You know another way out of the zone?" Tori asked. "Nowhere near where we came in. I'm really not feeling up to that Sergei guy at the moment."

"Me neither," Mateo muttered.

"He slugged you good," the smallest boy observed. No one commented on this.

"I know like seven or eight ways in and out of here," said the last boy, speaking for the first time.

"But then where are you going to go?" the smallest boy asked. "If you can't go home?" His face was all screwed up like he couldn't imagine anything worse than that. He looked like he might start crying next.

"I've got someplace else to go," Tori comforted the boy. "But it's all the way across town. And honestly, I don't know how I'm going to get there. Not on time." She glanced toward one of the windows and guessed the time as mid- to late afternoon.

Mateo looked at her like she was slightly daft. "My cousin's got a car," he said. "He's seventeen."

Tori cocked her head at him. "You mean I could. . ."

"It works some of the time," Mateo explained. His face brightened with the confidence a young kid has in teenaged relatives. "He fixes cars. I tell him what you did, he'll take you. I mean, if he can. If it's working."

The boy looked so happy that he might be able to do Tori a favor in return that she made herself grin at him as if she shared his excitement. Inside, she felt hollow and nearly dead already when she thought of her father. She ached to see him again. And, strangely, she missed Seth nearly as much, with a physical sensation of loss.

She wasn't sure she would care all that much whether she made it out of Philly or not if it weren't for one thing: If she got out and disappeared, Seth would be safe.

At least until he got another E to protect.

That thought brought another wave of loneliness flooding through her. She bent forward until she was eye level with the boys. "And you'll show me the way out of here?"

They nodded solemnly.

"Just one sec," Mateo said. He and the broomstick disappeared again into the other room. Tori didn't even wince as the stick whistled down through the air and something else—ribs? Skull? Kneecaps?—cracked.

Mateo re-emerged into the hallway. The wooden handle shone with fresh blood. He fell into position behind Tori at the top of the steps. He was a gutsy kid, she realized, but still a kid and it looked like all three of them expected the grown-up to take the lead here.

"Okay, then" she said, taking the first step down the stairway, knife blade shining dully above the bulk of her fist. "We're outta here."

« CHAPTER 44 »

THE TWO MEN in the front seat were saying something to her, but the blankness spreading through Wren's body crushed their voices. She let her head loll to one side, the leather upholstery burning her cheek.

She wasn't desperate for another cap, but she would be soon. The one they'd given her was corporate—seriously, capital C—better than any of the shit she or Owen ever bagged. But it was wearing off. She floated in a dead space. The halos that had warmed her when the cap first hit were gone. God was still inside her, but he was pawing the exits, one foot out the door. The two men were starting to scare her again.

The car paused at an intersection and the big guy behind the wheel—what was his name? Murray?—twisted around to stare at her. She saw him at the edge of her vision, but she was stuck in the dead space and she couldn't quite shift her eyes to meet his.

He snapped his fingers. "*Here,*" he told her. "Fuck it, I'm over *here,* you moron." His words drifted around her. She didn't move.

Murray's eyebrows clashed together. "Okay, look. You've had your snack. And now you gotta earn your pay. You said Jennings was gonna be at this safehouse and she wasn't."

Wren wanted to protest, but her mouth wouldn't cooperate. She'd never said Tori would be at the safehouse. She'd only said Tori might be. It was never a promise.

The car jerked into motion again. Wren's head snapped forward and back.

The little guy—Slater—not even turning around said, "You got another safehouse for us?"

"Another safehouse," Murray sneered. "You mean, another dead end?"

Wren wrenched her tongue into motion. "I think . . ."

"She thinks?" Murray japed.

The dead space slipped. The first hints of sickness tunneled into her. The first restlessness twitched her hands. Her hair was suddenly drenched. She thought about a cap dissolving on her tongue and licked her lips.

But she wasn't going to give them Tori. No matter what.

She could go all night without another cap. She could. She could do it. Maybe she could go all day tomorrow too. This time she'd push through the sickness and the need. Be done with all of it forever. Be done with Owen, too.

The car had stopped again. One of the back doors slung open. Murray leaned in, gripped the front of Wren's shirt, hauled her up from the seat and shook her. He dropped her back against the seat. A slap rocked her head, cracked her right temple against the window. Pain split her skull.

"Aah, she's useless," Murray said. "Let's dump her here."

Wren squinted out the open door. Where was here? She didn't recognize this block. She only knew that if they ditched her here, she had no caps stashed anywhere and no money to buy some.

She twitched upright. Better get one more cap out of these guys. Just one, for an emergency. As long as she didn't give them any real information, it was okay. She wasn't doing anything that would hurt Tori.

Murray was still outside, leaning hunched against the car. He had his comm clamped to the side of his head. He winced and soured his mouth like his head hurt as bad as Wren's.

Wren swallowed and stared at her lap. Her legs trembled. Her knees were quivering waves. Looking at them made her queasy. She shifted her gaze. The guy sitting in the front wasn't as scary as Murray. When she spoke, she leaned forward and pushed the words at the hairs curling against the back of the small guy's neck.

"When do I . . ." She swallowed harder. "When do I get a cap?"

The guy—Slitter? Slammer? What was it again?—swiveled his head just enough to eye her. His skull was narrow, his eyes tiny, his mouth a thin indentation. His face looked like a vacuum was slowly sucking in his features. "A cap?" he said. "When we get Jennings, I s'pose."

271

He shrugged and turned forward again. Wren hated him at that instant, hated how he could dismiss caps with a shrug. How he didn't need anything. Not like she needed a cap.

Murray slammed the back door shut. Wren jerked at the sudden noise. He wrenched the driver's door open again and dropped onto the seat. His meaty hands gripped the steering wheel, hairs crawling like black lice across the backs of his fingers.

Wren swayed back, tilted the crown of her head against the upholstery. She swallowed down vomit. Tears squeezed between her eyelids. It wasn't fair! Wasn't fair she needed another hit this soon. Wasn't fair that little Slitter—Slatter—*Slater* guy could just shrug and forget about her. Not give a shit if she was okay or dead.

At least Tori had understood. Tori got her a cap.

"So who was ridin' the comm?" Slater drawled.

"It's just Sergei," Murray said. "He's says he's ready for a little break from those two Guardian guys. Wants us to swing by again for a couple minutes."

"Then what?"

The car backed up in a sickening curve, gravel popping under the tires like gunshots straight into Wren's skull. "I guess he goes back to what he's doing. Jeez. Poor bastards. And us? We go wherever we get a bead on Jennings."

"Well, this one's shit out of beads." Slater, not bothering to look around, jabbed a thumb over his shoulder in Wren's direction.

Wren's sickness stalled, relented slightly. It was a truce she knew wouldn't last long. Her hair was soaked. Her hands fluttered against her thighs like spiders doused with fire. She had to get another cap.

"I know where the E's gonna be tonight," she blurted.

Murray hooked a glance at her in the rearview mirror. "Jeez, Whelk's got other contacts. Let's use 'em."

A bright red roar drove through Wren's head. She bent forward, forehead nearly to her thighs, her skull imprisoned in the tight cage of her arms. Sickness cramped her belly. Wave after wave gripped her. It was like giving birth, like the contractions that had smashed her in a vise, over and over, when she gave birth to the daughter she hadn't seen in years. She breathed in and out, nose and mouth, the same way she had then. Gradually, the pain eased.

The car stopped. A rear door opened. Someone slammed down next to Wren on the back seat.

"Don't bother, man," Slater said from the front seat. "She's got nothing. She's tapped out."

Wren jerked her head up. "I am not!" Bastard was going to cost her the caps she had coming.

Sergei was beside her, pressing in close. He slapped a hand against the headrest in front of him. "My sausages! It has been hard work today. And more hard work tonight."

Slater reached back, handing Sergei a package of thick sausages. It made Wren's stomach lurch to look at the bumpy tubes of meat, the spicy red casings. She leaned away.

Sergei tore the plastic open, jammed a sausage in his mouth, and chewed so vigorously that the mandible joints made an audible *snap* every time his jaws opened and shut.

Murray cleared his throat. "Uh, so you aren't done in there yet?"

Sergei swallowed noisily. "No. No. Those young men, just a little more time and I think they will tell me very helpful things."

"Have they said anything useful yet?" Murray turned halfway around in the driver's seat.

Sergei destroyed a second sausage. "No, they are bad boys. Try to hide things from me. But I have them right at the cliff. You know? Right on that edge. A little break for them to think about things and while they think, I enjoy my snack. It is a . . . what do they call it? Win-win!"

A muscle leaped at the corner of Murray's eye. He turned back around to stare out the windshield.

The last sausage vanished down Sergei's gullet.

"Now." His fingers closed on Wren's arm, tightened like he was going to crush her bones to powder. She stared at him in shock. Tears jolted from her eyes.

"Your last bit of information you give us—" He tutted and wagged a finger of his free hand in Wren's face. "It was not so good."

"But it was a safehouse!" Wren protested. "A Network safehouse, and I'm the one who got you in there."

The Russian widened his eyes. "But no Jennings." He gave Wren's arm a last, excruciating squeeze and dropped it, lifting his own palms in a so-what-can-we-do-about-this-situation gesture.

The caps were slipping away. A panic of words tumbled from Wren's mouth. "But she was there earlier. I saw her there. I swear I did."

Sergei leaned close, like he might swallow her next. A smell of sausage hung bloody on his breath. "You are not the one stringer. Stringers—they are—what do you say? A dime a dozen. We have many. Hmm? Better ones than you. They saw this Jennings themselves. Up on Olney this very morning."

Better ones. Did that mean they were about to cut her off? Wren's head clanged: *Get a cap, get a cap now now now*— Vomit simmered at the back of her throat and in the cauldron of her stomach.

"Yeah, but I'm the only one who knows where she's going to be tonight."

"Crazies will be cutting her throat in the North Philly no-go, I think," Sergei said, but his gaze never shifted from Wren's face.

"No. She'll be back down this way. She has an . . . an appointment."

Sergei's lips twisted. "With her what? Hairdresser?"

Up front, Slater snorted.

"With a coyote," Wren announced, stabbing the words out like a sword thrust. Then she sucked in her breath, clamped her mouth shut against a surge of sickness. Why the hell had she told them that? She really was as stupid as Owen said.

Sergei watched her, his face avid and alight. The energy crackling in his stare terrified Wren, but she'd caught his interest again. And that might mean a cap was in the offing.

It's okay—it's okay—Wren chanted in her head. She hadn't given Tori away. Not exactly. A thought crawled into her brain. She could fool the hitters, just like she'd fooled Owen. As long as she put the coyote pickup away from where it was really set to happen, Tori would be all right.

A fist snapped her head to one side.

"Come on now," Sergei coaxed, fist poised as if he was about to smash her head back the other direction.

Wren tried to think. She couldn't grasp anything, couldn't concentrate with her head aching from the blow and, far worse, the red hurricane roaring *capcapcap* against her skull.

Sergei ground Wren's lower jaw between the thumb and fingers of one hand. She yelped, tried to twist away. Couldn't. He shoved his face inches from hers. "Come now. Tell me."

The first place that shoved itself into her head was Mom's tent. "There's a big tent city, couple blocks from Hull Park. You know it?"

From the front, Slater remarked, "I've smelled it."

Sergei ignored the joke. "That's where she meets this coyote? Tonight?"

Wren tried to nod, but any movement made her jawbone feel like it was about to burst apart at the joints. Saliva unspooled from her mouth and slid across Sergei's fingers. His hand squeezed harder.

"What time?"

"Nine," Wren blurted, then clenched her eyes shut. Was that the real time? She couldn't remember. Maybe giving them the real time was better anyway. They'd be at the camp while Tori rode off in the coyote's van half a dozen blocks away.

Sergei was talking again. "Who is with her?"

"What?"

"You tell us she is using Guardian safehouses, yes? So she has a Guardian."

A Guardian who loves her, Wren thought, and wanted to weep. Did weep, tears unraveling down her cheeks, mingling with the saliva on Sergei's fingers.

The Russian eased the pressure on her jaw, held Wren's chin almost delicately. "Ah, our poor stringer. Poor girl. What is the word for her? Slater! Woesome?"

"Woebegone, maybe."

Sergei petted Wren's hair. She cried harder at the gentle touch of his hand, and relief that she hadn't done anything to hurt Tori. "Can I have a cap now?" she asked.

"That is a good girl."

"Can I?"

"A good, woebegone girl. Who is with little Victoria? Is it Seth Krey?"

Wren licked her upper lip, tasted snot. "Yeah."

"Very nice."

"He loves her." Wren's voice clutched, tore.

"Very sweet."

"Can I have my cap?"

Sergei put his face in front of hers. Stared hard into Wren's eyes. She blinked, ducked her head long enough to wipe her face on her forearm.

"You would only tell me the true, yes?" Sergei said.

Wren's arms quivered at her sides. The only true she knew was that she needed that cap. "Yeah," she whispered. "Only true."

"Because if this is not true? We find you. And this is your night of pain. Your longest night."

"Her last night," Slater commented.

275

Sergei blazed into a good-humored grin. "Yes. That also. Murray? Slater? You check on this tent city. If you see this Jennings there, you call me." He pushed open his door, sprang out of the car, leaned back in for a moment. "I will call you when I am done with our friends inside. But I will be here very late, I think."

"I thought you said they were right on the cliff," Murray muttered. "About to talk."

"Sometimes that fall over the cliff, it lasts many hours. And now I think we are done with our little stringer for awhile."

"Right." Murray lumbered out of the car, opened the door closest to Wren, and hauled her out by the back of her shirt. She tumbled onto the curb. Blood slowly darkened the knees of her pants. The skin beneath the bloody fabric stung, but she didn't care.

Where's the cap? Did they throw it? On hands and knees, she scrambled across concrete and dirt, searching for that tiny scarlet dot. She couldn't lose it. Could NOT lose it.

"Little girl."

She raised her head. Her hands paused, stopped clawing through the weeds that erupted from a crack in the sidewalk.

Sergei regarded her from across the trunk of the car. His face scrunched up with sadness. "My friends go look for that bad, nasty E now. They find her where you said? We give you five caps. And if they get to beat the shit out of her valentine boy? We give you three more caps. A bonus." The mournful lines sagging around his mouth and eyes burst into a gleeful grin. "I am so very excited. For you!" A last grin and Sergei strode to the apartment building again, disappeared inside.

The car pulled from the curb.

Wren stared down at the weeds. She rummaged through them another minute or two, ripping them up by the roots with her black-rimmed fingernails.

Nothing.

She pushed herself to her feet. She was crying again, tears and snot pouring down her face and dripping from her chin.

Her brain buzzed with need. Tori gave her a cap for hooking her up with the coyote. Maybe Tori would give her another one tonight.

A goodbye present.

Just the thought of it cleared a little of the fog from Wren's head. What time was it? She looked up at the broken streetlights. Almost full dark out. She wished her brain could pull out the time Tori was meeting the coyote.

Could be midnight. Could be now.

She jolted into motion.

« CHAPTER 45 »

MATEO'S COUSIN had a car, just as Mateo had promised. The car was rusty and farted black smoke and a stink of burning oil, but it ran, more or less. Well enough to get Tori back across town, at any rate, although it was a slow journey impeded not only by the car's uncertain health but by barricades of garbage, abandoned junkers, and roaming vandal-packs.

They let her out where she'd requested, two blocks from the Torresdale and Margaret intersection where she was supposed to meet the coyote. Mateo had obviously explained something about the no-go zone to his cousin. Before Tori climbed out of the car, the cousin grabbed her hands, enfolded them in his, and raised them to his mouth. His mustache was damp fuzz on her knuckles. She wrenched her mouth into a smile and drew herself free.

Out into the darkness. The car shuddered away, a wounded whale swallowed by murky water. Tori stood with her arms crossed and rubbed her elbows.

Every horrifying story she'd ever heard about treacherous coyotes and border crossings gone wrong swarmed into her head. Coyotes who sold their customers as sex slaves or used them in snuff films or raped and then abandoned them in the desert.

Problem was, she thought, giving herself a little shake, problem was that E's who stuck around ended up as hookers or in porn shoots or slinging street pharms or generally crawling in shit. Better to take a risk.

Anyway, Seth would be safer with her gone. That decided it right there. And it's not like her father was—

She pressed the back of one hand against her mouth, dammed back her grief.

She took her hand away. "What happens, happens," she said out loud.

Pivoting, she hurried along the street, following the gutters, afraid to get too close to the buildings with their black doorways and empty windows like hollows for killers to hide in. The broken streetlights pleased her. She couldn't see much, but neither could anyone else.

Well, unless hitters had nightvision implants.

At first, Tori thought Torresdale and Margaret was deserted. The intersection was dark. The few cars lodged along Margaret were equally dark, except for one that held a man and woman huddling over the gear shift with a flashlight. A couple of kids slept in the back seat.

Maybe they were waiting for the coyote too. They weren't hitters. Not unless hitters were using little kids as cover these days.

Ridiculous, but the idea made her uneasy enough that she walked faster, leaving the car behind. She didn't stop until she reached the street sign at the intersection. The pole tilted up from the cement at a jaunty, beach-umbrella angle. The air smelled metallic and rubbery, like the caged interstate a few blocks away.

Footsteps slapped the concrete. Tori whirled at the sound, poised to bolt. Someone ran down the middle of the empty street. Ran right toward her.

"Tori!" The person flailed closer. Voice scratchy, like she'd swallowed a bunch of tacks. Arms scarecrow-skinny and awkward. Frizzy hair rubberbanded into two limp horns.

Wren flung herself at Tori. Gripped those skinny arms around her. A stink of sweat and grime simmered from Wren's hair. The woman's entire body quivered, individual muscles in her arms popping and spasming. Tori, clamped in Wren's hug, could feel how the girl's body quivered, individual muscles popping and spasming.

Wren needed a hit, obviously. And soon.

"You okay?" Tori asked.

Wren still clung to her, but leaned her head back, met Tori's eyes. "I wanted to say goodbye." Wren was sweating through her clothes, sweating onto Tori.

Tori gently pulled free.

Wren blinked up at her. "Did I help you? Did I?

"Of course you did."

"I wish I could go with you." Wren looked as alone as Tori felt. Despite the pity Tori felt, she let silence gnaw Wren's words down to nothing. She glanced at the darkness heaped up around them. Only a few windows in the surrounding buildings glowed yellow, cracking the shadows apart. Where the hell was the coyote?

Wren hugged herself, shivering like it wasn't 90 degrees out. Like she wasn't already pouring off sweat. "I don't have the money anyway."

Tori, gaze flicking, comforted her. "And you wouldn't want to leave your boyfriend."

Wren shivered again, an extravagant, Arctic shudder that jolted her from head to toe. "He won't even give me a cap. You gave me a cap."

No surprise there. This wasn't about saying goodbye. Well, maybe it was—partially—but mainly it was about checking the state of Tori's possible supply.

"Look, I'd give you one now if I had one, but I don't," Tori said. "I don't use."

A man stepped from the darkness between two buildings. Tori's heart careened. Then she recognized him, the tall guy from the camper, the one who'd let her and Wren inside.

"Coyote's here," she told Wren who was too busy trembling and sweating to pay much attention. "Or his friend, anyway."

The man waved Tori closer. Wren stumbled just behind.

"Not her." The man held a palm up, blocking Wren's progress.

"She's just saying goodbye," Tori explained. "She's leaving."

Down the block, a car door thudded shut. The woman Tori had seen earlier, in the car with the sleeping children, walked toward the corner. The woman kept her head tucked down, her hair falling around her face. She'd jammed her hands in the front pockets of her jeans. When she got closer, Tori could see tears glinting on the woman's face.

"Van's a block away," the man said. "Coyote's with it. We head there together. You pay what you owe and get in the van. Use the rear doors. Right now, I want any guns."

"I don't have a gun," the other woman mumbled, her voice choked and gasping. She stared back at the car she'd left behind. That started her crying again, big noisy sobs.

"Shut it up," the man commanded. "I'm gonna check you real quick for weapons."

The woman barely seemed to notice he frisked her.

Finishing, he turned to Tori. Reluctantly, she extended her arms at her sides and spread her legs. The patdown was briskly efficient.

The man jerked his head at Wren. "Time for you to say your goodbye and get out of here."

Wren hurled herself against Tori, clinging to her again, almost knocking Tori over. "I don't want you to go," Wren said. "I don't want to be alone."

It was harder for Tori to work herself free this time. "You're not alone. Wren. Listen to me."

Wren groaned, swaying her head from side to side like an emaciated cow.

"You've got your boyfriend," Tori said.

"What, Owen?" Wren dragged her head upright.. "He doesn't love me. Not like Seth and you."

A painful twisting sensation turned within Tori's chest. She forced herself to give a careless shrug. "Seth doesn't love me."

"He's going to get messed up for you."

"No. Not anymore. He's not helping me anymore."

Wren squinted up at the dark sky like she was trying to remember something. Shivers ran through her. "They said they were going to mess him up."

Tori stopped trying to work herself free. She gripped Wren's arm, leaned in close enough to smell the dirt on the woman's face. "Who's they?"

"Hitters."

The man stepped in. "What hitters?"

Tori wanted to cover, wanted to say there were no hitters, that she wasn't an E, that Wren was obviously nuts, half psycho, a peelfreak in a delirium of withdrawal.

But even more, Tori wanted to know about Seth, and what was coming down.

She tightened her grip on Wren and gave the woman a hard shake. "What do you mean, they're going to mess him up?"

Wren squinted sideways now, mouth slack. "Sergei said—"

"Sergei!" Shit. It was all blowing up.

The man from the camper crossed his arms and stared at them both with a speculative, unhappy look. The crying woman who was his other client that evening shrank back and looked toward the car she'd come from like she was going to bolt toward it at any second.

"Just—let me think." Wren fluttered a hand, pinched up her face. "My head's not—it's hard to remember. Yeah. Sergei said they'd mess him up tonight."

Tori went completely still. "Are you sure he said tonight?"

Wren nodded her spastic head. Her eyes had a peculiar, unfocused quality. "At the camp. You know, where Mom is."

Coldness spread through Tori's body. If Seth was at the squatters' camp, it was all because of her. Her fault. She pulled back, trying to shake herself free.

Wren wouldn't let go of her. "Sergei—he thinks you're going to be at the tents tonight. That's all I told him. I never said anything about you being here. You're safe! I kept you safe."

Tori stood, frozen. Wren's fingers burned her arm. Seth would only go to the tent city that night if he expected to find Tori there. Wren—or someone—had given him that little nugget of information. And now Wren had led the hitters right to him.

Tori fixed Wren with a stare. "How do you know what a bunch of hitters are planning to do?"

The man from the camper grabbed Wren by both shoulders and ripped her away from Tori. "You tell these hitters about the coyote?"

Wren noisily snorted up the mucus in her nose. She ignored the man, snatched at Tori. Tori backed away in disgust. A snitch. Feeding both sides, most likely.

"Anything for a cap, Wren? Is that it?" Tori said.

Wren flailed for Tori again. Tori shoved Wren's hands away. "It's not like that," Wren pleaded. "I never told them anything real about tonight. I never told them you'd be here. I wouldn't. Never."

Tori was shaking almost as hard as Wren, but with anger. "Am I supposed to thank you?"

"No, but—"

"You tell Sergei, you tell that pack of killers where they can find Seth and then you want me to be grateful?"

Wren squeezed her eyes shut, pinched up her face. Her eyes slid open. She stared at Tori with a puzzled expression. "Is Seth going to be there?"

"For Christ's sake! Owen's right. You are pathetic." Tori flung herself around, bolted into the street.

"Hey!" the man from the camper yelled after her. "Get back here!"

Tori kept running. She dared a glance over her shoulder.

The man was raising his arm, straightening it. Gun, Tori thought, without seeing what he held. She turned forward, ran harder.

Ah the sound of a gunshot, she looked back again.

Wren—a scrawny silhouette—was throwing herself at the man, hurling her body full-force. Her skinny arms flitted and plunged, grabbing the man's legs, his back, his hair, anywhere she could reach him. Grabbing for the gun.

"Go!" Wren called out. "Go, Tor—"

A violent motion of the man's arms and Wren's scratchy voice cut off, mid-word. The gun exploded, a burst of light flaring briefly from the muzzle. Wren—the shadow of her—clutched at the man, slid down his torso, down his legs.

Tori ran.

« CHAPTER 46 »

TORI RAN all the way back to tent city, ran until her side cramped and her heart was about to explode out of her chest. Muggers, hitters, slingers: the dangers flared at the periphery of her mind and were instantly dismissed. The only thought that remained, pulsing in bright colors was Seth.

Guilt dug into her guts. She should have kept her distance from Wren, right from the start. Should have found somewhere else to sleep, found a coyote some other way.

But she'd been too chickenshit to go it alone. Too chickenshit to turn down an offer of help, even if it came from a peelfreak.

When she limped into the squatters' encampment, it looked exactly the way it had when she'd left it at dawn although she could hardly believe this was still the same day. Slingers lurked around the front. Men and women hunched over cooking pots in front of torn tents and refrigerator boxes. The air still stank of cabbage and beans and piss.

No sign of hitters. No sign of Seth. Not yet.

Tori headed straight for Mom's tent, pushed in through the flap.

The camplight burned. Mom was awake. Was, in fact, hunched over a bucket, puking into it. Tori halted at the stench and the splattering noise of vomit against plastic. Mom's grandson huddled crying in a back corner of the tent.

Mom looked up. Her mouth hung open, gray hair straggling through the strands of drool that unspooled from her chin. She just stared at Tori for a second, then lowered her head over the bucket again and waited, panting. Tori crouched beside her.

Mom's gaze slid sideways to touch briefly on her.

"You can't stay here," Mom muttered. "Didn't pay full for two nights yet." She looked like a crone, a fairy tale witch, her face carved with wrinkles and her hair wild.

"I'm not staying."

Mom's shoulders heaved slightly. She let her head hang and breathed noisily through her mouth. "Then what are you here for?"

"Did anybody come through asking about me?"

"I oughta ask for ten bucks to answer that."

Tori dropped back on her heels and stared at the grubby canvas three feet above her head. Is this what life always came down to? Caps or cash, cash or caps.

"I don't have ten bucks," she answered.

"Well, that's too ba—" Mom started, but her face clenched on the last word. Gripping the bucket with both hands, she retched into it. The little boy cried louder at the noises the old woman made.

When Mom finally lifted her head, blood streamed out of one nostril and dripped from her chin. Broken capillaries webbed her eyeballs. She fumbled for Tori's arm. "Get me some water?" Mom asked. Tears oozed past her eyelids. "It's all gone. I'm so thirsty. And I stink. " She pinched her mouth in, for a moment resembling the tight, controlled woman of the previous night.

"Nobody's come looking for you," she added. "Not in here anyway." Her mouth slid about a centimeter upward on one side. "No charge for that."

"Okay. Okay, thanks." Tori paused. "Is it food poisoning?"

"Naw, I've been having this for awhile. Comes and goes. Comes now, mainly." Contractions seized Mom's belly again. She dropped Tori's arm and grabbed the bucket. Tori understood why the little kid was sobbing. His grandma suddenly looked a hundred years old and on the brink of death. Maybe it was stomach cancer, something like that. What would happen to the boy if Mom was too sick to take care of him? Where would he go?

Tori hesitated. Her hand hovered an inch above the crown of Mom's head. Finally, she let her palm lightly rest on the coarse gray hair. "Sure, I'll get the water."

Tori found a couple of empty buckets and swung them up by their handles. Mom didn't glance at her. Tori stopped next to the boy on her way out. "It'll be okay." She wanted to ruffle his hair, but he was stiff, holding himself back, and she thought being touched might scare him. Break him: those were actually the words that came into her mind. "I'll be back in a few minutes."

She realized, when she reached the line for the water tap, that "a few minutes" was a lie. The line stretched, long and defeated. Lamps and firelight from the nearest hovels glinted in the stagnant water spreading underneath the tap. Squatters clutched empty water bottles, milk jugs, even a scrubbed-out pesticide tin. Tori slid into place behind a man who stank like a dirty litter box. A plastic trick-or-treat pumpkin, the black eyes and mouth long since peeled away, dangled from his fist.

Her stomach grumbled. She glanced around and wondered how likely she was to get the crap beaten out of her if she tried to jump line. Outside an elaborate construction of cardboard boxes, a girl squatted to play-walk her ratty doll across the mud. A motorized scooter and a gasoline canister leaned together, chained to the ground in front of the neighboring shack, the scooter so rusty it looked like it would crumble at a touch.

"Bastards, all of em, sonsabitches," muttered the man in front of Tori. He turned around and gave her a toothless glare. Then his stare flicked to something behind her.

Tori snapped around.

Three—no—four men hurtled toward her. She recognized the one in front despite the grimace contorting his face. He was the grabber who'd chased her and Seth into the alley, set the Hellhound on them.

"I got her, Owen!" another guy shouted, barreling ahead of the others.

Tori barely registered the name—*Wren's boyfriend*—before she drew back one of the empty buckets she carried and whaled it toward the man. The container glanced off the side of his head. But the bucket was only a lightweight plastic. The grabber yelped out a startled laugh and lunged. Missed.

Then Owen was beside her. Tori pivoted to face him. He cracked the barrel of his gun against her forearm. The shock vibrated from her hand to her shoulder and Mom's bucket dropped into the mud. Tori tried to plunge into the crowd, but there was no crowd, no chaos, just the endless line for the tap. The squatters stayed put, refusing to lose their place in line because of a few grabbers waving guns around.

Tori hesitated, glancing around frantically, trying to figure out which way to run. Three seconds and it was too late. The grabbers were on her.

Someone wrenched her arms together. Plastic cuffs closed around her wrists. Someone else kicked at the back of her knees, collapsing her legs. People were shouting and one of the men behind her said, "Okay, okay, we got her. Let's go!"

They dragged her to her feet. The mud captured one of her shoes. "Move it! Move it!" The four men surrounded her like bodyguards around a president.

"Get away from the girl!" Another voice—a man's, deep and rough—carried from the far side of the water tap.

The hands gripping Tori tightened. The grabber behind her kept pressure on the middle of her back, kept her walking. The pain in her shoulders barely registered as she looked over her shoulder, searching the shadowy faces behind her. Not—thank God—

Seth, not a voice she knew, but maybe someone from the Network.

Now the squatters waiting in line scrabbled apart. Through their midst strode a pair of men. The tall, thickset guy brandished a handgun. His shorter partner with the skinny face flourished something bigger and much more lethal-looking, like a small machine gun. Tori recognized the hitters who'd almost killed her at Sarah's house.

"I said, move away from her," the man with the handgun repeated.

"What part of that don't you get, assholes?" added the guy clutching the machine gun.

Neither of them broke stride, not for the water or the mud or for the small caliber arms brandished by the grabbers.

But the grabbers weren't giving up anything.

The first shot froze everyone for a split second. An instant later Tori was running, Owen shoving at her back, the grabber to her right pulling at her arm like he'd drag it out of its socket.

A fusillade of rounds from the miniature machine gun shredded the night. Tents collapsed. Shirts hanging on a clothesline flapped backward in smooth succession, one after another, like chorus girls. Someone screamed right in Tori's ear. She twisted around to see one of the grabbers down in the mud. The others never slowed their pace.

A tremendous whoosh. Fire tore into the sky. The heat smashed at Tori's back like a huge hand. It seemed like a sorcerer's trick at first, fire conjuring itself from the water and slime, but then Tori saw the scooter melting in the middle of the blaze and realized: A round must have hit the gas can and sparked the contents.

Flames jumped from tent to cardboard to trash heap. Squatters scrambled from their blazing shacks. The smoke and flame grew into a wall with the hitters somewhere on its other side. Figures flailed inside the blaze, their arms beating uselessly at tongues of fire.

The grabbers shoved Tori past the last of the shacks. A car waited among the weeds and broken glass beyond the encampment. When a sliver of glass sliced into the bottom of Tori's bare foot, she hissed with pain and tried to stop, but Owen shoved her and kneed her in the back. He forced her onto the floor of the car.

From the muddy carpet Tori stared up at the legs that bent above her like the bars on a cage. The car shrieked into motion.

"Stop looking at me, bitch," one of the grabbers sitting above her snapped. Before Tori could react, he raised a booted foot, smashed it down on Tori's left hand.

She screamed. Jerking her hand to her chest, she cradled it there, sobbing. The bones were on fire. Maybe broken. Tentatively, she opened and closed the fingers. Tears flooded her eyes.

"That'll keep her occupied," the same grabber said.

The grabber next to him in the back seat snorted. "Won't be long for her, anyway."

« CHAPTER 47 »

THE GRABBERS' CAR jolted onward through darkness interrupted only by the occasional functioning streetlight or a pawn shop's blazing neon.

They hadn't blindfolded Tori. She was grateful for that even though she knew that if they didn't care about her seeing their destination, it was because they didn't expect her to leave the place alive. Just the thought of traveling with her eyes smothered into complete blackness filled her with panic. They'd stuffed dry cotton wadding into her mouth and slapped tape across her lips. The cotton sucked every drop of moisture from her mouth. The carpet under her cheek stunk of smoke. Her left hand throbbed. She couldn't move the fingers. Or more precisely, when she did move them, pain momentarily obliterated the joints.

The car slowed. Through the windows above her, Tori made out the flat roofs of factories and high fences topped with barbed wire,.

The car stopped. In front of it, something metallic rattled and scraped. Tori raised her head, caught a glimpse of an industrial-sized gate sliding to the side of the roadway. A grabber shoved her down again.

"Pull over there," Owen directed from the front passenger seat. The car jolted over rough pavement. The same metal-on-concrete noise scraped from behind them now.

"Fucker," Owen said. "He was supposed to kill all the lights out here."

The car stopped again. The grabbers shoved the doors open.

"Me and Rafe got her," said the man who'd smashed Tori's hand. He was bald, his head shaped like a giant missile. He yanked her to her feet and pulled her out of the car. Cramps gripped her legs and she stumbled. Her right foot was numb, her naked left foot throbbing at the sliver still embedded in its sole. Pain hammered her left hand.

She swiveled her head, trying to take in the surroundings. Trying to see if there was any place to run if she miraculously slipped free for an instant. They stood in a barren parking lot enclosed by a ten-foot fence crested with razor wire, the fencing interrupted only by the wide metal gate, now shut again. Every third light in the parking lot buzzed with an orange haze. The concrete underfoot was half-rubble, littered with gravel that bit like teeth at Tori's bare foot. The only other car in the parking lot was a compact with a cracked window.

The grabbers were staring over at it too. "That the security guard's?" the grabber named Rafe asked. He had the jittery muscles of a peelfreak, his light brown arms quivering lightly and his stubble-scratched chin hitching up and down. He was spidery and thin, and never entirely stopped moving.

"Should be. Come on. He's supposed to meet us up there." Owen quickened the pace.

Rafe gripped Tori's wrist with fingers that were shockingly strong. She gasped, barely kept herself from crying out at the sudden twisting of her damaged left hand. "C'mon, you," he muttered and yanked at her to keep up. She staggered after him.

An illuminated sign hummed on the building's front wall: *Mori son P astics: Homel nd Proud.* The factory's dirty brown brick face had no windows and only a single door at the front. Massive vents erupted from the roof like smokestacks on an ocean liner. A second, inner fence, at least twelve-feet tall and as ferociously spined as the outer one, protected the building. This fence was interrupted only by a narrow gate directly in front of the factory's door and by a small sentry-box at one side.

The size of the building, the height and viciousness of the fences overwhelmed Tori. She didn't see any way out except through razor wire unless—like the no-go zone—someone had sliced the fence open somewhere along its length. But she'd never be able to find an opening fast enough, not with grabbers after her.

"Big place." The bald grabber echoed her thoughts. "Where's the workers?"

"All mechanical," Owen said. "Robots. Just the one security guard."

Tori swung her head around to look at Owen. There was a guard? If the guard was armed, if the guard had monitors on them right now, maybe she did have a chance. She'd run. Probably wouldn't get far, but she'd damn well try.

A buzzing sounded briefly from the narrow gate that led through the inner fence to the factory door.

"That guard just open it for us?" the bald grabber asked. "It electrified?"

"Just wait a minute, will you?" Owen surged forward and hovered about an inch from the gate.

The factory door opened. It was featureless, an unadorned steel rectangle streaked with gray. A man stepped outside.

He wore a security guard's uniform of dark blue pants and short-sleeved pale blue shirt, both shades of blue turned sickly by the orange lights. A truncheon wobbled against one hip, a pistol and stunner against the other. A gold badge clipped onto his shirt pocket glinted in the artificial light. He shuffled forward, ducking his head and peering out from beneath unruly eyebrows.

At the gate he paused. His hands didn't move toward the weapons at his belt.

Owen and the grabbers waited. "You coming out?" Owen finally snapped.

The guard flinched. "Yeah. Yeah. Of course."

If this was the guard, why didn't he guard the place? Tori sagged. Rafe's fingers dug harder into her arm, dragging her upright.

The grabbers had cut some kind of deal with the guy. Of course they had. The guard was on their side, even if he looked like a hard word from Owen would send him scurrying.

As soon as the guard's hand touched the gate, proving it harmless, Owen snatched the thing wide open. The bald grabber came forward to grip Tori's other arm. He and Rafe hustled her through the opening..

"You want to get rid of these lights out here?" Owen said.

"Sorry, I didn't think about that." The guard's forehead glinted as brightly as his badge. Wet patches spread from the armpits of his shirt, darkening the fabric in long ovals that stretched halfway to his waist. He glanced at Tori, his gaze trembling away the instant she met it. "So," he said with a short, forced laugh, "that's the E?"

"You lock that other one?" Owen pointed the nose of his gun at the wide, automated gate that had opened earlier to let their car into the parking lot.

The guard shuffled one foot forward and back, nodded hugely, like a seal. "Sure. Just like we agreed."

"Is it hot?" Owen asked.

"Hot?"

"Electric," the bald grabber clarified, earning an irritated glance from Owen. The bald man's grip tightened on Tori's wrist, compressing the base of each damaged finger. She let out a quick, high yelp of pain.

"Uh." The guard's gaze flickered to her again. "Uh, no. Used to be. The owner's never bothered getting anybody in to fix it."

Tori lifted her head at this. Not electrified? So if the fence had been sliced, it would be safe to slip through the gap. And if she had wire cutters, it would be safe to cut through the fence herself.

Yeah. Just pick up one of the pairs of wire cutters sure to be strewn around the place, give the grabbers the slip, and spend a leisurely quarter hour cutting an exit.

Owen jabbed a finger at the guard. "You said the property was secured. You said they make stuff for the military here." Owen's hand trembled. His mouth worked like he was trying to chew air.

Another one who needed a cap, Tori thought. Maybe he'd get unraveled enough to get careless. Hell, the way his teeth were grinding, he could cut through the fence with his mouth.

The guard edged back to the building's front door and held it open. "Uh, yeah, it's military. Uh, canteens, mess trays, stuff like that."

Tori didn't want to leave the humid outdoor air, the haloed lights. Entering the building felt like entering a tomb.

"Move it, will you?" Rafe tugged at her. His hand was sweaty and freezing at the same time.

The grabbers pressed inside. Rafe shoved Tori through the entrance.

The guard secured the door behind them. "I turned off all the internal surveillance so we're okay in here."

They stood in a lobby. Cheap paneling covered the walls. The suspended ceiling was gouged and chipped. The lobby had been turned into a storage room with old tables, chairs and boxes stacked inside it. The grabbers waited while the guard pressed ahead to an inner door separating the lobby from whatever lay beyond it, presumably the factory floor.

The guard keyed in a code, inserted a passcard, and offered his retina to a scanner. . The door slid open to a din of machinery.

Retina scans were bad, Tori thought. If you needed one to get out of the factory too, then she had zero chance of escaping this place once they got her through that doorway. Panic rose from her gut. She tried to cough, but the tape over her mouth and the cotton jammed inside it interfered. She heaved with stifled bursts that doubled her over. Terrified, she tasted vomit at the back of her throat, wondered if she would choke on it. She raised her gaze. Rafe looked annoyed by her, the bald guy disgusted. Owen didn't even seem to notice her existence.

The guard watched her with furtive, frantic eyes and tugged at the front of his collar. "Uh, is she gonna be okay?"

The vomit receded, along with the intense spike of panic. But the fear remained. Tori willed the guard not to look away. If she could get him to feel sorry for her, maybe he'd do something to help. She didn't know what exactly, but at least he had a gun and the right retinas.

She deliberately coughed harder, mixing in strangled choking noises.

"Can somebody do something?" the guard asked.

Rafe gave Tori's arm a vicious tug. "Stop it." Pain fried every nerve in her hand. She wallowed away from him.

"Just take the tape off her, will you?" Owen snapped. "Nobody's gonna be able to hear her inside this place anyway. Let her scream all she wants."

Rafe ripped the tape away from Tori's mouth. Her face stung. She spat the wad of cotton onto the floor. For a moment, all she could do was savor the sensation of breathing freely. She threw a pleading look at the guard who looked away again, rubbing his mouth with one hand, dragging the corners down.

Then, before Tori could do anything else, the grabbers massed around her and drove her into the factory's mechanized shriek.

« CHAPTER 48 »

IT WAS WELL after dark when Geoffrey Whelk got the summons he'd been expecting: Merle Edgers, of course. And Edgers was not at all pleased.

"You won't believe the call I just got," Edgers growled from Whelk's comm. Whelk eased himself away from Murray's car. Murray, in the driver's seat, plastered a salve on the burns that seared the back of his hand bright pink. Slater rested in the back, a bandage wrapped around a shallow flesh wound on his arm. Things hadn't gone quite as planned at the squatter's camp.

"If some moron living in a cardboard box hadn't left a can of gasoline sitting out on the front stoop, there would have been no inferno this evening," Whelk replied, reasonably enough he thought. "Murray and Slater suffered only minor injuries, but they'll be scouting about for the Jennings girl within the hour. Paden and Junior likewise. Sergei has been, ah, interrogating potential informants."

"You're a real piece of work, Geoff." Edgers' voice was steely, but Whelk detected a large vein of anxiety running just beneath it. "Your men missed Jennings, but I just got off the line with some old friends in the grabbing business. They had some good info on how and where we can get our hands on her. Specific information."

"Yes, Merle, but what are they asking in return?"

"Just a percentage." Edgers practically spat into the comm.

Smiling, Whelk continued to roll toward his own car, parked a dozen feet distant. The arthritis in his right leg had been quiescent all day, reason enough for good cheer. "Merle, I'd prefer we discuss this on another net. This particular one is too easy to tap and—"

"Fuck that cloak and dagger shit! Geoff, I want to know what you're doing about fulfilling your contract. Or should we just give the grabbers their percentage *and* your cut? Huh?"

Whelk reached his sedan. He leaned against the front. The suspension groaned. "We can accomplish our goal as soon as you tell me where these ruffians are."

"Where they are?" Edgers exploded. "You mean you don't know? Gee, I thought you had this situation under control."

"Feel free to omit the sarcasm, Merle. Just tell me where they are, and I'll take care of everything."

"Hell, maybe I should just pay them off. Get this job over with. Damn thing's been a pain in the neck ever since—"

"Merle, calm down," Whelk practically cooed into the unit. "Don't rush into foolish decisions. Is it Owen again, perchance?"

"We're talking a hell of a stiff percentage, Geoff."

"Yes, well, I'm sure that's true," Whelk answered. "Nothing comes cheap in our business these days. Especially when one is forced to deal with unsavory characters."

"Tell me about it. If half my staff hadn't screwed everything up already . . . If Paige had just taken it. Renz, he'd have taken it if she'd said yes."

"But they didn't pitch in when they were most needed, did they? They let you down, Merle. That's the problem with these young pups. No loyalty." When Edgers didn't respond, Whelk gave a short laugh to show he'd taken no offense at the reference to Paige and Mike's allegedly superior skills. "Well, Merle, are we going to continue dancing around insults, or are you going to allow me to deal with these insects?"

A moment's hesitation. "Seriously, Geoff, maybe paying them off is the best choice. Get it over with and then next time—"

"Ah, yes, next time," Whelk said. "Because when you start caving in to blackmailers, it's the slippery slope to financial ruin. I warned you last time, don't pay them off, don't encourage them, they'll only demand an even more onerous percentage on the next occasion. And they have, haven't they?"

"Oh, God," Edgers groaned.

"You have to nip this thing right now, Merle. No messy loose ends." Heaving his bulk away from the car, Whelk strolled around toward the trunk. "We'll pretend we're going to make the exchange. It just won't be quite the exchange they're anticipating. So. Where do they want the cash?"

"Morrison's Plastics. Down in the southern industrial ghetto. Military production. I'll have to get the money together for you."

"Actually, I'm still rather flush at the moment. You can reimburse me later." Whelk raised the lid of a long box inside the trunk, then removed the cloth that covered several rifles and a pair of handguns. "I'll see that Owen and his compatriots receive payment-in-full."

Edgers gave a short laugh. "Now that's the old Geoff talking." He sounded slightly more cheerful. "What do you have in mind?"

"The only reason Owen has Tori Jennings is because he and those maggots of his opened fire on some of my men." Whelk removed two clips of ammunition. "I have some people itching for a rematch."

"Okay, now, Geoff, I've got to warn you. You do something irresponsible, any cops step in again, I'm cutting all ties. You're on your own."

"Yes, well, you know, Merle, it's not too far-fetched to presume that these grabbers might be the very same men—or affiliates of the men—who shot your nephew. You have my condolences, by the way. For young Thomas's passing."

Whelk motioned Murray over and laid out several weapons for him to carry back to his car. "Any word on Mr. Krey's whereabouts, Merle? Or has Owen done us the service of removing that particular thorn from our collective side?"

"We've had some intercepts that indicate he got separated from her."

"Indeed?" Reaching into the trunk again, Whelk took out a nylon bag.

"He's not necessarily on the case anymore."

After shutting the trunk, Whelk carried the bag to the front seat of his sedan. "Oh, Mr. Krey will be on the case." He unzipped the bag to check the thick stacks of bills. "He's one of those types that stays on task. Solid, dogged, a touch on the boring side, if you ask me."

"Nobody did." Edgers sounded calmer now. "Just make it clean, Geoff. Keep it quiet. Reasonably quiet. Outside the factory. I don't want to pay out for damaged machinery."

"Not to worry."

"You do a good job here, Geoff, we may find a little reward for you for going the extra mile."

"I do believe we have sufficient motivation at this point in time." Whelk gave the other men a rotation of his hand. The driver, Paden, started the engine.

"Owen said to be in Morrison's parking lot at one a.m.," Edgers said. "He'll send somebody out front. They don't want to see more than one of you come forward. Sixty big, cash."

"Covered," Whelk answered. "All I require from you at present are blueprints for the complex. Good design specs, something with excellent detail."

"I'll put Spence right on it."

"We're assembling as I speak, Merle. I'll expect the information within the half-hour."

Whelk popped the air conditioning in his car to maximum and manipulated the vents to blast at his damp face. As he pulled into the street, the second car following him, Whelk sent an alert to Paden, then buzzed Sergei's comm. While he waited for Sergei to answer, he calculated numbers in his head: the shortest route to the industrial district; the size of the payment awaiting him at night's end; the amount of munitions currently at his disposal.

And, best of all, the quantity of intensely satisfying kills the evening promised.

« CHAPTER 49 »

IT WAS A LONG WALK to the house where Tori's father lived. Seth managed a couple dozen blocks on foot before he stopped. He leaned against the front of the nearest building, clung to it really, his sweaty forehead grinding against the warm bricks and his fingertips digging at the mortar. Every muscle of his body ached. His legs trembled. He pictured their muscles like brittle rubberbands stretched too far.

What time was it, anyway? Confusion sloshed inside his head. He wasn't sure when he'd taken that last injection or when he was supposed to have the next one. He hadn't brought the med box with him, hadn't even thought about it. Hadn't thought about much, really, except finding Tori. As foggy as his brain was, it was a miracle he'd actually remembered to bring his gun, although at the moment he'd rather have a car or some cash.

He had the comm with him and he'd sent Bobby and Kendall a slew of messages, begging for transportation. They weren't answering. Hell, Seth wouldn't care if Bobby was pissy and insulting as long as the Network coughed up some kind of junker Seth could use to get across town.

He sagged against the wall. Okay, the reality was he was in no shape to hike halfway across town. What he should do was keep trying Bobby and, in the meantime, go back to Singapore to get the meds.

Should, except that he felt so weak that he suddenly wasn't sure he could walk another block, much less all the way to Singapore.

He needed to rest first. Had to. He pushed off from the wall and lurched along the sidewalk. At the corner, he blinked up at the street sign.

Sydney was only another half a dozen blocks west. He shoved his hand into his back pocket. The access IDs and keycards were still there, bundled together with a rubber band.

That decided it. Sydney first. He'd rest, but not long. Thirty minutes, max. Every second he rested was another second Tori was on her own.

He kept his head down as he walked, focused on each forward swing of his feet. Concentrated on keeping a steady rhythm, keeping his balance. Focusing like that held the fiercest pain of the headache at bay.

The first thing that struck Seth when he opened Sydney's door and stumbled inside was the odor: sweat, burnt metal, and excrement. He froze in the doorway.

Two chairs. A body strapped to each of them. A knife on the table. A large square battery. On the floor, a plastic cup beaded with water.

A second later, Seth realized who the men were. He jolted forward, crossed the room without realizing he was in motion.

Kendall was unconscious. Blood spangled his hair. Seth gingerly touched his face, but Kendall's eyes didn't open. Seth grimaced, examining Kendall's sunken cheeks. He looked like an old man who'd forgotten to put in his dentures. When Kendall's mouth lolled open, Seth saw why. Most of Kendall's teeth were broken at the gum line or just above it.

"Jesus." Seth swung around to examine Bobby. Bobby's eyes were oozing slits, but they followed every movement Seth made.

Bobby wasn't looking behind him or to the side, as if watching a hitter's hiding place, but Seth suddenly realized how vulnerable he was. *Pitiful*, he castigated himself.. He hadn't made it this long as a Guardian by forgetting danger. He raised the gun and scanned the living room, the tiny galley kitchen, the bedroom and bath. There wasn't much to the place and no one hiding.

He returned to Bobby. Tiny wounds, thin as paper cuts, covered the man's chin and jaw.

"Sorry." Seth ran his fingers along the edge of the tape covering Bobby's mouth. "I've got to do this." Bobby blinked once, slowly, as if giving his permission and Seth tore the tape free. Bobby hunched forward and sucked in long, greedy breaths.

Seth touched his shoulder. Bobby reared up, wild-eyed.

"Hey, it's okay." Seth drew back, raised both hands, showing Bobby an empty palm and a gun pointed well away from everyone. "How bad's the damage?"

"Kendall's really bad." Bobby spoke with a lisp through cracked lips. Seth stared. Bobby obligingly drew his lips back from his gums. Four black slots gaped at the front.

"Jesus, Bobby." Seth stumbled to the table to retrieve the knife. He crouched beside Bobby's chair to saw through the cords. Bobby tried to stand, but his legs shook so hard that he immediately collapsed back onto the chair.

"Ken got it worse," he said. Kendall still hadn't moved or opened his eyes and he didn't react as, one by one, Seth cut the cords restraining him. "He talks too much," Bobby muttered. "Never has known when to shut up."

Kendall slumped forward on his chair. Seth caught him before he toppled to the floor and carried him to the couch. Straining to see, Bobby asked, "Is he breathing?"

"He's breathing." Seth pressed a hand beneath Kendall's jaw and circled the man's wrist with one hand. "His pulse seems kind of thready."

Bobby again tried, unsuccessfully, to stand. "Hospital," he lisped. "For Ken."

"Yeah. And you."

Bobby sagged. "There's no insurance. Not private." His mouth pulled into a ghastly imitation of a smile. Blood foamed from the empty sockets onto the adjoining teeth, coating them with a sheer pink film. "Public hospital."

Seth scrabbled for his comm and tried to get Public Emergency to answer. The first voice rerouted him to a second recording.

"Was it Sergei?" Seth asked. But he already knew.

Bobby tried to lick his lips. Seth took the plastic cup to the kitchen, dumped the contents, and filled it at the tap. Wincing, Bobby sipped the water. "Yeah. And another guy. Murray."

"Looking for Tori?"

"And you."

"So she's kept away from them." His sudden relief felt expansive, like someone had sliced him free of strangling cords as well. But the bindings refastened themselves tighter than before when Bobby added, "Grabbers got her."

Seth stared at him. "Wait. Are you sure?"

"Yeah."

Seth squeezed his eyes shut against the pain flaring inside his skull. Grabbers. He saw Riker's teeth, felt the way they sliced through skin and muscle. At least grabbers wouldn't kill Tori, not right away. That was the upside, but it wasn't much of one.

Snapping his eyes open, he tried Emergency again. No answer. He went to the kitchen and dug out a dishrag which he soaked under the tap. Returning to the living room, he swabbed carefully around the outside of Kendall's wound of a mouth, washed the sweat and blood from Kendall's face as if he could wipe away pain and terror at the same time.

"Somebody called Sergei while he was . . ." Bobby's face whitened and his glance ticked toward the battery. "Messing with *that*. I heard him talking."

"And he said what?" Seth asked. Kendall's cheek twitched under the damp cloth.

"Grabbers had her. A factory someplace. Uh—Morrison Plastics. Sergei tore out of here." Tears oozed from Bobby's eyes. "I was glad they got her, Seth. If it made him leave." Bobby sobbed. "I didn't care if they killed her. Eight years with the Network and I was praying that monster would go after her instead." Snot dripped from Bobby's nose. He didn't seem to notice.

Kendall suddenly groaned and twisted in his chair.

"Ken?" Bobby slid off his own chair and onto his knees. He crawled to Kendall.

"Hey, you're okay." Seth pulled the damp cloth back and put a hand against Kendall's cheek. "You're okay now."

Kendall, not opening his eyes, reached up and pressed his own hand down over Seth's and nodded once.

"We'll get you help," Seth told him.

Another nod.

Seth used his free hand to try Emergency again. A recording invited him to leave a message. He crammed the comm back into his pocket.

Kendall spoke. Through a mouthful of blood, he said, "Save Tori."

Bobby's head jerked up. "Hey, Tori's not the only one who needs help right now."

Kendall shook his head once, carefully, as if it were made of china and required delicate handling. "They'll kill her."

"We need to get you to a hospital," Bobby protested. "Now."

Kendall's lips stretched wide. A mixture of blood and saliva bubbled over the stumps of his broken teeth. He looked up at Seth through gluey eyelashes. "Don't let them kill her."

Seth dropped the cloth onto the floor and stood. His legs trembled and his balance was wobbly and out-of-whack and a headache was trying to chop his skull into splinters. Hope splintered through his dread. "Your car here?" he asked.

Bobby's hand twitched into a pocket. "I still think we need help now. I mean, Kendall does for sure." He pulled out an ignition card.

"What's the code?" Seth asked. "Bobby? Come on, man."

Behind them, Kendall mumbled, "Seven-X-two."

"Thanks." Seth pushed the ignition card into his pocket. "And I'll get you help as soon as I can. I swear. Just sit tight." He crammed the comm back into his pocket and swung around for the door.

Bobby scrambled to his feet. Panic seized his face. "What if they come back?"

Seth paused. It was hard to stand still. He wanted to get moving. "They won't come back. They're all going to be at that Morrison's factory, trying to kill Tori and collect their money."

Bobby's mouth turned down. He looked over at Kendall. Kendall offered another slow, painful nod.

"Ah, hell," Bobby muttered and twisted toward Seth again. "Go be a hero, whatever."

Seth, on his way out the door, heard him add: "Probably too late anyway."

« CHAPTER 50 »

"Hey!" Owen snapped at the security guard who jumped away from the door to the lobby. "You're not going anywhere till the exchange, got it? You're not going to ditch out on us. We're in this. You're in this."

The guard jerked his head up and down. "I'm in. You know that."

"Then get the hell over here."

The guard hurried to the open area where Tori and the grabbers stood between the door and the first of the machines. A conveyor belt hummed beneath the clamor of robotic tools striking metal. Tori's gaze scrabbled across the factory floor. Past the forest of moving mechanical arms, a large elevated platform at the back overlooked the factory floor. A black metal ladder rose from the floor to the platform where still more machines clanked and whirred. She couldn't tell if there was a rear exit at the back of the platform.

Owen jabbed a gun at the guard. The guard cringed. "This is the deal," Owen said. "I'll tell you when Regency's made contact. You'll go out by yourself and bring *one* Regency guy in to make the exchange. And we'll all be watching."

"Sure, uh, sure." The guard couldn't nod fast enough.

"Rafe, you cover the bitch." Owen shoved Tori so hard she stumbled into the grabber. The stink of Rafe's sweat filled her nostrils. Rafe drew back from her with a grimace, and she realized she probably smelled as bad as he did. With one needle-pocked arm, Rafe raised his own gun and pointed it at Tori's head. The barrel was so close she could feel the snout of it twitch against her hair.

"Jesus, you trying to kill her before we get our money?" Owen stalked over and shoved Rafe's arm down so the gun pointed at the concrete floor. Tori flinched, gritting her teeth, expecting to hear the explosive boom of the gun firing. A few feet away from her, the guard hunched his shoulders and bent forward, peering up to one side. He was obviously expecting the same explosion.

"Moron," Owen muttered, striding away. He stopped near the door, as far from the machinery noise as he could get—although the din echoed and clamored through the entire space—grabbed his comm out of his pocket, and glowered at the screen.

Tori dared a sideways look at Rafe. He was scowling at the floor, his lower lip thrust out, the gun pointed somewhere in the vicinity of his foot which was a hell of a lot better than pointed at her head. The muscles in his stringy biceps jumped and quaked. Fresh sweat streamed down his face even though the air inside the factory actually felt chilled, like it was kept well air-conditioned for the sake of the machinery.

The other three grabbers gradually spread out, lounging against the walls, sunk into their own pharmaceutical worlds. The guard stood a dozen paces away from Tori. He kept rubbing his hands rapidly together like someone lost in a frigid wilderness, trying to stave off frostbite and death.

He met Tori's gaze briefly, looked away, then returned his own gaze to her. His dark eyes looked were watery and pink. He hunched an apologetic smile in her direction.

Rafe appeared to be withdrawing into a twitching gloom. The gun was loose in his hand. He stared at the floor like he didn't actually see it. His left leg fidgeted all over the place, like it wanted to break into a hundred separate, jerky fragments. Every few seconds, he skinned his lips back like he was in momentary pain, revealing dull yellow teeth.

Tori edged sideways, nearer to the guard. Nearer, nearer, until her arm brushed his pale blue sleeve. The guard didn't shift away. His presence was a tiny seed of hope. Tori bit down hard on it.

"How close do you think it is?" she whispered. The guard was short, his face even with Tori's.

"How close is what?" he whispered back and Tori pressed her eyes briefly shut with relief that he'd acknowledged her.

"The exchange?"

The guard gave her a weak shrug and glanced down at the comm on his belt. "Uh, awhile, I guess." He paused. Tori waited. "You afraid?" he asked.

"Yeah." Tori crossed her arms. She was shaking. "I just wish I knew how they were going to do it."

"Uh, do it?" The guard gnawed his upper lip.

"Kill me."

Quiet. "Uh, right. Right."

"The company that's after me, their hitters are pretty brutal." Tori let him dwell on the word.

The guard ducked his head. "I'm, uh, Miss, I'm really sorry about all—you know—this."

"Yeah."

Another pause. Then the guard plucked a hand at her wrist. It was her damaged hand and Tori grimaced, squeezed her eyes shut against the pain that surged from her fingers.

"Wow, Jesus, sorry." He jerked his hand back.

Tori breathed, forced her eyes open. "It's okay."

The man's face looked like it was going to collapse on itself. "It's not okay. But I've gotta have the money. And you're going to get—I mean, eventually somebody's going to—so I might as well—I have to have that money." His face flamed. "My wife's sick." The guard swayed. "Aw, shit." His watery eyelids quivered.

"I just wish I could have a chance," Tori observed softly. "A fighting chance. That's all."

"I could—maybe I could—"

Tori carefully placed her ruined hand on his pudgy, thick-fingered one. Rolled that seed of hope around her teeth, under her tongue. Chasing it.

"They'll get me anyway." Her mouth trembled. "Like 99.9 percent. You'll get the money." She tried to squeeze his fingers. The pain made her gasp. "But you won't have to hate yourself."

The guard met her eyes.

"Hey! What the fuck?" Owen rampaged toward them across the open space, his gun jammed in their direction. "Keep your damn mouths shut!"

The guard shrank back, face pale. "We were just—"

Owen pushed the barrel at the man's throat. "You. Shut up. Stand over there until I tell you to move."

The guard scuttled to the spot Owen had indicated.

"Rafe! Wake up, you piece of crap." Owen whipped out his free hand and slapped Rafe hard across the middle of the face. Rafe jerked back, howling and grabbing at his eyes with one hand. "Your percentage just went down a couple of points, asswipe," Owen finished. "Jesus, I have to do everything? I'll take *her*."

Owen shoved Tori in front of him. A muzzle against the small of her back urged her to find a quick path through the machines. Except for the stink of smoke that clung to Owen and herself, the air smelled clean, almost sterile, and it was cool enough to freeze the sweat on Tori's skin. Her stomach oozed up into her throat.

"We're going upstairs." Owen's voice was close to her left ear. A knife in his other hand pushed against her right shoulder blade. He shoved her against the ladder. "Just you and me."

« CHAPTER 51 »

DR. SIMMONS HAD BEEN gone for more than two hours since drawing samples from Emily. Paige and Senator Logan waited in a small staff lounge at the back of the MyrexLabs complex. From one end of a sagging couch, Paige eyed the senator. Logan had finished feeding Emily and now cradled the infant in her arms as she paced back and forth.

Emily wore what looked like a satin onesie. Her blanket was a small square quilt, the colored blocks faded and soft. Antique, Paige thought, and swallowed down the edge of anger that rose through her chest. Put the baby—put the Senator—in Donny Oxlade's house and see how they managed.

Paige said: "At least she's sleeping okay."

Senator Logan frowned down at Emily's pinched cheeks. "Too well. And too much." The senator pressed her lips together as if she were blotting lipstick and lowered Emily into her carrier. The woman looked drained, a pouf of hair sticking up from the back of her head, her eyes flickering with anxiety.

Paige tried to feel a little sympathy. She uncrossed her legs and sat upright. "You want something to drink? The coffee's not bad." She made a toasting motion with her own waxy cup.

The senator put up a hand: *no*. She rearranged the blanket around the child's head. "I'm sorry, I never gave you a chance to tell me about your research. So just what is your area of expertise?"

"True crime, you could call it."

Senator Logan audibly caught her breath. "Forensics, you mean?" At Paige's shrug, she said, "You don't *write* true crime?"

"I'm researching a book." Paige's comm signaled an incoming message. She checked the locator: Renz. He was back in Philly, at Regency headquarters.

"A book about my grandson," the senator said in a flat voice.

No, Paige almost snapped, *no, you and your family aren't always the center of everybody's universe.* "Actually, it's about Tori Jennings." Paige stood. "Excuse me. I need to take this." She started for the hallway.

The senator's voice drove into her back: "You should have been up front about it. But you didn't dare tell me the truth, did you? Oh, I know just what angle you're going to take. The senator's family is a bunch of spoiled, rich monsters, the senator's a hypocrite. You think she's innocent."

Paige turned a measured look on the senator. "Don't you?"

The senator's face turned bone-white. She bent over the infant and fussed at the blanket again.

Paige strode out to the hallway. Taking a deep breath, she leaned against the wall, hunched over the comm like it was a match she was trying to keep the wind from blowing out.

On the screen, Mike lolled back in the assistant's chair in the anteroom to Edgers' office. He clasped his hands behind his head.

"I've just been talking to Spence." Mike glanced off to one side. "It looks like they've about got Jennings nailed."

A flicker of adrenaline tightened Paige's grip on the comm. She didn't want Whelk or Edgers to win this one. She didn't want everybody shitting all over Tori. Shitting all over the losers who never got a break in this world. "Whelk's killed her?" Her voice was tight.

"Not yet. Not quite. A bunch of grabbers have got her down at—uh, what was that place, Spence?" Mike looked sideways again. "Morrison's Plastics. Merle's got the Demolition Duo and the usual pack riding their tail."

"Grabbers?" Relief swept through Paige. Grabbers bought time. But almost immediately fresh anxiety crawled into her thoughts. Grabbers also meant unpredictability. Chaos. Although with hitters like Whelk and Sergei on Regency's roster, chaos was going corporate these days.

"Yeah."

"So Regency screwed up yet again."

Mike shrugged. "What else is new? You ready to start lining up some other jobs?"

Paige glanced down the long corridor. At its far end, a door opened and Dr. Simmons pushed through it. She wore a green smock and pants and a matching cap, as did the cytogeneticist who followed her.

"Give me a minute," Paige said and palmed the comm down against one thigh.

"It's positive," Simmons burst out. She stabbed a stack of printouts at the door to the lounge. "The senator's still waiting? Thank God."

The air went out of Paige's lungs. Positive. That meant . . . "Tori Jennings is innocent."

"And now we can get Emily into the hands of the proper specialist," Dr. Simmons answered. "Keep her from going down the same road as the other child." She paused. "Are you okay?"

Paige straightened. "I'm fine."

Simmons gave her a warm smile. "They'll have to help Tori Jennings now, won't they? Change her status. No more Executable." She paused with one hand on the door. "Don't you want to help me deliver the good news?"

Paige raised her comm. "You go ahead. I'll be with you in a minute."

Simmons and the cytogeneticist disappeared into the lounge.

Good news, sure. But nobody was going to be doing anything about Tori's status. The courts admit they'd made a mistake? No way. Especially if Jennings was already dead. But even if she wasn't, her innocence would cast a shadow over every hit by every execution company. Make people doubt.

Not that people cared enough to doubt, cared enough to question or make an effort that might take them away from their vidstreams for a couple of seconds.

The muscles of her face tightened. She brought the comm up close again. Mike still lounged in Spencer's chair, his feet propped comfortably on Spencer's desk.

"How about a job right there in Philly?" Paige suggested, biting off each word. "One night only."

Mike sat up. Paige heard a thud as the sole of his boot struck the floor. "Grabbers already have her, Paige. Whelk's probably already there." Mike leaned forward, squinted into the camera. "You okay, Paige?"

Why did people keep asking her that? Paige swiped a hand across her face, shoved her hair back. "One night."

"Okay. One night. Then what?" Mike's forehead creased.

Damn it. She was actually shaking. Her muscles so tight with fury, they quivered.

"Paige?"

Something inside her was breaking. Coming apart. A dam, a barricade with a crack zigzagging down its length, the structure's failure simultaneously terrifying and a relief.

"Then we'll talk," she said. "About—" She hesitated.

"About you?"

"Yes."

"About you and me?"

Her hand nearly crushed the comm. "Yes."

She returned to the waiting room. The senator had her own comm out. Struggling to keep her voice under control, the senator directed the device to contact Regency's main office.

Paige let out a deep breath. Assumed a poised, calm pose, hand on hip, leaning against the doorway. "Calling Merle Edgers?" she said.

"I'm canceling the contract," the senator answered.

Well, glory be. A rich politician with a shred of conscience. "He'll charge you an arm-and-a-leg to get out."

"I don't care."

Paige's tone darkened. "He'll pocket the cancellation fee, in addition to what you already paid, and let the hitters go ahead."

"I have to *try*."

The woman's anguish looked genuine. Paige straightened.

"Me too," she answered.

« CHAPTER 52 »

BEFORE HE DITCHED Bobby's car well down the street from the factory, Seth searched the trunk for anything that might prove useful. No weapons—not surprising, considering Bobby's previous attitude toward firearms—but Seth still carried his own gun so that was all right. He rummaged in the emergency toolbox, found wire cutters and pliers and jammed them under his belt.

The streets in the industrial district were deserted, but Seth kept his gun ready in his grip. Ten minutes walk and he was limping his way along the western perimeter of Morrison's parking lot. The factory's exterior lights were off. Only grainy shadow, tinged orange by the lights of surrounding buildings, fell across Morrison's property.

Several vehicles formed a black archipelago in the middle of the lot. He could see that there were people inside the cars, but not who they were. Regency, he assumed. Sweat dripped into his eyes, making them burn. His bad leg trembled under his weight. Dizziness batted at his head like a balloon.

Seth squinted up at the silhouette of barbed wire lacerating the sky. If he wanted to climb the fence that surrounded Morrison's, he'd have to find something pretty damn tough to wrap around his hands and legs or he'd be a mess of cuts by the time he dropped to the other side. And that was assuming he could muster the strength to attempt the climb in the first place.

He shook his head, trying to clear it.

Everything about the property correlated with the information Jared had transferred to him on the way over: the imposing perimeter fence, the second fence closer in that contained just the factory, and the factory itself, a building with no windows, no exterior access to the roof, a secured entrance at the front. He could go around to the back, but he was confident Jared had been right about that too, and he'd find nothing but loading dock doors, thick as missile silos and well-secured. Inside the building, Tori would be equally constrained by building security and the scarcity of exits.

Plus, of course, the grabbers probably had her tied up, handcuffed, lashed to a pipe, staring down a shotgun.

Seth studied the factory's dark walls. Chatter on Jared's Listening Post had indicated the grabbers were inside the factory, and they had Tori with them. According to Jared, Morrison kept security guards on the premises or, at least, had done so in the past. The grabbers had either subdued any guards or—more likely in Seth's opinion—cut them in on the deal.

He'd lost two Executables before, both to bullets. Clean, quick kills that had plunged him into days of guilt and solitude in safe houses before he could bear to reconnect with the Network. Those two deaths had sickened him, but if Tori died, it was going to be worse. A lot worse. The thought of failing her made him want to shut down. Himself. Everything.

Come on. She's not dead. So stop feeling sorry for yourself and get on with it.

He pushed himself into motion, gimping alongside the fence.

A narrow sentry-box interrupted the outer fence's progression. The box stood soldier-straight, its concrete walls rising to a sharply-angled roof. The windows were vertical slits. It had a forlorn and outdated air as if no one had used it for a very long time.

He'd hoped that the fence might be loose where it met the sides of the sentry box, but the connection was snug. Seth stared at the wire mesh. Electrified? Yes, according to Jared's information, at least at one time. Jared had noted that images of the factory grounds showed neglect and the fence most likely had suffered along with the other structures.

Seth continued past the guardhouse and several more feet along the fence. All intact, but a two-foot section along the fence's bottom edge had been bent upward. Seth crouched to examine it. The muscles in his legs quivered, exhausted and weak.

The gap between fence and concrete was only a few inches, too narrow for anyone older than a toddler to slither through it. Whoever had bent the fence couldn't possibly have made it through.

But if the fence had been electrified, the hopeful trespasser wouldn't have been alive long to work on bending up a two-foot long section of it.

That made up Seth's mind. Screw the pliers. He pulled the wire cutters out from under his belt. He held them near the turned-up bottom edge of the fence, the cutters' jaws wide like the mouth of a crocodile. Then he took a breath and snapped the jaws onto a section of wire.

Nothing. No sparks. No shock.

He let relief wash through him. Rested his forehead against the fence. But then he thought of Tori, raised his head, and got to work.

The wire was strong. Seth used every sweating ounce of strength in his arms and upper body to bring the cutters' jaws slicing back together again. Again. The effort made him tremble. His headache shot off like a Roman candle, fireballs exploding against the inside of his skull.

He pushed the edges of the gash he'd made as far apart as he could and crawled through the opening. Sharpened ends of snipped metal scraped painfully across the back of his shirt. Half-stooped and now allowing himself to hesitate, he hobbled to the sentry box.

As he'd expected, it was empty. The interior smelled like the damp leaves disintegrating in its corners. He leaned panting against one wall, jammed the clippers back under his belt. He repositioned himself until he could see the cars in the lot through one of the viewing slits in the sentry box's walls. Through another slit, he could see the inner fence and, just past it, the front door of the factory.

Someone on the inside was going to have to open that door eventually. Seth pictured the scene in his head, first visualizing a single man emerging, then a pair, then an entire pack of grabbers. He might be able to surprise them, take some of them down, but that wouldn't necessarily get him into the factory. If they kept Tori inside the factory, then killing some of the grabbers and hitters outside wouldn't help. If they brought her out with them, she would die in the gunfire. That simple.

The handle of his gun warmed in his grip. He needed to be patient. The grabbers weren't going to kill Tori, not on purpose; she was worth too big a payoff as long as they kept her alive. Until the Regency guys found a way inside, she'd be okay. Terrified, maybe even injured, but alive. If Regency *did* bust the place open, then it would be all over for Tori in a matter of minutes or, more likely, seconds.

He had to get in there before Regency got in. Before Tori came out.

A whirring, mechanical noise at the factory door made Seth tense and strain forward. This was it. The door slid open.

A short man with defeated shoulders and a pouched belly hesitated in the doorway. He took a dozen steps outside, leaving the door open behind it. Beyond the open door was a lobby of some sort where red security lights burned.

As the man passed the sentry box, Seth made out the markings of a uniform. A guard, then. The man reached the gate that led through the inner fence and into the parking lot. He hesitated, then opened the gate before pausing again.

Out in the parking lot, a car door swung open. A tall, thick-shouldered man climbed out and slung forward from the vehicles.

Now more car doors opened, more silhouettes unfolded from the interiors. They remained near the vehicles, watching.

"You want the money, or not?" the tall, big-shouldered hitter called out.

It took Seth a minute to remember where he'd heard that voice before: Arlington, the house where Tori's friend Sarah lived. Murray, that was his name. Seth tried to decipher the other shapes in the darkness. He saw only one silhouette larger than Murray's, and considerably bulkier. It had to be Whelk.

Another long hesitation, and the guard stepped through the gate and trailed Murray back toward the cars. The gate through the inner fence remained open. So did the doorway leading into the lobby. The open factory door seemed to yawn at an impossible distance although, in reality, it couldn't have been more than 50 feet away.

Seth swiftly considered his options. He had to get inside the inner fence while he could. After that? He could hunch back in the shadows, try to follow the guard and any hitters into the factory. Hope the factory door remained open—or unlocked—long enough for him to gain access and then pray to Christ that no hitters remaining outside would see him early enough to shoot.

Pretty lousy odds.

Or he could try to slip inside now, trusting not only in the bad lighting, but also that the hitters would be focused on the guard.

If they saw Seth? If he didn't make it? His mouth went dry. Then Tori wouldn't make it either. But if he never took a risk to get inside the building? She'd die then, too.

Seth wiped a fresh scrim of sweat from his forehead and slipped from the sentry box. He was still breathing hard, and his heart cramped in his chest every time it beat. Adrenaline or Riker's toxin? He didn't know.

Feeling far too exposed, he slipped through the open gate, then edged his way along the inner fence. The metal smelled warm and sharp, tangy with rust. At a plant somewhere down the street, a whistle blasted, made him flinch.

He reached the front of the factory. His foot brushed against a stunted shrub, not even knee-high. Its dead branches clicked together. Not allowing himself to glance over at the parking lot, he tracked even closer to the wall.

At the factory's open door, he didn't pause, but ducked into the lobby's bloody burgundy haze.

« CHAPTER 53 »

BESIDE THE CARS, the guard pushed back his cap and flicked on an oversized flashlight.

Geoffrey Whelk stepped forward from the shadows. "We don't need that kind of attention, son." The dim haze cast by the few parking lot lights that still functioned was plenty for this kind of work.

The guard flushed and fumbled the light off. "We're the ones with the girl," the guard protested, struggling to reattach the flashlight to his utility belt.

Whelk loomed nearer, holding up a zippered bag like a dog trainer raising a liver treat above a labrador.

The guard flicked his tongue to his lips like they were parched. He cast a pleading look from Whelk to Murray to the others gathered just behind them.

"Uh, okay," the guard finally squeaked when no one else spoke up. "Uh, there's no negotiating. We want the money, all of it. You're supposed to give me the money. I take it inside. If everything looks good, I'll bring the girl back out with me." He winced when he said those last words.

Whelk grunted and motioned Paden and Junior nearer to the guard. The guard tossed a frantic look over his shoulder at the expanse of empty parking lot behind him.

Time to set the pup straight. "Well," Whelk drawled, "that's not how it's going to happen. So what's your next option?"

"But that's how it's supposed to go down."

"I've not dealt with you before so allow me to educate you on how we do business in a situation like this."

"Now, just wait a minute." The guard tugged the flashlight free and snapped it on again.

Whelk stared directly into the beam. "Turn that off before someone gets hurt."

From the vicinity of Paden's meaty hand, a trigger clicked. The guard swung wildly toward the sound, the beam of light wobbling.

"Let me explain," Whelk said. "You're not getting this money until I'm confident that you have the girl and that she's still alive."

"Oh, she's here all right." Bravado bolstered the guard's voice. "And you know she is, or else you wouldn't be here." He stepped back as the other Regency staff approached.

Whelk closed in. "Keep that light out of my eyes, Mr.—?"

"My name's not important."

"No. It isn't." Whelk twisted his grin, made it menacing, clipped his words as neatly as if his tongue were a razorblade.

The guard flicked off the light. This time he didn't bother with the utility belt. He just crammed the butt end of the flashlight into his pants pocket.

"I'm only going to give you a taste of the full amount until you've satisfied my concerns," Whelk continued.

The guard cleared his throat. "How much is a taste?"

"Ten thousand. And one of my men is going in with you. To verify that the girl is here." When the guard hesitated, Whelk laughed. "I imagine your compatriot Mr. Owen Richter told you this was all or nothing."

The guard drew his shoulders back. "That's right. And maybe you need to get off the property if you don't accept those terms."

"Do you really think my men and I are going to disappear and let you drive out the way you came in?"

"Well, I don't think you'll be on the premises long if I hit an alarm. This factory puts out product for the Defense Department."

"Canteens and tin cups."

Silence. "Maybe we'll just sell her to one of your competitors," the guard dared.

Whelk practically yelped. "Competing execution firms don't have contracts with the family. Regency is the only wallet you can dip into. No one else has any stake in this matter whatsoever." He moved forward to pat the guard on the shoulder. "That's not the way it's done, young man."

The guard took a full step back. "I'm not kidding. I call in the alarm and they will disappear you."

"Very frightening. I confess I *am* more than a little curious as to what your employers think of your moonlighting venture."

"I'm not . . . uh . . . after tonight, I won't be working here anyway."

"After you divvy it up, what, five or six ways? Not much of a retirement."

The guard stayed silent for a moment, his forehead knotted. "I'm not telling you how many guys are in there if that's what you're trying to do."

With an elaborate sigh, Whelk unzipped the bag and pulled out a stack of money. "Here's what I want from you," he said. "I want you to inform Mr. Richter of my counter-offer. Tell him I want to send in one of my men here. Tell him it's in good faith."

The guard glanced uncertainly at the shadowy forms of the hitters waiting with their weapons in hand. "Just give me a minute," he muttered, shuffling several yards away to relay the message into his comm. When he came back, he was biting his lip. "He said ten thousand is okay, but you can only send one guy in with me. Alone. And no weapons, totally clean."

"Naturally. Murray?" Whelk motioned toward the darkness and Murray stepped forward. Murray gave his rifle to Paden, turned to the guard, crossed his arms and planted his legs.

"Uh . . ." the guard said.

Murray's face was stone. "Yeah?"

"I need to . . . uh, search you. Before I let you go in." Sweat ran down the guard's face. "That's what Owen said."

Murray's expression didn't soften, but Whelk pressed a hand to his shoulder. "Let the man do his job," Whelk said.

Murray slowly raised his arms. The guard searched him tentatively, pulling a handgun from Murray's belt and freeing a knife holstered underneath Murray's shirt. The guard gave Whelk an indignant look that disintegrated into an anxious frown.

Whelk directed a withering stare at the man. "Naturally, members of my staff tend to be well-armed. You expected otherwise?"

"No," the guard said. "No, I—"

"You really are quite the neophyte, aren't you?"

At Whelk's indulgent chuckle, the guard lowered his head and hurriedly skimmed his palms down Murray's arms and legs.

"Are you sure you don't want to strip search him?" Whelk asked. "Oral cavity, anal cavity—"

"Let's go," the guard mumbled and Murray, clasping the bundle of bills, followed.

The two men were shadows near the building when Whelk motioned for the rest of his team to draw close to him. "We need to be in position when Murray gets that inner lobby door jammed open. Ready to pour into that place. Kill anything that moves."

"Including Jennings?" Slater asked.

"We'll take our time with Jennings. But kill the grabbers immediately. Merle's orders."

"What about any workers?"

Sergei stepped around from the back of the van and slapped at the specs he clutched in one hand. "Robots," he answered on Whelk's behalf.

Murray and the guard disappeared into through the factory door into the lobby. "I need two men to give Murray backup. Paden. Junior. Go." Whelk gave them a gentle push in the factory's direction and started to follow when Sergei stopped him.

The Russian rattled the specs inches from Whelk's face. "How many, Geoff? Grabbers. How many?"

Whelk brushed the specs aside with one hand. "Four, five, half-a-dozen."

"And Murray, he will kill how many?"

"Half, if we're lucky," Whelk said. "Before they render him . . . how should I put it?"

"Dead?" Sergei leaned in closer until Whelk could smell the sauerkraut on his breath. "And the rest of the grabbers? They will sit there, they will wait for us to go in, yes? We are like ducks."

"Sitting ducks is the expression, and we won't be doing any of that. We'll be on the move, finishing up business."

Releasing a thin hiss of air between his teeth, Sergei spread the specs so Whelk could examine them. "There *were* windows. Here. You see?"

Whelk grunted as he bent forward to look. "They took them out, didn't they? When they switched to the fully-robotic line."

Sergei's face grew eager. "The building, it is weak, yes? Here." He jabbed at the paper. "And here. Where they cover over the windows."

Whelk pursed his lips thoughtfully. "So you're suggesting we go in through *two* entrances. A little surprise."

"Yes. Yes! We *make* the entrance, the second one."

"And, naturally, you have the munitions."

"I have already placed them."

Whelk's comm vibrated from the vicinity of his waist. He peered at the screen. "Ah. I expected Merle might be checking in."

"You and me and Slater." Sergei counted off on three fingers. "We go in the side of the building, yes?"

Whelk cast an appraising glance at the factory. "All right. I'll let Junior and Paden know what to expect, then I'll join you."

"For the big entrance, yes."

As Whelk strode after his team, he raised the quivering comm near his mouth, and murmured, "Accept transmission."

« CHAPTER 54 »

MUZZLE AT HER BACK, hands cuffed in front of her, Tori stumbled onto the lowest rung of the ladder.

"Move," Owen ordered.

The gun barrel stabbed between Tori's shoulder blades. She dragged herself crookedly from rung to rung. Flakes of black paint stippled her palms and drizzled down from her feet each time she slid another rung higher. Her left foot slipped. She gasped, grabbing blindly, and narrowly caught the rung in front of her chest. She tightened her grip and hunched there, sucking air in and out of her lungs.

Owen, climbing beneath her, slapped the side of the ladder. Black snow flurried down from the metal. "Fuck it!" he yelped. "Move your ass, will you?"

He crawled up behind her, pressing hard, forcing Tori into motion again. She was climbing too fast. She focused on each rung as if it filled the entire universe. Once, she darted a glance beneath her: Owen's black-speckled hair; the glint of the gun plowing forward and back, tracking with the skinny white hand that gripped it; and far beneath, mechanical arms gliding back and forth above the black stream of a conveyer belt.

Tori tumbled from the ladder onto the platform thirty feet up. The platform's cold metal floor bit through the knees of her jeans.

Owen followed right behind, bursting from the top of the ladder. He strode to Tori, aimed a short, vicious kick at her head. She rolled onto her side, barely avoiding contact.

"You almost fell," Owen said. "You could've killed yourself,"

"Would've saved you the trouble."

"It would've cost me sixty thousand bucks, you dumb bitch." He grabbed Tori at the elbow and yanked her upright. The violent motion tore at her shoulder. Tears burned her eyes.

"Move," he repeated, steering her away from the railing at the front edge of the platform. Below, the other grabbers fanned out with their guns, looking like underfed snipers. Rafe fumbled in his pocket, his arms shaking visibly, his head palsied. Looking for a cap, Tori thought. The guard hadn't returned.

Owen shoved her toward the rear of the platform where an array of locks secured a pair of massive loading doors. "Get in there." He motioned at a narrow gap between two large machines.

Tori held back. Thoughts vibrated, one on top of the next, each rejected until one snagged, caught.

Fear.

If something about the operation scared the grabbers enough, would they be willing to give up on the 60 thousand dollar ransom? Or at least delay handing her over? Give them some reason to doubt their plans, push them into uncertainty and confusion and maybe they'd get careless. Careless was good—careless might mean a chance to escape or to grab somebody's gun. Shove Owen off the platform.

"C'mon!" Owen rapped the gun barrel against Tori's already injured and throbbing wrist. Tears bit her eyes.

Tori swung around to face him. He jammed his gun an inch from her face. She smelled cold metal. The gray steel blurred as she gazed steadily at the grabber.

"You know you're going to die," she said, struggling to keep her voice as level as her stare.

Owen's lips slid back. "I know *you* are."

Tori flicked a glance at the factory floor thirty feet below. Rafe wasn't trembling anymore. He was swaying. Must've popped a cap.

Tori said: "All your guys, they're in here, aren't they?"

Owen's eyes narrowed. His bony shoulders lifted. "I told you to get in th—"

"You didn't leave anybody on the outside?" Tori interrupted. She raised her eyebrows, filleted the grabber with an expression of contempt. "Nobody on the perimeter? Nobody watching the hitters? Nobody ready to take them out the minute you see a problem?"

Owen's gaze skittered all over her face.

"Regency." Tori shook her head. Her mouth was dry. She wanted to lick her lips, but she was damned if she'd give any sign that she was nervous. Nervous? Scared semi-shitless. "Have you seen what those guys do to people?"

"They're gonna tear you up, for sure." But Owen's laugh was as thin and scratchy as his beard.

Tori kept her expression still. "Regency's done with paying out to grabbers. From now on, every deal they cut with grabbers is going to end with—"

"A dead Executable, yeah."

"Surrounded by a bunch of dead grabbers."

"Says the E." Another laugh, but Owen still hadn't looked away from her face, his gaze sliding and jerking like he was trying to see the lie written in the slipping away of her gaze, in the turn of her mouth.

Tori shrugged and turned to the niche between two machines where he'd been trying to herd her a minute ago. "I'm just telling you what I heard from being around Network people."

She had her back to the grabber, couldn't see his expression. Her heart beat out the seconds. Behind her, there was no sound but the vibration and whir of machines.

Then Owen said: "Your guardian told you that?"

Tori let her eyes shut briefly. Her relief at capturing Owen's interest was cut through with fresh anxiety. She had no special knowledge, was privy to no secrets. It was all pure bullshit. She turned to face Owen again. "I heard them talking."

Owen worked his jaw from side to side. He looked away from her, gaze twitching down at the other grabbers, then snapping against the barren concrete walls like he was hoping to see through them to the hitters outside. His hand was twitchy too, fidgeting the gun against his thigh.

Tori edged an inch closer. And another. If she could get close enough to grab the gun . . . She didn't care if she got shot in the process. Better than being gutted by Whelk and the Russian.

"The Network's got a lot of people in Philly," she said. Her lips were so dry they might have been sucking dirt in Death Valley. "If we let them know where we are, they'll be your outside guys. They'll do everything they can to get past Regency and get us out of here."

She held her breath. Did he believe her? And, Jesus, what if he did? It's not like she had some insta-number to the Network she could shoot up on his comm. She'd have to fake making the connection . . . which wasn't likely to be terribly convincing.

Forget that. Focus on the gun.

She edged closer. Started to raise her manacled hands from her belly toward her chest, preparing to lunge forward and make a grab for the weapon.

Owen's comm buzzed. He stepped back, shot Tori a look of disdain.

Her fingers curled hard into the palms of her hands. Sweat froze on her neck.

"You think I'm stupid?" Owen spat the words at her. "Yeah, the Network would do everything to get *you* out of here. Get *you* past Regency. They're not gonna do jack shit for us." Now his hand was tight on the gun again, jamming it pointblank at Tori's chest. It was no more than three feet from her heart. She imagined singed fabric, torn flesh.

"Get in there," Owen said. "Now."

Tori's self-control broke. "Please." Her voice surged out of her throat. Her face was suddenly wet.

"Move!"

Tori scrambled into the gap between two pieces of equipment and crouched there. Owen stood three feet distant, his stare fixed on her, his left hand jittering on the gun handle, his right hand scraping the comm from his pocket.

The side panels of the machinery surrounding Tori were cool and slick. They sent vibrations through her arms and back and deep into the hollow of her chest. She felt sick, scooped out. Somewhere nearby, a sound like a hatchet sliced the air, over and over, a sound of clean and efficient butchery that reminded her of the kill floor at Glynn River.

Tori hunched into a tighter ball. Nausea oozed from her belly all the way up her throat, past her eyes to the top of her skull. It was over. Or would be soon. She stared out from the cramped space with a sickly uninterest. A conveyor belt thrummed and rattled. A machine swiped a blade down onto squares of plastic gliding on the belt. The blade cut each square neatly in half.

Over.

"Oh, yeah, she's here," Owen was saying into the comm. Tori's gaze slid to him. "Yeah, she's alive. You think I'm dumb enough to kill the golden goose?" He paused. His left leg jigged up and down. He loosened his gun hand just long enough to scrap a couple of red pills out of his jeans pocket, dry swallowed them. His adam's apple rolled up and down. "No, let *me* tell *you* how this is gonna to work." His right leg started its own tarantella.

Swallowing caps when the meet-up with Regency was about to go down? Now that was careless. Tori straightened. The nausea sank low in her gut. Carelessness was exactly what she needed. How long before the cap really hit him?

Over? she thought. *Probably.*

But maybe not.

"Okay," Owen said into the comm. "The guard comes from the lobby into the factory with us in two minutes. Exactly. Your guy—what'd you say?—Murray?—Murray needs to stay right in front of the guard when they walk in here. Where we'll have a clean shot if this Murray guy of yours tries to fuck us over."

Tori watched through lowered eyelids at the blade as it sliced down again. She slowly twisted her wrists against the manacles. Plastic cuffs. Impossible to break. But very possible to cut.

If she could get away from the grabbers for ten seconds, fifteen, she could have her hands free.

Or cut off. If you screw up.

The ladder clattered. A second later, Rafe slipped over the top and onto the platform. He slouched across to where Tori squatted.

"You keep a good eye on her," Owen said, "if you want to keep your cut."

Owen clambered onto the ladder, sunk out of view. Rafe crouched a half dozen feet from Tori. He stared at her, not blinking, his mouth curled and his gun aimed toward her pelvis as if he wanted nothing more than to rape her with a dozen bullets. A grimy odor of old sweat, greasy hair, and onion billowed from him.

"You move, you're done," he said. She believed him.

She hunkered there, not daring to shift her weight from one leg to the other, until her feet cramped and her thigh muscles bunched and ached. The only thing she moved was her gaze, which slipped occasionally to the blade as it whickered up and down, up and down.

Ten feet away and it might as well have been in Baltimore. Tears filled her eyes, but she didn't dare raise her hands to wipe them away.

« CHAPTER 55 »

INSIDE THE LOBBY, SETH crouched behind a desk piled high with stacks of chairs at the north end of the room. He'd already examined the second, inner door that separated him from the factory floor, noting the security mechanisms. The thing had a retinal scan. That alone would be a major problem.

The exterior door shuddered, sliding open. Seth bent lower, pulse accelerating, his hand tight on his gun. Sweat dripped from his chin onto the back of his hand. A voice chattered nervously in the shadows out in front of the building. Something—a boot, maybe—scraped across concrete.

"Uh, there's a lot of clutter in here." The guard held back just outside the doorway.

"After you," another man said from the darkness. Murray. Big, bulky, lethal, but not psychopathic like his bosses.

Seth squeezed his eyes shut, tried to think over the ache clamoring inside his head and the fever that simmered every joint and muscle.

He could follow them into the factory when the guard opened the inner door—well, try to follow them—in which case he'd be seen too quickly to do anything. The odds of reaching Tori and bringing her safely out were miniscule.

Or he could wait here and ambush them when they brought Tori out. And what if they didn't bring her out? What if Murray just shot her right there on the factory floor the minute she and the money changed hands?

It was a risk, but he didn't think Whelk or Sergei would bring it down that way. They'd want to be involved, personally involved, in the kill. In the case of an Executable who'd eluded them for as long as Tori had, they'd want to linger over the process. The odds would still be terrible, but slightly better than if he tried to go in.

Hold on, Tori. He realized he was mouthing the words, over and over. *Hold on.*

« CHAPTER 56 »

MURRAY TAILED THE GUARD into the lobby. In the murky red emergency light, the place looked more like a flea market than a business establishment. Desks, busted lamps, chairs with broken backs, rolled up carpet that stank of mold. Lousy place to bite it. At least the guard's end would be fast. No car batteries or little electrodes or whatever the hell those things were that Sergei had attached to that hippie in the apartment. Nobody shitting their own pants with terror. This was the kind of job Murray liked.

The guard studied the time on his comm. "Okay." He stepped to the second, inner door, slipped a passcard through the reader, and hunched over the keypad to jab in a sequence of numbers. Murray pressed up behind him.

The guard dared a quick glance back. "What Owen said was, when this door opens, you move forward with me real slow. Okay?"

Murray briefly lifted his gaze to the ceiling. He could practically hear Whelk's voice oozing: *amateurs*.

"You—uh—you understand?" the guard said.

"Yeah. I got it."

The guard shuffled to the retinal scan. When the door slid open, he waved Murray through first, then followed. A pair of grabbers waited just inside the factory. While the guard re-secured the door, Murray surveyed the guns aimed at him.

The one who seemed to be the leader—at least by the way the other men kept glancing at him—moved closer. "You frisked him?" the guy asked the guard.

The guard's cheek twitched. "Uh, yeah, Owen, I sure did. Pulled a gun and a knife off him too."

"All right." Owen looked sweaty and distracted. The gun quivered in his hand. He reached for the banded money Murray held nestled against his chest.

Murray stepped neatly to one side. "Where's the girl? You don't get any money unless I see her for myself."

Owen flapped the gun at the platform. *Wasted*, Murray thought. *Totally dropped*. Probably more of a threat to shoot that gun off by accident than on purpose.

"I don't see her." Murray ostentatiously tightened his grip on the money.

Owen had a comm out. "Rafe. Rafe! Get her out where we can see her."

Above them, a man even skinnier than Owen slipped from behind a huge, clanking press of some sort. Rafe reached back to yank at something and a moment later Jennings, wrists fastened together, stumbled into view. She looked like shit, in Murray's humble opinion. Nice cheekbones though. Tall. Probably cleaned up nicely, if she'd ever got the chance. The grabber, Rafe, jerked her out of view again.

Murray nodded. " Okay. This is the way we do it."

"*You're* making the rules?" A smile spread like oil across Owen's face. "We're the ones with the prize."

Murray shrugged. "And we're the ones with the money. So listen up. The guard comes back out with me. I'll get the rest of the money. When we're ready to do the exchange, the guard'll call you from the parking lot. Your guy, *one* guy, brings Jennings out and the guard gets the cash at the same time." Murray pushed the bills at Owen. "Down payment."

Owen jabbed a finger at the guard. "Get back out there. I'll bring the girl down." Cradling the money, Owen turned and wound his way through the machinery toward the ladder.

Murray waited as the guard touched the passcard to the reader. "Hope Owen doesn't take off with all the money," Murray said.

The guard flinched, but he didn't look at Murray. A green light blinked and he reached for the keypad. "It's gonna be okay," the guard murmured. It sounded like he was trying to convince himself. Comfort himself. "My wife, she takes, Jesus, twenty pills a day. Half of them you can't even get at Uni-health. You got to go private. You have any idea how much that costs?"

Murray grunted and glanced behind him. Owen was almost at the top of the ladder. The grabber had taken off his shirt and knotted it around the money. With his emaciated back and his bluish-white skin, he looked like some kind of amphibian slithering up the rungs; at a distance, his tattoos resembled scales. Rafe waited at the top of the ladder.

The other two grabbers near Murray still had their guns trained in his general direction, but the barrels floated and twitched. One of the grabbers stared, glassy-eyed, right through Murray and the other sweated like he had faucets embedded in his skin. *Peelfreaks*, Murray thought with disgust and wiped an arm across his forehead as if he were hot. He rolled his right sleeve up to the elbow, then reached for the loose cuff of the left sleeve and then beneath the sleeve itself.

Under the sleeve, tape tugged lightly at the hairs on Murray's forearm. The tape held down a slim, flexible casing made of flesh-toned plastic.

The casing contained a razor, long and fiber-thin and just waiting for a throat to cut.

« CHAPTER 57 »

THE BREEZE HAD PICKED up, blowing a hot industrial stink of concrete, rubber, and chemicals across Morrison's lot. Whelk picked up his pace and turned the corner at one end of the building, heading toward the side where Sergei had parked the van. The fence hadn't put up much resistance to sundry items in Sergei's toolbox, to judge from the enormous, van-sized hole cut through it. Behind Whelk, Junior and Paden waited just outside the factory's front door. In front of him, Sergei and Slater toted explosives from the van to the wall.

On Whelk's comm screen, Merle Edgers glowered, face screwed-tight. Whelk thumbed the unit to audio-only. "Apologies, Merle. I wouldn't want to risk the light from the screen compromising this operation."

"What? What's going on up there? You don't answer my calls, you don't report in when you're supposed to."

"The girl is nearly in our grasp."

"Where is she?"

"Inside the facility, of course. We should be mopping up within ten, fifteen minutes," Whelk said.

"You got fifteen. What's your plan of attack?"

"Not to worry." Whelk pushed out a fat chuckle.

"I said, what's your plan?"

Time to throw the man a bone. "Murray has already penetrated the building's security."

Silence. Then what sounded like the thump of a glass bottle on a wooden desk. "Okay. And?"

"Paden and Junior will soon be positioning themselves in the lobby. The instant the interior door from the factory floor opens to—ah—disgorge Miss Jennings and her keepers, Paden, Junior, and your other fine employees will complete the operation."

All quite true. Paden and Junior had seemed to understand their instructions. Go on the attack the instant that interior door moved—not waiting to see who was walking through it—then make free use of their guns as necessary to advance into the factory proper. Whelk didn't mention the other prong of attack: the explosives Sergei would detonate following immediately on the heels of the lobby bloodletting.

The grabbers—not the most intelligent specimens to begin with—were sure to flail in the chaos until Regency wiped their sorry blackmailing glutei maximi across the concrete floor. Perhaps along the walls as well.

"Leave the unit on," Edgers ordered. "Don't even *try* to keep me in the dark."

"Of course, Merle, although I'm afraid the battery may be failing."

"Unh-unh. Don't you even think abou—"

Whelk swiped off the audio link as well. Then, swiftly, before Edgers would have even realized the connection was gone, Whelk set his comm to accept calls from Paden and Junior only.

He rolled his bulk to a stop near the van which was set well back from the wall. Sergei and Slater had finished placing the explosives. Sergei shot Whelk a cheery grin and a thumbs up and waved him behind the barricade of the van.

"It looks impressive," Whelk told him, nodding toward the wall. "That should give everyone inside a nice distraction."

"We take one or two out, yes," Sergei nodded eagerly and bent over the remote detonator. He glanced up. His expression reminded Whelk of a ten-year-old boy's. "And then? After we get in? Ha! We take out the rest."

« CHAPTER 58 »

MURRAY'S ARMS TENSED as he waited for the guard to finish the last of the security procedures. The guard stepped back from the retinal scan and the door leading back out to the lobby slid open.

"Uh, okay," the guard said. "I guess we can head back out now."

The guard stepped into the doorway. At the same instant, Murray jerked the tape loose and let the freed length of plastic razor wire slither out from beneath his sleeve. In one seamless motion, he grasped either end of the weapon, raised it, and passed it over the guard's head.

The blade lassoed the guard around the throat, slid through skin, muscle, and trachea. The guard's hands snatched at his neck. He stumbled halfway around. The wound curved across his throat like a thin red smile. He made a horrible, underwater sound. Shock drained his face as he thrashed at Murray.

The door started to glide shut. Hot blood spilled like a freshet over Murray's fists as he pulled the razor tighter. The guard collapsed, his torso wedged into the doorway.

From the factory behind him, Murray heard the grabbers' initial sluggish cries of alarm, followed by the first blast singing from a shotgun. He yanked the guard's sidearm from its holster and counted the seconds it was taking to do this, and it was taking too long, much too long. Where the hell were Paden and Junior?

Get down.

No sooner did the thought come than a bullet slipped like a burning tongue across the back of his shirt. Another short round exploded into the wall beside him. He had to get out of here, get to the lobby and out to the cars. In a half-crouch, shooting into the factory, he stumbled backward over the guard's body, but stopped, confused by gunfire and screams coming from *behind* him now, from the lobby.

Tearing off a couple of rounds that dropped one of the grabbers, Murray swung around. Paden sprawled on the lobby floor, half his throat gone. Junior slumped against an overturned desk; two neat bullet holes dimpled his forehead. For an instant, Murray forgot the grabbers and gaped at the man hurtling toward him from the lobby.

Fucking Krey. Where'd he come from?

As Murray slung his pistol around to fire at Seth, a bullet from a grabber's shotgun ripped into his shoulder, striking an inch away from the protection of his Grapamid tunic. The impact spun Murray around and down and another bullet tore into his thigh. He blinked up at the harsh white factory lights, disoriented, like a surfer tumbled by a strong wave. A third bullet drove through his wrist and his .38 spiraled into the air.

Murray stared up at Seth Krey vaulting over him into the factory. Krey turned to shove the guard's body with one foot, pushing it out to the lobby. No longer wedged open, the door immediately slid shut, trapping Murray and Seth both inside the factory.

Another explosion, this one overwhelming, blasted Murray's eardrums. He saw nothing but a burst of white radiance, swiftly swallowed by a blackness that engulfed him.

∞

Outside the factory, the blast dropped Whelk onto his hands and knees. The building roared and shook, pieces of brick and concrete showering the pavement. His ears rang. Dimly, through the ringing, he heard more shots from inside. From his comm: nothing. No alert from Paden or Junior that they were on their way into the factory yet.

That was Sergei for you. Always too eager with the detonator.

Okay, so Regency would only have this one entrance into the factory, not the two they'd planned. The grabbers would still be hurting. In shock.

Concrete dug into the butts of Whelk's hands and through the knees of his pants. He swung his chin up and blinked through air that was thick with grit and dust. Artificial light poured from a tremendous gash in the building's side. Figures—Sergei? Slater?—lurched across a small mountain of rubble and plunged through the smoky light into the factory.

334

« CHAPTER 59 »

THE EXPLOSION JOLTED the platform beneath Tori, flung her heart into instant overdrive. Blistering air punched her face. Her eyes reflexively squeezed shut. An alarm shredded the building's interior, the shrillness cutting through the clank and hum of the machinery that continued to function. Below, someone screamed. All the sounds were muffled.

"Shit shit shit," Rafe squealed nearby.

Tori blinked her eyes open. Rafe was on his knees, bent over, pawing at his oozing eyes. The lids were shut and already red and rapidly swelling. Dust painted his eyelashes white.

The cubbyhole the grabbers had crammed Tori into had protected her from the flying debris. Staggering to her feet, she stared out across the platform.

Thick clouds of dust obscured the work floor below. She could just make out an opening, like the ragged mouth of a cave, yawning in one of the walls. She couldn't see, at first, who was screaming, but then the billowing smoke parted for an instant and she glimpsed a body. The legs were gone, and one of the arms. The saliva in her mouth turned thick and sour. The screaming lost its shrillness, dwindled.

Stopped.

"I can't see! I can't—" Rafe crawled across the platform on his hands and knees, groping at the metal with clawed fingers. "Owen! Jake!" He looked half out of his mind, had obviously forgotten all about Tori.

She didn't make a sound—not that he would have heard her above the pulsing scream of the alarm. She let him go.

Rafe was almost to the platform when Owen scrambled up from the ladder. Owen didn't say anything to Rafe, didn't even seem to look at him, just raised his gun and broke for the vantage point at the railing.

Rafe raised his head as Owen's footsteps pounded past. Now Tori realized that the red around Rafe's eyes wasn't just from swelling. It was blood, smearing the man's eyelids and oozing down his cheeks. Rafe flailed out with both hands. Owen was only a half dozen feet away, but Rafe obviously couldn't see him.

Owen leaned out over the railing and shot at figures darting through the smoke below. Sweat drowned the tattoos on his back; a black dragon stared from his spine, its sapphire eye fixed on Tori.

Tori realized: no one was watching her. No one seemed to remember that she existed. But that might not last long.

Carefully, keeping an eye on the two grabbers, she sidled toward the machine she'd watched so intently earlier. For now, it continued to function with the same efficient rhythm. Its blade flashed down toward the conveyor belt, withdrew, guillotined down, whispered upward again.

Her fists rose to her chest. The plastic cuffs had dug thin channels into her flesh, giving each wrist a mottled purple-red bracelet. She strained her hands as far apart as she could until four inches of taut plastic vibrated between her wrists. She took one final glance at the grabbers. Rafe, still mewling and flailing, had crawled almost to the ladder. Owen kept firing his gun. The dragon on his back continued to glare.

Fear paralyzed Tori's lungs. She couldn't breathe. The blade rose and fell, cleaving the air.

Better not to wait. Better not to think too much.

She thrust her hands forward. Her head flinched down against one shoulder as the blade struck.

« CHAPTER 60 »

THE ECHO OF the explosion still rumbled through the floor beneath Seth's feet and rang from the walls. Shouts, wordless and desperate, ricocheted from every direction, obscured by the alarm's shriek. His earlier headache was nothing compared to the steel-on-steel agony now echoing through his skull. Dust covered him like a second gray skin. He tasted blood and salt, and the tang of metal and powder. His throat felt thick, his breath hot and smothered.

His hands were empty. The blast had knocked his gun clean away. Seth squinted through the smoke and fine debris sifting through the air. No sign of the weapon. He eased away from the closed lobby door and the dead men on its far side. His throat tightened at the memory of the shots he'd fired: a round that blew apart Paden's neck and two more bullets that plowed into Junior's forehead. He'd had no choice, not if Tori was going to survive.

Murray's body, half-a-dozen steps behind him, was already nothing more than an awkward mound beneath the charred air swirling around it. Another man, a grabber, his skull split wide, convulsed on the floor a half-dozen steps ahead.

Tori could be anywhere. If they'd held her too close to the explosion's impact . . . Involuntarily, Seth started in the direction of the blast, but pulled up almost at once. Someone was moving just ahead of him. The air had the smoky opacity of an old-fashioned battlefield. It took several seconds for Seth to discern that the figure was a man, short and thickset, with a squat neck and dark hair, but it took only an instant for him to realize the man was Sergei Chistyakov.

Sergei hadn't seen him yet. Seth dropped back, moving as unobtrusively as he could over a section of concrete floor strewn with rubble. He slipped behind a hulking piece of machinery. The machine was dead, a shower of bricks flung against its metal casing. He closed one hand around a half-brick. Not much of a weapon, but better than an empty hand.

Sergei swung momentarily closer, pushing the snout of a Kirkov handgun through the smoke before him and blasting out a dozen rounds. Somewhere, hidden in the smoke, a man screamed. Sergei wiped the back of his free hand across his mouth and pressed forward again.

Seth waited until the murky air had nearly swallowed the Russian. Then, brick in hand, he edged out of hiding.

« CHAPTER 61 »

THE EXPLOSION AT the Morrison plant shook Paige's car.

She was halfway across the parking lot, accelerating through potholes and broken glass when the blast hit. The steering wheel quivered in her hands. Her ears rang. The smoke that billowed up from the factory was only slightly darker than the sky.

She glanced in the rearview mirror. Mike was in his own car, maybe twenty feet behind hers. They'd met at the gate which someone—Regency people, presumably—had left open. More sloppiness. Mike had rolled down his window, frowned at Paige, opened his mouth. She'd shot forward into the lot before he could ask any questions. Now he was a shadow behind a tinted windshield.

Paige accelerated past a small cluster of parked cars. All dark, all empty as far as she could tell. The inner security fence loomed in front of her. She slammed the brake and jammed the shift into park at the same instant, and sprang out of the car. Mike pulled up beside her.

"Paige!"

The gate through the inner fence stood open. The stink of smoke and scorched chemicals filled Paige's nose and chewed up the lining of her throat. She sprinted for the gate.

"Paige!"

Something hooked her elbow, jerked her to a stop. She spun to look. Mike had a tight grip on her arm. He shook his head at her, wrinkles cutting his forehead.

She spread both hands open, quickly, like miniature white explosions. "I'm in a hurry."

"Yeah. I noticed." He stood almost a foot taller than her. He lowered his head, leaned closer. "Look, your situational awareness at the moment is shit. You're rushing into something, you have no idea who all is in there, how many, how they're spaced, how they're armed. That's not you, Paige. You don't work like that. What's the deal?"

She yanked her arm, hard. Mike gently released her. She was breathing hard—which was crazy, she'd gone hardly any distance at all—and she couldn't stop glancing at the smoke spreading upward from the building.

"Tori's in there," she said. "Maybe alive."

Mike just watched her. "Or maybe not."

Paige gave a deft little shrug that she didn't mean. "I know that." She started forward. "That's why I need to check it out. Now."

Mike fell into step beside her. "Because if you don't, then . . .?"

Anger flickered somewhere deep inside Paige. Anger at Mike, for not understanding. Anger at all the shoddy killers on Regency's employee roster, men with sadistic streaks a mile deep and integrity as flat as roadkill. Donny Oxlade would've fit right in with them.

And, she had to admit, anger at herself. She'd known Regency was cutting corners, taking suspect jobs, but she hadn't walked away soon enough. Or stepped in when she should have.

It isn't fair. Tori deserves a chance. Just like me.

Jesus, she was sick of it.

The factory's front entrance was shut and locked. Paige kept going, turning to the right where the smoke was thicker, caustic and biting. Her eyes streamed. With Mike still at her elbow, she rounded the corner of the building.

Geoffrey Whelk. Son of a bitch.

He stood beside a heap of toppled bricks, squinting at the building, one thick leg planted on the rubble like he was staking claim to the debris. Artificial light from the factory's interior burned through a ragged hole in the wall, tinting the smoke dirty yellow. Whelk's face glistened with sweat.

Paige tightened her fingers around her gun's grip and continued forward. Mike was a solid, comforting presence at her right elbow. The annoyance she'd felt for him disintegrated.

Whelk swung his bulk in their direction. "If you're looking for a bonus," he called, "I'm afraid you'll have to get in touch with Merle, have him check the assignment list." Whelk's voice was cool and damp. It made Paige think of snails, slugs, November rain. "This job is taken."

Instantly, fury slammed up from Paige's gut. "This job," she said, her jaw so tight it barely moved, "was cancelled."

Whelk's shoulders rose and dropped like a pair of tossed haybales as he turned back toward the smoke and the blasted-out wall. "I have my instructions from the main office."

Paige thrust the muzzle of her gun at Whelk. He only gazed at her and raised his eyebrows.

"I'm sorry," Whelk intoned, "but we seem to have a misunderstanding."

Paige kept the gun trained on him while she wiped her other hand on the front of her pants. Her palms were sweaty. But hell, it was a hot night, the sky itself bleeding out heat.

Inside the factory, something enormous crashed to the floor. Metal rang against brick, concrete cracked. Dust and ash gushed out of the break in the wall with fresh velocity. Through the tumbling roar of noise, someone screamed.

The gun jerked in Paige's hand.

Well . . . her hand jerked. Mike was right. She was blowing it. Losing control.

Mike pushed up beside her now. He stopped close to her, his arm pressing lightly against hers. He wore his usual white shirt, sleeves rolled unevenly above the elbows, and a pair of jeans. From the corner of her eye, Paige saw the solid white, solid blue, steady arm . . . and felt a little steadier herself.

Mike kept his eyes on Whelk and his own gun out, but loose in one hand. Casual. Like he and Whelk were just a pair of retired execution buddies who'd happened to run into each other on a street corner.

"What's going on in there, Geoff?" Mike asked.

"Oh, the usual. Sergei and the boys are just cleaning up a bit of debris at the moment."

Whelk gazed complacently toward the building. Smoke from the building puffed around him. Anger built inside Paige again.

"Grabber debris?" Mike asked, as laconic as Whelk was smug.

"And likely Jennings debris as well," Whelk answered, his expression never changing. "At this point."

Paige's muscles screwed even tighter. "That's the problem with you and your gang," she said. "There's always debris."

"And always a task successfully completed."

Before Paige would retort, Renz put in his own laconic comment: "That alarm been going on awhile? You worried about some police showing up and seeing this kind of property damage?"

Whelk shifted his shoulders. "It's just so much noise. The factory owner is in arrears to the security company. Ditto the police company that generally covers this industrial park. I use the word 'park' loosely, of course."

The distinctive high-pitched pop of a Kirkov fired inside the factory. Paige swung toward the sound.

"That would be Sergei, I believe," Whelk said, oozing a smile. "Must be a little more business that needs tending."

Bastard.

The Kirkov fired again. Paige stuttered a couple of steps toward the shattered opening in the wall, glanced back at Mike.

He nodded, gave her a relaxed thumbs up with his gun-hand. "Go ahead. I've got this."

Whelk cast his gaze heavenwards, gave a martyr's sigh.

"Put him down on his knees, hands on his head," Paige told Mike.

He just met her with his own level stare. "I said, I've got this."

"Right." Paige spun away, headed into the smoke, the stink of scorched rubble closing around her.

Behind her, Mike and Whelk bantered, laughing—*How can you bear to work with a female hitter, all that emotional stickiness? I dunno, how do you work with a crazy Russian psychopath?*—until the smoke swallowed them, and the churn of machinery and the occasional pop of the Kirkov chewed their voices down to nothing.

« CHAPTER 62 »

TORI REELED BACK from the blade. Stunned, she gawked from one hand to the other. The blade had sliced through the manacles a bare inch from her left hand. Although the cuffs themselves still ringed her wrists, she could move her hands freely now. She stretched her fingers, rolled her wrists in circles. The tendons and ligaments ached with relief.

She glanced around the platform. Rafe continued to fumble and crawl around the platform. He wasn't a problem. Owen, sending a frenzy of rounds into the smoke below, definitely was.

Tori would never be able to climb down the ladder without him seeing her. She gave the machinery behind her a wild glance. No loose tools that she could use as weapons, no crowbars or wrenches or hammers. Could she push Owen with enough force to get him over the railing? Skinny as he was, he probably outweighed her by fifty pounds. And he looked like he was in a state of mind to blast away anything that moved. She'd have to be quick and use every ounce of strength she possessed.

Her palms rose flat in front of her chest, like the blade on a snowplow. She imagined Owen's freefall, a battering of bones against concrete, and her mind's eye flashed to that day in Virginia when Seth taught her the rudiments of shooting. He'd taught her to shoot, but he'd never taught her how to kill.

In the moment that she hesitated, Owen turned halfway around, one hand digging in his pocket—for more ammunition, presumably—and saw her.

His face was blotched and striped with ash and soot, like war paint. He skinned his lips back from his teeth and strode toward her.

Tori's heart twisted like a wounded animal. She scrambled away across the platform, searching out the shadowed recesses between machines. She plunged farther back, toward the rear wall of the platform and the loading dock's chained metal doors. One heel slid across rollers set into the floor, setting the rollers into a frantic spin as she struggled to regain her balance. She skirted the rest of the rollers and glanced back. Owen stumped after her, fury screwed into his face.

She backed into a steel grating, tall and vertical, that stood like a gate separating the loading area from yet another line of machinery.

Trapped.

Owen came closer, relentless, pushing a clip into his gun. Tori spun around, dug her fingers through the grating's cold mesh. She shook it desperately. The grating had no handle, no knob. Over her own sobbing gasps, she heard Owen's furious grunts.

No way out. Tori gripped the grating so hard the metal cut into her fingers. She hurled the full weight of her body against it.

Something gave. A slight shifting. The grating gave way along one edge.

Tori almost fell on another row of rollers underfoot as she tucked her head down and shoved her way through the opening. The grating's thick steel edge scraped down the crown of her head, her neck, her back. She barely felt the track of pain that burned in its wake. All she knew was: she'd made it through.

She did her best to cram the grating back into place, but it resisted. She left it hanging crookedly behind her and vaulted between two sealed crates lodged on a stopped conveyor belt. The belt was chest-high, but adrenaline helped Tori scramble across it.

She glanced around, saw a gap beside one of the large machines. She bent low to crouch in the gap. The machine loomed to her right. To her left was a tremendous piece of steel that looked like the flat end of a hammer head, the surface almost two feet in diameter and positioned vertically. The steel was polished, gleaming like a dark mirror. On its far side two buttons, red and green, glowed on the wall.

Scrabbling sounds. From where she huddled, Tori could just make out Owen's hands spasming through the grate. "You're gonna—be sorry," he shouted. The words came in small eruptions, as spastic as his hands. "Cause me—so much trouble."

As Owen shoved the grating aside, Tori tightened her arms harder around her ribs. Making her body as compact as possible, she wedged herself another inch deeper into the shadows.

It wasn't good enough. Owen was coming right for her.

This hiding place was a trap. Tori bolted out, raced past the giant hammer head only to find that another mesh grate loomed five feet away. It was a twin of the first: steel and seemingly impenetrable. She knew, even before she gripped her fingers through the grate, that she'd never get through it.

Owen grinned at her like he'd just had the same realization. "I'm not losing this payout, bitch," he called out.

Only the stopped conveyor belt, studded with large crates, stood between them. Tori released the grate, glanced around, frantic to find a way out, another place to hide.

The green button. Even if it worked . . . even if it only bought her a few seconds . . . she smacked the button with the flat of her hand. The conveyor belt shuddered into motion. Beside her, something dark slammed forward, then slid back with a hiss. The metal hammer head.

A massive plastic crate glided past her on the belt and the metal plunger hammered forward again with a whoosh of cool air, shoving the crate onto metal rollers.

"Sixty big!" Owen crowed and dug in his pocket again. He pushed something between his lips. He shuddered, pleasure flashing across his face.

Tori was at the second metal grate, slamming herself at it, shaking it with both fists. It didn't budge. She closed her eyes—*please God please*—

Owen gave a startled yelp. Tori glanced across at him. Owen stumbled, rollers spinning and rattling under his feet. He flung his hands out, trying to save his balance. His gun discharged, aimed at nothing. Tori flinched away from the sound.

Owen grabbed the conveyor belt, clutched at it with both arms, slowly hauling himself up onto the black rubber surface, his feet still doing a crazy dance on the rollers.

The plunger erupted from the shadows like a shark from an underwater cave and rammed forward across the belt.

Owen never had a chance to scream.

His body sagged onto the rollers, slid across them, propelled by the plunger's force.

Before Tori even registered what had happened, another crate rattled in front of the plunger. The plunger punched crate after crate onto the rollers, toward a waiting wooden skid.

Tori's legs were numb as she slowly moved away from the stubborn grate and towards Owen. Her breath huffed loud and hard, the plunger drumming regularly through its erratic rhythm. She fumbled at the red button. The belt slowed; the plunger pulled back, stayed there.

Tori half-crawled across the stopped belt. Her knees sank into the rubber. She dropped down on the belt's other side, one elbow striking hard against the floor. Pain surged like an electric shock between her shoulder and fingertips. She lay still a moment, gritting her teeth and gathering her breath.

She tremblingly hauled herself upright, stood swaying and staring. From between a pair of crates on the rollers, a hand protruded. It was grimy, the nails filthy. The fingers curved against the floor.

Tori waited for the fingers to move. They didn't. Her breath barely skimmed through her throat.

Don't be so chickenshit. She jerked forward, until she could see between the crates—then stood there, sickened.

Owen sprawled on his back. The plunger had dented his forehead, smashed a cheekbone. His mouth was grotesquely bright, with random teeth driven through the smeared red lips.

Tori eased out a long breath and fixed her gaze on the floor. A strange, sickly feeling rose in her stomach, like she was plunging through midair, with no ground in sight. Dizziness washed over her. She shuddered, shut her eyes. She suddenly noticed the stink of smoke again, heard shouts below. Rafe was still moaning—*"Shit my eyes shit my eyes"*—and crawling around the platform.

When she was sure she wouldn't throw up, she opened her eyes. She slid her gaze to Owen, let it slide away again. The plunger's force had knocked his gun out of his hand. It lay a dozen feet away. Tori propelled herself into motion, snatched up the weapon. She gripped it just as Seth had taught her, her hands shaking, but the gun still seemed like an alien thing, out of her control.

Clutching it, nevertheless, she skirted around the machines, then around Rafe who was now rocking back and forth with hoarse inarticulate noises, tears leaking out of the swollen wreckage of his eyes and smearing the ashes on his face. He seemed to sense it when Tori passed him. He raised his head, like a dog smelling the air.

She paused, her mouth opening as if she would say something to him—she had no idea what—but then she shut it again and moved on. The man's cries broke like waves against her back.

At the railing, she stared down in shock at a mountain of toppled brick and pulverized concrete, a wide gash in one wall, headlights filtering in through the dust.

A movement of air momentarily pushed back the curtain of haze, and she saw him.

Tori couldn't move. Couldn't even breathe.

Seth.

He was down there, just a few paces behind a thick-set, ape-ish man with a gun and a buoyant expression unobscured by the five-o'clock shadow bristling across half his face. It was that Regency guy, the Russian. Sergei Chistyakov.

She must have moved without realizing it because Sergei and Seth both looked up at her at the same instant. Seth was pale, haggard, a sharp contrast to the Russian's aura of robust energy. At the sight of Tori, fresh glee surged across Sergei's face. Before Tori could drop—or even think to drop—flat to the floor, Sergei raised his gun.

« CHAPTER 63 »

TORI was alive.

Alive.

Alive.

The word pounded through Seth's head, overwhelming the headache cracking against his skull.

Tori's stare locked on him. She looked white, stunned. A few feet in front of Seth and still unaware of his presence, Sergei let out a joyous whoop and raised his gun arm.

No time to do this subtly. No time to try for Sergei's gun or go kicking through the rubble for a dead grabber's abandoned semi.

Tori made a feeble motion to lower herself to the platform. She wasn't going to make it.

Every nerve in Seth's body gave a painful twist. His fingers tightened around the chunk of brick. His muscles gathered themselves and launched him forward.

He brought the brick down as hard as he could, aiming at the back of Sergei's head. But at the last instant, Sergei twisted away and the brick smashed against his shoulder instead of his skull.

Still clutching the brick, Seth looped one arm around Sergei's neck and tightened it around the Russian's throat. In the same motion, he pinned Sergei's gun arm and weapon against the man's chest. His face was pushed against the back of Sergei's neck. The man reeked of smoke and bad cologne.

Sergei bared his teeth and let out a feral cry. He grabbed at Seth's arm. The Russian was strong, his short arms thick with muscle. Seth grimaced, gave an animal grunt. Jesus, the guy must drag tractors and toss tree trunks for fun.

The struggle didn't last long. The stalemate broke. Sergei dragged Seth's arm away from his throat and down toward his chest. He pressed Seth's wrist painfully back until the brick dropped to the floor.

Still positioned behind the Russian's back, Seth fought to regain a chokehold. He wouldn't be able to keep Sergei's gun arm restrained much longer. Seth's arms trembled with effort, but the Russian was too strong and Seth was still too sick. Sweat wrung itself from every inch of Seth's skin, making his hands slippery. Sergei fought to tighten his grip on the weapon, gradually turning the barrel. The gun quivered with the energy pouring from both men's bodies.

Sergei squeezed out a wild round. The bullet disappeared into the smoke. The veins of Sergei's neck stood out, thick and ropy, as he struggled to work the barrel of the gun in Seth's direction. Another centimeter, and another . . . Sergei's mouth strained into an agonized smile.

Sweat stung Seth's eyes as the black mouth of the barrel slowly edged into his view.

« CHAPTER 64 »

SERGEI WAS STRONGER. Even from up on the platform, that was obvious.

Tori realized that she'd raised Owen's gun straight out in front of her chest. She suddenly couldn't remember anything Seth had taught her about shooting. Her mind was frozen, numb. It seemed like the gun barrel was weaving and swaying. Maybe her extended arms were shaking. She didn't know. Didn't know anything except that below her, Sergei was grinning and eager and Seth was about to die.

An instant's panic flared—what if she missed Sergei and hit Seth? What if she missed everything?—but then her thoughts went stunned and silent again. Her finger ticked back and the gun roared.

Those first seconds after the shot were just like at the target shoot. She didn't know what she'd shot, or if she'd shot anything at all. Something dark spun away from the men like a singed bird. She watched, nonplussed, until she realized it was Sergei's gun wheeling through the air. It struck the floor and spun out of sight beneath a machine.

Sergei roared. That moment's inattention allowed Seth to lock one arm hard against the hitter's throat. The pressure broke Sergei's voice. Seth gritted his teeth as he tightened his arm. Sergei's face was turning pink, then red, veins knotting his forehead, his eyes starting to bulge.

Tori bolted across the platform and scuttled down the ladder, moving so fast that her feet kept sliding from the rungs. She dropped the last half-dozen feet.

Wind slipped in through the damaged wall. It cooled the sweat on Tori's skin, re-gathered and contorted the smoke, forced her breath from her in a choking cough. From the ashen haze in front of her came a guttural cry. It took her a second to recognize that the sound came from Seth's throat.

Tori's heart ate itself. She flung herself through the smoke, toward the noise, froze a half-dozen feet away from the men.

Sergei had lowered his head and was ripping into the meat of Seth's forearm with his teeth. The moment Seth's grip loosened, Sergei reared against him and pushed away. Sergei's mouth grinned blood, like he'd been eating raw steak. He reached across his chest with his left hand, pulling at something concealed beneath his shirt.

"Seth!" Tori cried out a warning as Sergei drew a knife free from a holster snugged beneath his armpit. Nine inches of powder-coated stainless steel gleamed above his grip. The final three inches of blade were deeply notched, the serrations chewing the air.

The Russian turned the knife on Seth with savage abruptness. The blade sliced at Seth's belly. Blood oozed into the fabric of his shirt.

Gasping, Seth spun away. Sergei followed him, relentless, dropping into a crouch that mimicked Seth's. The blade slashed the air. Seth held his bare palms in front of him as if they could somehow defend him from the knife. "Tori!" he shouted, never looking away from Sergei. "Get out of here!"

But Tori wasn't leaving him again. Not now. Not ever.

She raised Owen's gun. The barrel swam absurdly back and forth in front of her, following the men's constant motion.

The blade made another thrust at Seth; the tip caught the front of his shirt, tearing a six-inch gash in the cotton. Blood poured from the ragged wound in his forearm..

Tori felt the solidity of the gun in her grasp. There was no time. She lifted it and exhaled. Her eyes were clenched shut. *You're not going to hit anything with your eyes closed, Tori.* The memory of Seth's voice was so strong that, for a second, she thought she'd heard him speak.

She opened her eyes and fired.

The gun kicked, jerking her back. Sergei howled, lopsided, one hand flat to the concrete.

She must have hit him. Where? But he still gripped the knife. He staggered upright again. Then she saw the blood spreading across the sleeve of his opposite arm.

He grinned again. But there was no exuberance in it now, just flat, black fury. He took a step toward her. *Empty the clip*, she thought, keeping the gun trained on the Russian. *Center shot.* The gun was as steady as she could keep it. But Sergei's eyes went suddenly wild and he pivoted smartly, going for the gash in the wall.

She brought the gun down, the desire to take the man's life gone from her. Seth was on the ground and she went to him, fell to her knees next to him. "Oh, my God, oh, my God—"

She could hardly breathe as she lifted the hem of Seth's shirt. The slice across his stomach was long, but not deep. His forearm, with the chewed up skin and a chunk of meat torn out of it, looked uglier, but not fatal.

That was all that mattered.

Tori looked up questioningly, her eyes wet. "Are you all ri—" she said before Seth's arms closed around her.

« CHAPTER 65 »

SETH PULLED BACK and Tori could see his face, his fiercely-drawn eyebrows and pale, feverish skin. Exhaustion dug black graves under his eyes. Tremors rippled through his body.

"Where the hell have you been?" he asked. "Disappearing like that—"

"I just didn't want you to get hurt," Tori said. She looked down at his bloody shirt and ravaged arm. His blood dappled the front of her own shirt now.

Seth wheezed out a rusty laugh. Tori looked up. Turning his forearm to show off the savaged meat of it, he said, "Good plan."

"Obviously."

"Didn't you know I'd look for you?" he asked.

Tori leaned her head against his rough cheek, felt his fingers work through her hair, smelled the smoke that clung to him. She was trembling too, with shock and relief. "I thought you'd stop," she said. "I thought the Network would make you stop."

Seth cupped her chin and tilted her head up. "I was your Guardian, Tori. I still am." He managed another smile.

Almost as quickly, it melted away.

They both saw movement at the same time. Two figures made their way through the rubble, one moving forward, the other stumbling back. The closest to them, Sergei, had one hand raised, still holding a knife, while his other arm sagged lower, dripping blood. The newcomer—a slender woman with short blonde hair who stood as tall as the Russian—trained a handgun on him. She gave Tori and Seth a quick glance before settling her stare on the man before her. Her lips pressed tightly together. "You have the gun, Eisen. Not me." Sergei gave a brief wave with his knife hand toward Tori and Seth. "Go ahead. I let you take them. I even give you a percent of my bonus. Maybe."

Seth stiffened, shifting his weight. Preparing to lunge at the killers, Tori thought numbly. As if he had enough strength left to fight them.

Eisen. That name was familiar. She cast through her memory until it snagged on something: The book of photographs at the Virginia safehouse, the book that showed Regency's killers and the Executables they'd tortured to death.

Paige Eisen. Tori's heart squeezed all the blood out of itself.

Paige was shaking her head at Sergei, and holstering her gun. Then she removed her own knife from a sheath. The blade came to a cruel curving point. She stepped toward Sergei.

Recognition came into Sergei's face, first with surprise then brief amusement. "Eisen, Eisen," he tutted. "They tell me always you are a professional. And here we have a professional job to finish, yes?" He took another glance in Seth and Tori's direction.

Seth put his mouth against Tori's ear. Fever steamed off his skin and Tori wondered how many injections he'd missed. "Show him the gun," Seth muttered. She thrust the gun up in front of her like she was drinking a toast.

"Don't even think about going after her," Paige told Sergei. "Bring your knife to a gunfight? She'll take your head off." She moved closer to the Russian. "Let's go, Chistyakov. You and me."

"What're they doing?" Tori whispered to Seth who shook his head and sagged against her. Jesus, she got him the anti-venom and what did he do? Ignore it? Dump it in the trash like Riker's was some kind of joke?

Crouching slightly, the two hitters stalked each other in an ever-tightening circle. Sergei's knife wobbled awkwardly in the grip of his left hand and he slowly stretched the fingers of his other hand as if willing them to work properly. He blinked sweat from his eyes.

"So it is to be like the old times, then?" he spat at Paige, each of his movements a sidling squat-stride, like a sumo wrestler. "The training? Or do you have something else in your little girl's mind?" He chortled, lifting the knife blade up and down lewdly in his saber grip. Paige answered with a sudden step up, and the sound of the two blades coming together rang through the air.

"Yes, old times! Only now," he dropped his voice to a menacing purr. "Now no one to step between us, to stop the cutting." His eyes glittered. "I finish you for good." He reared a foot back and kicked a chunk of concrete in Paige's direction. She dodged, and settled back into her forward stance, eyes narrow, her breath soft and even.

They reversed direction, both alternating head fakes and quick steps as they drew even closer. But Sergei's breath was heavier and movements tighter and slower, his muscles tightening in reaction to his wounds. As he hesitated more at the feints, Paige gestured for him to come forward. *Come to me.*

He obliged, but his thrust was slow, a drunken man's. He gasped aloud in frustration. When Paige jabbed at him with two sudden thrusts, he backpedaled, stumbling for balance. He swung his own knife to parry, but Paige moved with the quick grace of a dancer, easily eluding Sergei's weapon and swiping her own blade down the length of his good arm.

The metal cut deep, seeking the artery. Howling, Sergei burst forward again, raking his blade sideways, slicing a crisscross pattern through the air. Paige stepped neatly away. Blood from the fresh cut on Sergei's arm flung toward her, spattering the floor an inch from the toe of her left boot.

Sergei's blade slashed at Paige, curving toward her abdomen, eager to release her intestines. She flung herself away from the blade and its tip caught the front of her shirt, tearing it. Buttons rolled across the floor.

Sergei lunged for her, throwing all his weight behind the thrust. Anticipating him, Paige was already drawing back as he vaulted into motion. Momentum drove him past her and, as he passed, Paige plunged her own knife deep into his side, just above where his body armor offered protection. Sergei fell to his knees with a shriek, and the blade slid out of him as he dropped face down to the floor. He groaned.

Tori stared, transfixed, at the knife Paige held upraised. Blood, brilliant and thick, covered the entirety of its once shining surface.

Paige hunkered down near the dying man, just out of range of his knife. Sergei's fingers convulsed around the handle. She waited until the knife clattered from his grip and he twisted fully onto his back. Blood choked from his mouth.

Then, leaning forward, Paige held her own knife poised straight above him.

Human sacrifice. The thought flared in Tori's brain. Her gorge rose. *She's really going to—*

The blade dropped like a dead-weight, entering Sergei's body just under the throat and slicing straight down. Paige gave the handle a quarter-twist and brought the blade out. She waited—one heartbeat, two—and stabbing the Russian through the center of the throat.

"*For good,*" she mocked, then booted his knife under the machines.

« CHAPTER 66 »

FOR JUST A MOMENT, the blond woman hovered there, wiggling her knife free while gazing down into the dead man's face. Whether she was reliving some past moment or memorizing how his corpse looked, Tori didn't know. She had no idea why one hitter would kill another hitter, but the way the woman had used the knife to dispatch her victim spoke volumes. Tori gripped the gun tighter as the woman looked over, taking notice of them. Her face was empty of emotion.

Then she wiped the gore from her blade onto the dead Russian's clothes and stood. She pivoted slightly to face them.

As soon as she moved a step in their direction, Seth spoke. "You can stop right there," he called out.

The woman rolled her shoulders slightly and took another insistent step in their direction. "I think you're just going to have to trust me. You've got no other way out of here." She gestured to her right, toward the huge opening in the wall. "I can walk you out. One last bridge to cross. It's almost over."

Her words were gentle, almost soothing, and Tori shivered. Was this the butcher's croon, the ease-you-into-death song? Seth shifted uncomfortably next to her. She could tell he wanted the gun. Not sure if he was in any condition to handle a weapon, she handed it to him nevertheless.

"And if we don't?" Seth asked, emboldened now with the gun in his hands.

Eisen shrugged. "You can try to go it alone, but I wouldn't advise it. Too many desperate people whose only skill set is murder. One of the worst is sitting outside right now."

"I'm guessing Geoffrey Whelk," Seth answered, checking the round in the gun's chamber. "But you're all getting paid by the same man. Forgive me for being a little bit skeptical."

"I don't blame you." Eisen, only a few steps away, eyed the gun pointed at her chest. "You're a Guardian. If you weren't suspicious, you'd be pretty lousy at your job. But like I said, you really don't have many options at this point." She held the knife in front of her and lowered her voice. "I'm a killer. But I don't kill innocent people." She looked at Tori. "Hold out your hands."

Something in the woman's face, in her manner seduced her; both of them, as Seth's hand on her shoulder eased a little. Tori's breaths were shallow as she held out her wrists to the woman. Her memories flashed on her former employers, how they'd just assumed the poor, crazy nanny must have attacked their baby out of some kind of demented envy. How the police had shoved her, pushed her, made fun of her tears and her pleas. How her lawyer had sagged defeatedly in his chair while the judge himself seemed to pick apart Tori's possible innocence one shredded bloody bit at a time. She remembered the Glynn River guards, the eyes watching while Tori changed into her prison jumpsuit, the snorting laughter during the frisks, hands lingering on her breasts and the body cavity searches that seemed, in her fire of humiliation and utter helplessness, to last for hours.

She still half-expected the worst. To be fooled again, only this time with the consequence being her own death.

But it didn't happen. Eisen slipped the curve of the blade inside each cuff and neatly sliced it clean. The plastic halves dropped to the concrete. When Tori looked into the woman's face, her gaze was friendly, and she sensed . . . almost *maternal*. Protective. The woman touched Tori's face, lifted her chin with a finger. She met the hitter's eyes and realized: Paige Eisen had felt similar humiliation, suffered the same helplessness.

"You're free, Tori," Eisen said, and slipped her weapon back into the sheath at her hip.

Tori held her hands up in front of her face. No cuffs, just deep red grooves around her wrists to show where the manacles had been. Relief gave way to something stronger—excitement, almost exhilaration. She was still an E, but at least for this moment, she felt free.

She offered a smile that felt like it wobbled and dipped. Paige's answering smile hooked slowly upward at one corner. The hitter suddenly looked much younger, barely more than a teenager.

Seth gestured at the dead man. "Killing your coworker is no way to advance your career, is it?" He shifted a bit on his unsteady legs and huffed his breath out with pain. "What was it, a professional disagreement?"

Just a moment, and the warmth drained from Eisen's face. She looked at Seth with a slip of an icy half-smile on her lips. "I don't work for Regency anymore."

They followed her into the humid night. Tori threw a last reeling glance at the platform, the blasted-out wall, the hulking machinery that could conceal a legion of killers. Moths poured against the ceiling lights, their tiny frantic bodies beating like snow flurries against the smoke.

Voices reached them from the vicinity of a van parked just beyond the last of the fallen bricks. The van's headlights fanned across the rubble. A man, mountainous and fleshy, hunched in that sweep of illumination. He kept shifting his weight from one knee to the other and his shirt rode up, exposing a luminous belly.

"C'mon, Geoff, you seriously never think about calling it a day?" A man's voice Tori didn't recognize. He spoke in an easy, casual tone, like he was relaxing on a patio with a beer. "A sugar beach, a little snorkeling, swordfish on the grill—man. Sign me up." The speaker lounged against the hood. All Tori could see of him were long legs in blue jeans and a pair of brown boots, crossed at the ankles.

"Some of us enjoy our labors," the big man in the headlights rumbled in response.

"Whelk," Seth muttered under his breath. "And Mike Renz, temporary zookeeper." He shook off Tori's hand and slipped into position just in front of her. She gave him an exasperated shake of the head. "I'm still your Guardian, Tor. That hasn't changed."

"Personally, I find my work very rewarding," Whelk pontificated. "Financially, of course, but it's gratifying in other ways."

"Even when the contract's been called off?" Paige interrupted, striding into the light. "Even when you have no legal right to finish the kill?"

Whelk swung his massive head in Paige's direction and scowled. "If I had to work with you, Eisen, I'd resign in a millisecond."

Paige drew up beside Renz.

"You okay?" he asked her.

"No scars yet."

Seth's mouth butterflied against Tori's ear. "Let's just slide past and get out of here."

They moved along the edge of the headlight's beam. Dull orange light oozed from the building's gaping wound behind them. It gave Seth's skin a sickly, leached color. Tori glanced down at her own hands. They had the same diseased tint.

As they passed, Renz gave them a casual nod. The gesture made Tori think, absurdly, of a cowboy tipping the brim of his hat. "Evening," the hitter said.

Seth let out an amused gust of air and Tori realized he must be having the same thought she did: this was surreal. "Jesus," Seth murmured. "Will wonders never—"

Whelk lunged. His hand came up from below his waist; it held something snub and black and ugly. At the same moment, Tori felt Seth's hand shove her back hard as he threw his body at the man. The night exploded with sudden gunfire. Two more shots crackled through the air. Seth shuddered and Tori realized he'd been hit. But he refused to turn, to stumble, to fall to earth and leave her exposed.

Renz dove forward, his own gun crackling, muzzle alight. Half-a-dozen rounds drove into a three-inch band of flesh where Whelk's body armor rode up over his gut.

A knife glittered, somersaulting across the divide between Paige and Whelk. The curved blade sank deep into Whelk's throat.

The big man seemed to collapse in slow motion, like a building imploding.

"*Seth!*" Tori screamed as he finally went down, collapsing into her arms. His weight pulled her down with him onto the pavement. She gestured frantically toward the others. "Help us! Please!" Her voice cracked. A terrible buzzing numbness filled her head.

But Renz was crouched over Whelk's motionless body. Paige had leaped forward, gun in hand now, the snout of it pointed at the hitter's enormous corpse.

Tori pulled Seth's shirt away from his chest. Her palms hovered an inch above the torn flesh. The night stank, all gunpowder and burned skin. Dimly: footsteps. Then Paige's voice.

Tori didn't understand what she said. Her head swayed. Tiny crimson dots pricked the air in front of her eyes.

Paige's hand brushed against her shoulder, and the cool touch of the woman's fingers brought Tori back from the edge of unconsciousness.

"What—?" Tori looked up.

Paige bent over her. The hitter's voice was calm, but a current of pain ran deep within it. "I'm sorry," she said to Tori. "This wasn't supposed to—I've contacted a private emergi-serv. They'll be here in a couple of minutes. If anyone can save him, they can." Paige's fingers slipped along Tori's cheek. Tori barely felt the touch. "But we can't stay here. There'll be a lot of questions. Too many."

Tori stared dumbly at her.

Renz stepped through the light and stood beside Paige.

Paige's hand slowly withdrew. "Tori." Paige faltered for a moment. "You should leave too. You can't do anything."

Renz pulled Paige away. Their footsteps diminished and disappeared.

Tori huddled closer to Seth.

Blood streamed from his nose and from one corner of his mouth, sliding down his cheek toward his ear. She couldn't hear him breathe, not even when she put her own ear close to his mouth, but she felt the faintest cloud of breath warm against her cheek.

A series of tremors shook him. Tori's felt her own face convulse, break apart. She hunkered back, her eyes blurred. She gripped his hand. "Seth?" For a moment, she thought that he'd tightened his own fingers in response. But then the spasms passed through his body, wave after wave, and his hand fell open.

In desperation, Tori rubbed his arms. She leaned close to his mouth again, but no mist of warm breath moved against her cheek now.

"No. C'mon. Help me out here." Turning her head, she touched her mouth to his. "*Seth.*"

There was nothing.

Then came a crush of tires on concrete and fresh headlights slicing the darkness. A car slammed to a stop a few feet from Tori and the door flung open. An instant later, Paige bent over Tori. The hitter took a firm grip on Tori's arm.

"You can't stay here," Paige said. "You have to leave."

Mute, Tori slopped her head from side to side, the movement enormous and uncontrolled. Leave? Go where? What was the point?

"Come on. Come with me." Paige dragged Tori up onto her knees. "We'll find a way to get you back with the Network people. I promise."

Tori tried to let her own body weight pull her back down to Seth's side, but the hitter was stubborn.

Paige's face was inches from her own. "He's gone," Paige said and Tori could see steel in the hitter's face. Hear iron in her voice. "And we're out of here."

Renz appeared, climbing out of a second car that Tori hadn't even noticed approaching. He gripped Tori's other arm. He was strong and possibly as stubborn as Paige.

Why? Tori thought.

Why not?

She let them raise her body from the concrete and stuff it into the back seat of Paige's car. But her life stayed behind, with Seth.

« CHAPTER 67 »

A COUPLE OF HOURS later, Paige and Mike were in the corridor outside Regency's office suite.

In her head, Paige kept seeing Tori kneeling over the Guardian, streaked with his blood. Paige's chest ached, deep inside, an untouchable place. If it had Mike sprawled there, guts leaking all over some crappy factory parking lot, she'd have...

Gone on, she told herself. Somehow she'd have gone on. Because she always had and she always would. Otherwise, the Donnie Oxlades won.

But she didn't like imagining it.

Mike leaned down to whisper to her. "You're sure about this?"

Paige met his gaze. It was steady. Close. It made the ache diminish, for a few seconds anyway.

"You're the one who should be answering that question," she said.

"You know what I always say." Mike cracked the grin she loved, but his gaze never shifted. The ache eased another notch. "If you're sure, I'm sure."

It was the middle of the night and the glass door leading into Regency's suite was locked, but the highest ranking hitters like Paige and Mike had passcodes and verified retinal ID. The door whispered open across plush eggplant-colored carpet. The reception desk was vacant, the high-end coffee maker empty. Paige touched her comm. Ledgers came up, numbers marching the length of the screen.

She nodded at Mike, then paced through the waiting area, past the conference room and pushed open the door to Merle's office.

Merle Edgers was at the far end of the room. He swung around, dropping a litter of blankets and pillows onto an assembled cot. Paige remembered that he kept sleeping supplies for late nights in the closet next to the wet bar.

"Oh. It's you." Edgers returned to the bedding. "Jesus, what a night. I'm done for." He reached for a faceted crystal glass winking under a table lamp and downed the amber liquid. The rest of the bottle stood open on his desk; a vodka bottle sat out on the bar.

Paige moved swiftly toward Edgers' desk without glancing up from the screen that illuminated her palm.

"Paige?" Edgers looked confused. Renz joined Paige and snapped a white smile at their boss. "Mike?" Edgers asked. Now the beginnings of alarm raised Edgers' eyebrows. He hustled toward the hitters. "Always good to have you stop by. Security didn't—ah—I never got a message you were coming up."

Weasly scum. How had she worked for this guy all this time? She should have known, even back when she'd started, what Edgers was. A drunk, a cheat, a tough talker who lounged in his air conditioned office all day. Arrogance and greed reeked from every flab and fold of his skin. Paige snubbed the comm shut and jabbed a button on the armrest of Edgers' leather executive chair. A thin screen rose noiselessly from the desk.

"Hey!" Shoving the chair aside, Edgers bellied up to the desk. "What the hell do you think you're doing? This is *my* office."

Paige ticked a glance toward the floor. The toe of Edgers' wingtip probed for the alarm button. Typical. Coward.

"I wouldn't bother," Paige told him and tapped the cool metal of her gun against his thigh, prodding him away from the alarm. His face swelled with furious heat. "Security's away from their desk at the moment."

"Yeah, well, they're supposed to check your guns at the door after business hours."

"Put it in a memo, Merle. Mike?"

Mike stepped in smoothly to take her place, his own gun directed at Edgers' head. Paige leaned into the desk to tap the screen with her finger. As a row of numbers appeared, Edgers made a sound somewhere between wheezing and snorting. She glanced at him. He tried to spread his hands in a placating gesture until a motion of Mike's gun told him to hold still.

"I don't know what's got into you two," Edgers said. "But I could use a little help. What I mean is, Whelk's not reporting in." He forced out a chuckle. "He's got me a little out of the loop tonight and the Jennings job was supposed to go down."

Renz's face was impassive. Paige murmured something at the screen and a new visual emerged: the very recognizable logo of the Hong Kong National Bank. Edgers choked.

Paige continued typing the numbers Edgers' assistant Spencer had given her after she'd encouraged him to compare his bonuses to Regency's revenues, and check the result against Edgers' promises. She was nearly into Regency's account. One more password and—

"Look," Edgers said, with an airy gesture, "why don't you guys head out there, see what's going on? Even if Whelk's already finished things off, I can give both of you a cut. And if Jennings is still alive, you go ahead and take over, get yourselves the full bonus."

"I heard the senator canceled the contract." Paige didn't look away from the screen. She didn't want him to see the poison rising from her gut. "And that she gave you twice the original amount for your trouble."

"Let me clarify," Edgers said. "You would each get a *full* bonus, both of you, the full amou—"

"Speaking of bonuses," Mike interrupted. "Paige has been checking over our finances and it looks like maybe you haven't paid out everything you *already* owe us."

"That's crazy." Edgers' breath puffed out with indignation. "Maybe you just dropped a few thou on strippers in Vegas and managed to forget about it."

Paige's mouth curled with disgust. Everything about the man was sleazy. Mike just laughed.

"You know," Edgers mused, "Spence is coming back in tonight. He should be here any time."

Mike laughed harder. Even Paige smiled.

Realization twisted Edgers face. "Hey, where'd you get all that, anyway?" He jerked a hand at the screen. "The passwords, you know—"

Mike clapped the man on the back with his free hand. "You should treat your staff better, Merle. Then maybe they'd treat you better, too."

Edgers visibly shuddered. Paige took pleasure in his anxiety, his anger. "You mind if I get something to drink?" he asked. "It's like a boiler room in here."

Mike briefly consulted his comm. "Sixty-two degrees."

"Look," Edgers said, "let's run through some numbers together. I'm sure that—"

"Cuff him, Mike." Paige pulled a chair around. She nodded for Edgers to sit.

He just stared at her, slowly swayed his head back and forth as if fury had made him sluggish.

Rage iced her. "Do it."

"Oh, come on, this is ridicu—"

"Sit," she ordered.

"—work something out, this is not an intractable kind of—"

Paige snapped: "Sit your butt down in that chair before Mike blows your skull into a jigsaw puzzle."

Blowing and puffing, Edgers lowered himself onto the seat. Paige drew out four sets of metal cuffs and shackled the man's wrists and ankles to the chair.

Returning to the screen, she gave Edgers a long look over her shoulder. He twisted against the restraints, his face so red it practically glowed. "The final password?" she said.

"You're a couple of lunatics, both of you."

"Lunatics with weapons," Mike observed and dug the muzzle hard into Edgers' right cheek, bruising the skin.

"I thought you were the assholes who prided yourself on your high-class morals," Edgers sputtered.

A click of the trigger and he relinquished the password. Then he closed his eyes as Mike kneed the chair forward so he could speak the necessary words into the bank's voice-recognition system. Mike pulled the chair away again.

Edgers licked his lips. "Making a few withdrawals?"

"Transfers," Paige observed. She spoke calmly, but doubt ate through her anger. She swallowed and the saliva seemed to stick in her throat. They were really doing this. Taking the money—which was rightfully theirs—and leaving everything. Regency, career, the U.S. She glanced up at Mike. Maybe he saw her uncertainty. He pumped an extra shot of warmth into his smile and his eyes. Sustained her.

Edgers shook his head. "So this is what it's come to. Theft. Embezzlement. Taking money at gunpoint like a couple of peelfreaks sticking up a liquor store."

"Just taking what's due to us," Paige managed.

"And then some, I'm sure." Edgers paused. "Can I at least have a friggin' scotch while I watch you rob me blind?"

"Least we could do," Mike said.

"Ain't that the truth? Top shelf. At the back."

Paige retrieved a tumbler and the bottle of scotch. She returned to the bank accounts.

"Ice?" Edgers snapped.

"Take it straight up, Merle," Mike said. He filled the tumbler and pressed it to Edgers' mouth. Edgers gulped it down in two huge swallows.

"You finding problems?" Mike asked Paige.

"I knew I would," she answered.

"You don't think you're going to work in this industry again, do you?" Edgers said.

"We're collecting our retirement," Paige said, watching Edgers grind his wrists against the manacles. "We've had some concerns for quite awhile. About how you're managing things. Accounting procedures. The long-term stability of our options. We're not interested in more than what Regency ultimately owes us. I think you have more than enough just in the operations' accounts. How much did you just deposit from Senator Logan?"

Edgers snorted. "Which goes for the bills. Do you know what insurance is costing me these days?" He belched, wincing at the explosion of air from his gullet. "I admit, we've had a few glitches. This is the thanks I get. All because you think you got stiffed on one lousy hit. And I *offered* you the hit."

"There's a lot more than 'one lousy hit' that's problematic," Paige said. Anger flared in her again. "Like the fact that Jennings didn't kill anyone."

Twisting his head to one side, Edgers glowered at Mike. "Without me, you'd be putting up siding somewhere in East Jesus, New Jersey." He made a hawking sound.

"Sorry, Merle, but it's time to cut the cord," Mike said. "We're thinking island. South Seas."

Paige stepped back from the desk. The screen slid from view.

"You really think you'll be safe?" Edgers said. "A couple of cut-rate runaways, lounging around some calypso hell? After what you're doing here?"

Paige leaned against the desk and regarded him. "Who were you planning to send after us?"

Edgers straightened in the chair. "Geoff."

"Geoff's dead."

"Sergei, then."

"Ditto."

"Hell, it doesn't matter. Any one of them has the potential to take you out. Paden, Murray, Junior . . ." His gaze clocked back and forth between their faces. "Aw, come on. You're shitting me. All of them?"

"All," Paige whispered and put a finger to her lips. She dumped Edgers' comm into the trashcan and used a stapler to smash his integrated deskphone and intervoice module. Edgers slumped, staring across the gleaming expanse of his desk. His head drifted toward the open bottle.

"You gonna pour me one more drink?" he bleated.

Paige followed Mike to the doorway. She paused there a moment. "You may not be able to get security to answer for a few hours," she said. "But the next shift comes on at six, doesn't it? Only two hours." She shut the door solidly behind her.

In the elevator, Mike drew his arm around Paige's shoulders. She let him, leaned back into his strength. Warm green water, white sugar beach: it sounded like everything she needed right now. That, and Mike.

The doors slid open. They stepped into the moist dimness of the parking garage. "I think—" Paige said, then stopped.

Mike's arm was still around her. "Yeah?"

"I think when we get there—" She hesitated, bit her lip. "Maybe I can show you one of those scars."

"I thought you didn't have any." But he pulled her closer against him.

"And maybe—"

"Yeah?"

"I might even have a margarita."

« CHAPTER 68 »

THE LISTENING POST in the Network's new location outside Pittsburgh was in a drafty attic rather than a claustrophobic basement, but much of the equipment was the same that Tori remembered from Virginia. Green and red lights blinked; the monitor she watched with Jared displayed a satellite image modified to clarify the topography around Glynn River. Tori was surprised by how narrow the ring of grassy field between the prison and the woods looked. When she'd been forced to walk through that emptiness, it had seemed endless.

Jared pulled back to give Tori an appraising look. "You sure you're okay with going back there?"

Tori nodded.

"I still don't know about this notion you've got," Jared said, "getting that close to the action."

"Not all that close."

"Last thing we need is our Guardians getting in gunfights with hitters right outside the prison grounds. I mean, it's legal for them to be there. But not for us." Jared chewed his lip. "Anyway, we'd lose too many Guardians that way."

"I'm not going that close," Tori lied. "Not as close as the hitters are going to be. But if the woman can get a couple of miles out, I'm going to be there for her."

Jared gave her a narrow look. She couldn't tell if he believed her or not. "So," he said. "Glynn River. We thought it might actually be an advantage for you your first time since you know the lay of the land."

Tori's nerves jumped up another few volts. "That's probably stretching it a little."

Jared's gaze intensified. "The disadvantage is the emotion between you and that place."

Tori tried to shrug this off with a forced smile. "Hey, I won the last round with Glynn River."

"True." Jared reached to shut off the monitor. "Did you know the E?"

"No. It's a big place. They have a lot of different work details, all around the clock. You don't really mix with very many prisoners. And it's not like you're encouraged to talk on the job."

Tori looked down at the battered, out-of-date comm the Network had outfitted her with. The visual still showed the gray, exhausted face of the woman who would be released from Glynn River the next day at five p.m. Just before the early October sunset, she mused, wondering if dusk would make it easier or harder for the E to get away from the hitters. If she focused on practical matters—location, logistics, weapon—maybe she would forget about the anxiety crawling around inside her stomach.

Jared picked up his empty coffee cup, stood, and stretched. As usual, he looked tired, unshaven, the skin under his eyes crinkly and thin. He swished around whatever muddiness remained at the bottom of the cup. "Well, you won't be dealing with Regency anyway."

"No."

Regency had folded a month after the mess at Morrison's. Edgers, according to Jared's sources, looked to be moving full-bore into his prison industry enterprises. In the months since Edgers had shuttered Regency, a number of ultra-budget execution outfits had swarmed into the field. "With killers straight out of the dollar store," Jared had remarked.

"Come on," he said now. "Let's go find something to eat."

Tori unfolded from her uncomfortable metal chair. An autumn wind beat the branches of a shaggy willow tree against the panes of the attic's single small window. Chilled air pressed through chinks in the window frame. When it came time to finding safe houses to use as Network HQ, Jared seemed to have an affinity for decaying farm properties.

"Hey, I almost forgot," Jared said. "Bobby said to tell you good luck."

Tori nodded acknowledgement. Queasiness oozed through her, stronger now, refusing to be ignored. She hadn't seen Bobby or Kendall since the 'Sergei incident,' as people in the Network generally called the beatings, electrocution, and torture. From what she'd heard, Bobby was missing half his teeth which he had no money to replace. The hearing in his left ear was damaged and he'd developed a twitch that routinely afflicted his face and hands. He provided information on the release venues, like the Glynn River package Tori had just been studying, but he insisted on working remotely and absolutely refused to ever be in the vicinity of an Executable. "Because Executables attract hitters, and he's never going through that again," was Jared's explanation.

Kendall had dropped entirely out of sight. Supposedly, he'd moved to some neo-pacifist commune in Oregon where the inhabitants tried to live entirely off the grid.

Jared touched Tori's arm. "Hey. You're gonna do fine." His smile was warm, but not entirely convincing. "Your last target practice, you did great."

Tori just nodded. After four months of practice, she damned well better be at ease with a gun. She wasn't the world's best shot, but Seth would have been proud of her progress.

The thought of him raised a bitter taste in her mouth, made her eyes ache.

"Hey." Jared gave her shoulder an awkward pat. "Come on," he said. "Let's go down to the kitchen and get you a cup of the worst cowboy coffee you've ever tasted."

He ushered Tori down the steep flight of steps from the attic to the second floor. A wet, moldy odor swelled from the hallway carpet, a brown-and-blue paisley blotched with assorted stains. Jared headed toward the stairs to the first floor, but Tori abruptly turned off into one of the old bedrooms.

She needed to see Seth. Before she left for Glynn River tonight, before she faced hitters again—this time as a Guardian, not an Executable—she needed to see him.

A monitor glowed on the card table in one corner of the room. An old vinyl chair slumped in front of the screen; the rollers attached to the chair's base had worn grooves in the yellowed linoleum floor. Jared had moved the binders from the abandoned Virginia house, the clippings and photos, and was digitizing and organizing everything when he had extra time.

Tori moved slowly across the room, her gaze locked on the framed photographs lining the back wall.

In his photograph, Seth looked very young. He wore a baggy jacket, army surplus. The fingers of his left hand disappeared into a front pocket of his jeans; his right hand was raised in front of his chest. He might have been waving or he might have been good-naturedly fending off the photographer. He was smiling, his mouth open like he'd just said something.

Probably *"C'mon guys, cut it out with the cameras, will you?"* Tori let out a breath, amusement mingled with that same persistent ache that pressed against her ribs every day, whenever she forgot to keep busy for a few minutes.

She took the picture from the wall. With one finger she traced through the light dust coating the glass.

Jared came to stand beside her. "I can take it down when you're here," he said. "I mean, if it upsets you to look at it. I wasn't sure how you'd—I mean, I know how much he meant to you."

Tori turned to meet Jared's gaze. "He's what keeps me going."

Jared leaned forward to scrutinize the other photographs still on the wall. His front teeth tugged thoughtfully at his lower lip. "He probably told you he was just another one of us, like anybody else in the Network. But he wasn't." Jared's hand swept across the row of pictures. "They were all great. Chen. Avery. Truth is, Seth was one of the best I ever worked with. He was willing to give up everything. You know that brother of his, the cop?"

"They're all cops."

"Yeah, but the one . . . Frank. You know, the one who came to the funeral?" Jared looked out the narrow window where black trees trembled under a night wind. "I told him outright: Seth was a hero to me. The guy just stared at me like I was talking Chinese, or something."

"Last of his kind," Tori said, a barely audible tremor running through her voice.

"Oh, I wouldn't necessarily say that," Jared answered.

Tori shot him a curious sideways glance. His confidence in her actually seemed sincere now. She felt the weight of it, the weight of the Network's confidence in her newly-learned skills. The burden of knowing that, just 21 hours from now, an Executable's life rested in her hands.

Tori stroked Seth's hair once, as if she could smoothe the cowlick on the right side even though it was just a photograph. She hung the picture back on its nail. The frame swung, glinting silver in the light before it came to rest. She thought of the small white stone cross above the weedy plot where his ashes were buried. The Network, at Tori's insistence, had found a spot for him in the same cemetery where his mother was buried although the only plot available had been on the opposite side of the property.

Which, Frank had remarked at the graveside, seemed like the most appropriate place for him, separated forever from the rest of the family. Close enough to almost reach them, but never quite making the connection.

Tori's father had been cremated, his ashes mixed with the powdery remains of a dozen other solitary or indigent or homeless corpses, poured into a communal urn, and buried in a pauper's plot donated for the county's use by the Catholic dioceses.

Jared clasped Tori's shoulder. He smiled at her. "Come on. Let's go raid the kitchen."

In the doorway, Tori stopped and turned, leaning forward as if she half-expected Seth to look back at her from the picture. His smile was hopeful, his eyes clear and unafraid.

A smile touched Tori's mouth. He'd be with her at Glynn River tomorrow. Her dad would be there too. They'd be with her wherever she went, and no matter what she faced.

Tapping the light switch, she made her way down the stairs to the brightly-lit kitchen.

ACKNOWLEDGEMENTS

With gratitude to Angela Cervantes, Victoria Dixon, Tessa Elwood, Janet Johnson, and Jane True for their insights and camaraderie, and with super-extra-thanks to Tessa for making the cover design process not only fruitful, but fun.

If you enjoyed **Executables**, be sure to read the companion stories in **Avenge Me**, available in electronic and print from your favorite online retailers.

About the Authors

Lisa Cindrich is the author of the children's historical novel, **In the Shadow of the Pali,** which was a selection of both the Junior Library Guild and the New York Public Library's Books for the Teen Age, as well as **Avenge Me,** a collection of stories set in the same world as **Executables**. She currently lives in the Kansas City area (on the Kansas side.)

Jay Sparks is the co-author of the **Avenge Me** collection. He also resides in the Kansas City metro area (on the Missouri side.)

Visit the authors at unmooredpress.com or shoot them an email at unmooredpress@gmail.com.

If you'd like to find out about releases and giveaways as soon as they become available, subscribe to Unmoored Press' electronic newsletter, available via the website.

www.ingramcontent.com/pod-product-compliance
Lightning Source LLC
Chambersburg PA
CBHW030547180626
46816CB00005B/1434